"Where am I?"
she asked hesitantly.

"In my bedchamber."

"Where are the other men?"

"I am not associated with the villains who attacked you."

"But you were watching me from the woods."

"Yes, well, I was rather bowled over to find a woman bathing in the stream. I'm not accustomed to the sight, you know?"

Sabrina steadied her irregular breathing and wiped away the moisture from her cheeks with the back of her hand. He had a soothing voice that broke through her mind's governing chaos, but his choice of words brought her even more unease. Unless otherwise invited by the lady of the house to give a palm or tarot card reading, she would never have ventured into such a home. And if anyone were to find her here, uninvited, she'd be tossed directly into jail.

Her eyes grew anxious. "I can't stay here," she asserted, momentarily overlooking the fact that she could barely move. "I have to leave."

Other **AVON ROMANCES**

Coming Soon

And Don't Miss These
ROMANTIC TREASURES
from Avon Books

ALEXANDRA BENEDICT

A Forbidden Love

AVON BOOKS
An Imprint of HarperCollinsPublishers

AVON BOOKS
An Imprint of HarperCollins*Publishers*
10 East 53rd Street
New York, New York 10022-5299

Copyright © 2006 by Alexandra Benedikt
ISBN-13: 978-0-06-084793-7
ISBN-10: 0-06-084793-X
www.avonromance.com

First Avon Books paperback printing: January 2006

Avon Trademark Reg. U.S. Pat. Off. and in Other Countries, Marca Registrada, Hecho en U.S.A.
HarperCollins® is a registered trademark of HarperCollins Publishers Inc.

Printed in the U.S.A.

10 9 8 7 6 5 4 3 2 1

For my grandparents:
healer and fortune-teller,
gendarme and dreamer.
Your lives are an inspiration.

Prologue

Dover, England
1812

The winter storm clouds tumbled across the midnight sky, masking the moon and stars from view. Only the distant murmur of the thrashing waves guided the cloaked figure toward the sea, where an anchored ship sat veiled in the mist, awaiting its precious cargo: a locket.

Tears streaked the woman's icy cheeks. She was so close to her sanctuary, within a league's eye of the blessed sandy shore. But she was also on foot, her steed maimed and killed in the hunt, and with the distant hail of galloping hooves fast approaching, it would not be long before her enemies descended upon her.

She gripped the small ornament in her icy palm. So seemingly insignificant. Yet the secret sealed between the two golden faces wielded enough might to knock a nation to its knees.

Frantic, she vowed if she could not get the locket out of the country, then at least her foes would be denied the peace and comfort afforded by its possession.

Her fingers unfurled. The locket sailed through the whirling winds and landed in a mound of snow. Minutes later, the muffled blast of a pistol brought the chase to a bloody end.

But the locket remained buried under the icy flakes. It was not until a month later, when the last remnants of winter had melted, and crocus and snowdrops poked through the thawing soil, that the glimmering speck of gold arrested the attention of a passing gypsy girl, who, wiping the dirt and grime away, fastened the locket around her neck.

Chapter 1

Sussex
1817

The young parlor maid bustled through the corridor, a bundle of white linens tucked firmly in her arms. It was but one of a dozen loads that needed to be washed within the next two days, and new to the estate, she was anxious to please her mistress with the timely deliverance of all the tablewear.

Unbeknownst to her, though, a distant pair of sensuous green eyes were roaming the corridor in search of some mild amusement. Those eyes happened to lock upon the fresh-faced maiden, and their evergreen hue brightened at the piquant sight of the well-rounded, petite form bustling along the passageway.

Lord Anthony Kennington, third Viscount Hastings, couldn't resist bestowing a suggestive wink and a dashing smile to the lovely young creature. Nor could the parlor maid resist heeding his flirtatious charm, and promptly stuffed her cheeks into her pile of laundry to conceal her blooming blush.

The two passed in silence. It was only when the servant had scurried far enough away that Anthony released the deep chuckle gurgling in his throat.

Meg, was it? Or maybe Mary? Her name eluded him. But she had proven a delightful treat the night before, when he'd found her, all alone, dusting in the study. Since his father spent much of the day shut up in that room, the maid had only the evening hours to tend to any housekeeping duties, and Anthony was much obliged for that shift in routine. His Mary-Meg was certainly merry, and after a few whispered words of amour on his part, they'd found themselves, under the waning candle glow, in a most exquisite position on his father's large mahogany desk.

Ah, to be in the country again! He must visit his Mary-Meg once more—twice, if time permitted. Such an accommodating, prime little piece was difficult to find within the boundaries of London's great walls.

Anthony's boots clicked softly, his greatcoat fluttering about his ankles with each long stride. He reached the sanctum of the parlor and flung open the door.

Lady Ashley Winthrop lowered her knitting needles to her lap and cast her assessing green eyes on the viscount. "And what, pray, do you find so amusing?"

Lush memories of his Mary-Meg, that's what, though Anthony thrust such mischievous sentiments aside to respond with more prudence, "Why, the sight of you knitting, of course."

Ashley pursed her lips and his grin only widened at her peevish countenance. He closed the door and approached his twin sister, offering her a kiss on the cheek before he settled in an opposite armchair to meditate on her painstaking stitches.

"Taken up a new pursuit, have you, Ash?"

Her response was to yank at the knotted yarn, prompting the tip of her finger to turn a bright crimson red.

His laughter rumbled throughout the room. "Why don't you leave the knitting to the spinsters and take a stroll through the grounds? The air will do you good."

"Don't be absurd." Brow wrinkled, she tugged and tugged until at last her finger was free. "I've come this far and I intend to finish the pair."

"The pair?"

She proudly held up two little misshapen boots of rose-colored yarn.

Anthony winced in sympathy for his infant niece, who was the likely recipient of her mother's valiant efforts. "Aren't those a little warm for Myra? It's the middle of April."

"And I should have the last stitch looped by November," she vowed with grim determination.

Shaking his head in light amusement, Anthony planted his elbows on the armrests, lacing his fingers together and resting them over his belly. "And where is my baby niece?"

"Out in the garden with her father and elder sister."

"So it's safe to assume the entire family has escaped to some refuge on the grounds?"

"All except for Mama and Cecelia, who seek out any commotion in which to immerse themselves."

Anthony withheld his snort, not the least surprised. He dipped his head back, until his neck nestled comfortably in the one sweeping groove of the ornately carved chair, and closed his eyes. "Well, there's certainly plenty of commotion. I've just come from the west wing and it's in utter shambles."

Ashley's eyes darted from her knitting to her brother. "Dare I ask what your eyes beheld?"

"Only the birth of Chaos herself. Orders were shouted over heads, reaching no one's ears. Bodies shuffled aimlessly, all appearing to be busy, but none really knowing where they were going or what needed to be done. The grand dining hall alone is in a frightful state."

"As is the ballroom."

He peeked inquisitively at his twin through the flaxen fringes of his faintly raised lashes. "And what, pray, is going on in the ballroom?"

"Nothing less than a cosmic feat. I've spent all morning overseeing its preparation, only mercifully to be excused by Mama's closest friend, who insisted on taking charge of the extravaganza herself."

"And so here you are."

"And so here I am," she reiterated with a sigh, fatigued at the mere thought of what she'd nearly undertaken. "It will be a miracle akin to biblical proportions to see this whole tiresome affair come together. Really, Anthony, I don't remember my début being nearly so exhausting."

Ashley had celebrated her come-out alone, despite their being twins, for he was not presented at court until after he'd completed his studies at Cambridge. As for their younger sister, Cecelia, the upcoming gala was to be her first formal affair, an introduction of sorts to her fellow peers prior to her official début at St. James's Palace.

"Your début was equally as exhausting, Ash. You just had a livelier spirit in your youth and a little disorder was always welcomed."

She crinkled her brow at him. "*We're* not that old, Anthony."

Another deep chuckle escaped his lips. "Considering the fact that we're hiding in a parlor to avoid the commotion of a ball, I'm afraid we are."

She *humphed* before returning to her knitting. "Well, this celebration is costing Papa a small fortune."

"I would imagine so. Do you know, I happened upon a cage of doves this morning?"

A startled Ashley soon burst out laughing, holding her hand over her belly. "Surely you jest?"

He teetered his head back and forth in the chair's groove. "I'm afraid not."

"Poor Papa," she empathized. "And poor us. I shall need a holiday after this festivity is over."

"You should have considered that before volunteering to be Cecelia's chaperone for the season."

Her golden brows cambered. "Volunteer? I was ordered to the post by our baby sister, and well you know it. At least Mama is accompanying us to London, so I won't have to be by Cecelia's side for every engagement." She paused her knitting to sigh longingly. "I had hoped to visit Paris this spring."

"You'd best postpone that hope for the distant future."

"Yes, well, you'd best postpone any of your future plans, as well. This season will demand all of our attentions, and if I'm not mistaken, Anthony, even you are not deprived of a duty."

"True indeed," he grumbled, recalling his obligation to scrutinize his sister's potential beaux before they progressed on to their father for the final inspection. Anthony had been spared such tedious obligation during Ashley's hunt for a husband, since he'd been too young to perform the task, but there was no such excuse this time around, and he was not the least bit looking forward to the chore.

His father, not surprisingly, was elated with the forthcoming state of affairs. And not for the obvious reason. As it was Anthony's responsibility to shift through the sea of unsuitable husbands, Reginald Kennington, the earl of Wenhem, had only to meet the handful of prospective suitors and make his final choice. Avoiding Cecelia's fustian callers was a joy unto itself, but the aging earl had another cause to be so content, and Anthony knew it. His father was agog at the prospect of heaping more responsibility onto his heir's shoulders, believing Anthony didn't have enough of it. And while that may be entirely true, the truant viscount did not appreciate the bestowal of *this* particular chore. Imagine the grueling demands of tending to his pleasures by night and then hightailing it over to the West End to fulfill his brotherly obligation by day. Just when exactly was he to sleep?

"It'll be a harrowing ordeal to get Cecelia married off," he repined. "The chit is bound to be finicky. I'll likely get a list of her husband's qualifications and have to acquaint myself with each and every credential."

"Oh, the agonies you shall have to endure!" A raised brow accompanied Ashley's insincere sympathy. "At least you are spared from attending dozens, if not a hundred, soirées this season."

Anthony grimaced at the thought. "Don't even mention such a ghastly fate."

His sister, at her wits' ends, finally tossed the knitting

needles and yarn aside, and slumped back into her chair. "Would you like some tea?"

He smiled. "I'd love some, thank you."

Heading for the wheeled serving cart, she poured a cup of the still-steaming refreshment, commenting aloud, "I missed you at breakfast this morning."

"I couldn't be bothered with inane chitchat over ballroom décor so early in the day. The vacant grounds were much more agreeable."

"Hmm." She handed him the cup and saucer. "In search of amusement, were you?"

Her suggestive tone had him smiling devilishly. "Nothing too wild, I assure you. The woods here are alive with faeries and elves, and the waters filled with playful nymphs. I thought I might ramble about in the hope of meeting one of the mystical creatures."

Ashley's staid glare never wavered from her brother as she settled back into her armchair. "And dare I ask if you found any nymphs or faeries?"

"Alas, no." He sighed with exaggeration. "Not a nymph or faerie was to be seen. A pity, too, for one might, perchance, have cast a spell over me and taken me away from all this madness."

She flitted her eyes heavenward. "Kindly recall this is Cecelia's début. It can't end in a scandalous debacle, so you just avoid any nymphs or fairies or whatever else flutters about in a skirt."

The twins were close enough that Anthony felt no modesty when posing his next question. "And just what am I to do with my time if not consort with fluttering skirts?"

"Oh, so ennui is the trouble." She tapped her finger

against her cheek, as though deep in thought, before her eyes lit with feigned enthusiasm. "I have the perfect solution—marriage."

The hair on the back of his neck bristled at the prospect. Anthony was well aware it was the goal of every woman and burden of every man to get oneself's leg shackled, but he saw no valid reason to hurl his bachelorhood away at his young age. His sister, on the other hand, considered matrimony to be the solution to all vice, and the sooner he found himself riveted the better.

"Ash, marriage is the most appalling suggestion to make to a man in the prime of his youth. You really *are* intent on capping all of my fun."

"Or at least curtailing it." Her critical gaze narrowed on him. "I think we both know neither vow nor iron manacle will wholly reign in your passion for the ladies."

He grinned, unrepentant, at that. "True indeed. God has simply made the fairer sex too beautiful to resist."

She gave an indelicate snort. "An excuse for debauchery since the time of Adam, I'm sure."

He chuckled. "Well, if man's nature is inherently flawed, and one must have a vice in life, a passion for the ladies is the most agreeable to have."

Ashley's eyes flashed toward the ceiling. "Yes, well, back to your pesky trouble with leisure. You need more responsibility, Anthony."

"And a wife should do the trick nicely," he replied without missing a beat, inured to the argument, having heard it countless times before.

There had once been a time when his twin sister

hadn't a priggish tendency to complain of, when she'd been downright indulgent of his escapades, believing her brother no different from other men, all of whom she'd deemed prone to a philandering instinct. And then she'd met her husband: a faithful, upright, respectable gent, and she'd reasoned *all* men were capable of such husbandly devotion if she just badgered them long enough.

"Certainly a wife will rid you of your spare time," his sister spoke with the astute wisdom of such a wife. "And I assure you, you won't have a moment's peace after the brood of children arrive."

Anthony didn't doubt that. Matrimony was a foreseeable damper to his own lustful disposition. The very reason Ashley was positively fixed on converting her brother from renowned bounder to loyal, straitlaced, faithful-to-the-core husband and father.

Now there was an image difficult to conjure. Him a reformed reprobate! Not for another twenty years at least. By then, he should have his fill of rollicking dalliances and be ripe to the point where the responsibility of a wife and children would be a welcome retreat.

"I'm sorry to disappoint you, Ash, but I've no intention of marrying for a good number of years."

She made a moue of annoyance. "Honestly, I don't know where you find the stamina to engage in such dissolute ways."

"Why all the censure? You're supposed to be *my* sister, remember? Kindly recall where your loyalty should lie."

"My loyalty is above reproach. Do you know the number of tales that have reached my ears concerning my rake of a brother? Had I mentioned even a fraction of them, I assure you, our parents would have had an apoplexy by now."

A skeptical look came her way.

"All right," Ashley amended with a shrug of her slender shoulders. "Only Mama would have had an apoplexy. But loyalty does not mean compliance, and I'll rebuke your sordid past whenever I get the chance."

But she didn't get the chance, much to Anthony's relief. The door burst open then, and in hopped Edith with her father and baby Myra following closely behind.

"So here you all are," Daniel Winthrop called out in his usual jovial spirit. He handed his gurgling daughter over to her mother and planted his lips to his wife's cheek. "How abominable of all of you to be hiding at such a merry time."

"Who said anything about hiding?" Ashley rested a fussing Myra over her shoulder and lightly tapped the infant's back. "We were only recuperating."

Daniel cracked a wide grin at his wife's response and dropped into a nearby chair. "Recuperating, eh?"

In the meantime, a rambunctious Edith had squirmed her way into her uncle's lap and shoved a hyacinth right under his nose. "Smell this," the four-year-old instructed.

Anthony set his tea aside and did as ordered, inhaling deeply. "Smells divine."

Smiling, Edith tucked the white bloom into his breast pocket, then patted his coat. "There, that looks better."

"I have one, too." Daniel pointed to his own blossom, veering out of his jacket pocket. "It adds a certain air of refinement, wouldn't you agree?"

"Most definitely," Anthony harmonized. "Brings out the gentleman in us all."

Ashley only grinned at the two indulgent men before asking her eldest daughter how her walk in the garden fared.

"It was dull," Edith said baldly. "Look at my shoes." She shot her small foot out from under her dress so her uncle and mother could inspect its virtually spotless appearances. "Papa wouldn't let me go near a bit of dirt." And then she buried her face in the crook of Anthony's neck and sighed.

"You poor thing," her uncle consoled, wrapping his burly arms tightly around the little creature and stroking her blond ringlets.

Daniel lifted his hands in defeat. "There is no possible solution to this predicament. If my daughter sets foot in the house with a single smudge on her clothes or person, my wife is upset. And if I don't allow my daughter to get a single smudge on her clothes or person, then she is upset. What is a man to do?"

"The dilemma you face, my dear," his wife remarked in mock pathos, still tapping a fidgety Myra.

"It most certainly is," Daniel affirmed, "since the affections of one of my girls will always be alien to me."

The solitude Anthony and Ashley had initially come in search of was eradicated by a door hurling open and an anxious Cecilia bounding into the parlor. "What are all of you doing in here?"

"Recuperating," Daniel supplied, only to receive a scolding look from his wife for his facetious remark.

Averting his eyes from his brother-in-law to suppress his mirth, Anthony slowly rose, allowing a giggling

Edith to slide down the length of his arms, and then moved over to greet his youngest sister.

"Good afternoon, Cecilia."

Anthony bent down and gave her a kiss on her flushed cheek. Since arriving on the estate a few days past, he'd seen Cecilia on no more than two occasions, she being utterly preoccupied with the arrangements to her début ball, which happened to coincide with her seventeenth birthday. But the estrangement benefited both siblings. Seven years apart, Anthony and Cecilia had never been close and had very little to say to one another. Ashley, too, had never developed a strong rapport with her baby sister, who was their mother's pride and joy.

A rather unexpected pregnancy, Cecilia had entered all their lives when no one believed the countess could have another child, and since that time she had become the shining star of their mother's world. Both women just loved pomp and ostentatious displays, not to mention being the center of attention, and a grand ball would be the perfect combination of both their lifelong passions.

The stunning young woman returned her brother's greeting, and then marched right up to her elder sister, her blond curls bouncing with each sprinted step. "The ballroom is in ruins!"

"What!?" a startled Ashley entreated.

Planting her slender arms akimbo, Cecilia compressed her rosy lips and lifted her button nose a notch. Her leaf-green eyes shone with accusation. "I asked you to oversee the arrangements to the ballroom."

"But Lady Hawthorn assured me she would tend to all the remaining details."

"Well, Lady Hawthorn has made a mess of everything. The floors aren't sufficiently polished; I can scarce see my face in them. There aren't nearly enough candles around the room. And do you know, Lady Hawthorn instructed the dark blue curtains to be hung instead of the pale yellow ones? It looks *horrid*."

Ashley rolled her eyes heavenward and sighed. "All right, I'll go and see what I can do."

"Cecilia!" resounded the bellowed name from the corridor.

"I'm in here, Mama," Cecilia called back.

At which point baby Myra belted out a loud wail of protest at all the commotion, and a desperate Ashley was left trying to calm the unsettled child.

Belinda, countess of Wenhem, scurried into the room. Her shoulders pulled back, her spine rigid, she poised her small, plump figure as though she were a member of the royal family, and demanded, projecting her voice so as to be heard over the crying child's: "Cecilia, did you call Lady Hawthorn a featherhead?"

"She ruined the ballroom, Mama," the young girl defended her choice of insult.

"That is no excuse for your behavior. Lady Hawthorn is your elder and my best friend. She is in a furious state and is threatening to leave the estate."

"Let her." Cecilia waved her hand to brush away the nuisance of Lady Hawthorn from her mind. "I have more important matters to worry over."

"Cecelia, you will march right back into the ballroom and apologize to Lady Hawthorn. You will also explain that your nerves are in a fragile state or the woman will think you daft for your insolence."

"I'll apologize only if Ashley can repair the damage done to the ballroom and make it presentable."

A still-bawling Myra left Ashley at a loss for words—
and wits. Her husband leapt to his feet and unburdened
his wife from the chore of tending to *two* whining infants by taking the fussing Myra into his arms.

Yet another botched family reunion, Anthony mused.
With his arrival from London, and Ashley's from
Northampton, the Kennington clan was together again
on their ancestral estate in the county of Sussex. Such
gatherings were growing more and more scarce. Once
Ashley had married and he had set up residence in London, the encounters with their parents and Cecilia had
been reduced to a yearly call at Christmas and a few dinner engagements during the London season. This break
in their normal family routine had proven to be far more
disruptive than any of them had initially imagined.

The clamoring voices jostled Anthony from his
mind's retreat. His mother continued to pursue the im-
propriety of Cecilia's behavior, Cecilia continued to
berate Ashley, Myra's cries only escalated in volume,
and Edith finally clamped her tiny hands to the sides of
her head to drown out all the racket.

Sensing the rhythmic thumping at his temples, Anthony furtively backed out of the room and made a dash
for his life.

Chapter 2

〜⌒◯◯⌒〜

Anthony stood alone, meditating on the secluded arched bridge, shadowed by the budding vines of weeping willows. He propped his elbows against the wide stone ledge and gazed below at the pristine waters, prattling in compliment to the lively twitter of nature's most vocal creatures.

An ash-blond curl slipped over his eye and he brushed the wayward lock aside. With the house in an abhorrent state of uproar, he had taken to the shelter of the trees for repose. But it appeared as though the whole of the property was abuzz with his sister's upcoming ball, for even the woodland critters seemed uncommonly garrulous.

Anthony was beginning to suspect that there was shrinking space in this world where a man could seek refuge from a throng of marriage-minded ladies. His sister's spectacular event was going to beckon to the fore every eligible miss in the county. Every aspiring maid in search of a mate was going to come calling—

and casting nets. But Anthony was determined no woman would snare him as her husband just yet. Marriage was such a sorry state to be reduced to. One had the added burden of a family to attend to, and then there was the whole problematic arrangement of an affair, which could no longer be pursued under one's own roof with a wife fussing about. It was all one miserable business, and were he not in need of an heir, he'd never succumb to such a suffocating fate.

Cecelia's extravaganza was a sour reminder of just how horrid his fate would be. Really, what mayhem! It was all nonsensical, the hoopla and dramatics to snag oneself a husband. But, then again, it was likely the mayhem that first attracted young ladies to the idea of matrimony, rather than the thought of an actual husband. He was apt to think that was the case with Cecelia at least. Anthony already pitied the poor bloke his baby sister was going to set her cap on, and he was thankful to be spared from a similar fate for another decade or two—though when his time to be leg-shackled finally rolled around, he thought with a slow-forming smile, he was greatly going to enjoy giving in to all the flirtatious charms of the female sex.

His musings interrupted, Anthony noticed a kerchief float by, decked in an array of lively colors.

He quirked a brow, and walked over to the other side of the bridge, in time to catch the brightly dyed cloth pass under the arched structure and continue to be washed away downstream.

A little out of the ordinary, to be sure, but nothing abnormal, or so he tried to convince himself. Despite that sound assessment, curiosity took root, and with a brisk walk in mind, he traversed the bridge and meandered along the shoreline, traveling against the current.

Minutes passed. Ducking the occasional straggling branch, clawing at his hair and clothes, he followed the windings of the stream until untamed waters morphed into a tender prattle, no more than a few inches deep. Climbing up a slight embankment, he turned the bend and paused.

Poised on a rock, her bare feet immersed in the icy stream, her willowy fingers combing through the long, wet strands of her ebony hair, sat a legendary nymph.

A raffish grin tugged at the corners of Anthony's lips. Here was the very reason why he had such a feeble disposition toward the fairer sex. Who in their right mind could resist such an unearthly being?

Folding his arms, he slumped a large shoulder against a tree, and with an admiring glint in his eye, studied the bathing creature in idle appraisal. The nymph's goose-fleshed skin glistened with dewy moisture. She wore only a pale ivory chemise, the hem yanked up over her knees and wedged firmly between her thighs, exposing the soft contours of well-rounded calves. But those were not the only curves to draw his attention. Shapely hips tapered to a narrow waist before his eyes rested upon a pair of supple breasts tucked snugly between the tight confines of bodice lace.

Delightful thoughts scampered through his mind. Randy images made more vivid by the lovely display of bountiful breasts and dark, puckering nipples jutting through the thin, damp fabric of her chemise. Despite the warm zephyr ruffling through the blossoming branches, the chill of the water had provoked her body's sensual response. And he couldn't help but mull over the enticing image of a plump breast cradled in his hand, his lips hemming round the chilled areola in soft, feathery kisses, smoothing away the wrinkles of the tightening bud before he welcomed the generous mound of flesh into his mouth.

Anthony dropped his lashes, taking in the sounds of the gurgling stream and loquacious birds, and inhaling the rich scent of birch wafting through the spring breeze.

Satisfied the blood was flowing more steadily through his veins, he opened his eyes. The twinkle of a gold locket, nestled between the cleft of her swollen breasts, caught his attention next, and when she moved to stroke her moist fingers along her neck and bust, her gold hoop earrings glinted under the random shafts of sunlight penetrating the forest canopy.

A more winsome sight he had never beheld.

Her hands welded to form a cup and she scooped the shimmering water into her crooked palms. As she bowed forward, he noted the birthmark etched on her right shoulder blade in the shape of a crescent moon, and his smile broadened. He couldn't resist wondering what other alluring secrets she had concealed beneath her wear.

The water splashed across her sun-bathed features, the residue raining back into the stream. Pearled globules dripped off high rounded cheekbones, dusted with a radiant shade of wind-whipped rose. Into the partially opened crevice of her mouth seeped some of nature's juice, and she licked her full lips to take in all the moisture.

Anthony's heart jounced, lurched right out of the confines of his chest, or so it seemed, at the tune drifting over the languid waters. He perked his ears to better hear the faint hum of her bewitching voice. The medley was foreign to him, but soothing, striking a vibrant chord in his heart, so each blood-pounding beat was a muffled thud. Hypnotized, he allowed her celestial voice to seep into his soul, to stir and rummage through the emotions buried deep within.

But the enchantment was not to last. As if sensing a penetrating gaze, the nymph's eyes soon shifted and suspiciously scanned her surroundings until settling on the intruder regarding her from the sanctuary of the woods.

It was those glistening eyes that lodged his breath in his throat: a brilliant shade of cobalt blue, fringed by thick, sooty lashes, flicking in wariness. Those eyes harbored a myriad of emotions, experiences, dreams, trials . . . secrets.

She was up, scrambling to the opposite bank, and dashed for the shelter of the trees. Only the distant hail of her footfalls, stomping over moldering leaves and twigs, permeated the deserted terrain.

Anthony sighed longingly. A pity to have lost such a whimsical vision so soon. And yet, he was delighted to have had the chance to witness such a charming diversion. Vivid memory of his water nymph would keep his thoughts pleasantly engaged for the next little while, and that was certainly agreeable.

The motley patch of colors flitted by his wandering gaze, and he narrowed his eyes on the assortment of clothes, boots, and a bag, all piled on his side of the shoreline.

Was the girl really so startled by his intrusion that she'd leave all her belongings behind and run barefoot and half naked through the woods? He couldn't let her go like that, all frightened and undressed. God only knew what would become of her in such an indecent state, and with a gallant grin, he decided to set out after the skittish creature, the bundle of garments secured in his arms.

She was a quick nymph, deft in ducking straggling branches and leaping over rotting logs. But his legs were longer, his strides wider, and he swiftly closed the gap between them. He reached for her.

"Let me go!" Swinging round, she pounded on his arm, then yanked one of her boots from his hold and struck him soundly in the shoulder.

His good humor steadily dwindled as he averred between hits, "I mean you no harm."

The hurdling boot halted in mid-air—for a second. She nailed her captor in the upper arm once more, and he was forced to dislodge the boot from her grip and toss it to the ground before she smashed his face in with the heel.

"I only wish to return your possessions." He quickly shoved the paraphernalia into her chest, expecting an apology and perhaps a little gratitude. He got neither.

The girl slammed her foot against his shin, her one liberated fist connecting with his jaw, and sprinted back into the bush.

Bewildered, Anthony stared at the quivering branches, all that was left of his impudent little nymph, and slowly reached for his tingling chin. Now prudence would dictate he leave the matter alone, but the viscount had none of that at the moment. Pure indignation compelled him to give chase, though he took no more than a step forward before he noticed his quarry cautiously backtracking hers. A brief glimpse over her head enlightened him with the reason for her sudden retreat.

Two men were approaching, their rapiers drawn.

"Wonderful," muttered Anthony, still fingering his chin.

Confronted with the nymph's envenomed glare, he was met with the accusation, "You meant no harm, did you?"

And he was forced to defend himself with a curt, "I most certainly did not."

Then to prove to her he was not a member of the villains' circle, Anthony took a step forward, with every intention of protecting her from the advancing fiends—only he wasn't swift enough.

The men lunged for their intended target. The girl's scream pierced through the rattle of twittering birds, and all three went crashing to the ground.

Blindly grabbing the first collar in his reach, Anthony yanked the brute into the air. A sound crack to the face followed, and the man collapsed in an unconscious heap.

The viscount swiped the fallen sword and turned to dispense with the second assailant, only to find a blade careening toward his head. He nimbly ducked to the side.

"Stay out of our affair," came the determined, and unmistakably lethal, warning.

"I think not," countered Anthony, and with a sound blow, sliced his opponent in the upper arm.

The blood spurted forth. The startled man winced and grabbed his wound, though he maintained a firm grip on his weapon. Eyes round in indignation, he promptly returned the blow.

"This is none of your concern!" the contender

blasted, with yet another failed swipe at his more skillful counterpart.

The rapiers clamored as the brandishing blades collided and the men stood locked in place.

Nose to nose, Anthony gritted through gnashed teeth, "I believe this is very much my concern," and with a powerful shove, dislodged the entangled swords.

His opponent staggered back before regaining his composure. "That filthy gypsy is a criminal! You have no right to interfere with her capture."

A gypsy? Yes, of course. He should have guessed. The colorful kerchief floating downstream, the style of her vibrant clothes, her exotic eyes, her long black hair. With her identity revealed, the threat to her life was even more apparent. There was no law prohibiting the mistreatment of gypsies, and therefore no repercussions should the men have captured her and done with her as they'd pleased.

Anthony's jaw instinctively flexed at the abhorrent images that trampled though his mind, and he demanded darkly, "What is her alleged crime?"

"She is a thief, and I intend to bring her to justice."

The viscount gave a soft snort. "A thief indeed." It was a sham of an excuse, as far as he was concerned, to harass an innocent lass. It certainly wouldn't be the first such attempt to persecute a gypsy.

"Move aside!" the fiend blasted. "That locket is mine!"

The locket? *That* plain bauble was the root of all the commotion? Surely not. Why, it was no more than a simple gold locket, easily replaced. Not much of a prize for a thief, and certainly not worth all the hysterics this particular scoundrel was making.

No, the brute was after the girl for more nefarious reasons, and Anthony wasn't about to let him anywhere near her.

His blade swooping across his rival's chest, Anthony came dangerously close to slicing his opponent from navel to nose. The antagonist jumped back, but not before Anthony's sword nicked him in the cheek, leaving yet another noticeable mark.

Bristling, the man slowly reached for his face and felt the drops of blood.

"I suggest you depart these grounds." Though the viscount's stringent remark could be construed as anything but a suggestion, especially with a blade aimed directly for his adversary's throat.

But the villain took no heed of the baleful monition and charged recklessly. "I'll not rest 'til I have that locket!"

Anthony, having had enough of the tiresome skirmish, briskly stepped aside, extending only his fist to soundly connect with the ruffian's face.

The man stumbled and plowed headfirst into the forest bed, joining his motionless comrade in unconscious bliss.

Jaw thrust forward, tense with the exertion of the afternoon skirmish, Anthony dropped his arm at his side and pivoted, expecting to find the gypsy had fled, but what he saw instead shoved his heart right up into his throat.

There she was, sprawled on the ground, completely still.

He drove the blade into the dirt and fell to his knees. Gently lifting her into his arms, he touched the bleeding wound at her forehead, then glanced down at the large bloody stone she'd struck her head against. With his ear close to her lips, he heard the shallow breathing and sighed.

"Well, my gypsy," he murmured, "let us hope I can carry you despite the swelling you so kindly bestowed on my shin."

Carefully, he lowered her back to the ground and shrugged his greatcoat off his shoulders, blanketing her. He then went over to collect her discarded clothing and boots, shoving the garments into the bag she'd been carrying before he slung the bundle of paraphernalia over his shoulder. Once more at her side, he gathered her wet body into his arms, and cautiously made his way back downstream and on toward the haven of the main house.

Chapter 3

Sabrina Kallos was lounging on a cloud—or so it seemed. Softness and warmth were all around her. A shaft of sunlight kissed her skin, rousing her from a deep slumber. No sooner had the stirrings of wakefulness touched her dreamy senses, than the rhythmic thumping swarmed her head.

She grimaced and cracked opened her eyes. It took some time for her misty vision to adjust and focus. The glaring light of the setting sun, shooting in through the row of tall windows, cast a fiery glow over much of her unfamiliar surroundings.

Titling her head to the side to avoid the brilliancy, she was struck by the sheer size of the room. It was massive. Everything inside it was massive. High ceilings, soaring windows, a giant bed with its sweeping canopy of fine dark fabric hovering above her. Why, the bed alone was of a greater size than the entire wagon she and her father lived in. Finely carved furniture filled the gaping space, as did figurines of polished bronze horses and many other knickknacks. Flames snapped in the hearth off to one side, the fireplace framed by glossy wood shelves, littered with books and other curious ornaments. The colorful walls displayed magnificent scenes of woodlands and a distant patch of hunters and hounds in pursuit of one unfortunate fox.

Sabrina didn't care much for the image. She felt like the very fox in the mural, and thoughts of the danger she was in suddenly overwhelmed her.

It was the *gajo's* shadowed figure standing by one of the windows that now seized her attention. His hefty body shifted to block out most of the sun's direct rays, allowing her a better opportunity to study him without having to strain her eyes too greatly.

Memories came rushing forth. She'd been attacked in the woods, that much she could recall, but beyond that, her mind was clouded in darkness. Where was she? Who was her captor? A quick glance to her wrists confirmed she was not bound. Blankets covered her body, and she sensed the linen coiled around her head, but her clothes were nowhere to be seen.

Heart battering in sync with the pulses in her skull, she tried to sit up, raising her head no more than a few inches off the pillow before a wave of discomfort attacked her senses and she dropped back with an anguished cry.

The dark figure abruptly turned at the sound of her sob and hastened to her side.

"Get away from me," she whispered raggedly.

The advancing *gajo* halted just short of the bed. "There is no cause for alarm."

"Where am I?"

"You're safe."

Sabrina, as of yet, could not entirely see the man's face, for he now had his back to the sun, a veil of shadows concealing much of his features. But she recognized his voice as belonging to one of the men who'd cornered her in the woods earlier that day. "My clothes?"

"Your chemise is drying in the adjacent bath." He indicated the direction with a gesture of his hand.

She was trembling, her voice quivering. "You took what you wanted. Now let me go!"

Soul-racking sobs congested her lungs, and she tried in vain to halt the surge of humiliating tears. She didn't want him to have the satisfaction of seeing her weep. Of seeing her dignity cut down to pieces. But try as she might to stave off the torrent of tears, rage and disgrace took their hold, her efforts to cap the sorrow dashed.

"Good heavens, woman, I never touched you! I carried you back to the house, to be sure, but I never laid an inappropriate hand on you."

She didn't hear him anymore, the tears streaking her cheeks, her breathing noisy as she gulped in drafts of much-needed air. She was tainted, by a *gajo*, no less. Her innocence brutally taken away from her. How could she ever go home? How could she ever explain this to her father? To her future husband? Oh, God! She had no memory of the ravishment, but it must have been brutal, for her whole body thrummed with pain.

"You brute," she sobbed and sputtered. "Just give me back my clothes!"

Muttering something under his breath, the *gajo* wove his fingers through his hair with a rough movement. "Stop with those tears. I give you my word of honor, as a gentleman, I have not mistreated you in any way, nor have I any intention of doing so in the future. I brought you here to recover. My sister removed your damp chemise so you wouldn't catch sickness. As for your other belongings, they are right here." He lifted her bag to prove his claim, then set it back on the floor at the foot of the bed.

The bout of misery that had swept over her only moments ago now dwindled. The tears still trickled down her face, but the suffocating sobs soon faded to occasional gulps of air.

Despite her grogginess and somewhat bleary vision, she managed to narrow her eyes to the shadowed figure hovering above her. "W-who are you?"

He sighed in apparent relief. "I am Anthony Kennington, Viscount Hastings, at your service."

"Where are the other men?"

"I am not associated with the villains who attacked you."

"But you were watching me from the woods."

"Yes, well, I was rather bowled over to find a woman bathing in the stream. I'm not accustomed to the sight, you know?"

Sabrina steadied her irregular breathing and wiped away the moisture from her cheeks with the back of her hand.

It was then that Anthony pivoted and strode over to a dresser to remove a white kerchief. He returned to the bed and handed it to her, but she wouldn't take it, so he just laid the silk cloth on the mattress beside her.

"Where am I?" she asked hesitantly.

"In my bedchamber."

He had a soothing voice that broke through her mind's governing chaos, but his choice of words brought her even more unease. A fretful notion came to her, that she would be swallowed up by the manor's walls and imprisoned eternally for daring to enter the sacred confines, even if it wasn't of her own accord. Unless otherwise invited by the lady of the house to give a palm or tarot card reading, she would never have ventured into such a home. And if anyone were to find her here, uninvited, she'd be tossed directly into the jail. Was this not taking the chains from her feet and placing them on her wrists instead? She may have eluded her attackers for the time being, but she now had to flee from the house before anyone else grew privy to her whereabouts.

Her eyes grew anxious. "I can't stay here," she asserted, momentarily overlooking the fact that she could barely move. "I have to leave."

"With your head wound? Impossible. But you are safe here."

So he kept insisting. But the thwack to her head hadn't left her witless. How could she trust a *gajo* . . . a stranger not of gypsy blood? For all she knew, it was Anthony who had struck her.

Sabrina slowly reached for her head. Somewhere beneath the layers of bandages was a tremendous lump, the culprit of her miserable headache. "What happened to me?"

"You were attacked and struck your head on a rock."

She didn't remember any of the assault, only the events leading up to it, so she had little other choice but to accept his version of events—for now. Truthfully, so little of it made any sense to her. "Why am I here?"

"I am bound to tend to your injury."

"You don't know who I am." Sniffing, she brushed away the last remnants of her tears. "A man like you doesn't bother with a woman like me."

"And who are you?"

Better she confess to him now and be done with it. To offset the inevitable wouldn't do her any good.

Her voice dwindled to a bitter whisper. "A gypsy."

"Yes, I already know that. I meant your name."

But she ignored his last statement to demand, "You already know?"

He nodded. "And by the way," he said softly, "a true gentleman comes to the aid of any woman in distress."

Doubt rekindled. Blinking up at him, her sea-blue eyes swept over him in a thorough assessment. Anthony stood with his hands behind his back and one leg bent casually at the knee. His attire consisted of a white linen shirt, the cravat spilling over the top buttons of his butter-yellow waistcoat, and it was then she realized just how broad-chested he really was, for even without the padded coat he'd worn in the woods, his shoulders spanned a good yard or so in width. Long, wiry legs were draped in tight brown breeches and tucked into knee-high, black leather boots. He was certainly formidable, towering above her like that. And the distrust in her eyes must have been evident, for he slowly lowered himself to one knee, the shadows fading the closer he came, and smiled.

He had a friendly smile. One that helped lessen some of those formidable attributes. Certainly one she rarely, if ever, saw from a *gajo*. Most outsiders never bothered to look at her with anything other than disdain, but his kind expression seemed sincere. Or perhaps it was the head injury making her see such things. Benevolent bluebloods did not go about the woods aiding gypsies in distress, no matter what Anthony claimed. And yet, his simple gesture of affection was enough to bring some comfort to her tormented soul. To find solace in another being, even one not a gypsy, who offered her compassion rather than brutality, helped to lessen the burden on her heart.

The smile also softened his features. His eyes were attentive, tranquil. No hatred burned beneath the dark green pools. Wavy, tawny-gold hair tapered evenly to his collar, a stray curl dangling over his brow. He was handsome—for a *gajo*. And he was big. She suddenly understood his need for such a large bed. And she suddenly remembered that she was lying in *his* large bed.

She couldn't stay here. Her life was no longer in peril, so there was no need to hide. If what Anthony said was true, then her attackers had no idea where she was, and that meant it was safe for her to return to her caravan. There was no trail left for the mongrels to follow and therefore no risk to her family's well-being. Her only concern over the last few days was that her relentless aggressors would uncover her camp and harm, even kill, some of her people in order to capture her. Knowing her fellow gypsies would band together to protect her, she wasn't willing to jeopardize anyone's life. It's why she'd left so abruptly, without a whisper of her intentions to anyone.

She knew her absence would cause her people much grief. How could it not? But she also knew her disappearance was the only reasonable choice. The men chasing after her were determined to find her, whatever the means. They had already proven that. Persistent as a pack of hounds, they'd not given up their pursuit of her in days, and would likely still be nipping at her heels had Anthony not interfered.

That brought another question to mind. Why had Anthony come to her aid? A man of his rank bothering to interfere on behalf of a gypsy? She'd never had a *gajo's* help before and didn't know what to make of the situation. From what she could remember, her attackers had been armed, and Anthony must have seen their swords as clearly as she had. Then why risk his welfare? He claimed it his duty, but Sabrina wasn't so convinced, which left her all the more mystified.

"I have to go home," she said again, her voice weak, and pressed the sheets to her chest once more, trying to sit up. "My family will be worried."

But he nudged her back against the cushions. "You are in no condition to travel."

Too lethargic to struggle, she didn't protest, and tried instead to subdue the throbbing spasms in her head by remaining perfectly still.

A light rap at the door diverted both their attentions.

Sabrina's eyes widened at the knocking intruder, but a reassuring gesture from Anthony put her skittish nerves at ease.

"Don't fret," he said. "It's only my sister, Ashley. She's here to help with your recovery."

Another caring soul? Sabrina found it difficult to believe in such kindness, especially coming from a pair of aristocrats, and as profound an instinct to run as she had, she was just too sore and dizzy to move.

Anthony left her side to unlock the door.

The *gaji* hastened into the chamber, a large ceramic bowl, crammed to the brim with supplies, nestled between her hands.

"Anthony, I hope you realize how difficult it was to amass all this with no one the wiser, especially with so many bustling bodies below."

"I appreciate this, Ash." Bolting the door behind her, he instructed, "Set everything on the desk."

The lady did as directed and began to arrange the articles on the table: a cloth, a bottle of liquor, small vials, a spoon.

Sabrina focused on the emerging ingredients, wondering what the duo were brewing.

When Anthony casually informed his sister that the patient was awake, Ashley whisked her head over her shoulder to stare at the bemused invalid, and Sabrina couldn't help but notice how very much she resembled her brother, with that same ash-blond hair and those same deep green eyes. The woman was by no means as tall as her sibling, but she wasn't short by any standards either, reaching a few inches past Anthony's shoulders. She wore a pale peach frock, the waistline circling just under her breasts, and her hair was tucked beneath a ruffled white cap, a few carefully positioned curls draped by her ears.

"How do you feel?" inquired Ashley.

Sabrina remained quiet. Those weren't the words she'd been prepared to hear. Rather, *get out of this house!* rang more sensible to her ears.

To curtail the stretching silence, Anthony responded on the patient's behalf with a confident, "She'll recover," then strode into the adjacent bath, reemerging with a pitcher. He dispensed the water into the basin.

Her attention back to her brother, Ashley indicated to the bottle. "Pour in about two ounces of the brandy."

With a soft clink, the glass stopper was plucked from the decanter and Anthony added what he estimated to be the correct amount of spirit.

Ashley gathered the utensil and measured two tea-spoons from one of the smaller vials. As the fumes drifted over to where Sabrina lay, she detected the potent scent of vinegar and wrinkled her nose.

The *gaji*, as of yet, had not demanded she leave her brother's bed, and little by little, Sabrina's heartbeats returned to a somewhat steady pace.

"Now for the salt." Ashley tended to the last ingredient before handing her brother the spoon. "Stir until the salt dissolves."

And so Anthony swooshed around the bowl, as Ashley resealed all the bottles, and Sabrina closed her drowsy lids, abandoning the siblings to prepare their mysterious concoction at their leisure.

Chapter 4

⟡

With a furtive glance, Ashley captured sight of the dozing gypsy, then looked back to her brother, whispering grimly, "You couldn't avoid causing a scandal this *one* time?"

He raised a brow. "Did you expect me to leave her in the woods?"

"Well, of course not." She lightly smacked his arm. "But the ball is in two days, the house is already in a state of uproar, and if our parents were to learn that a *gypsy* was now sleeping in their son's bed, heads would roll, yours and mine among them."

"Be easy, Ash. No one is going to lose their head."

"Why did you bring her here?" she insisted in quiet reproof. "Why not take her to the local physician instead?"

"I have a duty to take care of the girl *and* keep her assailants at bay."

"But to hide her in your room?"

"Where else was I to put her? The spare rooms will be occupied by guests on the night of the ball. Besides, no one is going to barge into *my* chamber without *my* permission. She is safe in here with me."

He glanced up at the sound of her huff and connected with her glare.

"Safe?" echoed Ashley. "With you?"

"Certainly."

"Really, Anthony, do you expect me to believe mere duty brought about this carte-blanche arrangement? That you had no other motive in bringing a beautiful girl to your bed?"

Up went another startled brow. The allure of a fair lady may be his Achilles heel, but to suggest he'd machinate this entire rescue just to seduce his vulnerable gypsy was a blow even to a man as jaded as Anthony. "You think me such a scoundrel?"

"I know you such a scoundrel," she corrected tersely. "Do you suppose I ignore all the accusations I hear from irate fathers and brothers and husbands and—"

"No need to continue," he quickly cut in before a tirade ensued. "I get the point, Ash. My reputation is deplorable."

"Then you understand my distress," she went on. "There is Cecelia's happiness to consider, and I intend to make sure her début is a smashing success."

"It *will* be a smashing success. Do you honestly think I would devastate my own sister's evening by announcing I have a gypsy in my bed?"

"I don't know what you intend," she grumbled warily.

"Really, Ash, I thought you would be more supportive of my efforts, always dictating I need more responsibility, and all."

"Hiding a nude woman in your bed is hardly the kind of responsibility I had in mind."

Indeed. Anthony knew perfectly well it was the responsibility of a husband his sister was referring to. And to counteract that dampening thought, he turned to a more wicked one, imagining himself caressing his nude gypsy in soothing ministrations. Now there was a responsibility *he* would greatly enjoy.

Ashley gave a short, fretful sigh. "How are you going to manage as caretaker?"

"With your help, of course."

"Of course," she returned dryly.

"Come now, Ash. Don't despair. The house is in a state of chaos, remember? No one will suspect anything out of the ordinary."

Ashley appeared to concede on those grounds, but was quick to point out, "And while we dine below, who will stand watch over the girl?"

"I simply won't leave my room. A few missed meals won't generate much attention, not with pandemonium already reigning throughout the house."

"And on the night of the ball?"

He paused to look over his shoulder at the slumbering gypsy. "Perhaps a few days of rest will restore her strength and mend her injury. She may yet be well enough to leave before the ball begins."

"And if she is not?"

"I will find a solution to that predicament should it arise." He glanced back at his troubled twin to underline, "But the girl isn't leaving until she has recovered."

There was a brevity of silence in which Ashley absently aligned the bottles on the desk.

"Anthony, if those men labeled her a criminal I don't see why you dismissed their claim so effortlessly. What evidence do you have of her innocence?"

"What evidence do I have of her guilt?"

"That isn't sufficient reason to conceal a possible offender."

He sighed heavily at that point. "I doubt very much *she* is the offender. Those men weren't seeking justice when they attacked an unarmed woman."

"Perhaps they were." Ashley glanced over to the bed. "For a poor gypsy, she wears a rather well-crafted gold locket."

Anthony paused his mixing to peer over his shoulder. Resting on the small table next to the bed was the gold ornament Ashley was referring to. "Then perhaps the girl is not so very poor after all. I'm not going to assume she has stolen the locket simply because you believe the piece is beyond her means."

"Why? Because you don't like to think poorly of a handsome woman?"

"No, because I refuse to believe those men would risk life and limb by fighting me for a mere trinket of a locket."

Her doubtful eyes lifted to connect with her brother's. "I do hope you know what you're doing, Anthony."

"I always do." An unladylike snort came his way, and he offered her a reassuring smile before setting the spoon back on the desk. "The salt has dissolved."

Peeking into the bowl to confirm her sibling's assessment, Ashley then took the scrap of linen and dipped it into the saline wash, wringing the excess liquid.

"I have another favor to ask of you," he began tentatively.

She quirked a questioning golden brow.

"Will you go below to prepare our patient a meal?"

Her shoulders slumped forward in dismay. "Do you really think you should be alone with the girl?"

"I don't believe my life is in any peril."

"I mean, it's improper for you to be tending to a woman not your wife," she qualified, somewhat annoyed.

"There is nothing improper about setting a compress over her brow. Now will you fetch her some food? She's likely to be famished after all this time."

Ashley's verdant green eyes darted between the patient and her brother, all the while mulling over the request. At last she sighed. "Oh, very well." Dropping the cloth into the basin, she headed for the door. "I'll be back soon." Then more sternly: "Behave yourself, Anthony."

He shook his head at his sister's monition. Honestly, did she expect him to act any other way?

Gathering the bowl, he treaded quietly toward the sleeping nymph. She looked so peaceful, he reflected, taking steady, even breaths, her eyes closed, the thick fringes of midnight-black lashes fluttering on occasion.

He placed the tonic on the nightstand, then proceeded to lock the door to stave off any unwelcome visitors. Back by his gypsy's side, he studied her for a long while. She seemed so vulnerable, adrift amidst the layers of blankets, dwarfed by the four-poster bed and looming canopy above. This wasn't to say she was petite—she was actually much taller and more firmly built than most of the delicate flowers of the *ton*—but she was seemingly fragile when sprawled over his vast bed, her spirited temperament subdued by dreams.

And she was stunning. His eyes were fixed to the soft

contours of her golden features. He took in more fully the dusty-rose tinge of her cheeks, the small rounded tip of her nose, the fine curve of her lush lips . . .

Steady, old boy, he heard a little voice inside him. *Remember your obligation. The girl is under your protection. You can't be an ass and seduce the vulnerable creature.*

Rightly so. Where had his mind gone? He wasn't *that* great a scoundrel, whatever his twin sister might say. The gentleman within him was strong enough to overcome the rogue, he was sure. It was just a bloody tragedy to have a veritable nymph in his bed, nude at that, and he could do naught but dream about her.

But it wasn't long before more sinister thoughts took hold of his imagination, and he wondered how long she'd been pursued in the woods and by whom. Why were those men so intent on causing her injury? Pure malevolence? Or was something more nefarious at work? He hoped to learn at least some of those answers in time.

But for now, thoughts of the future yielded to the priority at hand. He still had to tend to his gypsy's wound, and though he loathed to disturb her, he needed to unwind the linen coiled around her head in order to apply the compress. Perhaps, if she was in a deep enough sleep, he could remove the bandages without rousing her.

Or perhaps not.

Her hand latched onto his wrist, just as he was about to disentangle the knotted dressings.

"What are you doing?" she asked tersely. What remnants of lethargy still lingered, quickly vanished, and her deep blue eyes, alert and scrutinizing, pinned on him.

"I must remove your wrappings to apply the compress," was his steady reply. "It will help with the healing."

Her eyes shifted and narrowed on the basin. "What's in there?"

"There's some brandy, vinegar, and salt mixed in with water. It will ease your headache."

She appeared to study the bowl carefully before returning, "There should be apple cider mixed with vinegar and water, not salt and brandy."

"And why is that?"

She gave no response. Her attention was snagged elsewhere as she scanned the extensive chamber, then demanded brusquely, "Where is she?"

"Ashley has gone below to prepare your meal."

Her eyes were back on him. Such a deep shade of cobalt, he reflected, so riveting, so powerful, like a churning ocean revving before a storm.

At last, she released her hold on his wrist and slung her hand back over her belly.

"May I remove the wrappings?" he ventured to ask.

With no outward protest to dissuade him otherwise, he reached for the bandages a second time. Slowly unfastening the knot near her temple, he nudged the wrappings upward until they slipped over her head.

His fingers lightly brushed against her onyx-black hair, still damp and silky to the touch. The locks smelt of pine and birch and all the other fragrances of the woods.

He fetched the cloth from the bowl and squeezed it firmly. "This should provide you with some relief." He smoothed the moist linen so it spanned the entire length of her forehead. "I've never heard of apple cider used in cases of headache," he began off-handedly, hoping to draw her out of her reticent mood. "Do you know much about healing?"

In the wake of her prolonged silence and dissecting gaze, he pressed on, imploring, "At least allow me the pleasure of knowing your name."

Her skeptical gaze narrowed in further scrutiny.

He sunk to one knee, so their eyes were level, having noted earlier that the position appeared to bring her some mild comfort.

"I can appreciate the distress you must be feeling, but neither I nor Ashley mean you any harm."

There were a few long moments of thoughtful blinking before she broke her silence to state, "I heard whispering."

"Ashley and I were discussing your recovery."

"She doesn't want me to be here."

For someone who should have been asleep throughout the discussion, his gypsy was certainly perceptive. But she'd reached a rather uncomfortable—and unfortunately accurate—conclusion. Ashley definitely held doubts over his ability to handle the situation at hand, but Anthony felt it wise to downplay his sister's misgivings, without outright denying their existence. "Ashley is a little apprehensive—"

"Because of who I am."

"That isn't true."

Her features, circumspect in their make, told him she believed otherwise. "Then why are you hiding me in your room?"

"To protect you from your assailants."

She offered him a sad, ironic smile. "And from your family?"

He paused, ascertaining how best to respond. In the

end, he tilted his head to the side as a sign of reluctant concession. Why deny the obvious?

Intent on dismissing her fears of his family, he steered the conversation toward a more pressing concern, and asked, "What happened in the woods today? Why were those men chasing you?"

Her voice grew distant. "I don't know."

"You mean to say, they randomly selected you off the road to accost?"

"No."

"Then why?"

She reverted to silence. What was the girl hiding? He had never really considered her a criminal, as one aggressor had claimed, but if he'd misjudged the situation, and she was in some sort of legal muddle, he'd still not hand her over to the authorities.

"If you are a criminal, I will still protect—"

"I'm *not* a criminal!"

"I believe you," he said sincerely. "So tell me what really happened."

Sighing heavily at that point, her features grew somber, a dark cloud of torment spiraling in the despondent pools of her deep blue eyes. "A few days ago, I was at the county horse fair. My father was trading studs with the local farmers and gents, and I was telling fortunes to the women and children. These *gajos* walked by my wagon a few times during the day—"

"Excuse me, but what walked by your wagon?"

"*Gajo,* a man not of gypsy blood."

"I see. Please continue."

"I didn't think very much of them at the time," she resumed. "One finally asked for a card reading, but all the while, he couldn't stop staring at me. By the end of the reading I just wanted to get away from him, but he grabbed me and said I had nowhere to hide. He said I was too precious to lose again, as if we'd met before. I knew I was in trouble, so I kicked him in the groin."

Anthony cocked a brow. Well, she was spirited, and unabashed in her word choice, he'd give her that. But, then again, he was already acquainted with her lively spirit, for his chin still tingled from the sound blow she'd dealt him earlier in the day.

"I ran away," she continued with the harrowing tale. "Both men have been chasing me ever since."

"For how long?"

"It's been two days now. I stopped to wash in the stream, thinking I'd finally outrun them. But I was wrong."

His attentive green eyes grew thoughtful. Stolen locket indeed! In the end, the supposed crime his gypsy had committed was to deflect the unwanted advances of two pompous jackasses. Anthony had expected as much. With such savage fire in their eyes, the assailants were obsessed with something greatly personal, such as seeking "justice" for their battered prides. And he had no doubt their form of justice would have ended in the gypsy's ravishment.

His features darkened on that morbid note. "I'll see you safely home once you're well enough to travel."

She eyed him curiously. "Why?"

"Because you are under my protection."

Anthony rose and headed over to the writing desk to retrieve the matches. The sun had made its way into the underworld, leaving the sky in a limbo of twilight. The dwindling fire did not provide the room with enough light, so he lit the candle on the nightstand, a soft glow enveloping the immediate area.

The locket glinted under the luminescence, capturing his attention as it had earlier that day in the woods. He'd removed the adornment when he'd first brought his gypsy into the chamber, not wanting the chain to get tangled around her neck. He reached for the ornament now, fingering it with his thumb.

It was a simple oval, he observed, well crafted and somewhat larger than a traditional locket, but not overtly unusual. Dangling on a thin gold chain, the locket was plain, with only a small insignia of a lion's head carved into the center face.

He set the necklace back on the nightstand and looked down to find his gypsy watching him closely.

"Now that you've confessed your troubles, will you give me the honor of your name?"

A mist of indecision passed over her eyes, as though she'd already disclosed too much, and this one last detail was exceeding her confessional limits for the night. But, at last, as he'd hoped she would, she relented.

"My name is Sabrina Kallos."

Chapter 5

~~~OQO~~~

Sabrina detected his smile under the faint flicker of candle flame. She didn't understand why the smile had such an effect on her, why it had the ability to soothe her angst. Considering who Anthony was and where he had brought her, she should be more alert, more cautious as to when she allowed her guard to fall. But right then, with a throbbing headache and a somewhat drowsy temperament, a friendly smile was all it took to quiet her jitters.

Anthony treaded softly to the other side of the room and collected one of the armchairs. He positioned the seat next to the bed and sat down.

"For a gypsy, you have a very interesting name," he said.

"I was named after the river Sabrina."

"In Wales?"

"Yes, it's where I was born."

He nodded. "I was named after my grandfather."

"Do you have a large family?"

"It's steadily growing," he admitted with another grin. "Ashley and I are twins. She married some years ago and now has two children of her own. We have a younger sister, Cecilia, who is about to embark on the marriage market. That's what the 'bustle below' you heard Ashley mention earlier was all about. The house is gripped in the throes of preparation for a ball, introducing my youngest sister to the rest of society."

"When?"

"The day after tomorrow."

Her heart thumped faster. She quickly skimmed through the many catastrophes awaiting her on the day of the celebration, should she still find herself laid up in the viscount's bedchamber. Foremost on her mind was being discovered by one of the hundreds of guests no doubt scheduled to attend. She was no fool when it came to such grand spectacles, having often heard the tale of her cousin Gulseren's vicious treatment by the nobility.

It was last spring when her cousin had traveled through the countryside, offering her fortune-telling skills to the ladies of the more prestigious homes. Gulseren had unfortunately happened upon a stately dwelling the morning of a similar festivity, and was promptly run off the estate by the vengeful hostess, who summoned stablehand and footman alike to see the "filthy gypsy" off her land.

Sabrina shuddered at the prospect of a similar fate. "I have to leave before the ball begins."

His voice was authoritative. "You'll do no such thing. Don't fret," he added in a reassuring tone. "You're safe in here. The servants won't trouble you the day of the ball with so many guests to attend. Besides, the door will be locked."

The way in which he spoke, one would think it was an absolute truth she would be left in peace, but she had far too much experience with the mistreatment of gypsies to blindly accept his claim.

"No harm will come to you," he said, disturbing her wary thoughts. "Trust me."

Trust him? She didn't even know him. He wasn't even part of her blood. The man had no real obligation toward her. He would never stand by to protect her from a throng of angry bluebloods—his fellow bluebloods. He'd set a compress over her head and feed her and perhaps even escort her home, but beyond that, he would not side with her against his own kind.

His warm hand clamped down over hers, her heart missing a beat when he gently applied the pressure.

"Trust me," he said again, gruffly, more forcefully than before. His eyes narrowed intensely, the dance of candlelight reflecting in the deep green pools.

It was like a shock to her system, her response to such a simple gesture, and she didn't understand why she was reacting so oddly. The flips of her belly, the hammering of her heart? She must be hungry.

The knock on the door diverted Sabrina's attention, and her muddled gaze immediately sharpened on the entrance.

Anthony unlocked the barrier, allowing Ashley to slip inside.

"It's almost seven," she said, handing the server over to her brother. "Will you be joining the family for dinner?"

"I think not."

Ashley wrung her fingers. "What if Mama suspects you're ill and comes looking for you?"

Sabrina stiffened at the dreaded possibility.

"Simply assure Mother I'm in perfect health. Tell her I'm . . . immersed in a matter of business, that's it. I'll dine at a later hour—preferably when all have gone to bed."

Sabrina relaxed her braiding muscles.

"Very well," sighed Ashley. "I'll make your excuses. But, please, don't stalk down the corridors at night. I'll deliver your meal after dinner." Then, muttering as she turned to leave the room, "What will Daniel think when he sees me sneaking off with a tray of food?"

"Just don't let your husband see you," was her brother's sage advice.

Another sigh and Ashley was out the door, Anthony drawing the bolt behind her as he balanced the tray on one knee.

At the aromatic whiff of still piping-hot soup, the pains in her belly made Sabrina acutely aware of the fact that she was famished.

Anthony settled back into the armchair, the tray in his lap. "Are you hungry?"

"A little," she admitted, though her stomach almost reeled up to interject "a lot."

He took the spoon and dipped it into the bowl, sliding the utensil's underbelly along the porcelain rim to dispense with any dripping.

She crinkled her brow. "What are you doing?"

"Feeding you. I'm not blind to the look of pain on your face whenever you try to sit up. It's best this way."

She protested the feeding, claiming she was no helpless babe, but seeing as the spoon was already hovering near her mouth, and the strong scent of pheasant was ever so scrumptious, she merely surrendered with a sigh of annoyance and pried her lips apart. Her eyes closed, she savored the rich flavor. The soup tasted even better than she'd imagined.

And so the feeding went on for a while, with Anthony occasionally dabbing at her chin with a kerchief when a few drops strayed. And as the bowl's belly grew empty and hers grew full, he broke the lull in the conversation.

"You know, your English is very good."

She eyed him briefly before taking in another spoonful. "It was easy to learn. I've lived near *gajos* my whole life, trading with them, telling fortunes."

"I see." He brought another portion to her lips. "Since you're being so forthcoming, may I ask why you suggested apple cider in the saline wash? It puzzles me."

She swallowed. "Apple cider works better in a compress."

A blond brow arched. "Then you are a healer?"

"It is my destiny."

"And why do you think that?"

"Because I was marked at birth." When his brows stitched together in confusion, she elaborated, "I have a mark on my shoulder in the shape of a crescent moon. The council of elders always believed I was intended for some great purpose, and then, five years ago, when I cured my father of sickness, the council agreed it was my talent, that I should be trained as a future healer."

He nodded. "Then I must ask Ashley to scrounge up some apple cider." He set the tray aside and rinsed the linen in the saline wash before spreading the moist cloth back over her forehead. "Until tomorrow, though, this compress will have to suffice. Now try and get some sleep."

"And . . . ah . . . where will you be sleeping?"

"Over there." He indicated with a nod toward the hearth, where the plush, cinnamon-brown sofa was positioned. "Goodnight, Sabrina."

He rose to his feet, tray in hand.

She hoped it really would be a good night; she certainly longed for it. And on that wishful thought, she promptly gave way to the dreams already looming in her mind.

Chapter 6

❧◦◦◦❧

Anthony slumped a shoulder against the bedpost, his eyes tightly fixed on a still sleeping Sabrina. She appeared blissfully content, her slumbering features tranquil, her breathing deep and steady. Quite a contrast from the outbursts that had plagued her the night before.

Over the course of the evening, she'd muttered, cursed, prattled in some foreign language, and even wept. It had been the sound of her sobs that had finally prompted him to disturb her rest, but she'd soon drifted back into the realm of illusions, the dark images following suit, allowing her little, if any, peace.

In truth, his own sleep hadn't fared much better. For much of the night, he did little else than refresh the compress over her brow and listen to her incoherent ramblings, finding it bloody maddening that her assailants still pursued her in her dreams and he had no way of saving her this time. It wasn't until dawn broke that her nightmares had come to an end and she'd quieted, her remaining repose without further incident.

His gaze skipped over her to glance at the time. It was nearing ten o'clock. Breakfast was now being served below, and he was again conspicuously absent, though Ashley had assured him, when she'd come to deliver the morning meal, that she would tend to any concerns regarding his missing presence.

His sister might fuss too much—about everything—but he was greatly obliged to her for all her assistance. He could not have concealed Sabrina thus far without Ashley's help, and as soon as he was able to, he would demonstrate his gratitude by convincing her husband to take her on that trip to Paris she'd been longing for. Ashley certainly deserved the recuperation. And, with any luck, a holiday on the mainland might lessen her harried disposition and bring *him* some brotherly peace as well.

With recuperation still on his mind, his thoughtful gaze returned to Sabrina, and he debated internally over whether or not he should wake her. She needed her rest after a grueling evening overwhelmed with nightmares, but she also needed her strength, and he felt it best that she eat while the tea, eggs, and ham were still warm.

Having determined to rouse her, he pushed away from the bedpost. So as not to startle her by looming like some imposing titan, he dropped to one knee and gently nudged her arm.

It was a few more shakes before those midnight-black lashes fluttered, and dried lips parted to murmur unintelligibly. She burrowed her fists into her eyes and yawned. Sluggish lids half concealed those beautiful blue eyes that now pinned on him.

He smiled. "Good morning. How do you feel?"

"A little better," was her drowsy reply. "But my head still hurts."

"You need more time to recover." He removed the compress and dropped it into the saline wash to saturate. "Breakfast is waiting."

She sniffed, the air filled with the scent of freshly cooked fare. "I have to get up first."

"Why?"

"I had a bowl of soup for supper last night. Why do you think?"

His eyes rounded in comprehension. "Yes, of course, I should have anticipated . . . Do you need assistance? I can summon Ashley if—"

"I need my clothes," she cut in before he rambled on any further. "I can do this on my own."

"Let me fetch your chemise."

Anthony swiftly collected her undergarment from the privy. He should have considered such sensitivities, he rebuked himself. Why hadn't Ashley reminded him? But with so much hectic energy already coursing through the household, certain details in Sabrina's recovery were bound to be overlooked.

He laid the chemise atop her blanketed legs. "Can you sit up?"

"I think so."

With the bed sheets pressed tight to her chest, she struggled to raise her head, and he slipped a supportive hand behind her neck to aid in her efforts.

Ah, the feel of her warm skin cradled against his palm, damp from pressing up against his pillow. She was so soft. He would bet his legacy she was just as soft in other places too . . . maybe even softer.

The lascivious image of his fingers trailing over the

full swell of a magnificent breast invaded his mind with startling intensity. He could just feel the supple flesh cupped in his hand, his fingers kneading and caressing, his thumb swirling over the silky smooth patch of her rosy nipple, fast hardening under his solicitous touch.

He shuddered faintly, banishing the erotic fantasy before the slow stirrings of his cock grew more rampant.

Sabrina closed her eyes and heaved a deep sigh. His fingers were still entangled in the unruly locks of her ebony hair, holding her upright, so she didn't tip to any side in a bout of faintness.

"I'm not dizzy anymore." She lifted her lashes. "I can dress myself."

He didn't voice his doubts over her conviction. Rather, he put them to the test, and withdrew his hand from her neck. When she didn't topple over, he stepped away from the bed.

"I'll be by the window should you need my assistance."

As she reached for her chemise, he turned on his heels and made his way over to one of the tall panes of glass, giving her his back and subsequently her privacy.

He too needed some time, but to regain his scattered wits. How had lust overtaken him so swiftly just a moment ago? He had never experienced anything like it before, where the mere touch of a woman had kindled his desire. And it was unnerving to think it took so little effort to stir his blood, especially where Sabrina was concerned, for she just happened to be the one woman in the world whom he could never be with. He may be a degenerate, with a propensity for lifting a wanton woman's skirt, but he was not wholly without a sense of honor. Having Sabrina under his protection meant he had to guard her against all danger—including the danger of his predatory self.

Anthony didn't notice any of the estate through the draped sheers, his mind too engrossed with detecting Sabrina's movements. There were a few sighs and muttered remarks as she grappled with her garment, but so long as he could hear her, then he knew she was all right. And it was after a few combatant moments that her apparel seemed to be in place, for he next heard the rustle of bed sheets and the mattress shifting under her weight.

"May I turn around now?" he asked.

At the sound of her gasp, he pivoted, and found her clutching the bedpost for support. He was at her side in an instant, arms circling around her shoulders to keep her from slumping onto the floor. She sagged into his chest, and he sensed the shudder rip through her limbs, vibrating against his own.

"Are you cold?"

"I'm fine," her words clipped. "You're holding me too tight." And she braced her palms flat against his chest to push him back.

The pressure of her fingers digging into his body had the most disarming effect on him. The blood quickened through his veins. His heart thumped with awakened vigor. His grip tightened around her in possessive instinct.

There was a heavenly weight pushing against him in the form of a bountiful pair of breasts. Each deep breath she inhaled thrust those mounds harder into him, leaving his muscles stiffening, his body aching to feel more of her, aching to know her without the frustrating barrier of clothing between them.

Anthony released his hold before he took a leave of

his senses—if he hadn't already. She was in no further danger of fainting if she could wriggle so soundly in his arms. But there was still a good thirty feet to cross before she reached the privy, and he wouldn't risk another vertigo brush over her and send her face down into the carpet.

He cupped her elbow, and insisted, though in a slightly flustered voice, "I'll escort you."

"I can walk just fine," she muttered all the way to the privy, and once there, promptly shut the door in his face.

The wooden obstruction snapped him from his bemusement. He sighed. Headstrong and distrustful. An ideal combination of character traits indeed.

So curtly denied the opportunity to explain where the water closet was located, he hoped she'd figure that out on her own. But living out of doors, as was gypsy custom, he had to wonder if she had ever even seen a water closet.

He took to restless pacing in the minutes that followed, another conundrum occupying his thoughts. Could he really stay in the same room with Sabrina and not be able to touch her? It had never really occurred to him before, that abstinence could be so . . . painful. He was still trying to tamp the stiffening in his groin, but it was proving rather difficult. He had never refrained from anything in his life, was wont to doing as he pleased, with whomever he pleased. And now he wanted Sabrina. Never mind that he couldn't have her. His body was quite insistent that he take her. Bloody hell. Being a caregiver and a protector had an unforeseen, and rather agonizing, side effect.

Engrossed with his bewildering thoughts, he didn't realize how much time had passed, that his gypsy had yet to emerge from the privy. What if she had fainted, and in his absentminded state, he'd simply not heard her body collide with the floor?

"Sabrina, are you all right?"

He knocked again when there was no response. A brusque reply of perfect well-being followed this time around and he eased his twining muscles.

Pacing before the door, he offered her a few more moments of privacy, when he realized what must have her so preoccupied. He smiled at the thought. If the girl had never seen a water closet before, then it stood to reason she was unlikely to comprehend the nuances of the contraption.

With a light shake of his head, he reminded himself not to take anything for granted when it came to his gypsy.

He rapped on the door once more. "Pull the valve."

A muffled "What?" came through the barrier.

"The valve. Pull it."

Soon thereafter, the door creaked open. He was careful to do away with his grin before she took heed.

"Shall we have breakfast?"

He extended his elbow to guide her back to the bed, but she declined the invitation, and, tight-lipped, traversed the chamber on her own. He maintained a close proximity, to catch her should she fall, but his assistance was unnecessary. She didn't flounder once.

He realized then, there was something more than her beauty, something beneath those willful blue eyes, that relentless independence, that had him so intrigued. But thoughts of what that something was were put aside the moment Sabrina reached the bed and crawled over the covers, thrusting her posterior into the air.

An admiring, if not somewhat wolfish, grin touched his lips at the charming sight. Was she a virgin? He wondered. He had never found the despoiling of maids particularly appealing. They were far too abashed for his taste. He much preferred the allure of an experienced woman—and gypsies weren't known for being chaste. *His* gypsy certainly had no qualms about parading around in his bedchamber in only her chemise, and it was his understanding that a woman who found her body comfortable was very much accustomed to using it in a variety of ways.

The tempting thought took root. Wouldn't it be wonderful to be with *this* particular gypsy? And if the girl was willing, it'd be a marvelous match.

He closed his eyes, willing the yearnings into submission. He had a code of conduct to adhere to. He couldn't play the scoundrel and seduce his vulnerable ward. Honor demanded the utmost of gentlemanly behavior—though the sight of that tight derrière could certainly shake a man's sense of honor.

He quickly banished the thought.

Sabrina fumbled with the covers and at last slipped beneath them. She closed her eyes, sighing heavily, the short walk across the room having sapped some of her tenuous energy.

He took that moment in which to pour her a rejuvenating cup of tea and gather a few goods on a plate. He then set the food on the nightstand next to the basin.

Accepting the cup he offered with a nod of thanks, she sipped her tea without much effort, now able to sit up more comfortably than she had the previous night. And since he had already indulged in some eggs and ham this morning, he merely dispensed with another cup of tea for himself and hauled an armchair over to the bed.

Setting her own tea aside, she reached for the plate of food. "It's as rich in there"—she indicated to the privy—"as it is out here."

"Do you really think so?"

She sounded incredulous as she dipped into her eggs, mumbling, "There's a *fireplace* next to the tub. It's no bush in the woods."

The tea skewed down the wrong passage. "No, I suppose it isn't."

Oblivious to his throat clearing, she wondered aloud, a wistful note to her voice, "It must be nice taking a bath in winter with a fire raging nearby."

He silently admitted the thought had never crossed his mind, but he assumed it was indeed more comfortable.

"Aren't you going to have breakfast with your family?" she wondered next.

He shook his head. "Ashley will look after any questions regarding my absence, but with the house in an abhorrent state of uproar, it wouldn't surprise me to learn that no one took heed of my empty chair."

"You hate balls?"

"I despise disorderly conduct. Just the sight of all those bustling bodies, aimlessly scurrying from room to room, gives me an excruciating headache. I prefer to be as little troubled as possible."

"Then why trouble with me?"

He could feel those beautiful blue eyes carving up his soul in meticulous assessment, burrowing past his defenses, rousing within him what he was trying so hard to suppress.

"There's nothing cryptic about it," he said. "I simply deal with trouble as it finds me."

"So I was trouble?"

"I believe that label is more fitting for your assailants."

She nodded, her gaze averted to her plate, her voice taking on a more timid quality. "And does trouble often find you?"

His smile was suggestive, his response more oblique. "Not too often."

She said nothing more on the matter and returned to her breakfast. He studied her for a while, casually drinking his tea, admiring her like a work of art. His eyes didn't skip over a single detail, from the lone freckle on her neck to a short, stray lock of hair that curled under to tickle her chin. She was charming. She was lovely. She was every bit an alluring nymph . . . And she was in his bed.

He took in a deep breath. He would conquer this. He was strong enough to resist the nymph's enchanting call.

But the more he admired her, the more he felt like a jewel thief in the royal vault, appointed to be his own sentry.

Into the stretching silence he heard a throat clear, followed by a hesitant, "Um, how old is your youngest sister?"

Good. A wholesome question. He needed a sound kick in the arse, a blow to rattle and realign his scattered senses. "Cecelia will be seventeen on the day of her ball."

"And she is *now* being prepared for a husband?"

"Is she too young by gypsy standards?"

She scooped up another mouthful of egg and swallowed. "Too old."

"At what age do you marry?"

"Fourteen."

"That's quite young." And then his brows lifted at the prospect. "You must be near Cecelia's age. Are you married?"

She shook her head in response. "I'm one year older than your sister, but I'm not wed. The council of elders decided nothing should interfere with my training as a healer, even a husband."

"And when does your training come to an end?"

"It already has."

"So you'll be married soon?"

"In about a fortnight."

The teacup hovering near his lips struck the saucer with a faint clink. For some daft reason, he was annoyed to hear of her upcoming nuptials, and to dislodge the aberrant thought from his mind, he gave his head a rapid shake. Didn't do much good, though, the inexplicable irritation still lingered.

He set the china on the nightstand. "Who are you marrying?"

"My cousin, Istvan."

She said it so calmly, so indifferently, and certainly with none of the enthusiasm he'd expect from a prospective bride, that he had to wonder, "Do you love him?"

She shrugged.

"Then why marry the man?"

"Because the council has arranged our union."

A betrothal! So that was the culprit of her apathetic disposition. He could certainly sympathize. What a ghastly fate to be reduced to.

"Does your council of elders decide your future entirely?"

She nodded. "The elders must keep tradition. Because my father is the tribal leader, and I his only child, it's fitting that I marry my eldest cousin, who is destined to be the next tribal guardian."

"I see." Though a betrothal was not unheard of by any means, it was increasingly scarce in his sphere of company. Granted, a lady may not have complete autonomy in the choice of her husband, but she certainly had a say and could reject a suitor. Anthony knew as a certainty his father would never force Cecelia to marry a man for whom she had no regard, even if social rank and income were highly desirable. Then again Cecelia would never rebuff a gentleman of impeccable breeding, but that was a moot point. That his sister had the option to first set her cap on a potential beau was the issue. That Sabrina had not the same option was a little unsettling. But then, she was not a noble lady and thus afforded any of the privileges that accompany the title. Still, being a gypsy, wandering the countryside as a way of life, he'd expected her to have greater freedom when it came to formalizing a lifelong union.

"And you have no voice in such matters?" he wondered.

"I must honor the will of my people, as you must honor yours one day."

"Yes, but unlike you, I will have the freedom to choose my partner in life."

She set her empty plate aside and retrieved her tea, her voice surprisingly flat considering the prediction she was about to impart. "I have already foreseen your future wife."

He crooked an intrigued brow. "Prophetic and a healer? Very well, Sabrina, who will be my prospective bride?"

"A rich, titled *gaji*, respected by your people."

He felt that prophecy to be rather obvious. "Is there any other option?"

"You could marry a peasant."

Anthony looked at her, aghast, searching her features for signs of humor. But he found none. "That's preposterous!"

"So your wife must bring honor to your family?"

"Certainly."

"Then you are not truly free to choose anyone for your bride."

His expression grew thoughtful. "A man unwittingly in chains?"

"Those chains bind us all. I could never marry a man not of gypsy blood or I would be cast away forever."

"Complete expulsion? Rather harsh, is it not?"

"To bring a *gajo* into the tribe would taint the purity of gypsy blood. It is forbidden."

He offered a sympathetic nod. "That code of conduct certainly sounds familiar. It looks as though our worlds are not so very different after all." A short pause, then, "Would you ever leave your world?"

Their eyes met. Hers, a deep sea blue, darkened like a brewing tempest, drawing him into their stormy depths.

"To leave my family means never to return." She went to set the china on the nightstand, the teacup faintly rattling against the porcelain saucer. "I couldn't bear that."

Anthony nodded and lifted out of his chair. He wasn't sure why he'd asked the ridiculous question in the first place. He only knew her answer had triggered an unpleasant sensation to swirl in his gut.

"Why don't you get some rest." He recovered the compress still saturating in the basin, squeezing it firmly before setting it over her brow. "I'll wake you for luncheon."

Chapter 7

Luncheon was almost upon them and Sabrina had yet to get any sleep. She'd spent the remaining morning with her eyes closed, pretending to rest, though her mind was anything but at ease.

Anthony shuffled the papers on his writing desk, disturbing her thoughts, forever reminding her where she was and who was her caretaker. Each time he rustled a sheet, or shifted in his chair, she lifted her lashes to study his broad back, his arm teetering gently, as he scribbled away on the parchment or dipped his quill in the inkwell.

Her eyes skipped over his large frame and peered out through the row of tall windows to the cloudy sky beyond. The viscount had an unnerving effect on her. She didn't like to admit it, but the fluttering sensations in her belly made it difficult to ignore. It was ridiculous really, that the paltry and unintentional gestures of a lingering look or the mere touch of his hand should incite such peculiar jitters. But they did. And she tried to dismiss the wayward responses as quickly as they came, believing them the muddled results of her head injury and nothing more. She met with ill victory, though. Dismissing Anthony from her mind would prove to be far more complicated than mere reasoning alone.

She let out a faint sigh, careful not to attract the man's attention toward the bed. To look into his gem-green eyes at that point would only fan her irrational nerves further. And they were irrational. Weren't they?

Sabrina delved deep into her troubled thoughts, searching for a more practical reason for her pulsating innards. And then it came to her. Perhaps her nerves were on edge because of the feelings Anthony had stirred within her. Feelings of anxiety . . . and guilt.

It made more sense now, the tight thrumming of her heart whenever the viscount drew near. It was the man's bewildered expression, his insistence to know why she was marrying her cousin, that had her all quivering inside.

Lids heavy with shame, she closed her eyes. She had asked herself that very same rebellious question once before: Why did she have to marry her cousin Istvan? But she had felt guilty for even thinking it. She *had* to marry her cousin. Promised to each other five years ago, their marriage was postponed until her training in herbal lore was complete. That training at an end, she now had a duty to fulfill. If she didn't marry Istvan, it would disgrace her father. And she would never do anything to hurt such a proud and wonderful man. Her obligation was clear . . . and yet, her dormant doubts were roused again. She thought she had reconciled herself to her wifely fate, but apparently she had not or she wouldn't be feeling such absurd jitters.

"Is something wrong?"

Her gloomy thoughts disbanded at the sound of a guttural voice. She looked over to find Anthony had risen from his chair and was studying her intently from across the room. She didn't like it when he looked at her in that way. With such . . . fire in his eyes. She didn't like it at all. And then it happened again. The flurry of sensations mounted in her belly.

Anthony advanced toward the bed and she became tenser with each step he took. He slumped a shoulder against the bedpost, the structure quivering in response to his weight.

"Well?" came the rumbled query.

Well what? Had he asked her something? She quickly thought back. "Nothing's the matter," she said hastily, indicating otherwise, which he was quick to pick up on.

"Are you in pain?"

"No."

A blond brow lifted in obvious disbelief.

"I feel fine," she insisted.

He stepped away from the bedpost and went down on one knee, so close to her, she could smell the musk of his hair and feel his warm breath tingle her flesh as he exhaled.

Goose pimples broke out all over her skin. But she wasn't cold. If anything, she was stifled under the blankets, though she didn't dare kick them off.

He reached for her. Instinct intervened and she jerked away—too quickly. The spasms erupted in her neck. She hissed at the painful contractions.

Anthony *tisk*ed. "I only wanted to remove the compress."

And he did just that, taking the moist cloth from her forehead and dropping it into the basin next to the bed.

Serves her right, she supposed, for allowing her ridiculous jitters to rule her senses like that.

She reached for her neck, but his hand was there first, diving through the mess of her untamed hair, making its way over to her throbbing muscles. She stiffened at his powerful touch. But her nerves soon gave way to the pleasurable feel of his warm fingers rocking back and forth, his palm rising and falling, his grip tightening.

Her eyes fluttered closed. The man had a masterful touch, so soothing, so disarming. In slow, circular movements, his fingertips kneaded, the heat building on her skin, her body sinking into peaceful oblivion.

Her jitters were back, only this time more profound. And she couldn't help but reflect that there was something odd about the man. It had to be his character. She found it off-putting. A dutiful aristocrat she could fathom, but beyond that, she found undue empathy and consideration far-reaching. Anthony should more closely resemble his prim and guarded sister. But he was nothing like his twin. He was nothing like any *gajo* she had ever met before—or any gypsy.

"Do you feel better?"

The gruffness of his voice jostled her from her languid daze. Her eyes snapped open to connect with his. Those passionate green orbs seemed to dance with energy, and she found herself sighing again for no known reason.

She nodded.

Anthony gently withdrew his fingers to avoid the

tangles in her hair, and she was conscious, all of a sudden, that her hair *was* in a frightful state. What a ghastly sight she must be!

"What was that melody you were humming by the stream?"

She quickly brought to order her scattered wits. "Why do you ask?"

"I was only curious. The tune still plays in my mind and I'd like to give it a name."

"It has no name. None known to me," she corrected in a weak voice. "I heard it as a child."

"Who sang it to you?"

Ebony lashes sunk like wilted rose petals. "I can't say."

"And why not?"

"It is forbidden to speak of the dead."

There was a short pause, then, "Why?"

More questions? More poking and prodding into her life? She should be asking him that very question. Why? Why did he care to know anything about her?

Her heart was thumping, loud and fierce. "Because a ghost can return from the beyond and cause mischief if summoned by name."

"And you are afraid of ghosts?"

She couldn't hold his gaze any longer and looked away. "I would not be afraid of this one . . . but it is still forbidden."

When another pause settled between them, she thought perhaps Anthony had lost interest in the subject. But he soon offered her a suggestion that had her heart knocking a bit faster.

"Then whisper the name quietly so the ghost cannot hear."

He smiled when he said it. Such a beautiful smile meant to disguise such a devious suggestion. To break away from tradition? Could she really do such a thing? Sabrina longed to say the name. It had been so many years since she'd spoken it aloud.

Although she couldn't bring herself to say the name outright, she did admit it was her mother who had sung her the lullaby.

"When did she die?" he asked.

"Eight years ago."

She sighed, relief sweeping over her. It felt so good to speak of her mother again.

"How did your mother die?"

"Sickness took her away."

He nodded. "So you decided to become a healer."

She blinked at the concept. "It is my destiny," she repeated softly.

His voice was just as soft. "I think you had a hand in that destiny."

Those deep green eyes seemed to melt into her. The fluttering sensation in her belly was back, more overwhelming than ever. Anthony could bring peace or chaos to her heart at any given moment. She never knew which. Nor did she understand why he found anything about her ordinary life even remotely interesting. Now *she* had her curiosities about him, but the man claimed to be her protector, so her interest in him was natural. But he had no such reason to care anything about her. And other than the occasional inquiry into her health, he didn't need to speak with her at all.

There was a light rap at the door.

Sabrina twitched at the abrupt sound, for it was more akin to a blast in her tightly wound state.

She watched, leery eyed, as a lingering Anthony finally rose from his knee and headed for the entrance. She took that moment to compose her befuddled senses before Ashley bustled inside the chamber.

"I have the apple cider and vinegar."

The woman set the vials on the writing desk, along with a tray of food, pushing aside the parchment her brother had written upon, sparing it a curious glance.

"To whom are you writing, Anthony?"

He closed the door behind her and leaned against it. "To my butler in London."

"But you will see him in a few days."

"No, I won't. I intend to escort Sabrina home."

A quick glimpse toward the said patient, and Ashley returned her attention to her twin. She didn't respond to her brother's intended detour, though the tightening of her lips revealed her opinion of the excursion.

"You had best get below and join the others for luncheon," suggested his sister.

He shook his head. "I cannot leave Sabrina unattended."

"I will attend her."

Sabrina stiffened at the prospect of being left alone with Ashley.

"Forget it, Ash," he said. "You go ahead and make my excuses, as usual."

"Anthony, if you don't make at least one appearance before the ball, Mama will be beyond herself with worry."

"I often skip meals when Cecilia is in the room. Mother is perfectly aware I can't stand to listen to anymore drivel over debutante details."

"Yes, but she doesn't expect you to avoid *all* meals!

She'll panic if she thinks you're ill and cannot attend the ball. And she *will* search the entire house for you."

"All right." He sighed in defeat and approached the bed, offering the occupant a rueful expression. "I must go below. But you will be safe in here with Ashley."

Sabrina doubted his conviction, but restrained her qualms and merely nodded in response.

Instructions were dispensed, that Ashley was to see to her meal and stir up a new wash for the compress before Anthony finally consigned his charge over to his sister's care. He vacated the chamber, though not too willingly, for Ashley had to give him a firm push out the door when he continued to linger.

At the loud scraping of metal, the bolt was fastened over the door and the two women were left alone in the room.

Chapter 8

Edith let out a boisterous giggle. Her uncle dandled her on his knee, and the little chit was delighted with every moment of her imaginative play as a jockey on a race horse.

"More, more," she demanded when Anthony took a repose to sample his wine.

"That's enough, Edith," Daniel informed his eldest daughter. "Now off to the nursery with you. Hop to it."

Daniel signaled for the governess to fetch the child and escort her from the dining hall and into the nursery, where her meal awaited.

"But I don't want to go," whined Edith, and promptly latched onto her uncle's armrest to demonstrate her discontent. She refused to relinquish her hold, despite the persistent tugs of her governess.

"Now, Edith, behave yourself like a proper young lady."

Anthony heard the child snort in response to her father's command and withheld his grin. Daniel's most authoritative voice, in fact, held no authority at all. The man didn't have it in him to rule with a stern hand, and Edith was well aware of that truth. She stubbornly refused to give way, and an exasperated Daniel finally rose from his seat to pry the child's fingers loose himself. But Anthony gestured for his brother-in-law to hold steady for a moment, then whispered into his niece's ear.

Edith listened patiently, and with a wide, crooked grin, surrendered her grip on the armrest, and contently skipped from the room, governess in tow.

A dazzled Daniel sunk slowly into his seat. "Pray, *what* did you say to her?"

Anthony shrugged. "Just a few magical words."

"Well, out with them. There's been many a'times I've needed some magical words to handle that child, so don't keep them to yourself."

"I simply told her, if she behaved like a good little girl, her father would give her Guenevere for her upcoming birthday."

Reginald Kennington, the earl of Wenhem, seated at the head of the long rosewood table, let out a hoot of husky laughter at his son-in-law's plummeting jaw. "My boy's fixed you but good, hasn't he, Winthrop?"

Daniel continued to gawk. "But that pony will cost me in excess of three hundred pounds!"

Anthony only grinned. "A small price to pay for a child's happiness."

"I'm glad to hear her uncle thinks so, because he's going to pay for half the expense."

"Agreed."

The men reached over the table to clink glasses and cement the deal.

The old earl shook his head in light amusement. "That chit has you two gents coiled around her little finger."

Two sets of brows raised at the aging earl.

"I'm well aware of the irony," Reginald remarked curtly, his humor abating at the thought of the pending ball he was forced to finance. "But in my defense, Cecilia is much older and more skillful at manipulation."

It was unanimous. They were all docile when it came to the wishes of the females in their lives. No one was immune from tears, smiles, or batting eyelashes.

But warm memories soon faded, as a grousing Reginald interposed, "Speaking of the demands of ladies, I haven't had a moment's peace in days. There's a knock on my study door every two minutes. Something is always missing, or has yet to arrive, or has yet to be bought. I hate this blasted ball."

Daniel chuckled. "By tomorrow evening it will all be over."

The old man scoffed. "A veritable eternity for someone my age."

"You have many years left in you," said Anthony.

The seventy-two-year-old Reginald cast his son a dubious glance. "Humph. If this ball doesn't kill me, then we'll just see about your prediction. Your sister Ashley's début was decent, but Cecilia's will be a monstrosity."

A monstrosity indeed, making Anthony's attempts to veil Sabrina all the more intricate. But not impossible. With a little help from Ashley, he'd continue to keep his gypsy safely stowed away. Thus far, all was progressing as planned. His estrangement from the household, for instance, hadn't garnered much attention from his kin. The male members of the family, not surprisingly, thought nothing of his absence during the last two meals, quite envious, in fact, that he'd managed to escape the grueling ordeals, which consisted of little more than prolonged discussions over decorations, menus, and last-minute alterations to guest lists. As for the female members, his vacant chair had brought about a single demand before each dining as to his whereabouts, which Ashley had skillfully deflected to other more pressing concerns over the approaching revelry. And so, swiftly forgotten, the viscount had escaped any exhaustive questioning, while his present appearance at luncheon would summarily dispense with any lingering doubts as to his welfare.

"I hate to bring up such a subject at this time," said Reginald, the lull in the conversation having brought more solemn issues to his mind. "But it must be dealt with, and I see no reason to postpone the inevitable."

Anthony sighed, fully expecting to hear what his father was going to say next.

"I hope you will find time during your stay to speak with my steward, Anthony. You will one day inherit the estate and you must be well acquainted with all managerial affairs."

"I know, father," Anthony concurred, albeit reluctantly. Life in the country may bring with it more space to roam, but that space was dotted with naught but a humdrum assortment of blossoms and trees, neither of which sparked much exuberance in a man like Anthony, who'd always preferred to reside in the city, much to his father's displeasure. The earl had hoped his son and heir would eventually demonstrate some enthusiasm for the vast property he was destined to inherit, but Anthony's interests in the estate were minimal at best, and his father was well aware of that unfortunate reality. Unable to conform to the monotony of country life, the viscount tended to find his world shrinking whenever he was forced to review the accounting books or speak to the land steward. He saw no reason to diddle away his time hunched over an endless procession of numbers. That's *why* an administrator was hired to oversee the estate. And so long as the administrator counted every crop sold at market, Anthony need not have to.

"You must be especially stern when it comes to the finances of your future bride," Reginald resumed to narrate the list of imperative reasons why his son should continue with his tutelage. "The next Lady Wenhem will naturally live at a certain standard, but you mustn't allow her to cajole you into frivolous expenses—like the current Lady Wenhem," he grumbled with a hint of self-chastisement. "Our wealth isn't without limits. You must make that clear."

"I will, Father."

"Yes, well, so long as we understand each other. I expect this estate to be in our family for many generations to come." And then he uttered in all gravity, "I will haunt you from the grave should you fall into bankruptcy. Mark my words, I will."

Anthony swirled the wine in his glass. "I won't mind a ghostly visit from you once in a while."

"You'll mind when I bring your mother's spirit along to help with the haunting."

A dire threat indeed, Anthony reflected, as the image of his parents' specters trailing behind him for the rest of his life invaded his thoughts.

"I'll see your steward before I return to London."

Reginald gave a swift nod of approval, while Daniel

tried his damnedest to suppress his laughter, lifting his wine glass to conceal his smirk.

At the sound of approaching footsteps, the gentlemen rose from their seats to greet the arriving ladies, only to find it was the butler, Binste, who appeared in the doorway instead.

Three grumbling men returned to their chairs.

"A letter has arrived for you, Lord Hastings."

Silver tray in hand, Binste made his way over to the viscount and presented him with the illustrious platter.

With a nod of thanks, Anthony took the folded parchments before the stoic butler retracted his steps and disappeared back into the corridor.

"Who is it from?" came the curious query from his brother-in-law, who leaned over the table to try and catch a better glimpse of the correspondence.

Anthony had yet to determine that himself. The directions were a scrawling mess. It was a marvel the letter had found its way into his hands at all.

He broke open the red wax seal and stared at the rambling hieroglyphics, trying to make some sense of the letter's baffling content. Unable to comprehend anything, though, he quickly flipped to the last page and noted the signature.

He smiled. "It's from Vincent."

"And how is the old boy?" was heard from the earl.

"I'm not quite sure," said Anthony, still bewildered over his best friend's inscrutable penmanship.

Vincent Longhurst must have been foxed when he'd scribbled three parchments full of illegible handwriting. Anthony could decipher no more than a few fragments: *lady bird, hobble, return in time to* . . . He crinkled his brow at the mysterious last word. It was hopeless.

He folded the letter and tucked it away in his inner breast pocket. The epistle was unlikely to be all that important. Vincent loved to reveal the current *on-dit* of his life, especially when he was ape-drunk, and odds were, the pages contained another haphazard account of his latest torrid affair. Anthony would hear all about the tryst soon enough, once he returned to London and rejoined his comrade.

"Vincent's doing just fine," Anthony assured the other men at the table. "He sends his warm regards."

And so, with the mystery of the letter's author revealed, the gentlemen returned their attentions to more immediate concerns.

"By and by, where are the ladies?" Daniel inquired at that point, glancing over his shoulder to the wide open door and the empty corridor beyond.

"Heaven only knows," muttered Reginald, and set his furrowed hands atop his cane.

"Ashley will not be joining us for luncheon," said Anthony, hoping the fib he was about to impart would be accepted without much doubt, considering the hubbub reigning throughout the house. "Cecelia has set her to work on yet another decorative task."

"The poor dear," murmured her husband. "She's been overwrought these last few days. Do you know, I've observed her on one occasion pinching food to keep with her during the tiresome day."

An aghast Lord Wenhem slumped back into his chair. "Good gracious, but this ball will ruin us all."

Anthony lifted his wine to his lips. Eager to steer the discourse in a different direction, he decided it was time to tend to his other commitment and convince his brother-in-law to take his wife on that trip to Paris she'd been longing for. It was a few minutes later, with the help of the earl, that a thoroughly outnumbered and outwitted Daniel ungraciously conceded to the mainland trip. And when his absolute aversion to great bodies of water was taken into consideration, it was a sheer wonder that the two Kennington men were able to persuade their poor kin to embark on the voyage at all.

It was another few minutes before scurrying feet were heard making their way down the hall, and three famished gents rose in expectation of their remaining party, only to find a belated Cecelia appear under the doorframe.

"Where is your mother?" demanded Reginald.

"Looking for—" She stopped just short of the table when she noticed her brother. "Oh, here you are. Mama has gone in search of you for luncheon."

"Humph. I rescind my earlier prediction." Reginald sunk back into his seat. "It's not the ball which will kill me but starvation."

"Excuse me."

Anthony was already out of his chair and stalking toward the end of the elongated room, when Reginald called out, "What's wrong?"

But in his haste, Anthony offered no explanation, and three sets of curious gazes followed his large frame out the door.

"What was that all about?" Cecelia took her seat, and with a flick of her wrist, unfurled a white linen napkin and placed it over her lap, protecting the pale green of her muslin gown.

"Anthony's probably off to the kitchen to fetch his meal," surmised a disgruntled Daniel.

"Smart boy," came from Reginald. "If hobbling on

my cane didn't take so long, I'd make my way over to the kitchen to dine myself."

A bowl of cider wash nestled in her hands, Ashley stood by the bedpost, her sharp forest-green eyes honing in on the apprehensive occupant.

"My brother has taken great pains to protect you," came the stiff assertion. "I do hope you appreciate his efforts."

Sabrina said nothing in reply. Those so-called pains didn't seem all that great, not when she felt so unprotected.

Setting the bowl on the table beside the bed, Ashley wrung the excess liquid from the linen and placed it over the patient's brow. "You understand, of course, my brother should not have brought you here. A physician's care would have been more appropriate."

On that matter the two could agree. Sabrina might deplore the idea of being under the care of a *gajo* healer, for such men were often inept, but she'd much prefer that arrangement to her present predicament. Whatever it was that Anthony was making her feel, a physician could do no worse.

Ashley's staid glare soon withered. Her eyes darted from the bed to the floor, and she began to chew on her bottom lip.

"With you here, it's most . . . well, you see . . ."

The woman's newfound struggle for words brought more worries to Sabrina's mind, and she scrunched the bed sheets hard between her fingers. But then the obvious broke through her uneven thoughts and she whispered, "I know about the ball tomorrow."

"It's not the ball."

"Then what is it?"

"Anthony's reputation, is all." Ashley wrung her moist fingers. "Women tend to fall at his feet."

"I'm not clumsy."

Ashley gave her a blank look. "No, I mean to say women lose their hearts to the viscount. He has this irresistible allure when he smiles and ladies fall under his charms and my brother isn't one to resist an invitation . . . It's all rather fickle," she rounded off hastily.

Sabrina's dark brows pinned together in confusion. "An invitation?"

A tinge of color stretched over high-rounded cheekbones. "Oh, lud!" Ashley whirled around and hastened over to a window, muttering to herself, "This is all so vexing. My brother knows his place, surely. To think that he would . . . with a . . . even if she offered to . . ."

Ashley made her way back over to the bed, her steps steady and deliberate. She took in a deep breath, and said firmly, "This is most improper but it must be said, and the burden falls upon me to deliver the counsel. Anthony is a rake."

Sabrina blinked in surprise.

With that last tidbit of information now in the open, Ashley seemed a little more at ease and recommenced with her sermon. "My brother enjoys the company of a woman—more than he should—and you may find yourself unable to withstand his inherent charms. I would advise you to look past his smiles, for he treats all women in a similar fashion." Her fingers knitted tightly. "Furthermore, my brother is not one to refuse an invitation . . . to resist an affair with a fawning young lady—a vice I do not approve of. I recommend you keep your wits about you and my brother at bay. Think of him solely as your temporary guardian." The oration at an end, she let loose a long-winded sigh of relief. "I'll let you rest now."

Ashley hastened back to the writing desk, where she proceeded to cap the vials of ingredients used to prepare the cider wash.

Bemused, Sabrina could only stare at the pale violet of the muslin-clad figure. It took her another moment of reflection before the full impact of Ashley's words walloped her with startling clarity.

There was an unexpected rush of peculiar emotions that clustered in her chest, making it difficult to breathe. A fawning young lady? Is *that* what Ashley thought of her? A wanton ready to hurl herself at the viscount?

Sabrina didn't think it was possible, but her whole body was blushing at that point. She wanted to disappear under the covers and never emerge. To be considered something so shameless? Why, it was no better than being called a "filthy gypsy."

And then it struck her. Ashley *did* see her as nothing but a filthy gypsy. All those murmurings of one's proper "place" were her desperate attempts to convince herself of her brother's respectable behavior, that he would never stoop so far below his rank as to consort with a mere gypsy. But Ashley had failed to convince herself of such a thing, and had resolved to caution the trespassing gypsy instead.

If Ashley held her in such dismal esteem, what, then, must Anthony think of a half-naked gypsy in his bed? An easy conquest? Did he expect payment for all his efforts to conceal her with a night of . . .

She couldn't even bring herself to consider the thought. Oh, curse those blasted mongrels who'd chased her in the woods! Had it not been for their cruel persistence, she would never have found herself in this predicament, grappling with such a flurry of questions and fears.

There was a firm rap at the door. The mayhem in Sabrina's soul was abruptly put aside as her wide eyes darted to the entrance.

"Anthony, I insist you join the family for luncheon."

"Mama!" a panicked Ashley whispered.

The rattling of the door handle was followed by another persistent set of knocks. The trapped women exchanged horrified glances.

"Anthony? What is the matter? Open this door at once."

"Mother!" a distant voice echoed from the other side of the barrier.

There was a brief pause before a confused woman demanded, "Anthony, if you are out here, then who is in your room?"

"No one," was his swift reply. "The handle is stiff and has been difficult to turn for quite some time. It may appear to be locked, but a firmer push will eventually get you inside the chamber."

"Do you mean to say, I've been pleading with the *door* asking if anything was amiss?"

"Think nothing of it, Mother. The servants already suspect we're all mad, overworking them to such an extent. Your conversation with the door will only confirm their opinion."

"Why thank you for those words of comfort," came the dry retort.

The murmuring voices soon withdrew.

Two long-held sighs of relief burst into the room. The women glanced at each other before their discomfort resurfaced and both turned their attentions away.

Chapter 9

"It looks like rain."

Anthony stood by the window, observing the gathering storm clouds with mild curiosity. He released the pale sheers that swung back into position and turned away from the glass.

Sabrina was watching him intently. She'd grown quiet ever since his return from luncheon, more quiet than usual. Attempts to draw her out of her reticent mood had failed. His questions went unanswered. His comments went ignored. And if she wasn't studying him so profoundly, he might wonder if she even noticed him in the room at all.

"Sabrina, what's the matter?"

Silence.

"I know the near encounter with my mother was frightening, but it's over now."

Still nothing.

Women and their fastidious ways! Couldn't she just tell him what was wrong and be done with it?

Well, if she refused to be forthcoming, he'd just have to pry it out of her. He moved away from the window.

Was she sinking deeper into the feather mattress?

Anthony paused at the end of the bed, his eyes searching her features for clarity. *He* was the cause of her sudden angst? He bristled, indignant at the thought. How was it she still viewed him in the same vigilant light as a common stranger?

Bloody hell. It just wasn't right. Why should Sabrina spend the next few days in needless fear of him?

He had to do something. But what? What would it take to do away with her persistent suspicions? His word alone was obviously insufficient. But how to offer her proof of his just intentions? And then the thought came to him.

"Do you read palms?" he asked.

"What?"

He came around to the bedside and dropped to one knee. "It has occurred to me that gypsies often read palms to assess a person's character. Unless, of course, I am mistaken."

Those dubious blue spheres dimmed under the thick dark trim of her lowered lashes. "You're not mistaken. I'm gifted with the sight."

"Wonderful."

He promptly flipped his hand upside-down, presenting her his palm.

"What are you doing?" she demanded.

"I've never had my palm assessed. Curiosity beckons me."

Anthony had no idea whether a man's character was actually engraved in his palm, so he was taking a mighty risk in volunteering his hand. His gypsy might see nothing but a treacherous knave in the lines. Then where would he be? But since she already considered him a threat, he decided to go forth with his dodgy gamble. At worst, she'd continue to ignore him. With luck, however, she'd detect something other than an uncouth disposition, something more favorable to put her qualms to rest.

"Come now, Sabrina, you've done this many times before. What's one more palm?"

She studied him hard for a long while. Apparently his palm *was* one too much, for she made no outward movement to accept his challenge.

His voice low, he offered an encouraging smile before suggesting, "Wouldn't you prefer to know the kind of man I am?"

He was beginning to doubt the credence of his plan when she shrunk back against the cushions even further.

"Is something the matter?"

He already knew something *was* amiss, but he also knew his gypsy was too stubborn to admit to it. At last, she sighed in concession.

With faintly trembling fingers, she grasped the strong hand extended before her. His heart thudded a bit faster. It was such a thrilling sensation to feel her caressing his skin, even if her intentions were wholly innocent. Her touch was warm and soft as she gingerly trailed her forefinger along the grooves of his palm, assessing their merit, careful to avoid any contact with his eyes.

"This is your life line," her voice faint, she pointed to the etch nearest his thumb. "Its depth means you're passionate and enjoy a good challenge."

Right so far, though the challenges he preferred were reserved for the bedchamber. But Sabrina didn't need to know that.

His breathing deepened as her finger moved up to the middle line that slashed across his palm.

"This line stands for knowledge. It reveals you use your wisdom for a good cause."

This is progressing splendidly, he thought with confidence, unwilling to interrupt the girl with any comments of his own. She should consider him a saint by the end of the reading—though he hoped the reading was nearing an end. Being so close to her, feeling her feathery touch, a true healer's touch, was beginning to rouse within him passionate and wily emotions he had tried to restrain. He couldn't feel this way for her, aroused and possessive. He shouldn't want what he could not have. But therein lay the very trouble. There was nothing in life he could not have, at least there hadn't been before Sabrina had come along. And now here she was, a true temptation, touching him, her warm breath falling onto his palm, her beautiful body snugly tucked under *his* covers.

It was cruel, to be this near her, to want to reach out and feel the heat of her skin in return. It was devastating, feeling her hands cradle his palm so delicately. A simple gesture that provoked such a fiery response within him. The intensity was building inside him. He noticed her hand shaking, moving slowly over the last of the three lines that streaked across his palm.

Her voice dwindled, and he had to lean in to hear her whisper, "This is your heart line."

She stroked the heart line softly, as if mesmerized by what she saw. And he, in turn, was mesmerized by her.

He looked down at the groove, so meaningless to him, and wondered what she saw in it. His palm suddenly closed around her fingers, trapping them. She gave a quick gasp in surprise, her questioning eyes darting up to meet his. What beautiful eyes they were. How much he yearned to know what burned within them.

He found his voice, rough and urgent, almost pleading in its tone. "What do you see in my heart, Sabrina?"

He had never asked anyone such a fool thing. It was obvious to him who and what he was, an aristocrat, a lover, so few and simple terms. And he had never cared to know what anyone else had thought of him. But he did care to know what his gypsy thought. For some reason he had yet to understand, it mattered to him what she saw in his heart—if there was anything to even see.

"Well?" he urged her gently.

She stared intensely at him. "I see peace."

Peace? He crinkled his brow. "What do you mean?"

But she had no more left to say on the matter, and he realized, disgruntled, he would simply have to dwell upon her cryptic words.

Peace.

He couldn't comprehend the meaning. He certainly didn't feel very peaceful at the moment, such a torrent of passionate emotions battling inside him.

Sabrina wrenched her fingers away from him. She was displeased with the reading's outcome. It was there in her eyes, a brewing storm. But there wasn't a stitch of wicked intentions revealed in his palm, so he didn't understand why she was so upset.

He gathered his fingers together and pulled his hand away. "You doubt your own reading?"

She hesitated before admitting, "I don't know what to believe anymore."

"And why is that?"

She recoiled in silence. It appeared as though her suspicions of him would have to remain intact, much as he wished it were otherwise. He was just another *gajo* in her eyes, just another stranger to be anxious about, and that was all he would ever be. And he hated knowing it.

Anthony heaved out of his squatting position and headed over to his writing desk, intent on finishing the letter to his butler, there being nothing left to say to dissuade his gypsy of her relentless misgivings.

But it was a few minutes later that he heard the hesitant voice pipe up behind him.

"I'm thirsty."

Slowly, he turned around to look at the demure figure huddled under the blankets, the compress dipping below her brow so only the thin black slits of her eyes were visible.

He could feel those assessing blue eyes on him as he retrieved the pitcher from the privy and poured her a refreshing glass of water. She downed it greedily.

"Still thirsty?"

When she shook her head, he took the empty glass and set it aside. Back at his desk, he resumed the letter. But three lines later came the next interruption.

"I'm cold."

He didn't rise from his seat this time, only glanced at her from over his shoulder. Her features were inscrutable. What was the girl up to?

Hoisting out of his chair, he walked over to the trunk

at the foot of the bed and lifted the heavy lid to rummage through the articles buried inside. No blanket.

The lid thudded closed. Next he went over to the wardrobe and riffled through the paraphernalia there, again meeting with defeat. He didn't know where else to look. This was a task for a chambermaid. Perhaps his mother or even Ashley might know where the bed linens were stored, but he had no idea.

In the end, a cloak would have to suffice and he laid the garment over the blankets already piled atop his gypsy.

"Will there be anything else?" he asked.

"A book."

He lifted a brow at her ambiguous request, thinking perhaps he hadn't heard her correctly. "A book?"

When she made no effort to correct him, he traveled over to the bookshelves and randomly selected a title.

He returned to the bed and handed her the volume. "Will this suffice?"

She accepted the book of poetry and said not a word. Opening it to the first page, she began to read—upside down.

Without any irreverence, he plucked the book from her hands, flipped it right side up, and placed it back between her fingers. "Enjoy."

Anthony sat back down at his desk, still unable to fathom what had just happened. What purpose had all those errands served, other than to distract him? He sighed and stared at the half-written parchment, unable to recall what else he had intended to mention in the letter.

At last, unable to stir his memory, he set the note

aside and plopped the quill back into the inkwell. Hands clutching the armrests, he swiveled the chair around so he was facing the bed.

Sabrina was watching him, the book closed and resting in her lap.

"Was the poetry not to your liking?"

"I can't read," she said.

"So why did you ask for the book?"

"To see if you'd bring it to me." Then she added, her tone accusing, "You're too kind."

He chuckled at that. "So that is my crime."

"Your crime?"

"If your silence is a form of punishment, then I must assume you've condemned me for a crime. Though I admit, I'm taken aback by the charge of kindness."

"You mock me."

"Untrue." His voice deepened. "I merely wish to understand why you find my consideration so sinister. I am your protector, after all."

Her lips twisted, as though in dispute of that proclamation. "A man like you shouldn't care about a gypsy's comfort."

He stretched out his legs and wove his fingers together in his lap, his elbows positioned on the armrests. His eyes intent on the girl, he asked, "Must all nobles be villains?"

"No . . . but I don't want to be in your debt." There was a faint trembling in her voice as she spoke. "I can't repay you for saving my life, so if you expect anything—"

"I ask for no payment," he cut in, indignant at the thought that his chivalry was for hire. "My duty is to your well-being."

"And you want nothing in return? At all?"

"Certainly not."

He heard a sigh of what he assumed was relief, and wondered if perhaps he'd been tricked into offering a promise he couldn't keep. Though the thought of any monetary compensation was repugnant, a more personal reward, such as a parting kiss from the lovely young Sabrina, would not have been unwelcome. But he would never ask for such a gift now. Not after the promise he had just made.

Anthony sighed as well, not with relief, but with disappointment at his sealed fate.

Chapter 10

❧ ～◯◯～ ❧

A crooked flash of light split the dark sky. The distant groan of thunder followed seconds later.

Sabrina stared at the curtains, mesmerized by the dance of lightning, clutching the bedspread harder each time the grumbling thunder boomed.

It was nearing eleven o'clock. Time for sleep, though the rush of footsteps just outside the door indicated otherwise.

The occasional cry of a distraught Cecelia, followed by the firm reassurances of her mother, penetrated the room.

"Be thankful it rained tonight," Sabrina heard the consolation, "for tomorrow promises to be a beautiful day."

"And if the rain doesn't stop in time for the arriving guests?" was heard the sorrowful lament.

"Nonsense, child. It won't rain all night and then all day without break. And if by some act of God it does, we'll see to all the guests' comfort."

"Oh, Mama, what if a storm rages and the guests won't come?"

"Hush, Cecelia. That's rubbish! The whole county is privy to the great lengths we've gone to orchestrate this gala. So much so, this ball will be spoken of in St. James's court for weeks to come. No one will dare miss such an event for a few pelts of rain. Now off to bed with you, or your complexion will be sickly in the morning."

Another desperate cry was detected before the doleful voices withdrew.

Such mayhem governed the sky and land. Equal mayhem reigned within the walls of the house. And the mayhem gushing about in Sabrina's heart was no less powerful.

Anthony was asleep on the sofa, or so she presumed. He'd not stirred nor made a sound for more than an hour, though she couldn't understand how anyone could sleep under such conditions. She hated storms, always had since she was a child. Grand acts of nature were revered by her people as moments of great magic, but she'd never grown to admire a force so powerful it could shake the very earth. She felt so helpless and alone at such a time. So tiny and insignificant. And with the addition of soaring walls surrounding her, she felt even smaller.

The glass rattled as the wind howled and the rain beat against the panes. She scrunched her eyes tight and brought the covers up to her nose.

It was subtle at first, the images slinking through her mind, but soon, unabashed, she was envisioning the round, muscular contours of Anthony's formidable shoulders.

Sabrina's cheeks tinted at the unfitting thought, but the man happened to be more appealing to dwell upon than the wild tempest raging just outside the windows.

She'd seen him for the first time that night without his shirt. After the lights were extinguished, he'd removed his garments, all but his trousers, before sliding under the blankets. It was the repetitive streaks of lightning that had illuminated the darkened room, providing her with the startling vision of the vast expanse of muscle. Robust curves, shadowed by peaks and valleys of light and dark, made up the tightly built chest that had stolen her breath for a second before he'd disappeared behind the sofa.

What was wrong with her? Was she turning into a "fawning young lady," as Ashley had termed it? She dearly hoped not. But she couldn't seem to get Anthony out of her head. It didn't help matters that that afternoon's reading had served to highlight only honorable character traits, quite the opposite of what she was expecting to see in his palm, especially after Ashley's scalding assessment of her brother. And then Anthony had promised he wouldn't ask for compensation—of any kind—so *that*, along with the favorable palm reading, should have put her mind at ease about the man. But it did not. She still felt something in her belly every time she looked at him. She still felt those damn jitters and they were beginning to rule her senses.

It was what she had seen in his heart line that really troubled her. Peace. Her peace. Her future happiness and well-being was laid out before her in his hand. *His* hand. What could the man possibly have to offer that would bring her peace? He was an outsider. Everything in his world frightened her. But there it was, peace, staring back at her when she'd assessed his palm. It just didn't make any sense.

An ear-shattering clap of thunder jolted Sabrina upright. Her nerves rattled and her eyes sprang open, shooting instinctively to the sofa—and to Anthony. There he was, seated like a statue, staring straight at her. When he realized she was awake as well, he was on his feet.

That powerful body treaded softly toward her, and she felt an overwhelming rush of both giddiness and panic at his approach.

He stopped just short of the bed, his back to the windows, the entire front length of him masked in darkness.

"I had a dream," he murmured thickly, attesting to the fact that he had been asleep until only a short while ago.

She bent her knees and crossed her legs at the ankles, blinking up at the shadowed figure. "About what?"

Anthony settled on the bed, the mattress dipping with his newly imposed weight, and leaned over her.

"What are you doing?" she demanded hastily, only to find he was reaching for the candle.

He struck the match and lit the wick. She gulped hard at the feel of his bare shoulder rubbing against her breast, and the silk of his tawny-gold mane brushing against her naked arm, like feathers scraping softly over her skin.

He withdrew to his previous position, the mellow kindle of the low-burning flame illuminating his frame. A brooding faerie king, that's what he looked like, beautiful, dangerous, and mighty.

Her sea-blue eyes, brimming with wonder, poured over him in a keen, raking look. A tuft of hair spiraled from his belly, vanishing beneath his unfastened trousers, and a blush adorned her cheeks at the thought of where that hair ended up. Her eyes quickly skated up his wide chest, blanketed in a thick fleece of golden curls, and she suddenly wondered what those curls felt like. Were they soft? Or rough like the sonorous depth to his voice?

By the time her eyes elevated to meet Anthony's, it was to find he'd arched an amused brow at her examination. His lids were heavy with sleep, but his eyes were attentive and probing. Had she really gawked at him for so long? She was sure it had been only a few seconds, a quick survey of his build. But her sense of timing was apparently off.

Sabrina gave a tiny prayer of thanks for the dim light in the chamber. It helped to conceal the brightness of her flushing features.

"Your dream?" her voice cracked as she reminded him of his reason for coming over to the bed in the first place.

A faint smile touched his lips. She scooted further back against her pillow.

"I dreamt of you."

Those words, the gruff tone in which they were uttered, had an unnerving effect on her.

"I saw you amidst a sea of flickering lights," he went on. "You were disoriented. When I reached out for you, you vanished into the darkness. I searched everywhere for you, but the blackness and specks of light seemed to stretch on forever, and I finally had to admit, I had lost you."

Massive shoulders bowed forward. He brushed a knuckle gently across her cheek. It was like a streak of fire scorching her skin.

"I've never had such a disturbing dream," he murmured softly, still caressing her cheek, his eyes growing darker, more intense.

She was hypnotized. Her breath trapped in her throat. Her heart knocked hard against her ribs. She could only grip the bed sheets tightly in her lap, her knuckles turning white from the lack of blood flow.

"I won't let you fall into an abyss," he vowed. His thumb pressed tenderly over her mouth. "No one will hurt you, Sabrina."

She shuddered under the warmth of his words, and rebuked herself for allowing those words to affect her at all.

He was much too close, only inches from her. Panic prompted her to smack a hand flat against his chest to hold him at bay. Her pulse sprinted at the feel of the golden curls beneath her touch. The hair was soft. A pectoral muscle immediately jumped in response to the hand resting on top of it. Like wild horse hooves, his heart thundered beneath her palm, as a surge of heat invaded her finger tips, gliding up her wrist, her forearm . . .

Time stopped in that moment. She felt as if she'd melted into the dark pools of Anthony's eyes, lost in his soul for a fraction of a second. The moment was fleeting, but it was long enough to make her appreciate that she was treading over dangerous waters.

She hastily snatched her hand away, but before she could think to move again, his lips were over hers.

Soft, warm lips caressed her mouth, slowly at first, and then the kiss deepened. His lips parted and with rough urgency his mouth moved over hers. The strong scent of him filled her nostrils. The moist heat from his naked torso swathed her skin. The hungry movements of his mouth had her quivering right down to her toes.

She didn't know how to react to the kiss. She felt inept, gawky in her response. No man's lips had ever touched hers before. Forbidden to taint her gift of healing, such intimacy was denied her, so she was naïve when it came to the art of lovemaking. Not ignorant of the act itself, for the women in her caravan spoke candidly on the matter, but she lacked all personal experience. Her instincts didn't seem to be functioning. She didn't know what to do, how to hold him, how to return the intense feelings of pleasure he was giving her.

It was in that very moment she understood why a man's touch had been denied her for so many years. Anthony had the power to disorient her sense of being, to disrupt the very center of who she was and toss her amid a whirlwind of unique sensations.

His large, powerful hand slipped down her cheek, stroking her skin, beckoning goosebumps to erupt all over her body. Those long fingers scraped toward her midriff, caressing the wool crepe of her undergarment, teasing her sensitive skin, sending shudders of tickled delight throughout her weakened limbs.

"So sweet," he whispered thickly against her mouth. "So beautiful."

She blushed at his words. His touch, the sound of his deep and rich voice was doing things to her she had never felt before. Wonderful things. Things she had never even dreamed of. Emotions were all moving inside her, swirling together, colliding, erupting. It was like a dream. An intense, soul-wringing dream.

Wide-spread fingers rubbed up and down her ribs, massaging her sides, the pressure building against her skin. She shuddered in response. Her heart throbbed. A profound impulse to touch him in return eclipsed her, and she timidly reached for the firm muscles of his upper arms, gripping the taut biceps in inexplicable urgency.

At her hesitant touch, his hand began to move. Up and up it went, slowly, until his thumb and forefinger wedged under her breast and he cradled the swollen mound.

She inhaled sharply. What sweet pleasure it was to feel Anthony's hand caress such an intimate part of her. The heat in her belly was churning. A spark seemed to flare, as his thumb darted over her thrusting nipple, and he pressed down hard on the tightening bud.

There was an intense explosion of sensations. A startled cry escaped from the depth of her throat. He quickly slipped his hand back down to her waist, stroking her hip, soothing her skittish passions.

Something was happening inside her. A fluttering in her belly, more intense than anything she'd ever felt before. So great was the disruption to her being, that she took no heed of the falling world around her. Not until her head bumped into the wooden headboard, and she yelped in pain at the timely throbbing in her skull.

It was then the magical moment was shattered. Guilt and fear came rushing forward. Guilt at the pleasure she had found in another man's arms. And fear of what her father would say if he ever discovered her indulgence in such a wicked kiss.

The noise of the tempest must have muffled her common sense, she thought in alarm, or she would never have done such a thing. Hands trembling, she braced her palms flat against a pair of wide, muscular shoulders and shoved.

A breathless Anthony broke away from her lips. His eyes burned under the misty yellow candle glow. His chest, heaving, pushed against her breasts with each draft of air he inhaled.

Confusion descended. The look in his eyes altered to that of a man who had just awakened from a dream, bewildered and befuddled by his surroundings.

His hands slowly slipped away from her waist, the last caress sending one final, sensuous tremor vibrating throughout her limbs. When his warm body shifted upright, a distinct chill gripped her. The heat they shared was gone. The closeness severed.

The deafening drum of her heart filled the silent void, and she was sure Anthony could hear every erratic beat.

"I'm sorry if I offended you," he said hoarsely. "I didn't mean to be so bold."

He withdrew from the bed, running a quivering hand through his tawny hair to comb back the curls.

She needed another moment to steady her own irregular breathing. "Why did you kiss me?"

He hesitated before admitting, "It must have been the dream. I was not entirely awake when I, ah . . . I apologize. It will never happen again."

She sunk back against her pillow, pulling the bed linen up to her chin, and closely watched his tall, wiry frame make its way over to the sofa, where he sat down for a moment before spreading out along the furniture's length.

Those tender words he'd whispered, those soft caresses, had all been part of a waking dream? He'd meant nothing he'd said or done?

A single pearled tear pooled in the corner of her eye and she wiped the moist nuisance away, determined not to succumb to sobs. What a ridiculous state to be reduced to. Just what did she find so upsetting? That the man *hadn't* been trying to seduce her? She should be grateful to hear it was all just a mistake. One that would never happen again.

But the ache welled in her throat, making it difficult to breathe. She'd never felt so inadequate, so demoralized. The kiss may have been wrong, but it had been her first kiss, opening a whole new world of emotions for her, and that she'd shared it with Anthony was unexpected, but not worthy of an apology.

Yet there was no concealing the remorse in his voice. He was sorry to have opened his eyes to find his lips on hers . . . a gypsy's.

It looked as though Ashley's concerns were misplaced, for her brother did know his place in world, and it was not to consort with the likes of her.

She leaned over and blew out the candle. For a long time, she just stared into the darkness. The clattering panes of glass and shuddering earth faded into oblivion, as the ramble of her thoughts raved greater than the spring storm drenching the countryside beyond.

Chapter 11

What a ghastly old man.

Anthony studied the unsightly subject matter looming above the fireplace in the main salon. Great-great-grandfather Kennington, he presumed. He had always hated the image staring back at him from the canvas, but with such a prominent position in the room, one could hardly ignore the macabre figure. He tried to, though, slowly twirling the glass of brandy between his fingers, shifting through his muddled thoughts.

And what a muddle they were. There wasn't a moment in the day when he wasn't rapt with the memory of what had happened the night before. He had vowed, to both Sabrina and himself, not to inflict any harm on her. He had even offered the girl his palm to prove there was no reason to mistrust him. And then look what he had done? Aggrieved his gypsy by prowling about the bedchamber bestowing unwelcome kisses.

Those baffled blue eyes stared at him still. That flustered voice, demanding a reason for the kiss, revolved over and over again in his mind. He had made a sheer ass of himself. And there was no easy way to rectify his blunder. All he could do was keep his distance from the girl, hoping the estrangement would bring her some mild comfort.

He sighed. What had possessed him to resort to such scoundrel intentions? The answer eluded him. But a remote part of his being was obliged to admit his reasons might not be so obscure as he preferred to think. That his actions, though veiled in a light mist of drowsiness, were more deliberate than inadvertent.

To think that he lacked such control! It was difficult to accept. Whatever desire he felt for his gypsy, his gentleman's duty preceded it—or so he tried to convince himself.

It was all a bloody mess. He needed to redirect his energy, his thoughts. He needed a conduit to do away with his mounting lust so he could focus wholly on his duty.

And then in rushed the perfect solution to his frustrating predicament.

His Mary—Meg!

Polishing cloth in hand, the young maid set to work on the wood furnishings, buffing first a small side table to an illustrious sheen before she moved on to a larger piece.

She had yet to notice him in the room, so engrossed was she with her task. The salon had been designated a ladies' parlor for the evening and his Mary-Meg was clearly eager to brighten the room and thus please her mistress.

Anthony's smile was slow to form. He knew firsthand the merry maid would be eager in other ways, as well, and he slowly sensed his sullen mood dissipate in anticipation of the release he would soon have. Once rid of his distracting lust, his mind would be at peace, and there would be no more grueling battles between his duty and desire.

He set his brandy aside. The young parlor maid shuffled past him in her haste, and he reached out to grasp her wrist. She gave a startled gasp, her cheeks turning a bright sunset pink when their eyes met.

"I beg your pardon, your lordship."

"Not at all, my dear." His voice was thick, deliberately so, in his attempts to woo the pretty little maid. She was petite, blonde, with a soft set of pouting lips guaranteed to ease his suffering.

And the more he admired her well-rounded figure, the less inclined he was for words. He pulled the little creature down into his lap and curled his arms around her. She let out a bubbly squeak, and he brought his lips together to whisper a soothing "shhhh" before his mouth captured hers in long-suppressed hunger.

It felt so good to be with a woman again. He needed his merry maid and the energy gained from a passionate tussle. He needed it as much as he needed food or water to survive.

Giggling and wiggling in his lap, the maid fumbled with her skirt until it was hiked up over her knees and she straddled him with a familiarity he found invigorating.

Her derrière undulated against his groin in slow, sensuous motions, her fingers groping beneath her petticoat to unfasten his trousers. "What if someone sees us?" she breathed excitedly.

"Devil take them if they do." He slipped his hands beneath her livery to grip the naked flesh of her posterior.

Their kiss intensified. His cock hardened, ready to

plunge inside the merry maid . . . And then the most appalling thing occurred to distract him from the coupling. An image of Sabrina flashed through his mind, followed by an intense feeling of pain in his chest. A pain he could only assume was guilt. And since he had little experience with the emotion, he found it all the more baffling.

But he had no time to dwell on his puzzling guilt. Footsteps and cheerful whistling were coming down the hall.

Anthony hoisted his Mary-Meg off his lap. Muttering every vile word he knew, he shakily refastened his trousers, while the distraught maid skittishly smoothed her black skirt into its proper position. Her cheeks were a blooming pink blush, her lips swollen and red. She was a perfectly appealing sight—and he damn well didn't understand why he found it so hard to be with her.

Guilt?

What rubbish! What did he have to feel guilty about? Certainly not some daft notion that he was betraying Sabrina in some way. Why, the gypsy wasn't even his. And he definitely didn't belong to her. So where was there a betrayal?

Nowhere. He was just being ridiculous. He didn't get very much sleep last night, so no wonder he was such a mess.

With a quick curtsy, the merry maid scurried from the room, almost colliding with the strolling figure of Lord Winthrop. She gave an abrupt and mumbled apology before she hastened away, Daniel casting an odd look after her. But once he noticed his brother-in-law wedged in an armchair, Daniel's features brightened with mischievous amusement.

"Recuperating again are you, old boy?" Daniel strode into the salon with a jovial grin and settled into a cushioned seat opposite his brooding brother-in-law. "Hope I wasn't interrupting anything."

That got him a dark scowl, as Anthony tried to fight back the heat that still twisted and raged in his groin.

With an unrepentant chuckle, Daniel crossed his legs and removed his white gloves, slapping the pair over his bent knee. "Well, shift your attention for a moment. I've a piece of *on-dit* for you." He gave a roguish wink. "A little bird just whispered into my ear that an unexpected guest will be in attendance at the ball."

Since Anthony didn't give a fig for any of the soon-to-be-arriving guests, his frustrated passion making him sorely uncomfortable, his words were rather sharp and biting. "And this guest would be?"

"A marchioness."

"Am I to find this report engaging?"

"Well, you should," Daniel asserted, ignoring the viscount's darkening glower. "She's to be your next mistress, after all."

Anthony groaned and cupped his head in his hand. What ill-rotten timing! With a blasted ball to get through *and* ensuring Sabrina was safe *and* battling with his own swelling desire for the girl, he did not need the added distraction that this particular marchioness would impose upon him.

"It seems her ladyship is officially out of mourning," Daniel resumed. "And our dear Cecelia's début will be her first public presentation since the marquess's death. Word also has it that you and this particular marchioness are an intended lover's item." And then with his hand to his cheek, he whispered, "There's a discreet bet at White's over how many months the affair will last, or so I've been told."

"Not very discreet, is it?" he nearly growled.

"Come now, why the long face?"

"I'm not inclined to take a new mistress, is all—not yet anyway."

A disbelieving snort from his kin. "*You* not inclined? Become a monk, have you?"

In no affable temperament to engage in a badinage, Anthony glared at his brother-in-law. "Dare I confer with my sister on how encouraging you've been?"

Daniel's humor dwindled at that. "No need for threats, old boy. You know very well I'll not hear the end of it from Ashley if she suspects I've aided her brother in his philandering ways."

"So why are you *aiding* me?" he wondered dryly.

The man's grin returned. "Well, you see, I have it from another little bird—"

"You should get your head examined," he cut in tersely. "You have too many little birds fluttering about."

"That may be, but they do keep me thoroughly informed and entertained. Now, as I was saying, word is the marchioness is intent on having you for her next lover and this ball might prove to be the perfect forum to achieve her objective. Of course, your mother will have your head on a pike should you engage in a scandalous liaison during such a pinnacle time in our dear Cecelia's life."

"And you intend to watch me lose my head, is that it? A little retaliation for coercing you into that trip to Paris?"

"Consider it a parting gift before I set sail for the mainland."

"How very kind of you," he mumbled dryly.

Daniel's smile broadened. "Think nothing of it, old boy."

"We had best put this subject to rest."

"And why's that?"

"Your wife is on her way."

"How the devil do you know that?"

Ashley hastened into the room just then, her brisk steps so faint, the satin of her pale green gown barely whispered with a rustle.

Daniel shifted his bewildered gaze to his brother-in-law, but Anthony kept silent on the reflective glass of windows to his right, which allowed him a full view of the corridor, and thus his approaching sister.

"Mama bids us all to the front hall," said Ashley. "The guests are slowly arriving and we are to stand in the receiving line with the rest of the family."

A still-mystified Daniel slipped out of his chair. "Very well, my dear. Duty calls."

Anthony, too, hoisted himself from his seat, sure that the hardness in his groin had tapered enough so as not to offend any delicate miss and her mama. "Let us see this monstrosity to an end."

They all liberated a weary sigh in acquiescence, and then headed for the door, attending to any final adjustments in their accoutrements before stepping out into the corridor and proceeding toward the front hall to greet the arriving *ton*.

Anthony, his mood dark, his body still burdened with unfulfilled lust, straggled a short distance behind the chattering couple, mulling over the possibility he had rejected only moments ago.

A fling with the marchioness?

The lady was reportedly willing. His body was certainly willing. But could he cope with the demands of a mistress now? Could he afford to go without one might be the better question?

If he didn't find a way to rid himself of his distracting lust, Sabrina would be the recipient of all his attentions. And he wasn't going to make that mistake again.

A mistress it would have to be.

The sun drowsily slipped behind the distant crowd of trees. Vibrant shades of coral pink and magenta streaked the sky, like flaming arrows shot through the heavens.

Sabrina sat curled in an armchair, a blanket around her shoulders, fingering the locket hanging from her neck. Lined on either side of the window were heavy velvet drapes, a deep walnut brown in hue, tucked in swags and tied with golden chords. She skimmed her fingers lightly over the soft and supple fabric, warm from basking in the afternoon sun. Suspended from an iron rod and dangling to a pool on the floor, pale ivory sheers shrouded the barred panes of glass, and she peeked through the thin fabric to take note of the blossoming garden and the small lake in the distance, bouncing rippled sunbeams off its glasslike surface.

A perfect day to host a ball, she reflected, if the brilliant dusk foretold anything. Cecelia must be elated by the favorable outcome of the weather, and according to Anthony, close to three hundred guests would be in attendance for the dinner and ball scheduled to start at precisely seven o'clock.

Sabrina glanced over her shoulder to see the dials pointing to half past six, then returned her attention to the congested grounds. The windows in Anthony's room faced the rear of the estate, so she wasn't permitted a view of the arriving carriages, but many of the guests were enjoying a leisurely stroll through the garden before dinner was served.

The moving dots of colored gowns winding through the rows of spring blooms and shrubs, the hum of the orchestra rehearsing somewhere in the house, the patter of feet scurrying though the corridor as servants tended to last-minute details, injected a lively spark to Sabrina's otherwise dull spirit.

She'd been alone for much of the day. The solitude shouldn't bother her; she knew Anthony was needed elsewhere in the house. But still, a part of her suspected it wasn't brotherly duty keeping him at bay, but his desire to avoid her.

It was that damn kiss!

It was, wasn't it? The kiss? The root of all her troubles, her emotional angst? Had the kiss been a slobbering mess or Anthony's touch not nearly so artful, she'd have pulled away from him without a second thought and never ventured near the man again.

But the kiss had been none of those things, quite the opposite, leaving her innards all knotted and tense and still winding.

So many of her people had come to her throughout the years in search of love potions. But she'd never really understood what she was brewing. The herbal mixtures were intended to garner emotions she could not fathom . . . until now, that is.

Now there was such a raft of sensations still lingering, she almost wished there was a contrary potion to do away with them—almost. The feelings inside her weren't all that unpleasant. Her cousin Istvan certainly never incited such feelings. Though, truthfully, he'd never touched her in any real sense. But she knew, deep down in her gut, when he did press his lips to hers, Istvan would never be able evoke the emotions Anthony had.

And that troubled her. She hated to admit what the viscount could do to her with just one kiss, bringing her whole soul into disarray. She hated that the kiss had meant so much to her and nothing to him. She hated even more that he'd dismissed her from his mind, not offering her a look or more than a trivial word for much of the day.

Three swift raps on the door startled her from her meditation. There was a pause, followed by another two taps.

Sabrina sighed and glanced briefly at the time. Twenty minutes left in the hour. Anthony had promised to return before dinner, both to check in on her and to deliver her evening meal. To avoid calling out to her, he'd devised a series of knocks to let her know it was him at the door.

With the blanket still firmly wound around her body, Sabrina rose from the chair, her dizzy spells growing fewer and far less intense as the day progressed.

She shuffled over to the door, careful not to trip over the blanket's dangling ends, and unlocked the barrier, allowing Anthony to whisk inside the room before she fastened the bolt once more.

His long legs strode toward the small circular table, centered amidst a gathering of armchairs, where he deposited the meal.

"I apologize for my tardiness, but there was an endless procession of guests I had to greet before I could sneak away."

He glanced at the isolated chair positioned by the window, then turned to face her. She observed that the green silk of his waistcoat matched the hue of his eyes, and that his black, well-tailored garment emphasized his height and broadness of chest. She'd seen his attire earlier in the afternoon, but hadn't taken a good look at him then, for he'd rushed out the door the moment he was ready. Now she couldn't resist a quick comb of his frame, from the slicked curls of his tawny-gold hair to the shiny tips of his booted toes. He was stunning, all decked out in his finery.

For the first time that day, sharp, forest-green eyes darkened and regarded her with a hint of emotion. "You should be resting in bed."

Holding the blanket tightly around her shoulders, she returned quietly, "I prefer the chair."

He nodded thoughtfully, then gestured toward the window. "And what do you think of this extravaganza?"

"It seems peaceful."

"The ruckus is about to commence and I must be getting back to it. I will return in the early hours of the morning, after the last guest has departed or retired to bed."

She nodded in understanding and stepped aside when he advanced. He paused by the door, his fingers on the handle, as though he'd forgotten to say something, but then he turned the knob and slipped into the corridor.

Sabrina locked the door behind him and settled back into the armchair, ignoring her dinner for the time being.

She parted the sheers to view the grounds, just as an announcement was made that dinner was soon to be served.

The scurrying dots of color wove through the garden aisles, making their way toward the house, and she slumped back into her chair with another sigh.

It was some hours later that the buzz of the ball infused the entire household, and Sabrina found herself curled under the covers, a single candle burning by the bed. She'd spent the greater part of the evening listening to the murmur of three hundred celebratory guests, followed by the drone of the orchestra striking up dance after dance.

With sleep impossible, she delved into her imagination, thinking of what was happening below stairs. But her thoughts weren't very engaging. She didn't know what to envision, never having witnessed a *gajo* spectacle before.

The style of the dance couldn't be all that striking, she concluded, since the music was rather steadily paced without much of a lively tempo. And based on the rigid postures she'd seen strolling through the garden, the guests weren't likely to be all that spirited either. The richness of Anthony's room confirmed the ballroom was equally, if not more, lavishly adorned, though particular details were hard for her to imagine. Beyond that simple picture, she could think of little else.

Her imagination wanting, she wandered elsewhere in her thoughts, suddenly aware that her end of the house was relatively quiet except for the distant murmur of rambling guests. The servants were all likely crammed in the kitchen tending to a mountain of dishes. And that meant that the house was virtually deserted on the second level . . . and probably certain wings on the lower level.

It was a few seconds later that the blankets landed on the floor at the foot of the bed.

Sabrina was slow to sit up, wanting to avoid any light-headedness. It was perfect, she thought, the darkness outside, the many bodies huddled below, too densely packed to notice any one face in particular. She could leave without risk of discovery and be home in a couple of days. She would move slowly through the country-side, resting more often, delaying her return to her camp if she had to in order to offset any chance of faintness. But she didn't think risk of further injury was great. She felt fine, much better than she had two days ago.

Her excitement grew at the prospect of retreat with-out heart-aching confrontation. Freshly filled with en-ergy, she quickly located her belongings in the shadowed room and got dressed. When her boots were on, she pulled her hair back and tied the long tresses with a dark red kerchief she found tucked in her bag.

After a swift glance around the room to ensure she'd forgotten nothing, she patted her ears to feel that the gold hoops were still there and touched the locket at her breast. With a deep breath, she blew out the candle. Only moonlight spilled into the room. Her bag in her hands, she headed for the door.

Wait!

Could she really go through with this? Could she just leave without bothering to say thank you to Anthony? Whatever disaster may have befallen them on the night of the kiss, he *had* saved her life, nursed her back to health. It was cowardly to abandon him without a single word of gratitude.

She leaned against the door with a weary sigh. Her heart thumped loudly in her ears. To face Anthony tomorrow and the day after tomorrow, to spend more time dwelling on how awkward their relationship had become, required strength she simply did not possess. She wanted to go home. She wanted to be far away from all the bewildering emotions that consumed her. Anthony unsettled her more than he comforted her, and she was tired of the feelings battling inside her.

It's better this way, she thought.

Sabrina pushed away from the door and stepped toward the bed. She untied her scarf, her hair fanning free, and laid the red fabric over his pillow. She hoped he would understand.

The hinges squeaked, as the door opened wide enough for one blinking blue eye to peer into the corridor beyond. The wood barrier swung further back. She poked her head around the corner to inspect the other end of the long causeway. It was deserted, a far cry from the noisy, foot-stomping channel it'd been earlier in the day.

Tiptoeing out the door, she closed it softly behind her. It was the strangest feeling, entering the hallway, like stepping out of her skin. She was suddenly in a mysterious world, filled with unknown dangers, the sanctuary of Anthony's room instantly forgotten.

Her skittish nerves ruled her senses. Ignoring her elaborate surroundings, she listened instead for any advancing footsteps.

It was the music that steered her though the winding and unfamiliar passages. And try as she might to avoid it, the sounds only grew louder.

Minutes passed. Cautious to move stealthily along

the corridor's edge, her hand lightly skimming the candlelit walls, she ducked within a narrow passage, hoping the brief rest in dark seclusion would help ease her thundering heart.

Anthony hadn't exactly offered her a map of the dwelling's interior, and so she had no idea where she was going. Each hall looked the same, and for all she knew, she was traveling in circles. Where were the bloody stairs?

She took a deep breath, clutched her belongings tighter, and stuck her head back into the main corridor. She eased her way out from the shadows and froze. Voices were approaching, about to turn the corner.

Her back hit the wall and she slipped into the darkened passageway once more, her heart pounding, her blood rushing through her veins. She moved quickly to the aisle's end, listening to the clash of thrumming instruments, bubbling laughter, and lively chatter that invaded her narrow hideaway through a set of looming double doors.

Though her steps seemed deprived of strength, she crossed the inlet, with every intention of hiding until the corridor was clear. Her fingers quivering, she caressed the luminous brass handle before opening one of the glass doors.

The fanfare blasted her the moment she stepped over the balcony's threshold and into a world of privilege and pomp. She closed the door behind her. Instinct had her crouching on the floor, so only her assessing blue eyes veered over the balcony's stone ledge, scanning the remarkable mixture of twirling colors below.

It was overwhelming. Nothing could have prepared her for the brilliant array of gowns and elegant suits, or the bright torrent of jewels that winked under the blaze of candlelight with each graceful movement of the dancers. The music filled her soul, the scent of melted candle wax invaded her nostrils, the sparkling gleam from the crystal chandeliers flooded her vision.

The din took her breath away—and almost her senses—as the heat from the ballroom doused her with a cloud of dizziness. But the vertigo was fleeting, and the blurred sets of dancers, all advancing and retreating, holding hands and rotating, regained distinction in form.

Sabrina's eyes narrowed on one particular pair, standing off to the side, watching the celebration with mild interest, more intently focused on one another instead. The woman at Anthony's arm was laughing, her head tipped back so a few cinnamon-brown curls bobbed past her naked shoulders. Dark purple plumes trimmed the rest of the locks coiled atop her head. A brilliant gem sat tucked above the cleft of her tightly bound breasts, the much-too-low cut of her plum-colored bodice visible even to a balcony-perched Sabrina, and Anthony definitely had a better vantage point than she.

The sight was like a blow to the gut. What were the chances that that woman was just another relation to Anthony? Flimsy. No man looked at his kin like a rogue in a sea of beautiful maids. Besides, Anthony's family was blond.

She chided herself for her folly. What did she expect, to find Anthony off to the side, drink in hand, a look of boredom on his face? She scoffed. The viscount may deplore disruptions to his peace of mind, but some disruptions were evidently worth enduring.

Sabrina closed her eyes and turned away from the ball, her back against the balcony ledge, her bottom secured to the floor. She released a long, grated sigh. What did it matter whom Anthony talked with? It shouldn't, of that she was sure. That it did bother her, even a trifle, was troubling beyond words.

The music stopped. Sabrina lifted her dark lashes and focused on the reflective glass doors in front of her. Gathering her valor, she rolled onto her knees and cast her eyes back over the celebration.

Ladies were giggling and fanning themselves. Gents were playing the part of dutiful escorts, leading their partners away from the dance floor, while the orchestra set down their instruments for a brief repose.

The crowd parted slightly near the arched terrace doors, where an elderly nobleman stood, cane in one hand, tall glass in the other.

"Your attention, honored guests."

Sabrina found something about his countenance familiar.

"A toast."

Servants bustled through the masses, filling every empty hand with a glass of some sparkling spirit.

"To my daughter, Cecelia. May she have many happy and *peaceful* years before her."

There was a hearty laugh from the crowd. "Here, here," chimed, as hundreds clinked glasses in a concordant wish of contentment for the young debutante.

So the elder man was Anthony's father? Sabrina gave him a more thorough scan. No wonder she had found his features so familiar.

Upon the lord's signal, the orchestra resumed their

instruments and struck up another dance. Her gaze passed indifferently over the crowd, and returned to rest on Anthony and the same well-endowed lady, who was laughing again, this time over a remark Anthony was whispering into her bejeweled ear.

Sabrina saw red.

Chapter 12

❝**I**f Cecelia's life turns out to be peaceful, she will never forgive our father for that toast," Anthony remarked gruffly in Cassandra Livingston's dainty ear.

The woman's pearled smile and husky laughter were intended to dazzle the senses. "The dear girl would have every right to be in a dander. Imagine a life void of balls, luncheons, and picnics. What would she do with her time and fortune?"

"I hear the route to the Orient is adventurous."

"Abandon the London season to travel to the far side of the world? Good gracious, Anthony, you don't know your sister very well—or women in general for that matter."

He offered her a sly smile. "Untrue, madam. I know my sister very well indeed, and if not acquainted with the manner of all women, I do, at least, know you."

"Or you soon will."

Up went an amused blond brow at her brazenness. "Is that so?" he drawled.

Cassandra's only response was a falsely demure gesture, as she lifted her glass of champaign to conceal her amorous grin.

Anthony need not crawl into Cassandra Livingston's bed to know all the woman's secrets. Widowed one year past, the twenty-five-year-old marchioness had lost her husband, Percival, in a duel. It was all one sordid affair that had delighted much of the *ton* for months, and there hadn't been a scandal quite like it for some time. As the tale went, poor old Percival had fatuously issued a challenge to the much younger, and more experienced, Devlin Landcastle—Cassandra's lover at the time—proclaiming it his duty to recapture his wife's honor, as he had heard rumor of her alleged affair with Landcastle. Apparently, the marquess was as blind as he was old, for he staunchly believed his angelic Cassandra could do no wrong, and he laid down a challenge to the boastful Devlin: either desist from all slanderous remarks concerning his wife or meet him on the dueling field the following morning. By noon, the marquess was lying in state with a hole in his heart.

Anthony had never cared much for the whole tiring affair, there being one too many duels fought over a woman's supposed honor to ignite his interest—though none had ended as tragically as the marquess's in recent years—but the widowed Cassandra *had* caught his eye.

Though Anthony saw no honor in killing a man for the promiscuity of his wife, Cassandra no longer had a husband to object to any aspersions involving her repute, nor would she ever, having vowed to remain unattached for the rest of her days. She had her title, her fortune, and most importantly, her freedom. And with a respectable year of mourning now over, gossip placed the marchioness in the market for a new paramour.

It was the perfect solution to his predicament. The widow Cassandra clearly held no reservations about an illicit affair, and Anthony felt it high time he directed his desire on a more willing participant. Ideally, there was no obstruction to a liaison.

But for one hitch.

He was no longer fascinated by the woman. The sultry creature was at his fingertips and he felt not a stitch of passion stir his blood. Oh, the heat was still in his veins to be sure, only it wasn't stirred by Cassandra Livingston but by a certain gypsy he had tucked away in his bedchamber.

Bloody hell! It was becoming dismally clear that no one could replace his gypsy in his lustful cravings. He would not be satisfied until he'd had Sabrina. And that was a maddening thought, for he was beginning to fear that the gentleman within him was not strong enough to overcome the rogue after all.

"Is there an object to your discontent?"

The purr of Cassandra's voice breached his pensive thoughts, and Anthony shifted his gaze from the rows of dancers to the marchioness. "Pardon?"

"Your frown has steadily worsened these last few minutes. Is the chore of a dance really so atrocious to you?"

Unaware that his internal struggle was so clearly written on his face, he carefully composed his features into a bland expression. "I am not opposed to dancing."

"The company perhaps?"

"The company is radiant, as always."

She smiled seductively at that. "An unfulfilled yearning, perhaps?"

He stiffened. "I don't know what you mean, madam."

"Don't you?"

At her stealthy wink, he realized Cassandra believed he was pining over her and not . . . Blister it, he could *not* be with Sabrina! It was simply impossible. And he damn well had to accept that.

"Fret not, Anthony, the London season is upon us, and with it, a great many opportunities."

Her implication suddenly placed him in an uncomfortable position. Having previously hinted to a possible affair, he now had the irksome task of breaking away from their future engagement without outright offending the lady. Though, temporarily, he was spared from the bothersome undertaking by Cassandra's next comment.

"Follow Cecelia's lead," she suggested and nodded up ahead. "The girl is positively beaming at the success of her début . . . though one cannot say the same for your other sister."

Anthony's gaze immediately sharpened on an apprehensive Ashley at the other end of the ballroom. She was shaking her head at her husband's offer to dance, all the while twining her fingers, her eyes darting to the ballroom doors every so often, as though she were in anxious expectation of someone's arrival.

His twin's agitation evoked his own, and Anthony hastily implored, "Would you please excuse me, Lady Livingston?"

The marchioness nodded, and astutely watched the viscount make his way through the throng of guests to his sister's side.

"Ah, Anthony," a smiling Daniel called out when he noticed his brother-in-law's approach. "Didn't expect to see you all evening . . . not with Lady Livingston to attend to." At Ashley's darkening gaze, Daniel roughly cleared his throat. "Perhaps you could persuade my darling wife to lift that frown and join me out on the dance floor?"

"I'll do my best," was Anthony's hasty reply, and he promptly cupped his sister's elbow and steered her a few feet away from her husband. "What's wrong?"

"I've been trying to catch your attention for the last five minutes," she griped, "but you were too *engaged* with Lady Livingston."

He ignored her disapproving tone to demand, "Is something the matter?"

"A grave-looking Binste just walked by and went straight over to speak with Papa."

Their butler, Binste, always wore a grave face, as far as Anthony was concerned, so he saw no reason to suspect anything was amiss. "What of it?"

"I didn't hear the conversation's entirety, but I did overhear Binste insist that the house needed to be searched. He and Papa then left together. What if they suspect there is an intruder? The servants will eventually find the gypsy . . . Anthony, say something!"

Glaciation took over, numbing all his senses.

He was thundering toward the ballroom doors when Ashley grabbed him by the arm. "You can't leave! What will Mama say when she sees all the Kennington men disappearing? What will the guests think?"

"Tell Mother I have gone in search of the 'intruder.' As for the guests, I don't give a bloody damn what they think."

And with that, Anthony stalked off the dance floor, leaving a distressed Ashley and a curious Daniel gazing after him.

Anthony had never bounded up a flight of stairs so fast in his life. His heart was hammering, his thoughts reeling. He couldn't fathom how anyone had discovered his gypsy. But why else would Binste insist the house be searched?

He reached his chamber. The door was unlocked. He opened it and slipped into the moonlit room, his eyes shooting straight to the empty bed. There was nothing but a kerchief laid over the pillow.

His heart plummeted to his feet.

Fingering the scrap of fabric, he clutched it in his hand and brought it closer to his face. Sabrina's scent drifted all around him and he closed his eyes.

He had failed her.

Cramming the kerchief into his pocket, he spun on his heels, prepared to tear the entire house apart in his quest to find his gypsy.

"I'm still here."

Her voice, though faint, had the power to bring all his senses back to life. The dull ache in his heart vanished the moment he'd heard her words, and he scanned the dark chamber in search of her.

With only the moon glimmering through the windows, all objects in the room were cast in a milky hue, and it was hard to tell where the voice had come from. But then he saw her, curled in an armchair by one of the windows. She appeared to be part of the furniture, until he noticed her body shift and she rose from her seat.

Anthony released such a breath of relief, he was

sure she had heard the exhale from across the room. He weaved through the maze of armchairs to stand by her side.

"I thought something dreadful had happened to you," he said gruffly, then added in a stern tone, "Why was the door unlocked? Someone could have found you."

"I forgot to lock it."

Her voice was flat, her features dormant, and he felt his earlier apprehension stalk him once more. He also noticed that she was fully dressed.

He gripped her shoulders. "Has something happened?"

She stiffened at his touch and he recalled the fright he'd given her the night before, loosening his grip, and finally slipping his hands away from her altogether.

"Sabrina, what's the matter?"

Though her face was composed to appear indifferent, even cold, she could not hide the hurt in her voice. "I want to go home."

"I'll take you home just as soon as you're well enough to—"

"I want to go home *now*."

He murmured roughly, "Has someone hurt you?"

"I couldn't find my way out," was her shaky response. "I was lost. Someone chased me, but I disappeared in here before he could catch me."

He listened to her, bemused, unable to comprehend if what she was rambling about was real or a dream. "Sabrina, what's going on? Who's been chasing you? Did you dream of your attackers again? They can't hurt you anymore, you know?"

"I wasn't dreaming," she snapped. "I wanted to leave

before you came back, but I got lost in those rotten halls and couldn't find the stairs. And then I heard voices and had to hide on the balcony, and I caught you whispering to that woman, and . . . and . . ." She made some noise of frustration, then her arms slumped at her sides.

He dismissed the "caught" bit, as if he'd actually done anything to warrant a capture, to demand darkly, "You left this room?" She moved to turn away from him, but he grabbed her arms and this time he didn't let her go. "Why?"

"I'm not welcome here."

He could think of no reason, save one, why she would believe such a thing. "Did Ashley ask you to leave?"

"No, she doesn't have to say anything. I can sense what she's really feeling. And you can't stand the sight of me anymore." Her voice cracked. Some life sprung back into her arms and she crossed them under her breasts. "And you can't have a tryst with your mistress if *I'm* in your bed, so—"

"Enough." This time he cut her off, needing a moment of silence to gather his thoughts. "First of all, I don't have a mistress. And second, why do you believe I can't stand the sight of you?" His hands still firmly locked on her upper arms, he gave her a gentle shake when her silence persisted. "Sabrina, tell me why."

"You've ignored me all day."

"I wanted you to recover in peace."

"You wanted me gone from your sight!"

"That isn't true."

"Yes it is. You haven't been able to look at me since

the kiss . . . since you opened your eyes and found your lips on mine."

"What do you mean?"

"What do you think?" Her blue eyes were like liquid silver under the moon, so reflective, so luminous. He was entranced by the pair. "You want to forget all about kissing me . . . a gypsy."

It was unintelligible to his ears. She actually thought he felt nothing for her, was averse to ever having kissed her because of her bloodline? It was all he could do to keep his hands off the girl, and she thought his restraint out of loathing?

He shook his head in disbelief. "Sabrina, you don't understand."

Her lips trembled. "Yes, I do." She tried to wriggle free of his hold. "I know you feel some sense of duty to take care of me, but I feel fine, and I want to go home. I don't want to be in this house anymore. I don't want to be with you!"

He released her abruptly.

She looked up at him in a slight daze, as though surprised that he'd given in so quickly, but therein lay the deception, for Anthony had not given in. He wasn't about to let her go with such flagrant misconceptions.

Lightly, he grazed his thumb over her flushed features.

She gasped when his hands cupped her face and drew her near.

Planting her fists securely on his chest to brace herself, she demanded in a panicked whisper, "What are you doing?"

His voice was gruff. "I'm going to set things right." And then he pressed his lips over hers.

She squirmed, but he held her face firmly between

his palms, the kiss slow, deep and thorough, leaving her in no doubt as to his true desires.

It wasn't long before her muffled protests dwindled, and her body limped and sagged into his. The feel of those full breasts, pressing harder and harder into his chest as her need rose, incited chaos in his soul.

With some reserve, she hooked her arms around his neck, clinging to him, her fingers slowly digging and twisting into his hair.

He savored every exhilarating moment of it. But he was careful not to get too swept up in his own desire. He didn't want to unleash the full force of his passion, to frighten her into an early retreat. Little by little, with deliberate ease and control, he convinced himself. Be patient.

His arms circled her waist. He caressed her spine in slow, sensual motions, his fingers skimming the low curve of her back, just short of touching her posterior, before withdrawing and gliding up the ridges of her backbone. His hands kept swirling, dipping low on her back, then lifting to tangle through the thick fleece of her ebony hair.

A shudder ripped through her. A violent tremor, full of energy and excitement. And he felt every thrilling vibration.

The kiss deepened when he sensed she was eager, keen to feel more. His tongue skipped lightly over her lips again and again, knocking to gain entrance, and at last, she opened her mouth to the warm thrust of his tongue, inhaling sharply at the intrusion.

Pure, sweet heaven was all he could think of. And when she dared to engage in a lambent duel, her own tongue dipping and retreating, he felt the blood pool to his groin, the hardness beginning to build, and his next thought was that he'd soon be reduced to a pile of cinder.

"So this is where you hurried off to?"

The kiss was broken. Anthony and Sabrina split apart, both gasping for air, their bodies reeling in the aftermath of such an intense embrace.

Anthony pinned his eyes to the intruder under the doorway and detected the scent of perfume. He noticed the plume perched on the shadowed figure's head and gnashed his teeth. "Cassandra."

He cursed mentally for having forgotten to lock the blasted door. In his determination to locate Sabrina, such a triviality seemed inconsequential. Now it was anything but.

Sabrina backed away even further, likely anticipating a rather nasty confrontation was about to ensue. And his own guilt at his carelessness kept him from reaching out and drawing her back into his arms, since he doubted there was much comfort he could offer her at that point anyway. With that disagreeable thought on his mind, he faced the vengeful wrath of a slighted Cassandra Livingston, his own anger dangerously mounting.

Now that the other woman was aware of Sabrina's presence, it wouldn't be long before the rest of the household, never mind the *ton,* was privy to it as well. And when Cecelia and his mother heard about his clandestine "affair" on such an important night, pandemonium would be the unfortunate result.

And there was no hoping to avoid such commotion. Anthony knew Cassandra far too well for that. She wouldn't be so translucent as to admit she'd personally witnessed the embrace, for that would lead to a series of additional questions, such as what the marchioness was doing in Anthony's room in the first place? And contrary to expectation, it wouldn't be Cassandra's reputation at stake, but her sexual appeal. If word spread that Anthony didn't find her desirable enough to become his mistress, her enigmatic veil of seduction would flitter away. Too shrewd to allow such a disaster to befall her, and too vindictive to keep the encounter under wraps, Cassandra would find some sure way to sabotage his supposed liaison. The only question was how. And that question would be readily answered in time.

The marchioness stepped boldly into the room. Her eyes were deceptively stoic, like a dormant dragon awaiting the precise moment to unhinge its jaw and spurt forth a rush of fire. She raked her disdainful gaze thoroughly over Sabrina before returning her attention to the viscount.

"She's an uncultivated, rather wild-looking creature, Anthony. Your taste in a mistress has considerably declined."

"That's enough," he admonished darkly.

Cassandra lifted her slender shoulders in an indifferent shrug. "It is your misfortune if you prefer the company of a boorish peasant to that of a noble lady."

And with that incisive slander, Cassandra swept up the side of her gown and sashayed out of the room, her pride intact and Sabrina's in pieces.

Anthony hastened to the door and locked it after the conniving woman. He leaned against the barrier, regarding his gypsy's shadowed figure with remorse. He had failed to protect her after all. Now, with her presence known, they would have to leave before she could fully recover. He simply couldn't risk any further meddlers exposing her identity.

"Sabrina, I'm afraid we're going to have to make a run for it."

Anthony's words flitted in the air around her before dissolving into the darkness. The emotions battling inside her were making it impossible for any other sentiment to break through her thoughts.

Sabrina had trespassed into the land of the aristocracy, and she was neither welcomed nor tolerated in such a place. The inhabitants considered her nothing more than a wild creature. Uncultivated. Boorish. She did not belong here. She did not belong with Anthony. When had she forgotten her proper place in the world? When had she forgotten her duty to her people? When had she become such a fool, yearning for the touch of a man she had no hope of ever being with?

Her throat braided at the pending onslaught of tears. She choked on the obstruction and willfully maintained her stiff composure.

Anthony moved away from the door and lit the candle by the nightstand. "We have to get out of this house before Cassandra finds a way to inform the entire *ton* of your presence."

Her sentiments precisely. Only she would have omitted the "we" part. Voice flat and hollow, she said, "You don't have to come with me."

"I most certainly do."

Her nerves clattered. She couldn't bear to be with him any longer. Their kiss had ripped through her be-

ing with frightening intensity. Once she realized he had
no dream to blame for his conduct, that he *wanted* to
kiss her, all other reasonable thoughts had flickered
away. She didn't trust herself alone with the man. She
didn't trust him very much either. He had promised to
protect her from her attackers, but who would protect
her from him?

Her voice quivered. "And what will your family
think with you gone?"

He was back by the door, peeking into the corridor,
determining if it was deserted, she assumed.

"Don't trouble yourself with my family. I will explain everything to them once I return to London."

"Everything?"

He closed the door and faced her. "A reasonable account of some sort."

"So you'll lie."

"Most definitely. Now fetch your things."

Anthony scrambled through his chamber, gathering
together a few articles of clothing and stuffing them
into a small carrying case of some sort. His methodic
movements rattled her senses. He seemed intent on accompanying her, regardless of anything she said to dis-
courage him.

"But you have a ball to attend," she tried desperately
to reason with him.

"The ball will go on without me. My obligation is to
your safety."

"But a gypsy walking alongside a gent?"

"Walking? I'm afraid not. You're in no condition to
travel on foot."

"Well, then, riding alongside—"

"Riding together," he corrected and stuffed another

garment into his bag. "I can't manage two horses once you're gone."

Her palms were sweating at the thought of the two of them riding snugly together for days. "We'll only draw attention to ourselves. I'd be safer on my own. Those men are still out there—"

"Which is exactly why I'm accompanying you."

It was decisive and absolute. He was leaving—with her in tow—no matter what she had to say on the matter.

Anthony went over to his writing desk and shuffled through the parchments. With a frantic sigh, she did a little scrambling of her own, trying to locate her bag of belongings, which she'd tossed aimlessly aside when she'd last come into the room. She found the bundle wedged partly under the bed and yanked it out.

She had to get out of the house fast, and since Anthony was determined to come with her, she didn't think it wise to mulishly stand there, hoping he'd change his mind. For all she knew, a horde of guests were already mounting the steps and would be thundering at the door any moment now, intent on carting her out of the house and directly over to the magistrate's on a charge of trespassing. And if she had to choose between Anthony and the jail, she supposed the viscount was indeed the better option, though that logic did nothing to quiet her jangling nerves.

When she looked up again, it was to notice Anthony's arm moving swiftly, quill in hand.

"You're writing another letter *now*?"

"It's only a brief note for Ashley, to have the rest of my belongings packed and shipped back to London."

"And how will you deliver the note?"

"I won't," he returned simply. "I know my twin. She'll soon come in search of me and find the instructions on my desk."

He finished scribbling the message and propped the parchment upright against the inkwell to ensure his sister noticed it.

"Let's go." Anthony blew out the candle and cradled her hand.

At the touch of his warm palm, her heart jumped, smacked right against her ribs with a resounding thump. She tried to snatch her hand away, but he maintained a firm grip all the way to the door and into the deserted corridor.

She needed something other than his closeness to dwell upon, and blurted out the first thought that came to mind. "It's bad luck to start a journey on Friday."

He cast her a brief look over his shoulder. "My dear, I assure you it would be bad luck if we did *not* start our journey tonight."

He was right, of course, not that she cared, what with the endearment he'd just uttered still fluttering about in her head.

"Do you hear that?"

Sabrina gathered her wits about her and tried to focus on the situation at hand. Her ears caught sound of the muffled thuds of closing doors. "What's going on?"

"The servants believe there's an intruder in the house, and they're searching all the upper rooms."

"So where do we go?"

"I don't know. If we descend the servant stairwell, we'll end up in the kitchen amidst a throng of scullery maids. But if we use the main staircase, we'll come to within yards of the ballroom door and three hundred *very* questioning guests."

Another dilemma. She wasn't the least bit surprised. "Is there another way down?"

"Only the stairway in the east wing, but it's located at the other end of the house."

"So?"

"With so many bodies shuffling about, we're bound to come across one or more of them as we traipse through the winding halls."

"Then what do we do?"

Those large shoulders lifted and plummeted as he sighed. "We have no other choice, I suppose, but to risk the route to the east wing."

And risk it they did. Whenever a servant was heard coming their way, they ducked into one of the unoccupied rooms, waited until the maid or footman had entered a neighboring chamber to search through, and then bolted from the room and down the corridor.

It had been one of the more climactic moments of her life to finally reach the staircase without detection. And seeing as the eastern wing of the house was enshrouded in darkness, it provided the perfect camouflage for their escape.

Chapter 13

"**A**re you sure you don't want to ride up front?"
Sabrina didn't answer him. Probably because he'd already asked her the same question twice before and she'd already declined the offer both times. But aware of how sore her muscles must be, positioned on Shadow's rump for hours, where all the baggage was fastened, he couldn't help but repeat the question occasionally. And though he certainly didn't mind the feel of her warm body pressed snugly against his back, he did take issue with her physical discomfort throughout the long journey that lay ahead.

But there was not much he could do on the matter. Sabrina staunchly refused the more comfortable seat of his lap, and since her skirt wasn't wide enough for her to ride astride, she was obliged to travel sidesaddle behind him.

Anthony had to admit, if she was to change her mind and settle amid his legs, he'd likely lose all sense of direction and end up somewhere in Scotland. He was already having a difficult time keeping his steed in line, continually reflecting on the pair of slender arms coiled firmly around his waist, and he didn't need the added distraction of her soft, feminine posterior undulating against his groin.

He groaned mentally at the image he'd just evoked of her round hips rocking gracefully between his hard thighs. Damn, but it was growing harder and harder to control his responses to his gypsy's touch.

And Sabrina was apparently aware of his internal struggle. Before leaving the stables, she'd given him every conceivable reason why they shouldn't ride together, including that she got nauseous whenever she sat on a horse. Though she'd made no further reference to any sickness in the last hour of their leisurely journey, she'd also clammed up entirely.

He supposed he should get acquainted with her silence, for he sensed it was going to be his additional companion throughout the long ride back to Sabrina's camp. And it was going to be a long ride. Since she was situated so inelegantly, any increase in their speed would only jar her bones unnecessarily.

Anthony looked up at the sky. The moon was almost full. The stars danced like ebullient faeries at a midsummer night's soirée. There wasn't a cloud in the heavens, nor a gentle wind to breathe life into the slumbering earth. The night was perfectly still. Perfectly peaceful. So unlike the welter gushing about in his soul.

He closed his eyes and sighed. It was too much, the mishmash of conflicting feelings all battling inside him. There was his duty to contend with on the one hand and a preoccupation with his winsome gypsy on the other. It was even harder knowing Sabrina wasn't as against his kisses as he'd previously thought, that after a moment of surprise had passed, she was as keen and urgent with her lips as he was with his. And how those lips fascinated him. How much he yearned to taste them even now. Did she have the same yearning? He wondered. His gypsy had already proven how passionate she could be when coaxed from her shy and reserved shell. Could all her distance and agitation be no more than unfulfilled longing?

The rogue within him took an immediate liking to that idea. Sabrina had falsely believed he'd wanted nothing to do with her because of her gypsy blood, but now she knew the truth. Now she knew how much he truly wanted her. And he knew that deep down she wanted him as well. There was nothing keeping them apart. Nothing save that blasted gentleman's code of conduct he had to adhere to . . .

Oh, to hell with it! He was a rake. The whole world knew it. And if the girl was willing, and he was willing, why shouldn't they have a delightful tussle in bed? Why should he deny them both their passions and be frustrated? He had seen to Sabrina's recovery and he was now escorting her home. She was safe, protected, and healthy. He had done his gentleman's duty. Whatever else might pass between them would in no way be a breach of honor on his part.

He opened his eyes, his soul a little more at peace. The answer was clear to him now. He would tend to both his duty and desire, having concluded that one was in no way an infringement upon the other.

But first, he had to cap the heat still rising in his blood. A neutral discussion seemed the best option, and he broke through the silence with the first chaste thought to grace his mind—though it took him about a minute to come up with one.

"We should be there shortly," he said.

"Where?"

"The township. We'll stop at the local inn for the night."

"Why in town? What's wrong with out here?"

Anthony cast his eyes over the desolate country terrain. "Out here? On the ground? I prefer a comfortable bed in town."

The implication escaped his lips before he could catch it. He sensed her body stiffen.

Bloody hell.

It was going to take a subtle seduction to draw his passionate gypsy out of her shell, not a blatant invitation to bed.

This night just wasn't going smoothly for him.

Sabrina lifted the candle high to ward off the darkness.

She stared at the bed. Though large enough to accommodate two bodies, there was only *one* in the room Anthony had rented for the night.

This won't do.

She set the candle aside, along with her bag, and grabbed a pillow and a blanket off the musty mattress, dropping the articles onto the scuffed, hardwood floor.

Much better.

A hard bed was nothing uncommon for her, and since Anthony had paid for the room, he could sleep on the feathers.

Truthfully, she'd much prefer to spend the night somewhere—anywhere—else. But her escort had insisted they share quarters so he could "maintain her safety."

Anthony had followed her into the chamber long enough to drop off his carrying case before returning outside to tend to his horse, leaving her in the darkness to fret at her will.

The bouncing light from the candle flame snagged her attention, and she narrowed her eyes to the mirror on the wall. Something had changed. Something in her reflection she wasn't able to pinpoint. And it wasn't just the distress of the last few days that had appeared in her features, it was something more.

She brushed the wind-whipped strands of her ebony hair behind her ears, and skimmed her fingertips over her flushed cheeks. She did look almost wild, didn't she? Her hair was rumpled and her face all pink from the brisk spring air.

Running her fingers through the long, knotted tresses, she wondered what Anthony saw in her. She didn't possess the striking beauty of Cassandra or the regal manner of any of the ladies who'd been in attendance at the ball. She didn't have any brilliant gowns or sparkling jewels to adorn her. She didn't have much of anything a man like Anthony would find enticing. So what did he want with a gypsy?

It was a few anxious minutes later that the door swung open, Anthony's large frame filling the doorway.

His eyes immediately narrowed to the pillow and blanket at his feet. "What are you doing?"

"Getting ready for sleep."

Slowly, his piercing gaze lifted to meet hers. "On the floor?"

He sounded so incredulous that she began to suspect

he earnestly believed she'd spend the night somewhere else—like in his arms. The thought of finding herself under the covers with him, sharing in *his* heat, sensing *his* every turn, feeling the touch of *his* body, convinced her she'd never make it through the night with her wits intact.

Somewhat flustered, she pointed out, "You asked for only one room. Where else am I to sleep?"

He studied her intently for a long while, his eyes mesmerizing under the soft candle glow, before he closed the door and leaned against it. "I'll take the floor. You can have the bed."

She shook her head. "You paid for the room, so the bed is yours."

"I paid for the room, so I decide who gets the bed, and I choose you."

"I don't want the bed," she said flatly.

"Then I suppose we'll both have to share that space on the floor."

She bristled. He wouldn't dare join her! On second thought, why risk it? This particular aristocrat never did anything the way he was supposed to. He might just be stubborn enough to forsake the comfortable bed and take the floor beside her.

"Fine," she said, and headed over to the bed. She scooped up all the remaining blankets, dropping them onto the floor, then crouched and began to arrange the linen to form a makeshift bed.

Anthony remained stationed by the door throughout the preparation, his arms folded across his chest.

Finally, he asked, "What are you doing?"

"Making your bed. I don't need your broken back on my conscience."

"Pardon?"

She straightened when she was satisfied with the comfortable pile she had arranged. "You'll twist your back on the hard ground. You're not used to sleeping on anything but feathers."

She glanced up to determine if he was insulted by her suggestion that he was, in essence, a dandy and could never withstand a night on the floor. But his features remained unreadable, though the dark kindle in his eye didn't foretell of good tidings.

Sabrina yanked off her black boots and tossed them into a corner before heading over to the window and pushing open the pane of glass. A fresh country breeze bathed her body in the aromatic scents of wild flowers and bales of hay. Energetic crickets chirped in the distance, providing a vocal concert to help carry her off to sleep.

She took a moment to absorb the sounds and fragrances of the night, and closed her eyes, inhaling deeply. After a brief pause, she went straight over to the bed, with no intention of disrobing, and collapsed onto the mattress. She curled into a ball, wedged her fist under the pillow, and dearly hoped her dreams would come soon to take her away from all her troubles.

It was a few moments later she detected the soft click of boot heels striking the hardwood floor.

She kept her eyes shut tight, her back to Anthony, and heard him mutter something about a "stubborn minx" before she opened her eyes in time to see one of the blankets descend over her body. He then headed back over to the other side of the room.

Scrunching the corner of the woolly fabric between her fingers, she pulled the cover up to her nose.

He was doing it again. Playing the part of the gallant gentleman. The only trouble was she wasn't a noble lady. Their relationship, such as it was, would be so much simpler if he treated her with the same contempt the rest of his kind so effortlessly bestowed. There would be no fluttering heartbeats then, no desire . . . and no feelings of guilt for that desire.

Moonlight filled the room, the candle extinguished. Anthony settled onto the floor.

"Goodnight, Sabrina," he said softly.

Muffled against the blanket, she returned, "Goodnight."

It would not come, sleep that is. She opened her eyes to gawk at the window. The guilt was gnawing at her. Just how was she supposed to sleep with the knowledge that Anthony was lying on the floor, not used to the rigid planks beneath his back, prone to the aches and pains he'd undoubtedly feel in the morning?

The man's pride, or chivalry, or sense of duty, or whatever it was that had sent him to the ground in the first place, would also prevent him from taking the bed, unless she did something to change that.

Seeing as her guilt already prevented her from getting any sleep, Sabrina quietly slipped off the mattress.

"What are you doing?" came the quizzical demand from the darkness.

Wrapped in her pillow and blanket, she curled up onto the floor. "Take the bed! I'm fine right here on the ground."

Silence. Only the crickets chirped in the distance. Then she heard his big body shift. Finally, she thought, the man would listen to reason. But she should have known better.

Sabrina shrieked. Scooped up off the floor and into Anthony's arms, she found herself dropped back onto the feathers with a stern warning.

"Stay in the bed until morning. I don't want to see you on the floor again."

With that, he sauntered back over to his side of the room.

"But your back—"

"Will be perfectly fine," he cut in impatiently, and settled onto the floor for the second time that night.

But they both knew that wasn't true, that his back would be crooked come dawn.

"All right," she grit through her teeth. "We'll share the bed."

His shadowed head slowly peeked over the mattress to gaze at her. He shrugged at last. "Have it your way."

Oh, charming. Have it her way? If things went her way, he'd be in the bed—alone. Better yet, he'd be sleeping in *his* bed, in *his* house, and not in here with her at all.

Sabrina hustled to collect every spare blanket, then dropped the pile onto the bed, constructing a dense wall.

For what she hoped would be the last time that evening, she crawled onto her side of the bed and closed her eyes, giving Anthony her back again. She could feel those intense green eyes watching her, burrowing a hole right through her. She ignored the faint tremors dancing along her spine.

The mattress dipped at his sinking weight, and she rolled into the depression. Quickly scooting forward, she virtually teetered on the edge of the bed.

Wide-eyed, alert to every movement or change in sound, she waited for her bed partner to drift off to sleep, though if the passing minutes were any indication, it would be a long wait. Anthony tossed to one side, then rolled onto his other, where he was still for all of two seconds before flopping onto his back. When the wall of blankets was shoved up against her own back, she realized he'd moved again, and this time he was far too close to her side of the bed.

"What are you doing?" she demanded stiffly.

"Just trying to get comfortable."

His gruff voice was unnervingly close.

"Well, stop it," she hissed.

"You'd rather I be uncomfortable?"

"I'd rather you lie still."

He sighed. "I'll never be able to fall asleep with those damned crickets."

"They're the sounds of the night and I can't sleep without them."

"They're more the sounds of my nightmares."

"It takes some getting used to," she mumbled.

"Can you really ever get used to it?"

"One day, maybe. The noises are as calming to me as any silence."

He grumbled, "I think I'll always prefer the silence."

"Then this will be an interesting night for you."

"Will it?"

An abrupt innocence crept into his voice, and her insides did a full-about turn at the sound of his playfulness. She'd not expected his mood to shift so quickly, nor had she meant to suggest anything. Her cheeks tinted. How the devil had that remark slipped passed her lips?

She rushed to move their talk in a different direction. "I'll close the window if you can't sleep."

His hand shot over the wall of blankets to brace

against her shoulder and push her back down against the bed.

"It's all right. Like you said, it takes some getting used to."

That he'd reached her so effortlessly proved how poor the wall she'd built really was—not that she'd consider tearing it down.

"Sabrina."

She gripped her pillow. "What?"

"Since neither of us can sleep . . . I suggest we finish our interrupted kiss."

The pillow smacked across his face.

Anthony reached over the barrier, dove his arm under her back, and hoisted her right up over the divider.

She hit the wall of muscle and gasped at the alarming feel of hard pectorals quivering under the weight of her body. Fingers wove tightly through her hair. Another hand clamped over her lower back, making it impossible for her to push away.

Her breath trapped in her throat at the smile he bestowed. In the moonlight, it was a devilish smile, not sinister in nature, but certainly roguish, and definitely handsome. But the man had lost his mind if he believed she'd actually consent to such a suggestion. And since the shock of what was happening deprived her of words, she responded by wiggling soundly in his arms. The more she struggled to get away, though, the more rigid his muscles grew, until she heard the deep, rumbling groan.

She stopped squirming, still as stone, and stifled a groan of her own, though it had nothing to do with her mounting desire, and everything to do with her foolishness for having ignited his.

"Anthony, I—"

"Shhhh," he whispered against her lips, caressing her hair, the lower curve of her spine. "Don't fight it."

That won't be too hard, she thought dismally. Hot, sultry breaths warmed her already flushed features, and she found herself sinking even deeper into the dark pools of his hypnotic eyes. If she didn't pull away in the next instant, to hell with reason, she would lose herself to the tempest threatening to consume them both.

An instant passed.

Into the swirling waters she leapt.

Gripping the silk of his shirt, as though it were her lifeline, she didn't resist when he gently lowered her head and pressed his lips to hers, thrilling her, alarming her, leaving her clinging desperately to him for guidance.

She had never dreamed anything could feel so wonderful. An upsurge of sensations soaked through her every pore. No gypsy wives' tale had ever been so vivid. No one had ever mentioned just how heart-pounding, soul-wrenching such an experience could be.

The moist tip of his tongue skipped over her lips, once, twice, and on the third flick, he dipped into her mouth. A rush of air filled her lungs. Her pulse sprinted at the hot feel of him delving inside her. Each probing thrust of his tongue grew more urgent than the last, and her lips were eager, possessive, hungry in return.

"Anthony," she breathed heavily against his mouth.

In an instant, the wall of blankets was kicked clean off the bed and their coiled bodies spun once, so Sabrina found herself pinned under his weight instead. And what a difference it made to feel *his* body on top of hers. A glorious tension twined in her belly. Her inner thighs prickled and ached, as the slow, feathery touch of his hand slid along her calf, lifting her skirt up over her knees. A surge of cold air whooshed over her legs. Goose pimples tickled her flesh and she shuddered violently.

It was frightening, the storm of emotions inside her. How could he make her feel this way? How could she cope with the thought of losing her heart, her very soul to this man? And what of the devastation she would feel when it came time for her and Anthony to part? What of the devastation she would cause her father if she was to return to her camp in disgrace?

A sudden panic overtook her. "Anthony!"

But his mouth clamped down harder over hers, bringing a decisive end to her lapse into reason.

Sabrina gulped in drafts of much-needed air when his lips finally left hers to tend to her neck, her chest . . .

The laces at her collar already loose, he merely slipped her blouse down one shoulder to expose a bare breast to his parted lips.

"So beautiful," he whispered raggedly, reverently, a deep crimson blush springing into her cheeks at the awe she heard in his voice.

His hot mouth covered her nipple, fast hardening under the languid caress of his tongue. She whimpered at the intense feelings bubbling inside her and clawed at his shoulders. Pure heaven was all she could think of. Her fingers moved to knit tightly through his golden mane, and she pressed his head harder against her breast in an instinctive cry for more. He appeased her demand most willingly, drawing her deep into his mouth and suckling, sending a hand under her blouse to attentively knead her other breast.

A whip of heat lashed her skin at the feel of those powerful fingers rocking the mound. His thumb rubbed the sensitive bud of her nipple, already tightening, shrinking between the friction of each deft and eager stroke.

She wanted to weep between the disparity of her own desire and her sense of duty. The act of love may be cherished and celebrated by her people—and with good reason—but *only* between a husband and wife. She could not go home dishonored. She would have to live with that dishonor for the rest of her life.

A second break in the sensuous storm provided her with a chance for escape, and this time she was more adamant.

She grasped the sides of his head and forced him to meet her gaze. "Anthony, I can't."

Her voice was heavy, smoky, and yet crackled with apprehension. He looked into her eyes so passionately, she felt an overwhelming impulse to move her fingers to his wet brow and brush away the moist curl dangling over his eye. She did so lightly, tenderly.

They just held each other for a time, waiting for the surge of passion to subside, neither willing to let the other go.

With a deep sigh, Anthony dropped his head to her shoulder and eventually nestled against her breast.

She didn't make one word of protest when he went to sleep in her arms that night, his ear pressed snugly over her heart. It stomped so loudly in her chest, she was sure he had heard every resounding beat.

Chapter 14

⌢⌒⌒⌒⌢

"Do you intend to peel the skin away?"

Crouching by the stream, a bemused Sabrina suddenly demanded, "What?"

"Your face," said Anthony. "You've been scrubbing it for the last five minutes."

Had she? She looked down at her wet hands. He must be exaggerating. It didn't seem like five minutes had passed.

Lifting the hem of her skirt, she patted her face dry, and cast one final look at her distorted reflection in the rippled water before moving away from the shoreline.

She turned to find Anthony kneeling a little ways off, Shadow's hoof in his lap. He was digging out the pebbles that had wedged themselves in between the metal shoe. Her heart fairly tripped at the sight of him. It had been doing that all morning. She had yet to bring the erratic beats under control. It was midday and still her jitters were as strong as ever. Since setting out from the inn at dawn, her nerves were on constant edge. Memory of the night she and Anthony had shared—or almost shared—tumbled through her mind even now, sending color blooming to her cheeks.

She had tried to hide the adorning blush by dabbing some cold water over her flushed features, but the heat glowing from her skin could not be doused. It didn't help matters that Anthony looked so dashing. His formal evening wear tucked away in his bag, he'd replaced the elegant garments with the more ordinary garb of dark britches and a riding coat, though the snug fit of leather over hard muscled thighs was anything but ordinary in her eyes.

Shadow snorted when his hoof was released. With a pat on the rump to encourage him, the horse stepped toward the bank and dipped his muzzle into the icy stream.

Anthony's gaze then settled on her. The sunlight danced in his eyes, the reflective pools flashing like emerald gems, winking in full brilliancy.

He advanced.

Her stomach knotted.

"Should we reach your camp by tomorrow, do you think?"

She struggled for words. "Tomorrow night, perhaps, or the morning after."

"And you're sure the caravan will still be there?"

"My people would never leave without me," she insisted.

"I only wanted to make sure you had a home to go to."

The softness of his voice sent her pulse tapping. Swift, energetic little beats. And when his eyes darkened at their prolonged stares, and her pulse pattered even faster, she found something else to occupy her attention, narrowing in on Anthony's horse.

He followed her gaze. "We should get going."

She let out a weary sigh, as he sauntered over to the animal. It was hard being so close to Anthony, feeling those intense green eyes burrowing through her, wanting to reach out and stroke that finely chiseled face, and press her fingertips over a pair of soft lips. Lips that had given her so much pleasure the night before . . .

She curled her hands into fists, just in case she was daft enough to try anything so absurd.

Anthony stood next to Shadow and waited for the animal to have his fill of water. When the horse reared his head and nuzzled his chin over his master's unruly curls, he let out a deep, hearty chuckle, patting the great beast's neck in return for the affectionate gesture.

Sabrina's eyes never wavered from the pair.

First to mount, Anthony nudged the horse forward and extended his hand for her to climb up behind him.

"Are you sure you'd rather not ride up front?"

She just stared at the open palm. What was the matter with her? She'd ridden all morning behind Anthony with no catastrophic results. Why now, all of a sudden, was she so hesitant?

"I'll walk," she said brusquely, and headed through the sparse brush, back toward the main road.

Shadow's muzzle veered over her shoulder as the animal fell in step behind her.

"You're not walking back to your camp," he objected. "You've been laid up for days and are still too weak."

"I don't intend to walk all the way home, just a few miles. I feel fine."

She heard a sigh behind her and was sure it hadn't come from the horse.

She was right. Anthony dismounted and took Shadow by the reins. He was at her side, so close, they bumped arms, and she took one giant step away from him to avoid any more jolts along the way.

A quick glance at him and she caught the mellow lines of his profile shift into a smile. Damn that rogue! He found her anxiety amusing, and she wasn't the least bit indulgent of his humor. She was having enough trouble keeping her wits about her without his laughing at her to make matters worse. What's more, his smile was always the most disarming of all his qualities.

When she next risked a sidelong glimpse at him, it was to find his features were inscrutable. Gone was that wicked smile, but the mischievous gleam in his bright green eyes still sparkled.

She wanted to ignore him, but she wanted him back on his horse even more.

"What are you doing?" she demanded.

"Walking alongside you."

At that hedging response, she inquired impatiently, "Why?"

"If you insist on being stubborn, then I'll prove equally as headstrong. What if you faint? Someone has to catch you."

But his unnerving presence faded into the back of her mind just then, as her attention was snagged elsewhere. With a sense of delight, her eyes narrowed on what appeared to be a cluster of knotted vines. She walked over to the bush for a closer inspection. It was!

"Sabrina, what's the matter with you?"

It did look rather odd, her tugging and tugging, and the willful branches refusing to give way. But she didn't care. She ignored his question and bent each of the three stems until they snapped, the knotted cluster of intersecting vines falling into her palm.

With a triumphant smile, she looked up to find a perplexed Anthony watching her with interest.

"Did you just do battle with a bush?"

"More like battle with the faeries," she clarified.

"I beg your pardon?"

She held up the tangled vines. "See how they're knotted?"

Narrowing in on the interwoven mess, he nodded. "So?"

"It means the faeries have tied them." Fastened to the horse was her bag, and she tucked the tiny bundle of vines inside. "It's a powerful charm."

He gave her an odd look. "I think you've gone too long without food. Perhaps we should break for luncheon before moving on."

Since she was rather hungry, she readily agreed, though not before she gave him an annoyed look for his dry remark.

Anthony tethered his horse to a nearby bush and collected a small bundle of food wrapped in white linen. He had purchased the fare from the inn before they'd departed.

Settling onto the mossy grass, sheltered by a light canopy of sparsely lined trees, they broke their fast, dividing the smoked ham and bread between them. Neither said a word to the other for the first little while, content with their meal and the tranquil surroundings. But that all changed soon enough.

"Do you often see faeries?"

His voice was smooth. It was deep and rich to be sure, but she couldn't tell by his tone if he was merely curious in his inquiry or if he was humoring her.

"The faeries don't show themselves to gypsies, or to anyone else for that matter. They like to cause mischief when no one's looking."

"Where do they live?"

"Some live in the forest, others in the fields, and there are those that live in the water."

A blond brow arched. "Nymphs, you mean?"

She nodded.

"Ah, then they do show themselves to man, for I have seen one."

He was smiling. She'd seen that smile before. It was a boyish grin, charming, with the strength to knock the very breath from her lungs. Her voice dropped to a whisper. "You've seen one?"

Anthony broke his bread, the crumbs raining down over his black leather boots. "Some time ago, I was walking through the woods when I came upon a stream and beheld a water nymph."

He sounded sincere, like a boy with a secret he readily wished to impart. She forgot all about her food as she leaned in to better hear him. "What did the nymph look like?"

"She was very beautiful," he said softly, the hue of his green eyes darkening. "Glistening water drops bathed her body like a torrent of jewels. Her long, flowing hair was as black as soot, her eyes as blue as the sea."

There was an unexpected jolt in the pit of her stomach, followed by a scarlet tint that crept into her cheeks. He was talking about *her*. No one had ever said such . . . nice things about her. To hear herself described with reverence and in such flowery terms left her heart thumping in her ears and her limbs refusing to move.

Slowly, his hand came up to caress her cheek. It was a tender touch, leaving her skin prickling all over. "The nymph was every bit as enchanting as legend claims." His powerful fingers moved to brush over her mouth in feathery strokes. "I've never come across anyone so lovely. She will haunt my memory for some time to come."

Sabrina seemed to fall into his heavenly green eyes. And it was a swift, deep fall. She realized then she wanted to spend the rest of her life with him and be happy. And deep down in her heart she knew she could be—if only there was a place on earth where they could be together.

But there wasn't.

She could no more break with the traditions of her world than he could with his. And short of creating their own world, they could never be together.

The bleak truth struck her soundly. The sadness of it all overwhelmed her, as though a weight was crushing her chest. And then the fear of growing too fond of a man she could never be with encouraged her to break away from his entrancing eyes.

She pulled back. The look in Anthony's eyes was that of a glowing fire, vowing to consume her. She could feel herself being pulled into that fire and quickly scrambled to her feet.

But the bond between them wasn't broken. She wondered if it ever would be. A small part of her hoped not.

"I think we should keep going," she said after a long and tense pause.

He nodded and rose to his feet, his deep green eyes never wavering from her.

Chapter 15

~~~~~~∽◯◯◯∽~~~~~~

The somber hues of the gloaming sky swirled together, as the last rays of sunlight streaked over the distant horizon. An unusually warm wind weaved gently through the meadow, the rustling blades of grass bowing in unison to the will of the breeze. There was the scent of wild flowers in the air, coupled with the soft fragrance of acacia shrubs. Nighttime critters chirped, hummed, or croaked their evening concertos. Not that Anthony noticed any of it.

He was absorbed with the fading sun. Twenty minutes had gone by, he estimated, since Sabrina had ambled down to the nearby creek for her bath. It being such a pleasant evening, she had insisted upon one, and after promising to stay within a reasonable distance of him, she had meandered off into the bush unescorted. He'd reckoned it was safe enough for her to do so, that no dangers lurked behind any shrubs. But still, he wouldn't leave her unattended for too long. Another five minutes and then he would go in search of her.

Though why the girl preferred to bathe in the wild rather than in the privacy of a nearby inn was beyond him. Perhaps habit was just too hard to break.

His own lustful habits were indeed too hard to break. Proof was in the images now invading his mind. Images of his beautiful gypsy dipping into the wrinkled waters of the creek, her smooth skin textured with tiny goose bumps, her full breasts growing cold in the nippy waters. He pictured himself warming those beautiful breasts, caressing the heavy mounds, kissing away the chill from the tight, puckering nipples.

He closed his eyes and shuddered at the erotic vision. God, how he wanted Sabrina. His whole body ached for her. And he knew she wanted him in return. Her response to him the other night took care of any lingering doubts on the matter.

So why had their night of passion come to such a swift end?

It baffled him. The girl knew he wanted her regardless of her bloodline, so that wasn't the root of her enduring reservations. Perhaps she was accustomed to making love outdoors? No, she wasn't the kind to be so finicky. Besides, one word from her and he'd have taken her out onto the nearest hilltop without a qualm.

So what was it then? Why did her hesitation persist? And then it came to him. Perhaps it was her first time—with a *gajo*. Was she nervous about being with an outsider? It was beginning to make some sense. She wanted him, and yet she didn't trust him enough to be with him. And if such was the case, then he would simply have to put an end to her misgivings once and for all.

His gaze went back to the dusky horizon. Five minutes had gone by and still there was no sign of Sabrina.

Checking to see his horse was still securely tethered to the tree, Anthony set out after his tardy gypsy to make sure she was all right.

The murmur of the trickling creek guided him toward the shoreline, where he followed the windings of the bank, scanning the surrounding terrain for any sign of her.

Searching for some movement in the water, he almost ended up strolling right past Sabrina. She was seated so still, curled in a ball with her arms hooked around her bent knees. In the hovering darkness he had mistaken her for a boulder embedded along the shoreline. On closer inspection, though, he noted the faint ripples in the water where her toes skimmed over the surface in lambent strokes. Apart from those graceful movements, she was perfectly inert, rapt with such intense thoughts that she didn't even notice his approach.

A twig crunched beneath his booted heel, and the meditating water nymph scrambled to her feet in alarm.

"It's only me," he said to reassure her. "I was worried when you didn't return to the meadow."

Taut-limbed and flustered from her interrupted solitude, she wondered, "How long have I been gone?"

"Half an hour or so."

His voice faded to a gruff whisper, as his eyes narrowed on her damp and snuggly twined chemise. The garment was fitted wantonly over her frame, a loose strap slumped down her arm, slightly exposing the smooth mound of her swelling breast.

It stirred his blood, to see her in such clinging attire, where every delicious curve was candidly outlined. Instinct propelled him to reach out and hook his forefinger around the straggling wet strap, tenderly sliding it back over her shoulder.

"You'll catch cold," he murmured, feeling her shiver under his languorous caress.

She wrapped her hands around her arms. "I'll heal myself."

He grinned at her riposte, but then he heard the chattering sound and his grin vanished. Her teeth were striking together, and he swiftly shrugged his riding coat off his shoulders.

"You foolish girl," he chastised. "You're frozen."

Blanketing her in his coat, he folded her into his arms. Ah, what a feeling! Pure bliss was all that came to mind.

He could feel the shivers coasting along her spine, and tightened his embrace, his cheek brushing softly across her damp and icy brow.

"Anthony!"

"Protest all you want, my dear. I'm not letting go 'til you stop shaking."

And to prove it, he rubbed his hands up and down her back in brisk, swirling motions.

The friction was causing him some heat as well, despite the cold, wet garb pressed up against him, and he was gripped with a powerful need to taste her. Well, he always had that urge. But now it was even more consuming.

His lips went to her brow, then to the icy tip of her nose.

"I want you," he said softly.

She gasped. His mouth closed tightly over hers. She wiggled soundly in his arms, for all of two seconds, before she sighed, the tension draining from her limbs, her body sagging forward into his chest.

She shuddered and he felt every thrilling tremor. "I need you," he whispered hoarsely, captured her lips in an ardent kiss, then broke away again. "Let me love you tonight."

It was a whimper she let loose. A whimper of defeat. The sweetest sound he had ever heard. He wanted to cry out with joy at her surrender. It was about bloody time they both gave in to their overriding passions. He was certainly at his wit's end with desire.

"Anthony, please," she whispered.

"Am I really such a scoundrel for finding you so beautiful?" he breathed against her skin, kissing her between words. "Am I really such a blackguard for wanting to taste those sweet lips of yours?"

"I can't," came the quiet protest. Her voice was quivering. "My father—"

"Will never know," he cut in quickly.

"But my future husband will!"

"Devil take your future husband! . . . How will the man know? You don't intend on telling him, do you?"

"He'll know," she insisted. "On our wedding night, he'll know. Oh, can't you men tell when a woman is a . . . a . . ."

Anthony abruptly released his hold and she staggered back. She was flustered, her chest billowing with each eager pant. And she was striking, with the silver moonlight bouncing off her glossy wet hair.

"You're a virgin?" He couldn't tell if it was a blush or the fading moonlight, shadowed by a cloud, darkening her cheeks just then. "But you can't be. You're a gypsy."

She bristled. "What does *that* have to do with anything?"

"Well, I mean . . . the way you paraded around my

room in only your chemise with no hint of modesty. You just never acted as though you were chaste."

"Gypsies don't find shame in their bodies. So long as my legs were covered, I *was* being modest."

Perturbed, he ran his fingers roughly through his hair. He hadn't counted on a clash of cultures to pollute all his notions about her. Suddenly, he didn't know what to think anymore. He felt as if he didn't know her at all.

"Why are you saving yourself for a man you care nothing about?" he asked, at a complete loss to understand her motives.

"I have my father's honor to think of."

"And why would your father care?"

"It would disgrace my entire family if I were not a . . ."

"Virgin?"

"On my wedding night," she rounded off hastily. "Why do you sound so surprised? Doesn't your future wife have to be chaste?"

"Well, naturally, but issues of rank and reputation, wealth and heirs are at stake."

She stuck her arms through the sleeves of his coat and crossed them under her breasts. "And I suppose my father's honor is worthless because he's a gypsy?"

"I did not mean—"

"I know what you meant," she cut in sharply. "Because I have no fortune, my father shouldn't care whom I bed."

All right, perhaps that was what he meant. But in his defense, a gentleman had to be selective in his choice of a bride. One couldn't risk ignominy by marrying anything less than perfect breeding. But a gypsy being so finicky? Did it really matter all that much whom she bedded? She had no social standing to protect or noble family name to dishonor.

He was at a loss for words. Sabrina, on the other hand, had no such difficulty in finding her voice.

Chanting a few unintelligible words, she spit at his feet.

He looked at his boots, then back up to her, storm clouds gathering in his eyes, and demanded, "What did you just do?"

Her lips were trembling. "I put a curse on you."

"You cursed me?" Incredulous, he suddenly thundered, "What the hell for?!"

"Because you thought me a whore!" she cried back. "You wanted nothing more than to bed me. You didn't even care that it might ruin the rest of my life!" Moisture swelled to the brim of her sooty lashes. "I thought I meant something more to you. But I don't. I'm nothing but a poor, worthless gypsy to you."

"That isn't true!"

"Yes, it is. It's all you'll ever see in me. You're just like all the others."

His anger vanished at the sight of those tear-filled eyes. He realized then the girl *had* trusted him. At some point in time, she'd stopped looking upon him with suspicion, but he'd been too self-absorbed in his lust to notice. And now, he'd shattered her confidence in him. He'd never done that before: devastated a woman's trust. Come to think of it, no one except Sabrina had ever placed such faith in him to begin with, so that was why there was never a crushed spirit or broken heart to contend with.

But now, to see that disillusioned face stained with tears—tears he had caused—was piercing to the soul.

She spit at his feet once more.

"There. I took off the curse. I shouldn't be angry

with you anyway. *I'm* the fool." She pointed to her chest. "*I* thought you were different from other *gajos*. But you're not. You care only about yourself."

Something unpleasant swirled in his gut at her cutting words. He quickly closed the space between them and grabbed her arms. "Sabrina, listen to me."

"Get away from me." She broke free of his hold. "I don't want anything to do with you."

It wasn't in his nature to leave a woman irate with him. A smile or charming remark usually did away with any feminine pout or frown. But Sabrina wasn't wounded because he was tardy for a ball or absentminded in complimenting her dress, and he sensed such a trivial reparation wouldn't suffice in this instance.

"Sabrina, I . . ."

She stalked away. He heard her ragged breaths grow faint, saw her silhouette disappear into the shadows.

That wretched feeling stirring in his gut grew worse. It consumed him. He felt the overwhelming need to make amends. But how?

And then an alarming thought intruded, that they would part company on such ghastly terms. He couldn't bear the thought of his atrocious conduct haunting him for the rest of his days. He certainly couldn't bear the thought of Sabrina always hating him. She had been the only one to ever see in him something more than a rogue. To believe he was honorable. To place her very safety in his hands. He wouldn't let her go home thinking she had been a fool to ever trust him. He would set things right between them . . . somehow. He swore to himself she would have no regrets in having met him.

Chapter 16

⟡～⟡⟡⟡～⟡

She was nearly home. The thought was strange to Sabrina. It had been almost a fortnight since she'd disappeared from her camp. No great length of time. And yet it seemed like she'd been away for ages. She felt changed. Older. She felt as if she didn't belong with her people any more than she belonged with *gajos*.

It was such a wretched feeling, to have no sense of belonging. She had never felt that way before. Her path in life had always been so clear, lit by the wisdom of the tribal elders. They had guided her for so many years, and she had grown dependent on them. Without an elder near to instruct her, she was lost. The path she now walked in her heart was dark and frightening, and she couldn't see what was waiting for her at the other end.

But the elders would steer her back on course, she was sure. As soon as she was home, they would set everything to right. She would begin her life as a healer, a wife, and eventually a mother: the very destiny she had tried to thwart. She would no longer try to avoid what was meant to be. She had been punished for her reckless behavior, for stepping beyond the boundaries of her world and consorting with a *gajo*. She would not be such a fool again.

It shamed her to think of what she had done—or almost done. To have trusted a *gajo* was beyond reckless. Children knew better than to trust an outsider. And *she*, daughter of the tribal leader, should have obeyed gypsy teachings. She should have accepted that an outsider was akin to an enemy. Had she done so, she would never have developed feelings for Anthony. She would never have risked dishonoring her father—or herself— for a heartless rake.

The sky rumbled in the distance. She shivered at the sight of the threatening clouds. She didn't want to be alone and trapped under the angry heavens when the storm came pouring down. But then the horse snorted some distance behind her, and she sighed, remembering she was not alone after all.

A quick glance over her shoulder and she caught sight of Anthony's trailing figure, leading the horse by the reins. Why the man was still following her, she didn't know. But he hadn't said a word to her since the other night. She was thankful for that. The sound of his voice only stirred to life intimate emotions she wanted stifled. But knowing he was there, feeling his eyes on her, seemed to affect her just as powerfully.

It wasn't fair that one brief, wandering figure in her life should have such a great impact on the rest of her days; that she should have changed so much, in such a short period of time, and all because of one man.

That unhappy thought remained with her until she

felt the tiny, cold drops of water strike her skin. She scanned the countryside with an eager eye and an attentive ear. Her camp was nearby. The land looked so familiar.

And then she heard it, the laughter. Children's laughter. And her eyes fell upon the distant moving dots dashing toward the nearby hilltop. Her camp. It was just over that hill.

Her heart thumped faster. She was home. She would soon see her father. Would he be angry with her for disappearing from the caravan? Would he be able to see the change in her? And would he be able to guess the reason for her change?

Her lackluster pace allowed Anthony to close the gap between them. Her gaze so intent upon the hillside, she was startled to hear the deep voice by her ear.

"Are you home?"

She turned to look at him. A hesitant wind ruffled his golden hair, causing a stray curl to dance over his bright and piercing eyes. It made her chest hurt to see that handsome face, so noble in appearance. Her heart cried out at the image—an image she now knew was nothing but an illusion.

"My camp is nearby," she said. "I have to go the rest of the way by myself."

He nodded in understanding. Should anyone see him traveling with her, it would lead to too many questions. Questions she did not want to answer.

She couldn't bear to keep her eyes on him anymore. She turned away, but he cupped her face between his strong fingers and forced her to confront him.

"Sabrina, I never meant to hurt you."

Did he have to sound so earnest? Those blasted tears were gathering again. Curse them! She would sooner bite her tongue and make it bleed than shed another tear for the unfeeling scoundrel.

"Forgive me," he said sincerely. "I only wanted to help you. My desire for you was . . . real. But it should never have interfered with my duty."

Why was he doing this to her? In moments, they would part company for good. Words of forgiveness would get him nothing, he had to know that. She would never be so foolish as to trust him again.

"I wanted nothing from you," he said next, as though he had heard her thoughts, but then he sighed. "That isn't entirely true. I wanted you. I still do. I cannot help how I feel."

Why was her heart stomping so loudly in her ears? *Why* couldn't she break away from his hold?

"But one intention was always honorable," he whispered. "I always meant to protect you and see you safely home. Perhaps I am just more of a rogue than I care to admit." He pressed a warm and tender kiss to her brow. "Goodbye, Sabrina."

And that was it. He took his horse by the reins and walked away. Words were swimming around in her throat, drowning, and by the time she'd mustered enough control to say something, Anthony was gone. He was no more than a moving shadow in the distance.

The soft sprinkle of rain soon turned into a steady shower, the kiss on her brow washed clean away.

The din of bubbly chatter meshed with the notes of the jigging fiddlers, as all united in celebration of the healer's safe return. There were many tender smiles, many joyful voices, many spirited laughs and tight, bone-crushing hugs. But there was one gypsy in the camp who didn't feel like celebrating.

Sabrina's gaze flitted between the spinning dancers, the musicians, the giggling children poking sticks at the birds roasting over the snapping flames. Her eyes moved along the row of brightly adorned wagons, wrapped around the camp to protect the festive dwellers within from the rest of the dark world. And then her eyes skipped over the roofs of the wagons and she stared out into that dark beyond.

It was such a clear, crisp night. The storm clouds had faded. Flickering white lights spotted the heavens, as though the stars themselves were chattering as exuberantly as the gypsies. Sabrina wondered what those stars were whispering. What secrets were shooting across the sky? What did the stars think when they looked down upon the earth to find her amid such revelry and yet feeling so alone? Or did those stars see her at all?

Sabrina brushed her fingers over her brow where Anthony had kissed her goodbye. An ache entered her heart as soon as she thought of the viscount. An ache borne of doubt. Doubt about everything that had passed between them. She had been so sure that morning that Anthony was nothing more than a scoundrel. Despite all the hopeful traits she had once observed in his palm, she'd concluded he was a bounder through and through, just as his sister had proclaimed. Those lines of honor etched in his palm were an illusion, one she'd conjured in her befuddled state of mind. After all, she was recovering from a head injury, and it made perfect sense that her gift of sight should remain clouded until her wound had fully healed. But now, she was not so sure of her belief. Now, as she sat on a fallen log, bundled in her bright green shawl, watching the festivities unfold before her, she wondered if the traits she had seen in his palm were indeed buried somewhere deep within his heart.

Anthony's parting words were making it hard for her to ignore that she might have been mistaken about the viscount's true nature, that the man had potential after all, though he had yet to express it. She almost wished there was no chance of such a mistake. That he was nothing but a heartless rogue and could never be anything more. It would make her own grief much more bearable. She wouldn't dwell on such a wretched being for very long. But if he wasn't so wretched? If he'd meant all those tender words he'd uttered in his good-bye, then what was she to think? To feel?

The ache in her heart grew stronger. Was Anthony a misguided but noble man at heart? Or a skilled trickster? The question would surely haunt her for some time to come.

"You are not dancing, daughter."

Sabrina looked up to the towering figure of her father and smiled. "I'm tired," she said in her native Romany, though just the sight of the spinning dancers made her head hurt. She didn't mention that to her father, though. No one knew of her head injury and she intended to keep it that way. To speak of her wound would lead to questions about her recovery, and she did *not* want to tell her father that she had spent the last few days in a *gajo's* bed. Just the thought of mentioning that to him had her shivering all over. And the man was quick to take notice.

Vardar Kallos sat next to his daughter, hooking a

protective arm around her shoulder and squeezing. "You seem unwell," he said with concern, his dark blue eyes fixed tightly on her.

She kissed his thick black beard and rested her head on his shoulder in reply.

"You think to appease my distress with a kiss?" He sighed when she snuggled closer to him, then chuckled. "Clever child."

Clever? Perhaps evasive was a better word, she thought with some guilt, though she had not withheld everything from her father. He and the rest of the camp knew of her attackers and why she had fled. They knew she had spent days in hiding before she'd made her way back home. They just didn't know where and with whom she had hidden.

"How did the talk with your betrothed fare?" he asked.

"It went well," she admitted. After a tearful reunion with her family and friends, it had come time for the dreaded talk regarding her disobedience. Despite the circumstances under which she had disappeared, the grief she'd caused her people had to be addressed, and her father was the obvious choice to chastise her and administer any proper punishment. But it wouldn't be his place to reprimand her for very long. With her approaching wedding, the responsibility would soon belong to her husband. And Vardar thought it best if her betrothed took on that responsibility a little sooner than expected.

"Istvan was as forgiving as you, Father. He did not think to scold me. He said he was just happy to see me home."

"Perhaps there was more wisdom in your cousin's

heart than forgiveness? To scold you before the wedding ceremony would pollute the marriage bed. That might bring bad luck on the heads of your future children."

Sabrina couldn't help but wonder what kind of luck the marriage would have if the wife's heart belonged to another man. She closed her eyes, banishing the wicked thought.

"I am sorry," she said again, "for leaving you so suddenly."

"I know, child." He kissed the top of her head. "My days were filled with dread while you were gone, but now that you are home safe, I am proud to call you my daughter. You risked your life to protect your people. Your courage will make you a great healer and a great leader. Our people will one day look up to you as the wife of the tribal guardian. You have a very sacred duty."

A sacred duty? She supposed that was true. Wife. Mother. Healer. They were all roles she had to fulfill to ensure order and stability and peace. Who would heal body and soul alike if not her? Who would marry the next tribal guardian and serve as an example of tradition if not her? Who would bear a son to inherit the guardian's position if not her? To fall short of a duty, any duty, would incite turmoil within the tribe.

"When will I be wed?" she asked quietly.

"The elders and I have spoken. We believe you should be wed on the next full moon. It is a good time to begin a new life . . . unless your recent troubles have so upset you, you wish to postpone—"

"No, Father," she was quick to cut in. She would not avoid her fate. Doing so would only lead to further heartache. The more time she spent thinking about Anthony, the more miserable she became. It was better to just throw herself into her new life and never look back on the old. "I will marry Istvan on the next full moon."

But she felt her heart twist with each word that she uttered.

Chapter 17

The creaking carriage wheels, trampling over sooty, cobblestone roads, lulled an already listless Anthony. He had been traveling for days. On foot, on horseback, and now by carriage. He was tired. Or that was the excuse he used to explain away his morose mood.

But fatigue alone could not account for his pensiveness. There was something else gnawing at him. And he didn't have to delve too far into his thoughts to discover what that something was.

Sabrina.

She haunted him. Her brilliant blue eyes gazed at him from the darkness of the carriage. He blinked a few times to dismiss the vision, but it lingered a while before fading away.

He'd never been so crass with a woman in all his life. It'd all been unintentional, of course, and he'd said what he could, what he thought was best, to make amends. But he didn't know whether his words of contrition had had any effect on her. Did she still despise him? Or did the truth enlighten her, make her realize his boorish behavior had been unintended?

He would never know. She was home. Safe. She would be married soon. She would have a new life. And he would be dismissed from her old one like a bad dream.

Anthony stretched out his long legs. It was better that she forgot all about him. It would be just as well that he forgot all about her. Guilt and regret did not sit very comfortably with him. They downright suffocated him, and he hated the unfamiliar sensations.

He'd been an utter ass toward a woman. So what? It was bound to have happened eventually. He didn't need to suffer for it unnecessarily. He had made a mistake, pure and simple . . . So why the hell *did* it matter so much? Why couldn't he get Sabrina out of his head? And why did the thought of another man touching her, even her husband, make him want to send his fist through the carriage window?

Anthony was spared the trouble of searching for answers when the carriage rolled to a halt. He was home. Finally. He needed a good night's sleep. He needed to prepare himself for what the morning would bring.

Chaos.

Now that he was back in the city, he would have to face the wrath of three particular females, all to whom he was related. His mother and Cecelia would demand an explanation for his disappearance from the ball, while Ashley would demand to know what had happened with the gypsy.

Bloody hell. It was going to be an infernal morning.

Anthony ordered the coachman to put away the carriage in the back stables, and after a sound crack of the whip, the horses trotted off, the creaking carriage wheels fading around the deserted street corner.

Anthony stood at the base of the stone steps and looked up to find the windows of his stately dwelling dark as pitch. Well, it was late. He wasn't sure how late—he had no pocket watch with him—but with the streets vacant of all stirrings, save for the misty crawling fog, he assumed it was well into the early hours of the morning.

Slowly, he made his way up the stone steps, fumbling through his pockets, searching for the key to his home. After turning his coat inside out in his quest, he finally found the key and went to insert it through the lock.

But the light sound of footsteps treading the pavement behind him snagged his attention.

He stiffened, listening. And waited. Waited for the steps to grow close. When he sensed the shadow was near, he whirled around, grabbed the assailant by the shoulders and spun him about.

His unfortunate foe had no opportunity to defend himself, could only grasp in vain at the bulk coiled around his windpipe, halting the flow of precious air to his lungs.

"Anthony!" The man wheezed between desperate breaths. "Let me go!"

"Vincent?!"

The choke hold was instantly broken and Vincent Longhurst slumped to his knees, coughing, wheezing, and fighting for air.

"Good God, Vincent!" Anthony knelt beside his best friend to inspect how badly he was injured, and was thankful to find that nothing was crushed or broken, just bruised. "What the hell are you doing lurking in the shadows? I could have killed you."

"You very nearly did," muttered Vincent, still coughing and rubbing his tender throat.

With care, Anthony hoisted his injured comrade to his feet, and swung the man's arm over his shoulder to better support him. It was then he noticed the stench. After a quick glance to Vincent's appalling apparel, he confirmed his sense of smell had not deceived him.

"What the devil happened to you?" Anthony demanded. "You look like a vagrant."

"I've been living like one for the last few days," his friend admitted, still clearing his throat and massaging his sore glands. "Didn't you get my letter? I spent my last farthing on a messenger."

"I got the letter," Anthony confirmed.

"So why didn't you come home? I begged for your return."

"Is that what the letter was about? Vincent, I didn't come home because I couldn't read a bloody word you'd written. Now tell me what's going on?"

"Let me inside first. Someone might be watching us."

The pleading in his friend's voice suspended Anthony's curiosity for a moment, and he unlocked the front door, ushering a fearful Vincent inside.

It was some time later, ensconced in an armchair, a large wool blanket draped over his shoulders, that Vincent held a shot of brandy between his shivering hands. He was affectionately referred to as the "dear boy" by the rest of the Kennington family—all except for the countess, who was dismayed by her son's choice of a comrade.

Since Vincent was the third son of a baron, he was devoid of both title and fortune. The so-called dear boy thus had to make his own way in the world. Necessity had propelled him to join a regiment; active duty on the mainland nearly cost him his neck. Now back home in London, having vowed never to set foot on another battlefield, Vincent had returned to his old truant ways, immersed in the luxury and pleasure of the many gambling halls throughout the city, in the hopes of winning his fortune rather than having to earn it.

Anthony studied his somnolent comrade, seated by the glowing hearth, and took notice that those typical bright and spirited brown eyes of his were now a befuddled, gloomy version of their former self. Even his butler, Dobbs, hadn't recognized his best friend.

After all the racket he and Vincent had made, fumbling in the dark, trying to make their way into the study, Dobbs had come scrambling down the stairs with two footmen in tow, fearing there was an intruder in the house, only to find it was his master come home with a rather vile-looking vagrant in his company. Since Vincent had made no effort to correct the misguided assumptions of the staff, Anthony had followed his friend's lead, remaining silent on the issue of his identity, as well. He'd merely dismissed the staff back to bed, and now he and Vincent sat alone in the study, silence between them.

Food and a bowl of water for cleansing had been brought in for Vincent's use, but his friend had yet to accept the refreshment, and the fare remained untouched on the desk.

Anthony didn't press him to partake in any of the offerings. He allowed Vincent some much-needed time to recover. He only watched his friend from across the room, wondering what the devil had happened to the man in such a short period of time.

"Vincent, what's going on?"

The man rubbed his tired eyes. "I explained so much in my letter."

"Just recount what you wrote, as best you can."

He sighed. "The whole thing happened a fortnight ago. I was issued an invitation to an exclusive gaming club, in a well-respected part of the city, where I met a woman, Emma Kingsley."

"Ah, the ladybird," said Anthony. "One of the few words I managed to decipher from your letter."

"The very one. I fell head over heels for Emma."

"You fall head over heels for every woman you meet." A tendency Anthony himself was prone to.

"Yes, but Emma was different," Vincent insisted. "She was incredibly beautiful and witty and clever."

"Are you *still* infatuated with this woman?"

His friend's chagrined shrug was answer enough.

Anthony shook his head. "So what did Emma do to you?"

"She inspired me."

"Pardon?"

"Emma was like lady luck herself. With her at my side, I couldn't lose a hand. I was so sure I'd win my fortune that very night and never have to worry about money again."

The loud groan that stemmed from Anthony halted the flow of the story for a moment. The viscount slumped his face in his palm and mumbled, "I think I know how this story ends."

"I wish I had your foresight. But at the time, I was just too eager to amass my wealth, and I just, well . . ."

"Didn't know when to quit." Anthony sighed. "Just how much did you lose?"

"Anthony, you must understand. I couldn't forsake the money I had already invested, and then I got this winning hand and I was sure I'd recoup everything, but—"

"How much, Vincent?" he demanded again, his tone none too approving.

"Five."

"Hundred?"

"Thousand."

"*What?!*" Anthony sprang to his feet and stalked over to the hearth. He paced briskly before the fire, his long, ominous shadow crossing over Vincent again and again. "Are you mad?!"

"I told you, I had to try to win back my money."

"But five thousand pounds!"

"I was sure my good fortune would eventually return if I just stuck it out long enough," bemoaned Vincent. "But it never did. At the end of the game, the club wanted its money. I promised to pay off the debt in a few days, but I had no real idea where the blunt would come from. And then, three days later, there was a knock at my door. I ducked out the back and went for a stroll."

"You thought to avoid payment?"

"For a little while. Just until I could gather the required sum. But when I returned, the bloke was still standing across the street, watching the entrance. I went out again and returned, and *still* he remained standing just outside my apartment. Anthony, there is *always* someone watching my home."

"So where have you been staying all this time?"

"I've been forced to hide in a miserable little flat. I sold my watch, gold-tipped cane and ring, everything I had on me when I first left my apartment for a walk. I've been living off the few pounds those items have brought me, but the money's run out. I finally caught word of your pending return and have been waiting for you these last two days."

"What? In the streets?"

"Where else could I go?"

"What about your father?"

"I could never ask my father for help. He would sooner shoot me than offer a saving hand."

"I'm sorely tempted to do the same," the viscount growled.

There was a pleading look in his friend's eyes. "Anthony, they want their money—all of it—in one sum. No installments. I can't pay such an exorbitant amount. What am I going to do?"

"*You* are going to do nothing. *I* am going to that club tomorrow to pay off your debt."

Vincent gave a long-winded sigh of relief. "I don't know how to thank you for this, old chum. I swear, I'll pay you back every shilling."

And Anthony predicted the debt would be fulfilled by his eightieth year, though he refrained from making the prediction aloud.

Instead, he stalked over to his comrade until he towered above him, and in a hard tone, advised, "As part of your debt to me, you will also swear to give up gambling—for good."

The man nodded in quick accord. "I swear."

That was one small consolation, Anthony supposed. "Come along, Vincent," he grumbled. "I'll see you to one of the guestrooms. We'll get this whole mess sorted out in the morning."

213 Cullen Lane.

Anthony glanced up from the scrap of paper he held in his hand to the ironcast numbers nailed above the door.

This must be it, he thought to himself, and shoved the paper into his pocket. He mounted the steps of the regal apartment and was met by a high, well-polished mahogany entrance. He knocked on the door of the Lion's Gate establishment. No response. He knocked again, and when his admittance was still denied, he pounded on the wood with his fist. He'd be damned before he'd stand there all morning, requesting the attention of some lowly gaming hell owner.

At last, he heard the latch lift on the other side of the door. The entrance creaked open.

"May I help you?" came the stiff offer from a rather pale, ornery old man, who was not the least bit intimidated by the grave gentleman hovering above him.

"I am here to see Luther Gillingham," Anthony said tightly.

"Mr. Gillingham is not available. The club opens at eight o'clock every evening. You may come back to see him then."

Anthony's fist landed on the closing door. "Mr. Gillingham will either see me right now or he will forfeit the five thousand pounds owed to him by Mr. Longhurst."

That got the old guard dog's attention, and he stepped aside with a sweeping gesture, extending his arm into the main hall. "This way, your lordship."

It was a few minutes later that Anthony found himself in the manager's opulent study. The room was filled with the highest standard of goods. Leatherbound books lined the one shelved wall. Pale yellow drapes, satin by the sheen of them, adorned the tall arched windows. And only the softest, most comfortable silk upholstered the armchairs. It was a chamber fit for a noble—which Luther Gillingham was unquestionably not.

"Here you are, my good lord."

Anthony accepted the offered drink, though the man's condescending civility was prickling his ire.

Gillingham settled behind his large desk and puffed on his cigar. A gold ring, embedded with a brilliant emerald, winked when his hand twisted and caught the light. "How is Mr. Longhurst? I haven't seen him in a while."

"Mr. Longhurst is well," Anthony returned in feigned propriety, then tasted the brandy. He recognized the vintage. The very best, no less.

"We enjoyed his company greatly." Another deep intake of smoke before he released it slowly. "I do hope to see the good fellow again. Our tables are always open to him."

Anthony ignored the invitation. "I am here to pay off Mr. Longhurst's debt."

"A man who likes to get right down to business." Gillingham came forward in his chair and placed his elbows on the desk. "I admire that. No sense chitchatting when there's money involved."

Reaching into his breast pocket, Anthony pulled out the bank draft. "Five thousand pounds."

The folded paper landed in front of Gillingham. He eyed the funds for a moment, picked up the draft, then tucked it away in his desk drawer.

"You won't even read the draft?" said Anthony.

"My good viscount, I would never insult you in such a way." Then adding in a devilish grin, "I trust you implicitly."

Anthony restrained his urge to wipe that abrasive grin off the scoundrel's face. "The debt is paid. You will call off your hounds."

"But, of course. Business is business, you understand. I had nothing personally against Mr. Longhurst."

Setting his empty glass aside, Anthony rose from his chair. "Mr. Longhurst has retired from gambling. You will not see him in here again."

Gillingham also stood in a mock show of courteous respect. "Pity. A delightful chap to the core. We shall miss him." He came around the desk and extended his hand. "Good day to you, Lord Hastings. I hope to see you again one day, if not your friend."

Anthony bit back his growl and grabbed the fustian scoundrel's hand in a firm, brief handshake. "I think not."

"A great pity indeed. But I extend the invitation to you nonetheless."

On opening the door for his guest, Gillingham beckoned a beautiful young woman to approach. "Emma is one of our finest hostesses. She will show you to the door, my lord." Then, with a wink, "Perhaps she will tempt you to return after all."

Anthony bristled at the mere mention of the

woman's name: the very temptress who had "inspired" Vincent to squander five thousand pounds—*his* five thousand pounds. Though he had to admit, with one look at the finely dressed whore, he was beginning to understand how his best friend had been lulled into losing the hefty sum in the first place.

But Emma's ringlets of gold and pouty lips were soon dismissed from Anthony's mind, his attention snagged elsewhere. It was the glimmering jewel cushioned snuggly between the two bountiful mounds of her breasts that caught his eye. A jewel that looked strikingly familiar.

The memory struck him soundly. It was the very same gold locket that Sabrina always wore, complete with a lion's head engraved in the oval face.

Anthony was baffled. How could Sabrina have the exact same necklace as Emma Kingsley? It made no sense.

But he had lingered too long on the locket, he realized, and promptly composed himself. Gillingham was watching him with avid curiosity, so he made a quick reference to his moment of pause.

"Very tempting indeed," said Anthony, indicating to the woman's breasts, hoping Gillingham would accept the aloof explanation at face value. "Good day to you."

He promptly turned on his heels, and in long, arrogant strides, trailed after Emma's swinging hips, all the while mulling over what he had just seen. It wasn't until the temptress had shown him to the door, and he'd glanced once more at her locket and then to the brass knocker in the shape of a lion's head, that he made the connection.

Anthony smothered the sprouting fear inside him,

and with a few parting words to Emma, to throw off any suspicions he might have aroused, he ducked into his waiting carriage and ordered the driver to take him home directly, though he didn't intend to remain there for very long.

It was clear to him now. Those two scoundrels in the woods really *had* been chasing after the locket. That meant they worked for Gillingham. It also meant Sabrina was still in danger, for a ruthless man like Luther Gillingham would never give up his search for a prize he greatly valued.

Anthony had to go back to the gypsy camp.

He had to warn Sabrina.

Back inside the Lion's Gate, at the far end of the corridor, an inquisitive Luther Gillingham remained standing, regarding the tall silhouette of Lord Hastings disappear from view.

When Emma eventually made her way back down the hall, he grabbed her by the arm, demanding harshly, "What did the viscount say to you?"

She jerked her arm free. "He only asked how much it would cost to spend the night with me. But I don't think he is of any great value to us."

She flounced off, Gillingham glaring after her. But he was no longer convinced it was Emma's breasts that the viscount had found so enticing.

Chapter 18

"You'll beat the skirt to shreds."

So startled by the interruption to her solitude, Sabrina released said skirt, and then clambered after it before it drifted away downstream. By the time she made her way back to her washing spot, she was met with a fit of giggles.

"You frightened me," Sabrina accused.

"Did I?" chuckled Gulseren, as she came to squat beside her cousin. "You are too sensitive. What is the matter?"

Sabrina went on with her work, smacking the skirt against the rock, trying to break up the stubborn mud clustered around the hem. "Nothing's the matter. I'm distracted, is all."

"Hmm. I wonder what's distracting you." Gulseren tapped a finger against her chin. "Did an elf scurry by, flooding your ears with tales of hidden gold? No? Let me think. I know! A dancing bear was just entertaining you! Not that either? Well, what else could it be . . . ?"

"Don't tease me, cousin. You know the wedding is on my mind."

"Ah, the wedding." There was a giggle by her ear before Sabrina felt a pair of slender arms coil around her neck. "I forgot all about the wedding. The very wedding that will soon make us sisters."

Sabrina looked over her shoulder at her cousin with a helpless smile. She already loved Gulseren like a sister, but becoming a wife would bring the two of them even closer together, and not just in terms of kinship, but in friendship as well.

Gulseren was already married, and Sabrina had never really understood what life was like for her cousin, her existence being one of lonely freedom. Now she would. In three days time, she too would become a wife. No more would she sit idly by and listen to the women talk about things she knew nothing about. Soon she would join in those talks herself, finally able to understand a sacred part of gypsy life.

"Your father is worried about you, Sabrina. He thinks you're not behaving as a proper bride should."

There was a sudden pang in her heart. Her nerves threaded to form a taut knot in her belly. "Why does he think that?"

"Because you have been very quiet of late."

"I'm always quiet."

"Yes, but you are also a bride, and brides are never quiet."

The knot in Sabrina's belly tightened. She had tried, she really had, to mask her gloomy mood from her father. She'd stayed away from the man as best she could, so he wouldn't notice her sullen features. But he could always tell when something was troubling her. Now he'd sent her cousin to investigate what that something was, and Sabrina didn't know what to say. How could she explain the feelings of turmoil inside her without revealing *who* had triggered them? How could she admit that a man haunted her dreams—a man not her betrothed?

"Is something bothering you, Sabrina?"

"No," she was quick to refute, and gave her head a firm shake for good measure. "I'm just nervous about the wedding."

That got her a kiss on the cheek. "I was nervous too. But don't worry. Everything will be all right."

Sabrina dearly hoped so. As her wedding day approached, foreboding shadowed her thoughts. She was sure she would betray her encounter with Anthony in some careless way, and then she would be shunned and scorned by her people.

Sabrina kept her fingers busy, wringing the water from her skirt, and her thoughts away from doom. "I'll speak with my father when I return to the camp."

"Good. Saves me the trouble of being a messenger." Gulseren unhooked her arms from around her cousin's neck and moved to crouch beside her again. "I have a surprise for you."

"What is it?"

"An early wedding gift."

Eyes filling with appreciation, Sabrina looked down to the beautifully beaded leather pouch, perfect for storing all her charms and herbs.

She dried her wet hands against her skirt before she accepted the gift. "Thank you," Sabrina said softly, and fastened the pouch around her waist. "I'll wear it always."

"See that you do. I didn't spend weeks fiddling with the beads to have all my hard effort hidden away."

With a grin, Sabrina reached for another piece of clothing and dipped it into the stream.

"Do you need any help with your wedding clothes?" her cousin asked.

She gave her head a brisk shake. "I'm almost finished. There are only a few more coins to sew into the hemline of the skirt."

With a sly smile, Gulseren replied, "Don't forget to sew a few coins into the wedding sheets, too. It will bring your future children good luck."

Cheeks brightening at the mention of such a thing, Sabrina immersed herself in her laundry, trying to ignore the spirited laughter coming from her cousin.

"Perhaps you shouldn't look behind you," Gulseren chuckled. "Your cheeks might darken even more."

But, of course, Sabrina now had to look, and her eyes pinned on the slowly approaching figure of her betrothed. Her blush deepened.

Istvan was heading toward the two young women with a timid smile on his face. He was tall, like his father and her father and all Kallos men in general, with the same dark brown hair and soft blue eyes. He was also slender for his height, but then, so too had her father been at his age, and he'd eventually developed into a strong and robust man—though Anthony was already strong and robust.

There it was again, that wicked thought. She had to forget about Anthony. Guilt slashed through her for making a comparison between her betrothed and the viscount. Istvan didn't deserve such treatment in her thoughts. He was a good man. He would make a good husband . . . so why couldn't she see him as *her* husband?

"I have come to speak with my betrothed," he said hesitantly, his eyes darting between Sabrina and the ground.

Gulseren nodded, smiling at her brother, and then winked at Sabrina before she skipped away. Sabrina wanted to reach out and stop her cousin from leaving, but she realized how foolish that would seem, and instead, turned her eyes to the water and her clothes.

Crouching beside his betrothed, Istvan cast her a wary smile. "More and more caravans are arriving by the day," he said shyly. "My father says there will be up to two hundred gypsies gathered here in time for the wedding celebration."

Sabrina gave him a half smile in return and continued with her laundry. Guilt kept her from saying anything. She had yet to be married, and already she had betrayed her husband in her heart. It was hard to look at Istvan without feeling her remorse increase tenfold.

But Istvan wanted her attention, and the gentle pressure of his fingers on her wrist forced her to surrender it.

His eyes were searching, even eager, as he waited to learn of her reaction to his pending gesture. "I have something for you." He unfurled his palm to reveal a gold bracelet with a tiny horseshoe charm dangling from it.

"It's beautiful, Istvan," she said quietly, and allowed him to fasten the clasp around her wrist, her hand shaking the entire time.

She felt shame welling up in her breast. Everyone was thrilled about the approaching wedding. There would be much feasting and drinking and dancing in three days time. Hearts were merry—all those except for the bride's. And she hated being the *only* miserable one.

With dismay, she realized she'd need far more luck than a golden horseshoe charm to make her future life with Istvan a pleasant one.

"I will leave you to finish your chores," he said and walked away.

Sabrina looked after him, her heart in chaos. Misery gave way to anger. This was *her* wedding. Was she really going to spend it sulking? Was she going to pine away for some viscount she would never see again?

What a ridiculous thing to do.

With newfound resolve, she decided to partake in the festivities and enjoy herself. She was going to learn to love her husband as a wife should. She was going to be happy. Her encounter with Anthony would not cloud her future contentment. She was determined not to let it.

It was the crescendos that guided Anthony toward the gypsy campsite. He had heard the music before he saw the signs of smoke coming from the bonfires dotting the encampment.

He now crouched on the hilltop, masked by the darkness, gazing below at the bubbling festivities. He recognized the sounds of fiddles and tambourines, and there was laughter and singing voices. Clapping hands served as drums, beating in time to the lively music, as the dancers twirled in each other's arms, their bright garments mixing in a brilliant display of whirling color.

It was a large camp, larger than he had imagined. There were so many wagons that he wondered how he was ever going to find Sabrina amid such commotion.

But his quandary was short lived. He spotted the long flowing locks of sable black hair, and then he heard the sparkling and spirited laughter. He had never heard her laugh before. Such an infectious sound that filled him with indescribable warmth.

She was happy . . . and he was going to shatter that happiness with his barged interruption. But he didn't have a choice. He had to warn her of Gillingham's intentions. He had to make sure she was safe. He owed her that much.

She was dancing in a young man's arms, her movements fluid in her long, bright green skirt. Something sparkled from the hemline, something he wasn't able to discern from a distance. He only saw the glittering adornments as she spun and spun by the fire's light.

It was like a solid punch to his gut. Was this her wedding? Is that what all the dancing and feasting was about? Is that why she was dressed so colorfully? He had come too late . . . No, wait. What was the matter with him? He hadn't come to interrupt her life, to stop her from getting wed. That she was married didn't change his intention. He still had to warn her of the danger she was in.

But how? He couldn't just amble down the hillside and join in the carousing. He knew how much gypsies distrusted outsiders. They might even mistake him for one of Sabrina's former aggressors, and he hadn't come this far to get his head cracked wide open.

He would have to flag down Sabrina's attention. He only needed a few words alone with her, to caution her, and then he would be on his way.

His horse secured to a tree, Anthony made the slow

and solitary descent. He steered clear of the cluster of dancers and roasting pits, where most of the gypsies were gathered. He lurked instead in the shadows of the brightly adorned wagons that circled the encampment.

Ducking behind each wagon, he made his way closer to Sabrina.

It took him a few minutes to pass by the wagons without detection. He stopped behind a bright red one, situated closest to where Sabrina was dancing. And now he need only capture her attention.

That was going to prove difficult, though, even from his more advantageous position. He couldn't call to her, she would never hear him with all the boisterous music and laughter swarming around her. And if he was to shout, well, he'd garner a trifle more attention than he was really after. A hand signal seemed appropriate, but she would have to be looking directly at him to notice a few flickering fingers in the darkness.

He would have to wait, he supposed, until the ideal moment, when he was sure to gain her notice. And so that was what he did. He hunkered low, to remain unobtrusive, and watched her.

She was as beautiful as ever. Her cheeks were aglow from the exertion of the dance, her eyes bright and glistening like sapphires. When she moved close to the fire, her ebony locks were streaked with orange highlights, but when she moved away, and the moonlight broke through a pocket in the clouds, her hair seemed to glow the darkest shade of cobalt. She was like a chameleon changing her colors, and he was enraptured by her every movement and transformation.

He had missed her. He hadn't realized how much until he saw her now. He'd certainly missed her more than he should. And for some inexplicable reason, he ached at the sight of her so content.

The loud barking behind his ear had Anthony whirling around and narrowing his eyes on a whelp of a mutt no larger than his boot.

"Bloody hell," he grumbled, and then hissed for the irritating canine to be silent. But the mutt refused to halt his high-pitched assault, and Anthony grew worried that someone was eventually going to come along to see what all the commotion was about. Even with the mighty din going on all around him, a passing gypsy would soon hear the little whelp's cries and come to investigate.

Having no other recourse, Anthony decided to try his hand at charming the incorrigible ball of fluff. He sunk down to his knees, his voice soft, his hand opened in a friendly manner.

"Come now, that's a good whelp. Don't cause a stir. I'm not here to hurt you, or anyone else for that matter."

When he saw the flash of tiny white teeth, he realized he was going to have to be a bit more forceful with his charms, and reached out for the canine, intent on muffling his snout.

But the whelp scurried off in a panic before Anthony had a chance to tackle it, and he cursed under his breath as he watched the little mongrel dance about and bark hysterically at a young girl, who must have been his mistress.

The girl put her finger to her lips, ordering the mutt to be quiet, and then ignored the rest of his antics. Once the whelp realized he would get no more attention, he stoutly pranced back over to the bright red wagon and a thoroughly exasperated Anthony.

"Damnation, what do you want?" Anthony whispered sternly. "I have no bones for you. There is all the food." And he pointed in the direction of the roasting pits for good measure.

But the whelp wasn't interested in the roasting pits— or perhaps he was just interested in seeing *Anthony* roasting over the pits.

The viscount readied his hands, prepared to make another attempt at muffling the animated mutt, when he heard a voice calling—a male's voice, and an older male by the sound of it. He was speaking in some foreign tongue, but his tone was openly scolding.

Anthony peeked past the wagon to see a big, burly gypsy approaching. "Bloody hell. Now look what you've done." He pinned his flashing eyes on the triumphant whelp before he desperately searched the terrain for somewhere to hide. But the valley was deserted of trees or shrubs, at least any that were close enough for him to duck behind. So Anthony was left with only one option. And he dearly hoped no gypsy had been left uninvited to the wedding.

Without giving it another thought, he sprung open the back door of the wagon and jumped inside the darkness. He crashed into something, God only knew what it was, and then steadied his vigorous breathing, listening for any signs of movement.

The whelp continued his tirade, now barking at the closed wagon door, and Anthony irately wondered if the curse Sabrina had once put on him would work on a dog.

There were a few loud commands, again in a foreign tongue, and Anthony only hoped the gypsy didn't think to look inside the wagon. If he did, Anthony would be left with no other recourse but to send a fist hurling into the man's face, and then to drag both him and the little dog into the wagon. Anthony simply couldn't allow anyone but Sabrina to see him. He could not devastate her life further by revealing to her caravan that he knew her. As mistrustful as her people were of *gajos,* they would invariably shun her for her association with him. And he couldn't let that happen to her.

Anthony held his breath when he no longer heard the whelp's cries. He waited to see if the door to the wagon would open. It was silent for a time, though he still heard some movement from the other side of the door. And then, moonlight peeked into the wagon.

He stifled a curse. He'd really hoped to avoid hurting one of Sabrina's kinsmen, but he was left with no other choice.

The door drew back.

Anthony curled his fingers into a fist.

But the woman's cry of alarm startled him, and then the door slammed shut in his face.

His heart was pounding. He listened to the swift and lively chatter at the other end of the wooden barrier, but he was unable to understand a word. It wasn't long before the male voice withdrew and all was quiet again.

He curled his hand into a fist once more, not knowing what to expect, and then the wagon was flooded with pale moonlight, and Sabrina was standing before him, fury flashing in those spirited blue eyes of hers.

The relief that came over him was instant and all-consuming. He grabbed her and pulled her inside the wagon, and though she gasped in surprise at his sudden movements, she didn't protest.

It wasn't until the door was closed, and they were both huddled inside the pitch darkness, that she released her fury. "What the hell are you doing inside my wagon?"

The space inside was so cramped, she was virtually in his lap when she'd made the demand, though he hadn't heard her, so overcome by the feelings of bliss and passion that welled up inside him. He wrapped his arms around her and drew her near. It was instinct, the need to hold her close to him. And before he realized what he was doing, he took her lips in his with a savage possession he didn't know he was capable of.

She stiffened, then squirmed, then her arms went tight around his neck in a desperate hold, and Anthony thought he was going to die before he could have his fill of her. He had never missed nor wanted a woman as badly as Sabrina, and the desire to be with her overtook all his senses. He was consumed with the sweet taste of her, invigorated by her energy. The harder she clung to him, the hotter his blood became and the more fierce his kiss grew. He couldn't get enough of her. It was as if he'd been starved, and it was only when a bountiful feast was presented before him that he realized just how hungry he had truly been.

His hands locked in her hair, his tongue thrusting with desperate strokes into the hot, moist cavern of her mouth. God, she felt so good. She tasted of wine and he was utterly intoxicated.

Sabrina suddenly grabbed a fistful of his hair and jerked him back. She held his head at bay.

"Why are you here?" she demanded breathlessly.

In the darkness, he could see nothing of her. And yet

it was such an intimate moment. He could hear her deep breathing; feel her heart thundering under her breast.

"I had to see you again." His own voice was low and gruff. "I had to warn you. I didn't mean to ruin your wedding." And then he thought to ask and clarify, "Are you married?"

He heard her take in a breath, about to answer, but the sudden pain in his heart prompted him to silence her with another hard kiss. "No, don't answer that. It doesn't matter. I've come to warn you that you're still in danger."

She was holding his head back again, her warm, sultry breaths bathing his face. "Danger? From what?"

"From whom," he corrected. "There is a man in London, Luther Gillingham. He runs a gambling hall and employs a number of high-end doxies to work in his club. Sabrina, one of those women wears the very same locket as you."

He waited to hear her reaction. He was not prepared for her scalding tone. "And just what were you doing with the doxy?"

"Never mind that," he almost growled, but then the agreeable thought hit him, and his tone dramatically altered. "Are you jealous?"

"Of course not," she insisted indignantly, if in a somewhat shaky tone. "But don't tell me you've gone about London, spending your time with doxies, all with the purpose of helping me."

He grinned. She *was* jealous. And it delighted him to the very core of his being. He was fortunate the wagon was so dark inside that she couldn't see his victorious smile, or she might have clobbered him with something just then.

"Sabrina, it doesn't matter how I came across the knowledge. What matters is that you're still in danger. The men chasing after you want the locket."

And to emphasize his point, he reached between them to grasp the locket around her neck, only his hand grazed the full swell of her breast in the process, and she shivered at his touch, leaving his own body in painful pangs of want.

"This is what Gillingham wants," he whispered and tugged on the locket. "And he is a dangerous man. He will do anything to get this locket. You have to stop wearing it. You have to go away for a time, so Gillingham will lose all trace of you."

"I will," she promised, and Anthony felt his body stiffen at the vulnerable sound of her voice. Cursed damnation, *he* wanted to be the one to protect her. And it was going to take great fortitude indeed for him to let her go a second time.

But he wouldn't release her just yet. "Where did you get the locket?"

"I found it, five years ago, by the seashore. I've worn it ever since. I thought it would bring me good fortune."

Her voice cracked. His grip tightened around her in soothing comfort. "It will be all right." He kissed her lips tenderly. "No one will hurt you, I—"

He was about to promise he would always take care of her, but he realized that was not his place—it was her husband's.

"Sabrina, you have to get away from here as soon as you can. Gillingham's men are still searching for you, I'm sure of it."

The grip on his hair loosened. "You should go before anyone sees you."

He would go—soon. His mouth touched hers in a passionate kiss. "Have you forgiven me?" he breathed against her lips, desperate to know whether his previous words of contrition had had any effect on her at all.

But she didn't get the chance to answer him. He should have gone when she had asked him to. But now it was too late.

The door to the wagon swung wide open.

Chapter 19

Sabrina stifled a horrified scream and swung her head over her shoulder. "Father!" she gasped in her native Romany, the tears already swimming in her eyes.

The man was livid. His fingers shook at a frightening pace. His whole body quaked with unmistakable rage and horror and disgrace.

She scrambled out of Anthony's lap, the tears now streaking her hot cheeks. "Father, please, let me—"

She got no further. The man grabbed her roughly by the arm and jerked her clear out of the wagon. She ended up sprawled on the ground.

Anthony jumped out after her, yelling, "Get away from her!"

"Anthony, please!" she cried. "He's my father. Don't hurt him."

That gave the viscount pause, but it only enraged her father more to hear her use the *gajo's* given name, betraying further their already obvious level of intimacy.

Everything happened so quickly then. The commotion by her wagon attracted more curious gypsies to investigate, and soon a small crowd had gathered around her.

"This is all my fault," said Anthony. "Please, let me explain."

Vardar ordered for Anthony to be seized, and two men stepped forward to grab him by the arms. Anthony didn't protest, for her sake. Her pleading eyes were begging with him not to hurt her kinsmen.

Nobody knew who Anthony was yet. His attire consisted of simple riding gear. Her father would never accost a peer of the realm, fearing any legal retribution, but in his current state of wrath, he wouldn't hesitate to offend a mere country gent.

Sabrina intended to reveal Anthony's true identity, to save the viscount from any real harm, but confessions on her part would have to hold off for a while.

She was suddenly being dragged by her father to the very center of the festivities, and was tossed back onto her knees before the great bonfire.

The music stopped. The alarmed gypsies staggered back in fear and dismay. Anthony was dragged out into the light alongside her, but he was kept at a slight distance, so all eyes were on Sabrina and her father for the moment.

Istvan made his way through the crowd, demanding to know what had happened.

"She is a disgrace," came the ragged, tortured words from her father. And each word pierced her heart like a slashing sword. "She tells me she is tired and wishes to rest, and I find her in the arms of an outsider."

The last word was uttered with such vehemence, it was hissed. And Sabrina felt it sear her ears. Tears drenched her soul. Her whole life was falling to pieces, fading into oblivion, and she could do nothing to stop the spiraled descent. There was nothing she could grab hold of to save herself.

Istvan looked between her and Anthony, disbelief in his eyes. "Is this true?"

Sobs wracked her lungs, strangling her words. She could scarcely breathe, her fear and humiliation were so great.

"How could you do this?" Istvan whispered, heart-broken, shame burning in his eyes that she had been found in the arms of another man.

"Nothing happened," she vowed between sobs, try-ing to explain she had not lost herself completely to an-other man, but her words were of no help to her now.

"Nothing happened!" roared her father, and dropped to his knees, grabbing a fistful of her hair. She could see the alabaster white of his eyes fill with tiny red veins. Tears pooled to the corners of his eyes, his voice crack-ling with suppressed agony. "I find you, in the darkness of my wagon, in the embrace of another man, and you tell me nothing happened? You disgrace me, child." His teeth were clenched, his tears now flowing freely. "You are not my daughter anymore."

It was like ice, gradually splintering, a crack here, a fissure there, and then the whole sheet broke apart, dev-astated beyond recognition. She felt cold, shattering pain. "Father, please, I made a mistake. Forgive me."

He gnashed his teeth to keep his composure from crumbling. "How can I forgive you? You have dishon-ored me." And then quietly, so no one else could hear, "How could you do this to me, Sabrina?"

She could feel a wrenching ache in her chest. "I'm so sorry, Father," she whispered, trembling all over.

The pain that flashed through his dark blue eyes was replaced with rage. Black, simmering rage.

Vardar rose to his feet and looked at Anthony with unveiled, consuming hate before he returned his gaze to his daughter. "You are banished from this tribe."

A great murmur arose. Weeping was heard all around her. Sabrina couldn't believe it. She shook her head fervently in denial. "No, you cannot mean that. I love you, Father. I don't want to leave."

His composure cracked ever so slightly at her words, but hardened again in the next instance. "You know the laws of our people. You have shamed me. You cannot make amends."

"But where will I go?"

He took a brisk step toward her and wove his fingers through her hair, blasting: "You have chosen the bed of an outsider and now you will sleep in it!"

"But I haven't chosen him!" she cried.

"Do not lie to me!"

"Please, listen. He helped me when I was in trouble—"

"And you have chosen to repay him with your body."

"No!"

He let go of her hair. "Get out of my sight."

"Father—"

"I am not your father!" Again he snatched her by the arm and dragged her back to their wagon. He started to stuff her clothes into a bag, mindlessly grabbing whatever was in his reach. "Now leave," he ordered and threw the bag at her.

"Please, do not send me away," she begged, panicking, the tears blearing her vision.

"Get out of my sight," he whispered harshly and stalked away from her.

Sabrina flew after her father in a desperate attempt to change his mind, but he shrugged off her grip, and gave her a sound smack across the cheek.

Instant regret filled his eyes, then pain, then fury. "I said leave!" he bellowed.

Anthony struggled against his captors, enraged by the brutal sight, and received a solid punch in the gut for his trouble.

"Let him go," bade Vardar, and Anthony was instantly released.

The strike had dazzled Sabrina's senses. She touched her wet, stinging face in shock. Her father had never hit her before. She couldn't believe what was happening. Her distressed eyes roamed over the hushed crowd, and she saw the astonished, weeping face of Gulseren, of a devastated Istvan, of her heartbroken father, and of all the horrified gypsies gaping at her.

She turned on her heels and fled, ran through the darkness, blinded by her tears. She staggered up the hillside, stumbled, then pushed on. She floundered again, but forced herself to continue. Coming down the hill, she dropped to her knees a third time, and remained where she was. She felt all the strength drain from her limbs.

The racket in her head was unbearable. Weeping voices meshed with sharp, jarring sounds of reproof. Sadness poured through her veins like cold, numbing water. She had lost everything. Her family, her home, her life in an instant. It was all gone—forever.

What an impenetrable word. Forever. She couldn't

grasp the meaning. It sounded like a very long time, but she couldn't really go on for the rest of her days without ever hearing the voice of her father. She couldn't really go about the world alone. One day she would be forgiven. One day the anger would pass. It had to. Her father loved her. She knew it. He was angry now, but he wouldn't be always. She would come home again when a little time had passed, and ask for forgiveness. Her father wouldn't be able to stay furious with her forever. He simply couldn't. She would die alone in the harsh world. He wouldn't let her die. Would he?

She was shaking so hard her teeth were striking in swift, loud successions. She felt cold. Lost. The grief was so great, she didn't think she could stomach it.

What was she going to do? Where was she going to go? No other gypsy caravan in England would take her now. Word would spread of what she had done, of the shame she had brought upon her father, herself, her people. She would have to leave England and join with another caravan on the mainland. She would have to go to the ends of the earth to find a place where she would be welcomed. She just couldn't be alone. The world was cold and cruel. She was hated by *gajos* just for being a gypsy. She would never be safe anywhere but with another caravan. Only fellow gypsies would protect her. Only her own kind would love her.

The arms that wrapped around her shoulders were strong and gentle, and such an aching contrast to the horror of what she had just been through, that her silent cries soon turned to loud, soul-wrenching wails.

She didn't notice the tender embrace that scooped her up and carried her away. She didn't notice the movement beneath her, as she found herself on a horse, trotting steadily through the dark, deserted valley. She didn't notice the arms that kept a firm hold of her the entire time she wept, never letting go for even a moment.

It was only after the tears had stopped flowing, it was only after the sorrow had washed away and an empty void taken its place, that she thought to ask, "Where are we going?"

"To London," said the soothing voice by her ear.

She didn't say anything more. She didn't care where she went. It didn't matter. Nothing mattered anymore.

Two nights later, Sabrina found herself slumped against the squabs of an enclosed carriage, traveling through the gloomy streets of London.

The journey to the city had been a quiet one. Her spirits dark, her thoughts bleak, she had very little to say to Anthony. He made no effort to coax her from her doleful mood. Instead, he remained by her side. A silent shadow watching over her. It was comforting, without being distracting.

But now in London, she had a flurry of new troubles to face. It was such a big, imposing city, full of twisting alleyways—and *gajos*. Lots of *gajos* who hated gypsies. How was she ever going to find her way in such a threatening place?

The dark silhouette of brooding buildings reached far into the misty skyline. Chimneys galore puffed their sooty ash and smoke, blanketing the city in a hazy fog. It was like a disturbing dream. And she was trapped in it. Never again would she awaken and find herself in the safe confines of her father's wagon.

Her heart tightened at the mere thought of her father. Grief poured into her empty heart, and poured and poured, and would have poured on forever, it seemed, had she not put a cap on her sorrow and forced the tears into submission. Is this what her life was going to be like from now on? A drab existence of endless pain and regret and sorrow?

She looked over at Anthony, a discreet peek before she turned away again. He had everything he could ever want in this world. Did he even realize or care that she had lost so much?

It would be so easy to lash out at him; so simple to blame him and rail at him and make him feel every murky emotion crushing her own spirit. But she couldn't do that. It was troubling to admit, but Anthony was now the closest thing she had to a friend in this world, and she was afraid of losing him too. Besides, he hadn't come to her camp to destroy her life, but to save it from Gillingham. It would be unfair of her to scream at him.

Sabrina sighed, shifting her attention to the window, staring absently at the clustered homes, all ghostly quiet for the night. Suddenly, her thoughtful reflection in the glass morphed into a grimace.

The carriage whizzed by a ragged figure, but not so quickly that she couldn't recognize an old gypsy peddler woman, all her charms and talismans dangling from her hip, white wisps of her hair escaping from under her bright red kerchief.

She was a wretched vision, hobbling the dark and empty streets, and Sabrina's heart squeezed at the fleeting sight of her, as she saw a glimpse of her own lonely future.

It was Anthony who noticed her stray tear and asked gruffly, "What's wrong?"

She tore her eyes away from the glass, fearful of what else she might see. "I'll be alone for the rest of my life," she said quietly.

His voice softened. "Can you really never go home?"

She shook her head. "My father banished me."

"Do you have family elsewhere?"

"Yes, but I can't stay with them. Word of what I did will spread to other caravans, and I won't be welcomed anywhere in England soon."

"I'll take care of you."

Her eyes filled with a mixture of surprise and suspicion. "You?"

"I'll make sure you're always safe. I won't abandon you to the streets."

Dabbing at her moist eyes with her fingertips, she said, with a trace of bitterness, "You can't give me another home and family."

He was quiet for a moment, his features staid and masked in shadows. And then his voice filled the dark space of the carriage, so deep and determined. "I'm sorry, Sabrina. I didn't mean to take you away from your father or your husband or anyone else you love."

She sniffed. "I have no husband."

"What?"

"I'm not married."

He sounded bewildered. "But the celebration I witnessed?"

"I'm not married anymore," she amended. "I was banished, remember?"

"And just like that your marriage is dissolved, without even a ceremony of divorce?"

"The tribal elders will grant my cousin the right to remarry. He deserves to be happy and have a family."

After a long pause, he said gently, "You deserve to be happy, too, Sabrina. You know that, don't you? This was all a mistake, an accident. You didn't do anything wrong."

If only she could believe in that conviction with all her heart. Perhaps, then, her misery wouldn't be so unbearable.

But she couldn't believe in such a fanciful thing, not for too long anyway. The guilt always came back to rest on her conscience, despite her best attempts to shoo it away.

She had wanted Anthony, longed for him secretly in her heart. *She* had betrayed her father, and her betrothed, with that will-o'-the-wisp longing. It wasn't easy to dismiss the blame from herself. Not easy at all.

The carriage came to a teetered halt. It was late. There was no real risk of being seen—not by anyone important—so neither Sabrina nor Anthony took any precautions when stepping down from the carriage. The driver was ordered around the back, and then Sabrina was whisked up the stairs and ushered into the home without a word.

But both the viscount and the gypsy were oblivious to the figure skulking in the shadows just across the street, watching the late arrival of the couple with avid interest.

Chapter 20

❝**A**re you hungry?❞

Sabrina shook her head and wrapped her arms around her shoulders. Her gaze wandered until settling on a window at the far end of the room.

"Tired?" Anthony wondered next.

She shook her head again. She didn't feel much of anything, except for a dull ache in her chest.

Anthony set the oil lamp on a nearby table and proceeded to light a few additional candles around the room, bringing more and more of her lavish surroundings into better view. The more wicks he lit, the more the shine of brass and the glitter of white marble pierced her vision.

Sabrina was right back where the whole ordeal with Anthony had begun—in his bedchamber.

She looked to the large bed, blanketed in blue velvet splendor.

She wasn't supposed to be here.

Not again.

Anthony approached, his glossy green eyes reflecting the dots of candle flames throughout the room.

He placed his hands on her upper arms and gave a light squeeze. "It will be all right."

The low, decisive tone of his voice was strangely comforting, despite the vagueness of his words. And the feel of his hands on her, so warm and soothing, made her skin prickle and dance. She realized then her spirit was not as dead as she had previously believed.

"If you're not very tired, we should talk about this." He touched the locket at her neck, his fingers grazing her skin ever so softly.

Her own fingers, trembling slightly in the wake of his tender touch, went around the locket, clasping the cursed piece of gold that had ruined her life.

"Here." She whisked the locket up over her head and dragged it through her long hair. "Have it." She dropped the gold into his open palm.

He stared at her for a moment, his green eyes aglow with sympathy, before he brought the locket to his face for a closer inspection, murmuring, "To think, such a little thing could cause so much trouble." He thoughtfully twirled the gold between his fingers. Then his eyes shifted back to her. "Unlikely as it seems, Gillingham must have lost this locket years ago, then one of his cohorts simply found it around your neck."

Bad luck! Her life was ruined because of a mere chance encounter. It was enough to make her want to weep again. She didn't, though. She firmly turned her attention to the locket, wanting to know everything about it. In particular, why it had brought about her demise.

"It's welded shut," he observed curiously.

She nodded. "I found it that way. I didn't want to tarnish the gold by breaking it open. I didn't think there was anything important inside anyway."

"Then perhaps it's time we took a look inside. Do you mind?"

Her words were curt, her voice bitter. "You can melt it for all I care."

Anthony offered her another compassionate glance before he headed over to his writing desk and shuffled through the drawers. He pulled out a brass letter opener, long and slender with a relatively sharp end. "This will have to do. I don't think there's a jeweler open at this late hour."

He propped the locket on its side and positioned the letter opener between the two clenched faces. Both hands bracing the opener, he pushed down hard.

The locket shot across the room and smacked into the opposite wall with a resounding thwack.

They both flinched at the loud blast in the stone-silent house, then exchanged bewildered glances.

"I think we'll need a hammer," he reasoned, and walked across the room to retrieve the locket.

And so the search began for a blunt object in the room. But with everything made from fragile porcelain, or polished wood, or refined brass, or gilded gold, there wasn't much in the way of a hammer to choose from.

Sabrina finally slipped off one of her boots. "Use the heel."

He cocked a blond brow at the unanticipated suggestion, then smiled. She suddenly felt as if *she* had been hammered, the breath knocked from her very lungs. She had forgotten how beautiful the man was when he smiled.

Fortunately, he took the dangling boot from her hand

just then and set to work, giving her a much-needed moment to compose herself.

Again he balanced the locket on its side, with the letter opener serving as a chisel, and tapped the heel against the head of the opener.

At the pathetic first strike, she folded her arms under her breasts. "You'll have to hit it harder than that."

He cast her a quick, indecisive glance. "I don't want to damage whatever's inside."

"We'll never *know* what's inside if you don't break it open."

He appeared to concede on that point. In the next instant, he gave the letter opener a forceful whack. The locket didn't open, but neither did it sail across the room this time. Another two poundings and Sabrina heard the faint clink of metal snapping.

She shuffled over to stand by Anthony's side, and looked down at the stained and folded piece of parchment that had spilled out of the locket.

Disappointment swamped her. She wasn't sure why. What else did she expect to find in such a tiny compartment?

But still, when nothing grand and valuable tumbled out, she felt somewhat desperate at the thought that her life had been ravaged over a mere scrap of paper.

"This better be a treasure map." It was a terse retort, to offset the sorrow she felt rising and clawing in her throat.

Anthony carefully peeled back the stiff edges of the paper. No treasure map. Just a few garbled characters she had no hope of understanding.

She looked to him in anticipation.

"Well?" she prodded when he still said nothing. "What is it?"

His brows pinned together. "I'm not quite sure."

"You can read," she said curtly. "What does it say?"

"It's an . . . address."

"A what?!"

"It's just an address."

She gawked at him in disbelief. But she could tell by the expression in his eyes that he was just as baffled by the insignificant discovery as she was.

She whirled around to stalk about the room in quick, agitated strides. Her thoughts were spinning. Her heart was thumping at a mad rate. Grief was welling up in her breast, making it hard for her to breathe.

Everything in her life was gone. Her home, her family, her friends. And for what? A trivial missive?

A set of thick arms folded around her shoulders, squeezing the grief from her bones, bringing her nervous pacing to an end.

She needed something to grab on to, and Anthony's deep and steady voice was the only semblance of sanity there was in the room.

"It will be all right," he murmured by her ear.

He had already said that once before. Whether he was making her a promise or just offering consolation, she didn't know. A part of her didn't care. Words held little meaning to her at that moment. All she knew for sure was that she didn't feel quite so alone and hopeless when in Anthony's arms.

Anthony could hear the bed sheets rustling. He'd been listening to that same faint swooshing sound for the last hour or so. It was obvious neither he nor his gypsy could sleep. And whereas Sabrina tossed restlessly about in bed, he lay still on the sofa, one hand tucked behind his head, the other slung over his naked midriff. He had a foot planted on the cold floor, and another propped up on a small pillow, his bare toes peeking out from the end of his blanket.

It was dark inside the room. Only a pale, misty glow from the kerosene street lamps down below filtered in through the window sheers, casting the furnishings in a ghostly silhouette.

He stared out that dimly glowing window, trying to come up with a reasonable account of why a nefarious scoundrel like Luther Gillingham would bother to undertake the enormous effort of obtaining a tiny piece of gold and a scrap of paper. Even with the mysterious address scribbled on that scrap of paper, it didn't seem like a very bountiful prize.

But Anthony knew that conclusion was illusive. As poor a treasure as that locket seemed, Gillingham was not the kind of man to waste his time, energy, and money on a venture that was anything less than extraordinarily profitable. And with that indisputable premise in mind, Anthony had the irksome task of trying to decipher just what was written on that scrap of paper. What was *really* written on it, that is.

The address was unfamiliar to him. It could be a location anywhere in the world. And staring at the paper or reciting the village name over and over again in his head would get him nowhere. To learn what secrets Gillingham wanted so desperately to get ahold of, he would have to come to know Gillingham better. And that meant he would have to return to the Lion's Gate.

The sound of quiet weeping interrupted Anthony's thoughts.

He sat up slowly, peering into the misty darkness. He hated to hear her distress. The muffled cries were piercing to his ears and wrenching to his gut.

Without another thought, he tossed his blanket aside and treaded softly toward the bed, crouching beside it.

Sabrina had her back to him. She was trying to muffle her tears by burying her face in his pillow, but he could see her quivering shoulders, and the sight ignited a deep desire within him to wipe away all her grief.

He reached out and grazed her hair, whispering, "Dry your eyes."

She stiffened at his touch. "I can't. The tears won't stop."

He didn't pull his hand away from her cool and silky locks. If his touch was disturbing her, she would have smacked his hand away. And so, he continued to stroke her hair idly. It wasn't long before he noted the tension fade from her muscles.

"I miss my family." She sniffed, and slowly turned around to face him.

He settled both knees on the floor and propped his elbows on the mattress. His fingers lazily flicked at the ebony fleece of her hair, strewn across the pillow in a wild, silky wave.

He gazed into her shadowed eyes, so doleful, and thought about his own family and how fortunate he was. Whatever scandal he had instigated in the past, he had never been shunned by his family for it. There was great comfort in that security. A security Sabrina now lacked in her own life.

"I can't change the past," he said in a somber voice, "but I can try to make your future a better one."

It was dark inside the room, but not so dark that he couldn't see her brow furrow. "How?"

"I'll buy you a house."

It was his protective instinct that had prompted him to admit that. He hadn't really thought too much about what he was going to do with her, now that she had nowhere else to go. His first priority was to her welfare, and with Gillingham still searching for her, her welfare was not yet secure.

But his gypsy had no real fear of Gillingham, he realized. She had never met the man. He was just a name to her. But the predicament of finding herself homeless and alone was very real to her, and he should have addressed that issue sooner.

But the ad hoc solution he'd just come up with seemed to be as reasonable as any. With all the money he possessed, why shouldn't he give her a new home? She would be safe and he could always look after her.

"You'll buy me a house?" she said in confusion.

"A little cottage," he clarified, the idea taking firmer root. "Anywhere in England. It'll be yours. Always. No one will ever make you leave it. And you'll be safe. Far away from Gillingham and his prying eyes."

She propped herself up on one elbow, so their eyes were level. "A cottage without a family isn't a home."

He heard the plaintive note in her voice. It made his next suggestion all the more vehement. "I'll visit you often. You won't have to be alone."

"Often? Will your future wife and children let you visit with a gypsy?"

"I don't intend to marry anytime soon," he was swift to refute.

"But when you do, I'll be alone. You're not going to spend your time with me when you have a family to look after."

He could hear her quickness of breath as she tried to fight back her despair, and he took her face, already wet with tears, between his hands. "Sabrina, I won't abandon you."

"Yes, you will." Her voice was trembling. "I'll lose you one day, just like I lost everyone else in my life."

"No, you won't!" His lips took hers in a passionate vow of assurance. He could taste the salty tears still lingering on those supple lips, and he drank in her sorrow, determined to quell all remnants of her grief. Grief he had helped to cause. And he knew of no other way to deal with her briny tears except to kiss them away.

But the longer his lips moved over hers, the harder her breathing grew and the more her tears fell, dripping onto the backs of his hands and drizzling down his wrists.

He pulled away from her. "I'm sorry," he whispered hoarsely, still holding her moist cheeks between his palms. "I shouldn't have done that. I didn't mean to hurt you even more."

"D-don't."

"I won't touch you again," he promised, furious with himself for letting his passion overtake his sense of reason yet again.

He let go of her tear-stained face and rocked back on

his heels, prepared to move away from the bedside, when her hand reached out and circled his wrist.

"No," she said in a small, hesitant voice. "Don't stop. I don't want to be alone tonight."

He looked down at the feminine fingers gently pressing his skin, then up to the glossy wet eyes staring at him through the hazy darkness.

He couldn't have heard her correctly, he thought. She couldn't have said to him what he'd been dreaming about since the day he'd met her. She couldn't *want* him to make love to her after everything they'd been through. Could she?

Not about to misinterpret her actions—again—and end up doing or saying something he'd later regret, Anthony took her hand in his and asked carefully, "Sabrina, do you want me to—"

He never finished what he was going to say. She leaned into him and kissed him softly—giving him all the answer he needed.

It was instant, the heat that spilled through his veins. Drinking in her salty tears, his lips moved over hers with all the passion that was ransacking his soul.

He sensed what she wanted from him. Solace. A way to forget about every dreadful thing that had happened to her. And giving in to their frustrated passions was certainly one way to forget. And he would make sure she did forget—for a time, at least. He was going to take away her pain and make her feel every exhilarating emotion he was experiencing.

Anthony peeled back the blanket and joined Sabrina on the bed. As much as he wanted her, as much as his muscles ached for her, he restrained what he was truly feeling. He wouldn't take her in a bout of hard lust. He wouldn't let the moment whisk by them in an unfulfilled burst of instinct. Sabrina wasn't one of his licentious mistresses. She was an innocent. No other man had ever touched her. And he was going to take his time caressing her, lulling her senses, giving her that solace he knew she wanted.

But first he had to ease her jitters. She quivered beneath him, and he wanted her to quiver with desire—and only desire—the very same desire that was tearing him apart inside.

"Don't be frightened, Sabrina."

"I'm not," was her stout reply, but when his fingers closed around her breast, she inhaled sharply, amending her earlier claim in a soft and shaky voice, "Perhaps I'm a little frightened."

But he didn't want her to be scared, even a little. He wanted her to trust him, to let go of her fears and doubts, to let him love her as she deserved to be loved—reverently.

"I won't let you be afraid," he whispered, lips moving over hers in slow and deft exploration.

To soothe her anxiety, he would tantalize a most sensitive part of her. A part he himself adored. A part that was cushioned beneath him, causing him to give a heavenly sigh.

Anthony could just imagine her sensitive breasts chafe from rubbing up against the coarse confines of her wool chemise, and with a sudden urge to free those beautiful mounds, he slipped a hand between their meshed bodies and slowly unfastened the laces of her undergarment.

Her breathing deepened. His fingers worked neatly

to loosen the lace bindings of her chemise, and expose more fully the sweet globes of flesh he so longed to savor.

God, how he loved her breasts. They were full and proud, and he wanted to feel them against his hand, to taste them deep in his mouth.

The laces came free, the chemise parted enough to expose one of the generous mounds to the chilly night air.

His hand went to the breast.

She gasped against his lips.

He felt her nipple shrink and tighten in the brisk night air, and he rubbed the flesh back and forth, massaging her, warming her skin, evoking a low, whimpering moan from the depth of her throat.

"Oh, Sabrina, what you do to me . . . I am the one who should be frightened."

"But I haven't done anything."

It was a husky retort. An innocent retort. The girl really believed she'd done nothing to arouse him. But her very touch, the very warmth of her skin, the scent of her hair, the feel of her lush lips on his own, was more than he could bear. The temptation she provoked tore at his resolve. And he would need all his strength to maintain control of his lust.

The firm and bountiful breasts wiggling beneath his chest were like irons branding his skin. He had to taste them, and he kissed a path of sleek wetness down her neck to the protruding tip of one plump breast.

Anthony licked the taut nipple before he took the generous mound into his mouth and suckled.

Fingers digging deep into his hair, Sabrina whimpered and arched her body forward, sending her breast even deeper into his mouth.

He groaned at the exquisite feel of her, and locked his arm under the small of her back to hold her in place, his other hand cupping her breast, keeping it to his mouth as he sucked and kissed the rosy tip, feeling as though he would never have enough of her.

He was already hard and ready for her, but she was only at the start of what promised to be a very divine experience, and he wasn't going to rush her. He would bring his gypsy to the very summit of her desire before he'd join her on that peak.

But the feel of her satiny breast in his mouth had a riotous effect on him, making it a grueling challenge to hold in his passion. His lips took in more of the thrusting peak, teasing the coral tip with his swirling tongue, tearing a deep-rooted moan from her throat.

Those wanton sounds of need had his cock throbbing for her comfort. She was slowly unleashing her every pent-up emotion, and he was burning up inside as a result. She'd have him scorched to a heap of cinder in no time at all, he was sure of it.

Sabrina was moving beneath him, twisting, arching, silently demanding that he give her more. And he intended to. With a swift movement, he whisked both straps of her chemise off her shoulders and pulled the garment down to her waist, so their bodies touched, flesh to flesh.

She dragged him back down and his lips instantly sought out her other breast, clamping over her nipple in avid hunger, whirling his tongue over the coral tip in slow, sensual caresses.

Her passionate whimpers grew louder and longer. Her hands held his head tight, so tight, he sensed his hair curling around her fingers in taut tension.

He let her breast slip free between his teeth. She wasn't appreciative of that, if the protesting moan she gave was any indication. And he smiled to know her desire was as great as his.

"I want you so much," he said in a ragged whisper, giving her a long and intense kiss. "I've wanted you since the day we met."

"And I want you," she breathed weakly, her breasts rising high to meet his chest with each labored breath she inhaled.

That brief, honest admission brought him a burst of satisfaction. "I'm going to love you tonight." He kissed her tenderly. "Like I've dreamed of doing for so long."

His mouth went back over hers, his tongue thrusting and flicking over her own in deft and eager strokes. He gingerly slipped his hand down her silken belly and rounded her hip, only his fingertips grazing the softness of her warm skin.

Gradually, he moved downward, reaching for the hem of her chemise, tangled around her knees. He grabbed a fistful of the fabric and began the steady ascent, gliding the thick material up along her thighs, pushing it higher and higher, exposing more and more of her body to him, until the dark patch of curls at her apex was bare to his touch.

She was trembling. He was going to make sure she quivered with desire and not fear. He shoved her chemise up to her hips and then braced his hand between her legs.

"Let me show you true pleasure, Sabrina."

Sabrina shivered at his whispered words, at the husky timbre of his voice wound tight with desire.

It felt so good to be touched by Anthony again. Too good, perhaps. It was pure chaos in her heart to feel the power of his strength surging through his brawny arms, to inhale the familiar musk of his hair, stirring her senses into a whirling fit.

But she was glad for the distraction from all her woe. She was glad to give in to the desire that had haunted her for so long without worry of the consequences anymore.

There was a burning, twisting need inside her now, stoked by the slow, sensual movements of Anthony's fingers between her legs. It was a feathery touch, but a determined one, stroking over and over again, teasing her sensitive skin, making her pulse sprint and her body throb and her breathing quicken.

She abandoned herself to the pleasure of the experience, wishing it could last a lifetime and beyond. But her thoughts were soon shot into blissful disarray as one powerful finger slipped inside her.

She cried out, her whole body shuddering. Her hips arched forward to meet his touch in an instinctual cry for more. And he gave it to her. A second finger joined the first, and plunged deep inside her sleek passage, slow at first, then he hastened the pace, and the faster he thrust, the more the heat swelled in her loins, and the more she cried out in want.

Her hips were moving up to meet each thrust of his fingers. He was making her feel so much and with such intensity, she thought she would lose her senses.

"Anthony," she gasped.

His lips crushed hers, hot and possessive in their movements. It thrilled her to be caressed in such a way by him. It made her tremble to know that he wanted her, that he had longed for her since the day they'd first met. Her heart beat faster at the thought. Her arms folded tighter around his shoulders to keep him even closer to her.

She could feel his heart stomping against her breast. Rhythmic drumbeats sounded in her own ears. With his fingers still diving into her, she felt a sense of urgency building. A tight, thrumming ache swelled in her loins, and a desperate need for release consumed her.

But Anthony wasn't prepared to give her any relief yet. His fingers plunged into her, slow and steady, and then swift and determined. He continued to alter his tempo.

She moaned against his lips in helpless want. His tongue clashed with hers in a rivaled battle of passions.

What the man could do to her with his body was frightening. But it was also heavenly. And soon he proved just how heavenly it could get. Fingers still driving into her, he let go of her lips, and dropped his head to her breast, where he embraced her nipple, his tongue licking the jutting bud.

She gasped at the feel of his hot lips suckling at her breast. Her lashes fluttered, her head arched back against the pillow, her nails dug harder into his back.

She groaned. It was a loud, demanding sound for appeasement. But his movements only hastened the more vocal she became. His fingers moved swifter, his mouth sucked harder, and she was ready to weep at the desire tearing her up inside.

"Anthony, please," she begged breathlessly. She didn't even know what she was asking for, but he, blessedly, realized she needed to be doused, and he was finally ready to comply.

His fingers slipped out of her. She whimpered instantly at the feel of him leaving her when she wasn't ready for it yet. But he soothed her frustrations with a sound kiss and a reassuring, "It's not over yet. I'll give you what you want."

Anthony shifted his weight. He settled between her throbbing thighs, and what a glorious feeling *that* was, to have his weight anchored so snuggly against her pulsing core.

He unfastened his trousers and lowered them slightly. It was too dark inside the room for her to see anything clearly, but she could definitely *feel* his turgid flesh pressing against her. And she was suddenly alarmed by its size.

Good heavens, was *that* supposed to fit inside her? She didn't think it would, not without causing her enormous pain.

A sudden apprehension stalked her. She scrunched her eyes in expectation of the discomfort soon to come.

But then, with a warmth that tore at her heart, she heard him whisper, his voice hoarse and strained, "I won't hurt you, Sabrina. I could never hurt you."

She believed him. In that moment, she completely trusted him. Her eyes opened and adjusted to the faintly lit room. She looked up to find a pair of dark, smoldering eyes gazing down at her. So tender, so passionate, so needful—of her.

The thunderous thumps of her heart steadied. Her body thrummed on a chord identical to his own. In tune, in hunger, he joined with her.

The pain was minimal compared to the intensity with

which she wanted him, and her first cry of shock was attentively stifled by his soothing lips. He didn't move once he was inside her, giving her tense muscles time to ease, and her body time to grow adjusted to his length, his thickness.

Being one with Anthony was unlike anything she had ever imagined. Soon the heat filled her and he began to stir. It was slow at first. He withdrew from inside her, not fully, but part way. Her legs locked behind him, holding him in place. She wasn't willing to let the moment end so quickly, not when she was just growing accustomed to it and feeling immense pleasure overtake her senses.

He chuckled softly by her ear. "Trust me," he said roughly.

She eased her grip, giving him the room he needed to pull partly out of her before he thrust back inside. He did it again. Withdrew halfway and then plunged deep inside her. Then he did it again. And again. Slow and steady at first, he pulled out and thrust back in.

She closed her eyes and moaned softly. Tingling anticipation tickled through her limbs. The tension in her body grew stronger and stronger. She clung to him harder and harder, digging her fingers into his hair. His slow thrusts deepened, quickened. Soon he was moving in and out of her in steady plunges. He was breathing hard against her neck. His back was slick with sweat.

Their bodies moved together in waves, his full girth filling her. The tight, pleasurable knot that had formed within her tightened even more. His rocking thighs rubbed hard against hers, the chafing movement leaving her throbbing and burning inside.

"Anthony," she gasped between panting breaths.

His movements quickened. Swift, piercing strokes that brought her unbearable pleasure. And then she felt it, her muscles contracting around him in quick succession. There was a pulsating wave of glorious gratification that coursed through her veins, and she cried out at the intensity of what she was feeling. Anthony let out a fierce groan of his own soon after, and thrust hard into her.

She was breathing loudly. They both were. Anthony was slumped against her, though he braced his weight on his elbows so as not to crush her, and buried his face in the crook of her neck, his body still joined with hers.

She loosened her tight hold on him, feeling dizzying blissful. In an idle gesture, she stroked his damp hair, smoothing back the tousled curls. She just wanted to be near him. To enjoy the feel of him without the urgency inside her commanding all her other senses. It was such a wonderful feeling to just hold him, to hear him breathing deeply by her ear, to sense his weight nestled on top of her. And she wistfully wished that she could feel this way for the very rest of her days.

Chapter 21

$\sim\!\!\!\infty\!\!\!\sim$

Raven-black locks rested over his midriff, blanketing him in a fleece of silken strands.

Anthony gazed down at the beautiful nymph in his arms. He was propped up against a pillow, his knees bent like two mountainous peaks, shielding a slumbering Sabrina between them. Her smooth cheek rested over his bare belly, and he could feel her soft, warm breath stir and tickle the fine hairs on his abdomen.

He had never seen her sleep so soundly. Nor had he ever been so at peace as when she was curled in his arms.

He twisted a lock of her hair around his finger, thinking about the little cottage he was going to buy for her, and how he would come to visit her and continue to share her bed. It was nice to imagine she would remain an intimate part of his life for years to come. He didn't like the thought of losing her. He was content to have her as his mistress.

Mistress. Would she consent to such an arrangement? He wasn't sure. He had poor judgment when it came to *this* particular female's thoughts. All he knew was that she felt an obligation toward her father to honor her arranged marriage. But according to Sabrina, she had neither a father nor a marriage anymore. Did she now consider her obligation void? Would she be willing to engage in an affair with him?

He'd have to broach the matter carefully with her. The timing had to be exact or he risked the proposition coming across as an insult. It might appear he was offering his help in exchange for her favors, and he didn't want her to think him a callous brute. He was her protector. And he would take care of her regardless of her response to his offer.

But it was a delightful thought to have her as his paramour. And he hoped that thought would one day come to fruition. He saw no reason why their liaison should come to an abrupt end, not when they both found such comfort and pleasure in one another's arms.

Sabrina stirred and murmured unintelligibly. He could feel her lashes whisking across his skin in rhythmic blinking.

Rousing her somnolent head, her midnight blue eyes lifted to meet his and he gave her a lazy smile. "Good morning."

She offered him a shy, half smile in return, and he chuckled softly at her newfound bashfulness. "You slept well. I didn't feel you stir in my arms all night."

A soft pink blush adorned her cheeks. She was delightfully whimsical in her temperament. So candid and passionate in one moment and so quiet and reserved in another.

She wiggled in his arms, trying to pull away from

him, but the movement of her grinding body sparked new life into his own drowsy limbs.

"Anthony!" she gasped, as she found herself tumbling across the bed, her hands pinned high above her head.

He positioned himself on top of her and grinned roguishly. "I like it when you cry out my name."

Hot pigment darkened her cheeks even more, and he couldn't resist kissing her when she was so charmingly chagrined. Ah, but what a sweet mistake that was, for one taste of her enticing lips and he had to taste even more of her—all of her. His mouth sought out an adorable earlobe.

"Anthony," she clipped out, an anxious tinge to her voice, "we have to get up."

"Not at all, my dear," he said in a husky drawl, nibbling her ear. "We can stay in bed all morning if we choose." He moved on to nip at her neck.

She flinched, and he soothed the innocent bite with a languorous caress of his tongue. She shuddered beneath him. He liked the feel of her excitement rippling against his every muscle. With her hands stretched taut above her head, her breasts were pressed hard into his chest, and he liked the feel of that even more. The only thing he didn't like were the fibers of her wool chemise rubbing up against his skin instead of her own silken flesh. But he took care of that minor irritant with a quick flick of his wrists.

Her hands released, he tugged at the straps of her garment and yanked them down to her waist.

"That's much better," he rasped with carnal hunger, staring down at the two beautiful mounds of her exposed breasts. God, they were even more stunning in the daylight when he could see every magnificent inch of them.

She gave a brief, startled cry of protest at being disrobed with such speed, but when his ravenous lips took a plump breast into his mouth, her protests turned to moans of pleasure.

He chuckled at the feel of her anxious fingers weaving through his hair, holding him tight to her breast. He loved it when she gave him an uninhibited response. Her honest and so powerful desire made his all the more intense.

He thoroughly tended to both her breasts, caressing them, kissing them, suckling them, bringing her to such a state of arousal, her grip tightened on his hair until his scalp pinched.

To relieve the building pressure in both his head and his groin, he slipped between her warm legs. He was already naked, his trousers discarded during the course of the night. He had only to adjust her chemise, so it was crumpled up around her hips, and then he dove into her in one swift and steady stroke.

She was hot and wet inside. It was pure ecstasy to join with her. His body tight and ready, he began to move in slow undulations.

Her face was a lovely mixture of need and pleasure, and he watched her expression intently, aroused even more by the patent feelings of lust he was able to incite in her.

Lush lips parted and panting, she let out a soft, aching moan, and he lost all intention of a deliberate coupling, his hips rocking with greater urgency against her own. He thrust into her over and over again, his muscles flexed and straining, as he held his own climax in check. When he heard her cry of release and sensed her body spasm around him, he let go of his own restraint, driving into her in swift successions, letting out a loud, guttural cry of pure physical fulfillment.

His breaths were quick and heavy, his heart a thundering drum beating. He took a moment to steady the thudding organ before he slowly pulled out of her comforting heat.

"We can't keep doing this," she said in a quiet voice, her own breathing swift and raspy.

"Ah, but we can, my dear." His lips went to her forehead and he could feel the hot flush of her skin. "We can do this for as long and as often as we like." When he sensed her brow furrow beneath his lips, he gave her another quick kiss on the mouth. "But now is not the time to talk about it." Now was definitely *not* the time to ask her to be his mistress. "We have another important matter to deal with."

With another kiss on her lips, he left the bed and went to gather his discarded trousers from the floor. Sabrina scrambled to cover herself, wiggling back into her chemise, and a light smile touched his lips at her sudden modesty after the intimacy they had just shared. His smiled only broadened when she finished fiddling with her chemise and happened to look up to find him still in his natural state.

Her eyes quickly averted to the bed, her cheeks a blooming pink blush.

He chuckled softly and said in jest, "*Now* you are ashamed to look at me?"

"I'm not ashamed. I'm just not used to seeing you, well, any man—" Flustered, she paused for a moment and took a deep breath. "I'm not used to looking at anyone unclothed."

He dropped the pants on the floor again and sauntered back over to the bed.

Sabrina's eyes widened at his approach. "What are
you doing?" she demanded in alarm, scooting across
the bed.

But he caught her ankles and yanked her forward.
"Perhaps you should get accustomed to looking at a
nude man—especially this man."

He lifted her to her feet, so she stood opposite him,
enough distance between them to reveal every male
part of him to her innocent gaze. But she kept those
heavenly blue eyes pinned fixedly on his face.

He grinned down at her, his fingers cupping her chin.
"You can look at the rest of me, too," he said in a teasing manner. And when her hesitant eyes did just as he
suggested, and combed over his frame in a long and curious assessment, stirring the heat in his groin, he added
in a more critical tone, "And you can touch any part of
me that you desire."

Her lingering gaze snapped up to connect with his
eyes. His whispered words brought another disconcert-
ing flush to her cheeks, telling him she had been thinking of doing that very thing.

His lips brushed hers lightly. "Really," he said
gruffly, "I won't mind if your hands roam all over me."

"I believe you," she was quick to respond, albeit a little dryly, and he chuckled softly at her terse tone. But it
was no great secret to her that he adored the pleasures
of a woman.

He turned around to retrieve his trousers yet again,
slipping into them, giving her the gained security of his
covered torso which she so obviously needed.

What a capricious creature she was. So candid and willful, even violent at times, and so frightened and meek when it came to the pleasures of the body. A true bashful maid in the one sense, though she had none of the other timid qualities of a genteel bred miss. He liked that about her. And if she consented to being his mistress, he intended to do away with her penchant for blushing at all things lustful.

They both busied themselves getting dressed.

When they were in a state of near-decent attire, Sabrina ventured to ask, "What are you going to do about the locket?"

"Nothing, I'm afraid." He sat down to pull on one of his leather riding boots. "I can't make any sense of the address we found in it, so I'll have to resort to another means of investigation."

"Such as?"

"I'm going back to see Gillingham."

Fumbling with the last button of her blouse, she froze upon hearing his confession. "Alone?"

"Did you expect to come along?"

Her eyes narrowed sharply on him. "I expect you to be careful."

"I intend to be."

"Then why go to Gillingham?"

He pulled on his other boot. "I have to learn more about the man. How else am I to understand why he's chasing after you?"

"But he's not chasing me," she pointed out with some unease. "He's chasing after the locket."

"Yes, but he thinks *you* have the locket, and he's determined to get you both."

"Why do you think that?"

"Gillingham isn't a man to be crossed injudiciously." He stood up and fastened his green vest over his crisp white shirt. "If he believes he's been wronged, he will seek vengeance. And he likely believes *you've* wronged him by stealing the locket."

"But I found it!" she objected hastily and struggled to put on her own boots.

"I know that, but Gillingham does not. He's still looking for you *and* the locket. And I have to find out why."

"What are you going to do, ask him?"

He smiled at her dry wit. "Nothing quite so forward, I assure you."

Anthony headed for the door. But he never reached it, his path blocked by one very determined-looking gypsy.

A finger poked into his chest. "You're not leaving this room."

He arched an intrigued golden brow. He realized she thought he'd meant to leave and see Gillingham this very instant, but that hadn't been his intent. Having arrived home late the other night, he'd missed the opportunity to announce his return to the staff. He was about to rectify that, when the striking face staring up at him, glowing with a mixture of alarm and anger, changed his mind.

"I'm not leaving, am I?" he inquired coyly, playing into her misconnection.

She shoved him back a few paces. "No, you're not."

He stepped forward again. "Really?"

"Really," she reiterated tightly, her palms smacking flat against his chest. "You're not going anywhere 'til you tell me what you intend to do with Gillingham."

His voice dropped to a husky whisper. "And just how do you intend to stop me from leaving?"

She pushed hard on his chest. He grabbed her wrists and crossed her hands behind her back, dragging her snuggly up against his chest. "You'll have to do better than that."

Fire sparked in her cobalt blue eyes. She clenched her teeth and grit out, "Fine." In one swift movement, she wedged her foot behind his ankle and twisted her body so her shoulder jabbed him in the chest, shoving him back toward the bed.

He lost his balance at the unanticipated assault and went crashing down to the mattress, bringing a struggling Sabrina along with him.

She gave a shriek of surprise as they both landed on the feathered comforter, and Anthony let out a deep and rumbling laugh. "Now *this* will definitely detain me from an encounter with Gillingham."

She wriggled on top of him. "Let me go, Anthony."

He gave her a wolfish grin. "I'd rather not."

"Anthony!"

With a disappointed sigh, he released her, and she scrambled back to her feet, her eyes as inclement as ever. "Now tell me what you intend to do."

"I intend to inform my staff that I'm home." He lazily got up off the bed. "I'm not going to see Gillingham at this very moment, though your concern for me is touching," he added with a wink.

Her lips pursed in obvious annoyance of his trickery, but before she could assuage herself of that annoyance with some cutting remark, he quickly instructed, "Now wait in here for me. I'll be back in a few minutes."

He reached the door in three long strides and looked over his shoulder. "And remember to—"

"Lock the door behind you," she cut in succinctly, her arms crossed under her breasts in a magnificent display of pique. "Yes, I know the routine."

He gave her another smile and then dashed from the room.

But Anthony was prepared to dash right back up into his room when he reached the bottom of the staircase and heard the squabbling voices coming from the main hall.

"I demand to see him this instant," rattled a familiar female voice.

"But your ladyship," was heard the earnest entreat of his butler, "Lord Hastings isn't here."

"Rubbish. He's hiding from me. I know it. And I won't stand for it a moment longer."

A patter of hasty footsteps approached.

Anthony wavered, considering his options: to take the staircase again or to confront the wrath of one very cantankerous female. He made the indecorous decision to mount the steps. He couldn't deal with the irascible woman just yet. He had so many other duties to attend.

But alas, his escape was belatedly orchestrated. He wasn't even halfway up the stairs when the incisive remark arrested him to the spot. "Going somewhere, Lord Hastings?"

Apparently not. He turned around and flashed his sister a placating smile. "Good morning, Ashley."

"It's anything but a good morning," she clipped out.

"Lord Hastings!" The butler sounded alarmed.

"You're home. I would never have attempted to bar her ladyship entrance had I known—"

"It's quite all right, Dobbs," drawled a dispassionate Anthony, as he made his way back down the steps. "I returned late last night. Please inform the rest of the staff that I have arrived."

"Very good, my lord."

With a curt nod, Anthony dismissed the servant, and then advanced toward his sister, pausing just short of her arms' reach, for the woman looked ready to clobber him.

"You just couldn't help yourself, could you?" came the biting reproof.

"Not out here, Ash," he warned in a low voice, and risked that clobbering by cupping her elbow and escorting her into the nearby study.

She didn't clout him, but once safely ensconced inside the room, she let loose her tirade.

"I've come to demand an accounting from you, Anthony."

"Yes, I would imagine so."

"How can you sound so blasé?" she dropped her reticule and parasol onto his desk so her hands were free to brandish in his face. "Do you realize what you've done? And after all that ranting and raving about duty. I just *knew* you couldn't resist the gypsy."

So the slighted Marchioness Livingston had had her revenge, he thought with scorn. "How did you hear?"

"From Lady Flemming, who'd heard it from Lady Camelford, who'd heard it from—"

"Yes, yes, I have the picture," he interrupted dryly. "The tale's gone round the *ton*."

"How could you do this to Cecelia? How could you tarnish her début in such a vile manner? Rumors are flying of your latest torrid affair with some unseemly wench."

Unseemly! He scoffed. Anthony headed over to the window to survey the morning traffic parading by.

His sister resumed her rant. "Gossip dictates you were so enamored by some peasant girl, that you stalked off the middle of the dance floor for a tussle. Cecelia is livid. She won't have you come near the townhouse."

"Well, perhaps this whole fiasco has a bright side to it after all," he drawled.

Ashley gasped. "If you disgraced your own sister just to get out of your obligation—"

"Don't be absurd," he chastised and turned away from the window, locking his hands behind his rigid back. "What's done is done. But I had no intention of ruining Cecelia's evening."

"Your intention is irrelevant. Cecelia's perfectly planned evening had a blemish. And that blemish is the talk of the *ton* rather than her ball."

He let out a deep, frustrated sigh. "I'll make it up to Cecelia."

"How?"

"I'll buy her a piece of jewelry."

"A trinket will hardly make amends for the girl's disastrous début."

"Then I'll make sure to give her sapphires or diamonds," he said in exasperation. "That should nicely exonerate me."

"*Why* did you do it in the first place?"

"I didn't *do* anything," he countered sharply.

She scoffed. "You wouldn't have gone into hiding if you truly believed you'd done nothing wrong."

"I wasn't hiding, damn it!" he snapped, both in guilt and frustration. "I had to escort Sabrina home, remember?" Though he purposefully failed to mention that his gypsy was again securely locked away in his bedchamber. He could just imagine his twin sister's reaction to that tidbit of news.

"I knew you couldn't keep your hands off the gypsy," she rebuked. "And after all the mortification I went through to try and avert this very fiasco."

At her unexpected revelation, his voice dropped a notch, his eyes narrowing with intent. "What mortification?"

"Oh, never mind."

Her sudden sheepish look had him demanding in a dire tone, "Out with it, Ash."

"Well, I had no other choice," she was quick to defend herself. "I had to try to avoid a scandal."

"Just what did you do?"

"Nothing too distasteful. I only cautioned the gypsy to keep her wits about her." Then, in disapproval, "Every other woman tends to lose hers when around you."

His guilt vanished as his anger simmered. "You *what*?"

"You didn't leave me much choice," she insisted, flustered.

"And how is that?"

"You have a disreputable nature. There was no point in confronting *you* about the essence of propriety. But I had to say something to the girl. I couldn't very well have it known that Lord Hastings diddles his time away with a gypsy!"

"I trusted you," he said, and not without a hint of hurt in his voice at his sister's betrayal of confidence. He thought back to the time when Ashley had watched over his gypsy while he'd dined with the rest of the family. He remembered returning to his room and finding Sabrina mute and apprehensive. He remembered thinking how odd it was that she still considered him a threat after all he'd done for her.

But now he understood the girl's timid disposition. She had spent her time with Ashley, listening to heaps of ghastly tales concerning his character. She had been censured and warned to keep her gypsy hands off him. Was it a wonder she'd been rendered speechless by the time he'd come back into the room?

"You can still trust me," Ashley insisted defiantly. "I did what I thought was best."

"You made me look like a liar," he said in a tight voice. "I'd promised Sabrina she would be safe with you and you attacked her the moment I left the room."

"I would hardly call a prudent caution an attack. But it doesn't matter now, does it? The whole of London is whispering about your little tryst the night of your sister's début ball, so my advice to the gypsy obviously went unheeded."

He stiffened. "I'll have you know I never bedded Sabrina the night of the ball."

Too angry with his sister's perfidy, he hadn't realized how awkward his assertion sounded, implying he had bedded Sabrina on some other night instead. But, thankfully, Ashley was too wound up to notice his little faux pas.

She pressed on with her complaint. "Oh, what difference does that triviality make? The whole of London *thinks* you bedded a peasant on the night of the ball. And now we have to salvage this season for Cecelia."

He sighed again, shelving his anger for the moment. "What do you propose we do?"

"You are to come to Papa's townhouse tomorrow morning."

His brow crinkled. "But I thought Cecelia didn't want me anywhere near it?"

"She doesn't, but Mama insists." Ashley headed over to his desk to recover her reticule and parasol. "Mama isn't about to cause a greater stir by letting everyone think her son has been banished because of his transgression. She wants the rumors squelched, and so she intends to go on with Cecelia's come-out as scheduled. You're expected in the West End at ten o'clock sharp."

Her peremptory tone made it clear the issue was not negotiable, and he mentally cursed that conniving witch of a marchioness for spreading the whole sordid tale of his "transgression" across London. Now he had to do what he could to appease his kin, and see to it that his sister married well, despite the shaky ground on which her début had been launched. Though he was curious. "Just why am I expected in the morning?"

"Cecelia is to be presented at court."

"Oh, good God," he groaned and brought his fingers to his temples.

"You're not wiggling out of this, Anthony," she said tersely, and touched the curls at her temples to ensure nothing had been disturbed during their heated exchange. "Nor can you avoid the other obligation you're expected to perform later that very same day."

"Which is?" he all but growled, dreading to hear what else she was going to stack upon him.

"We are both to escort Cecelia to Vauxhall."

Bloody hell. A visit to St. James's Palace *and* a night out among the *ton*. He had never had the urge to do a woman harm before, but throttling the conniving Marchioness Livingston was suddenly an appealing thought.

"Fine," he relented with total ill grace. "I'll be there." But where would he tuck Sabrina while he was off gallivanting the whole day? And when would he get the chance to visit with Gillingham and learn more about that cursed locket? He was going to have to do some quick thinking.

Ashley gave him a swift nod of approval and headed for the door. He escorted her to the front entrance.

"I will see you tomorrow, Anthony." Then, she added sternly, "Don't be late."

He let loose an exasperated sigh when his officious sister finally departed. God, that woman was becoming a handful. He hadn't realized just how much until now.

Anthony headed back for the sanctum of his study, pondering what he was going to do about Sabrina. He couldn't return to his room and confess the mess he was in without also confessing a handy solution to that mess.

If only he could go to see Gillingham tonight, then tomorrow's gadding about wouldn't matter all that much. But what would he do with his gypsy for the few hours that he was gone? Should he inform the butler that he had her concealed in his room? Or should he just give the order that his bedchamber was not to be disturbed for the night? The servants might think the command a little odd, but then again, he was a wealthy bachelor, and they just might conclude his peculiar request was nothing more than the whim of a pampered lord. He could always hope.

Anthony would be able to think with a clearer head if it wasn't for the blasted incessant whistling in his ears.

He was about to castigate whichever fool servant was making the ungodly racket, when his eyes rounded in surprise at the approaching figure. "Vincent?"

The whistling stopped and his best friend gave him a jovial grin, apparently well recovered from his previous degenerate state. "Ah, there you are, old chum. Missed you these last few days. Where have you been?"

He was incredulous. "Vincent, are you still living here?"

"And where else would I be?"

"Where indeed?" The sarcasm was unmasked. "It's been three days. Why aren't you back in your apartment?"

"Well, I couldn't go home," he said with resolve. "Not yet anyway."

"And why ever not?"

"Hadn't heard from you, old chum."

Anthony doubted his ears. "I told you I would pay your gambling debt."

"Yes, and then I never saw you again. How was I supposed to know that everything had gone as planned, and it was safe for me to go home? I wasn't going to risk my neck again . . . Besides the food here is so much more delicious than the meager rations I'm accustomed to."

"Out, Vincent!" he ordered in a perspicuous tone. "Your hide cost me five thousand pounds and is perfectly safe—at least from Gillingham."

"All right, all right." The man whirled around and

ambled back in the direction he had come from, grumbling all the while, "What has you in a tizzy?"

Anthony studied his comrade's retreating figure, mulling over the sheer audacity of the man, when the thought suddenly struck him. "Vincent, come back here!"

The flummoxed man spun around again and strolled over to the viscount. "What is it now?"

"You're not going anywhere."

Vincent sighed heavily. "Do make up your mind, old chum."

Chapter 22

The viscount prowled his bedchamber in search of his cravat. Sabrina knew that was what he was looking for because he kept muttering about it under his breath.

Apparently, his lordship was accustomed to *being* dressed, and the task of dressing himself was proving a mite irksome.

Compelled to dismiss the servants from his room, for her sake, he had to do much for himself, and watching him try was rather amusing.

Sabrina didn't laugh, though. She didn't even smile. She just sat in the middle of the large bed, her knees pulled up to her chin, her arms wrapped around her legs, and her eyes following the viscount's every move in merriment.

He was a handsome sight. Tight-fitting trousers, a walnut brown in hue, cupped and caressed his every muscular curve. The bone white of his shirt contrasted with the deep forest green of his waistcoat, bejeweled with shiny gold buttons. Tipped off with high black leather boots, and the dark green coat he had draped over the back of a chair, he would make a fine vision as soon as he was all put together.

She found pleasure in just watching him. She liked being unobserved, free to let her eyes roam over his masculine figure with no worry of reproof for her shameless admiration. Not that Anthony would think her admiration of his body shameless. Certainly not. The man would be honored, thrilled, excited to have her looking at him in such a wondrous way.

But no one else would approve. Not on his side of the family and definitely not on hers. Though she didn't have to worry anymore about what her people would think. She needn't concern herself with censure from her father or the tribal elders. Ever again.

Her amusement dwindled as a tight knot slowly formed in her belly.

She was alone.

The wretched truth of her predicament, forgotten for a moment, came back to strike her with stinging intensity. She had no one to care for her anymore. Oh, sure, Anthony had vowed he wouldn't abandon her, but she knew better. She had seen the magnificent ladies of his world, adorned with their jewels and gowns. Such splendor would entice any man. And Anthony was no different. Her simple ways and her wild gypsy looks had no hold over him. At least, no lasting hold. He would forget all about her in time. He would stick her in some cottage in the middle of nowhere and leave her there. All alone. And she would feel the pain of that loss greatly, now that she had grown so close to him.

She gulped in a deep breath, blinking back the moisture pooling in her eyes. She had to come to terms with the ghastly truth. There was no one left in her life to guide her. No elders to steer her down the path of her destiny. No father to instruct her in the old ways. No husband to comfort and protect her. No friends to offer her advice and confidence. For the first time, she had to look to herself for all her needs.

"Found it. Blasted nuisance . . ."

Sabrina glanced over to the mirrored dresser to find Anthony, elusive cravat in hand, muttering and fastening the scrap of cloth around his neck.

It was dark outside. Soon he would be off to the Lion's Gate. She'd been told that was the name of Gillingham's club, though what Anthony intended to do once he arrived at the club was still a mystery to her. And she intended to solve it before he set foot out of doors.

She eased off the bed and approached him from behind, her eyes meeting his in the reflection of the mirror. "What do you plan to do at the club?"

Still fumbling with his cravat, he returned, "I plan to learn all that I can about Gillingham."

"How? He isn't likely to tell you about himself."

"True. Which is why I don't intend to ask him."

Her brow furrowed. "So who will you ask?"

"Emma Kingsley."

Sabrina had no idea who the woman was, but just the mention of her name had her palms fisting. "And who is Emma Kingsley?"

He gave the cravat a few finishing tweaks. "One of the doxies working at the Lion's Gate."

"The same doxy you visited before?"

Smoldering green eyes narrowed on her. She regretted her harsh tone the moment she saw the dark look in his eyes.

"Is that a streak of jealousy I hear in your voice, my dear?"

Yes!

"No," she bit out mulishly.

A blond brow arched. "Really?" He turned around to face her. Those brilliant green eyes seemed to dance with laughter. "I had hoped it was jealousy."

Since he was taking a step toward her, Sabrina thought it wise if she took one back. And to keep from dwelling on the giddy panic storming her breast, she demanded, "Why ever for?"

"If you were jealous, then I'd know you care for me."

Her back bumped into one of the bedposts, and she looked up at the towering figure of masculine energy, undaunted. "Why would it matter to you if I cared?"

Her question seemed to give him pause. A spark of indecision flashed through his mesmeric green eyes before a faint and roguish smile touched his beautiful lips. "It'd just be nice to know."

He brushed a knuckle softly across her cheek and she shivered at his touch.

"I'm not jealous," she insisted then, belatedly and a little breathlessly. Heavens, the man was stunning under lamplight, glowing like a faerie king surrounded by sparkling faerie dust. "I'm upset," she went on to clarify. "While you're hopping into Emma's bed again, I'll be all alone—"

His voice was low and a little rough, making her shiver, as he cut in, "I never hopped into Emma's bed the first time I met her."

"So how did you find out about the locket she wears?"

Like a magical spell, he entranced her to the spot with his heated gaze. His knuckle strayed to her neck, stroking softly, sending more shivers of tickled delight throughout her weakening limbs.

"I only saw Emma wearing the locket," he drawled, his lips so close to hers, she could feel his warm breath bathing her skin.

"Then *what* were you doing in Gillingham's club if not chasing after skirts?"

He chuckled softly, his voice thick. "I don't spend *all* my time chasing after skirts."

"I find that hard to believe."

"I can't imagine why."

She gasped at the hot feel of his palm cupping her breast, his splayed fingers kneading the supple flesh.

He murmured roughly, with false injury in his tone, "It's rather unjust to have such an undeserving reputation."

Undeserving indeed! But the feelings brewing inside her overshadowed her cynicism just then.

Gripping his face in her hands, she guided him down to her lips, opening her mouth to the aggressive thrust of his tongue.

It was a hard, steamy kiss. And with Anthony grinding against the front of her, and the wooden bedpost digging into the back of her, she was being rubbed and stroked and caressed into a dizzying frenzy.

An abrupt knock at the door.

She gasped. Anthony plunged his tongue deeper into her mouth before he broke away from the kiss with a growled oath.

She clutched the bedpost for support, dazed. Heavens, would she ever get used to the man's kisses?

A smoky pair of deep green eyes raked over her from head to toe. After a brief, piercing survey of her figure, he sauntered over to the door and opened it.

"For once, Vincent, I wish you'd arrived late."

At Anthony's curt words, Sabrina's gaze flitted to the clock to see that it was half past seven. Just who was Anthony expecting?

"What the devil is wrong with you, old chum? First you mysteriously summon me to your room, then you go into a dander when I arrive. You've been acting rather . . ."

The man's scowl morphed into a lazy smile as soon as he spotted the third occupant in the room.

"Well, hello there." Vincent swept an assessing eye over a thoroughly flustered Sabrina. "No wonder you've been so distracted, old chum. Been hiding a ladybird—"

A sound punch to the shoulder diverted Vincent's attention. He grabbed his arm, massaging the muscle, glaring back at Anthony. "Haven't I suffered enough bruises at your hands?"

"Apparently not," the viscount said sternly.

"Well, then, why don't you tell me what's going on?" His eyes, more alert, skipped back over to Sabrina, and he added with a dashing grin, "And explain who this lovely creature is."

"Sabrina's no ladybird," Anthony rectified tersely, closing the door. "She's staying in my room, under *my* protection. So behave yourself and tell no one that she is here."

"A damsel in distress?" Vincent's eyes reverted to the viscount. "Why do you always have such good fortune?"

Sabrina almost choked on that. Her life was ruined and it was Anthony's *good* fortune? She refrained from making any comment.

Moving deeper into the room, Anthony gestured toward the other man. "This is Vincent," he completed the introductions. "He's a good friend of mine and he's going to watch over you while I'm away."

Sabrina's eyes flew back to the miscreant in alarm. "He will?"

"I will?" said Vincent, a devilish smile tugging at the corners of his lips. "I say, old chum, are you sure you want *me* looking after her?"

Anthony spun about, eyes sizzling. "*You,* Vincent, owe me a rather large sum of money, if I remember correctly."

The other man winced.

"And you will begin paying off the debt by keeping Sabrina safe," the viscount continued in a firm tone. "Tell no one that she is here. I should be back in a few hours."

Anthony took his coat from the chair and slipped into the garment.

The sight of him preparing to leave caused Sabrina's heart to knock frantically against her breast. By the time he made his way over to her, her heart was making so much racket, she could scarce hear her own desperate pleading.

"Anthony, you can't leave me alone with this man."

"It'll be all right." He gathered her into his arms, pressing a kiss to her brow. "I know he seems a bit of a . . . scoundrel. But I trust him. You'll be safe, I promise."

And with those few soothingly whispered words, he

was striding for the door, shooting Vincent one last, admonishing look in the process. "Take good care of her."

Vincent nodded. "Right, old chum."

The door closed with a soft thud, leaving the two occupants in the room to stare at one another in dismal uncertainty.

Anthony stood in the entrance to the gaming hall. The gusty laughter of male carousers had guided him to the spacious and opulent arena. Now on the threshold, he witnessed the hedonistic revelry firsthand.

At each of the gaming tables, adoring doxies regaled their patrons with bawdy humor and sensual caresses. Drinks and wealth drained from glasses and pockets respectively. And a piano in a corner provided the already animated atmosphere with a bubbly jig, inducing some of the more besotted patrons to belt out a rather slurred chorus in accompaniment.

It was a glorious display of debauchery—and for once in his life, Anthony wasn't tempted to immerse himself in it.

Tacking on an engaging smile, he sauntered into the room. He thoroughly scanned the arena for any sign of Gillingham, but the man was nowhere to be seen. An advantage to Anthony. He wasn't interested in speaking with the elusive club owner directly. Quite simply, he needed a woman. His charms weren't likely to coax any answers from a reticent male employee standing guard in the club. He needed a more malleable target for all his smiles. He needed Emma Kingsley in all preference.

He glanced around the room again, this time in search of a particular doxy. But as chance would have it, a particular doxy was in search of him.

Slender fingers rounded his shoulder in a lascivious caress. He looked down at his side to find the stunning Emma Kingsley circling him, a broad and amorous smile hooked on her rosy lips.

"Good evening, Lord Hastings," the seductive creature purred.

"Good evening," he returned in the same throaty vein. Gillingham was sure to hear of his return to the Lion's Gate, and would naturally wonder why the viscount had come back after so thoroughly expressing a desire to never do so. If Anthony could convince Emma he had returned because of her, there was no cause for Gillingham to think anything was amiss. A lustful viscount was hardly a menace.

He pried Emma's fingers off his shoulder, and brought the back of her hand to his lips in a playful display of gallant behavior. "You are a dangerous temptress, madam."

A slender blond brow cocked ever so slightly. "Am I?"

"I vowed never to return after forfeiting a great sum of money to your employer, and yet here I am, unable to endure another night without gazing into your lovely eyes."

She gave a husky and spirited laugh, and hooked her hand through the viscount's arm, steering him through the room. "Lord Hastings, I do believe you are mistaken. If memory serves, it was not my eyes that captivated your attention during our last encounter."

"I stand corrected, madam." His eyes went to the decadent display of her abundant breasts—and narrowed on the familiar gold locket engraved with the face of a lion. He resumed his roguish manner with a downright wicked grin. "It was another lovely pair that captivated my attention."

Emma ushered him to one of the cushioned love

seats that dotted the outskirts of the arena. Cupping two glasses of spirits from an attentive server, she then snuggled next to him in the seat, her fine lavender fragrance drifting all around him.

She handed him the glass. Even with a drink in hand, a firm body pressed close to him, and a soft scent tickling his senses, Anthony wasn't lulled by the deftly orchestrated seduction. He knew the game well. It was all intended to loosen a patron's purse strings. But he wasn't there to get his pockets bled. He was there to get some answers.

"And what is your desire, Lord Hastings?" Emma inclined her head toward the gaming tables. "To try your luck at cards?"

Anthony followed her gaze to the center arena and the cluster of men at each table. His eyes drifted over the faces, some familiar, some not. He recognized Jeremy Fielding, third marquess of Winbourne, a renowned rake and wastrel in his own right. And then there was General-Major Archibald Adington, whose exemplary service during the Battle of Waterloo had gained him laurels galore. There was also Lord Bradford Derwent, a political man in the House of Lords, and a known thorn to the house for some of his radical views on reform. All in all, it was a rather eclectic mix of patrons.

And then Anthony's gaze narrowed to the doxies hanging over the men's arms. His muscles stiffened at the sight. The women all wore the very same locket as Emma Kingsley! He couldn't believe his eyes. Was Gillingham marking his whores? If so, why?

To quell the sudden apprehension rising in his chest, Anthony flashed Emma a dashing smile. "You are much more alluring than a mere game of cards."

"Am I?" she coyly quipped again.

"Most definitely, madam." And to prove it, his eyes went back to caress the full swell of her breasts. But he couldn't play this flirtatious game indefinitely. It was time he steered their discourse in a more useful direction.

In a daring gesture, he fingered the locket cushioned between her breasts, his voice a lazy drawl. "My, what a simple ornament for such a striking creature."

Emma's fingers came up to intertwine with his. "I have always believed, if the ornament glittered and sparkled too greatly, it might detract attention from . . . my lovely eyes."

He chuckled at her double-entendre. But in his gut, frustration was slowly forming. Emma wasn't being very forthcoming. And he couldn't continue asking questions about the locket, not when he was supposedly there to dote on her "lovely eyes." He would end up arousing the woman's suspicion if he continued with any interrogation.

Anthony dismissed all further mention of the locket for the time being, and pressed on. "And what will it cost me to gaze into your 'lovely eyes' at my leisure?"

She leaned even closer to him, her breasts pushing up against his arm. "One hundred pounds."

Anthony gave her a look of genuine incredulity. He had never heard of such an exorbitant rate. And to spend one night with a whore?!

"One night with you must rival an eternity in heaven," he said.

Her smile was enigmatic. "You shall have to forfeit the figure to find out, my lord."

He gave a soft grunt. He would have to forfeit the figure indeed. And he wasn't the least bit looking forward to it. Imagine dropping another small fortune into Gillingham's pockets, just so he could ask the woman a few questions in private.

And then another thorny thought took root in his mind. Once he and Emma were alone, and he had a few answers from her, could he just leave the room, offering the excuse of a forgotten engagement? Or would that appear too suspicious? Would he have to spend a few hours in bed with the woman? And why the devil was he even fretting over the dilemma? Better yet, why did he consider it a dilemma at all? He may be here to learn more about Gillingham, but he couldn't go about his investigation in a heady manner. He wanted to convince Emma he had returned to the club because of her. If he had to have a tussle with the doxy to prove it, then so be it.

And yet dread or guilt or apprehension stalked him. He wasn't sure which of the three it was. It might even be a combination of the trio. He only knew he had never felt this way before. So . . . nervous about being with a woman.

What the deuces was wrong with him? He didn't often pass up an opportunity to sleep with a beautiful wench, especially since he had to pay a hundred bloody pounds to be with her!

But that unpleasant sensation in his gut continued to gnaw at him, despite his sound attempts to reason it away.

With some discomfort, he forced a roguish grin to his lips. "I accept your price, madam."

Chapter 23

❦❦

"**H**ow about a game?" Vincent uncrossed his legs and moved away from the sofa, where he'd been sitting for the last half hour. "Why gawk at one another in silence the whole night? A game will melt away the time."

Sabrina cast him a wary look. They weren't children. What kind of a suggestion was that? And then she remembered where she was. In the land of the *ton*. Of course Vincent would suggest the diversion. What else did wealthy *gajos* do with their spare time except play games and throw parties and chase after skirts?

An image of Anthony dallying with some buxom wench skipped through her head just then. His mouth pressed on another woman's lips stabbed through her thoughts. She could see the two lovers tumbling in bed. She could hear the doxy's giggles and Anthony's husky laughter. Sabrina could even sense what the other woman must be feeling right about now; Anthony's touch on her breast, his hands stroking her thighs in a rhythmic caress, making her gasp and pant as he trailed his fingers to the inside of her . . .

Sabrina took in a sharp breath of her own, banishing the disturbing vision. The distraction of a silly amusement suddenly held appeal.

"How about Piquet?" suggested Vincent.

She shook her head, never having heard of it.

"*Vingt et un?*"

Another shake of the head.

"Hazard?" he offered hopefully. When she still said nothing, he sighed and waved a dismissive hand. "Then I'll just teach you the rules of Hazard. Do you have any blunt?"

Her brows pinned together. "Any what?"

"Coins?"

"Oh!" She nodded this time.

That brought an eager smile to Vincent's face. "Wonderful. I'll just duck back into my room and gather a few coins. Be back in a moment."

Sabrina found herself staring at the closed bedroom door, mulling over the need for coins in a game, and also pondering why Vincent had a room in Anthony's townhouse. Surely the man didn't live here?

But she would have to wait until Vincent's return to learn the answer to that mystery. In the meantime, she busied herself with scraping together what few coins she had.

Rummaging through the clutter of her bag, she yanked out the bright green skirt she had worn on the night of her wedding celebration. She gazed at the skirt with a pang of longing, thinking of all she had lost. Fondling the velvety fabric in her hands, she bit back her tears and went to work, tearing out the coins she had sewn into the hemline. So much for gold bringing a gypsy good fortune!

Vincent soon returned to the room and locked the door behind him. "Help me move these chairs."

She did as he asked, pushing aside one of the armchairs positioned in front of the fireplace, while he pushed away another, leaving a gap in the carpet.

He settled onto the floor and motioned for her to do the same. She did, reluctantly sinking to her knees opposite him.

"Now, all we need are two of these." His palm unfurled to reveal a pair of dice.

Sabrina arched a brow. "And what do we do with those?"

"Well, the rules are . . ."

And it was two hours later that the dice were still quietly spilling onto the cushioned carpet.

Sabrina watched in anticipation as the little ivory blocks tumbled and tumbled, and finally teetered to a stop, revealing the combined number of seven.

"It's the main!" she cried with glee.

A dismayed Vincent could do naught but stare as the last of his coins were cheerfully scooped up by his more fortunate opponent. "Bloody hell," he muttered.

"Shall we play again?"

"Lord, no!" He shook his head passionately. "You've reduced me to a pauper."

With a smile, she clumped her winnings together in her hand, and opened the beaded leather pouch tied at her waistband, dropping in her spoils. It was a pity the game couldn't go on. It had been fun to play—for her anyway. And she'd learned a lot about her appointed guardian during the course of the evening.

Readily willing to spill forth his life's troubles to a sympathetic ear, Vincent had revealed much about himself through idle chitchat, and she'd soon discovered he was no more than a harmless, somewhat misguided, wastrel.

A wastrel who happened to be in a similar bind as herself. It seems they were *both* in hiding from Gillingham, though for different reasons, but Vincent didn't know that. While he was content to gush about his recent plight, she was content to just listen to him. In so doing, she realized a lot. For instance, it was through helping Vincent that Anthony had come across Gillingham—and the doxy. The viscount hadn't been scouring London's brothels for amusement like she'd first thought, and for some inexplicable reason, she was relieved to hear that.

There was a quick rap at the door.

The two occupants of the room exchanged anxious glances.

"Who is it?" wondered Vincent, slowly approaching the door.

"Who do you think?" came back the muffled, yet terse, retort.

"Oh, God," Vincent gave a soft, but nonetheless desperate, cry. "Hurry!" He motioned to Sabrina. "Put the chairs back."

She scrambled to her feet in obedience, wondering what was wrong. Anthony was back. Surely that wasn't cause for alarm? They'd been awaiting his return after all.

The chairs were pushed back to their former places. The dice disappeared into Vincent's pocket.

But he still didn't unlock the door.

Vincent gave her a pleading look. "You mustn't tell Anthony that we were gambling."

"Why not?"

"You simply mustn't," he beseeched. "Promise me."

"I promise," she said in haste, the rapping at the door growing louder and more determined. "Now open the door before he makes any more noise."

Vincent let loose a quick sigh of relief and turned the key. He had to leap aside to avoid the swinging door from clobbering him in the face.

"What the devil's going on?" demanded Anthony, striding into the bedchamber, his eyes searching for Sabrina. The moment he spotted her in the room, he scanned her from head to foot in a thorough assessment, his heated gaze leaving her feeling ravished. "What took so long to open the door?"

"Nothing, old chum," Vincent was quick to dismiss the notion. "It took a few seconds to reach the door, is all. Don't be in such a tizzy."

Anthony's smoldering gaze moved from Sabrina over to Vincent. "Everything went well, then?"

"Perfectly delightful," chimed his friend, who then shifted his uncomfortable gaze away from the viscount's penetrating one. "You have a very charming ward. Now, if you'll excuse me, I believe I'll retire to bed." He swiveled on his heels. "I have an early start in the morning."

"And just where do you think you're going in the morning?" demanded Anthony, bringing his comrade to a dead halt.

"Why home, of course." The man spun about. "The deed is done. The girl is in prime health. What else am I to do here?"

"You're not leaving until I say so. I still need you to look after Sabrina."

"But—"

"Goodnight, Vincent."

The man gave a weary sigh. "Goodnight, then."

At the sound of the key rotating in the lock, Sabrina knitted her arms under her breasts, pinning her fiery gaze on Anthony

He turned to confront her, a single blond brow arching. "Is something the matter?"

"Just how long do you intend to keep me locked away in here?"

"Not too long," he said in assurance.

But she wasn't mollified. "*How* long? I'm not going to sit in this room night after night, while you go off to dally with some doxy at Gillingham's club."

A vision of Anthony doing to another woman what he had done to her—the very vision she had tried to forget all about by indulging in a distracting game of Hazard with Vincent—came back to haunt her now.

"I'm not dallying with any doxy," he insisted.

But she could smell the untruth. The air was filled with the fragrance of lavender, and unless he'd spent the evening picking flowers, it was perfume she sensed. And Sabrina didn't wear any perfume.

"I can smell her all over you." Her heart throbbed as she made the accusation. She had no right to feel territorial over Anthony. He didn't belonged to her. He could do as he pleased, with whomever he pleased. She knew that. So why did she feel so betrayed?

He moved toward a nearby chair and shrugged off his coat, draping it over the head rest. "You may be able to smell the doxy all over me, but she wasn't *under* me."

The tight ache in her heart convinced her it was time to change the subject. The current one was just too painful. Anthony would only persist in his lies and she'd have to fight even harder to get the truth from him. Trouble was, she didn't deserve the truth, not about this matter. It was his business what had happened at the Lion's Gate. And although she felt like screeching and hurling something at him, she also realized her desire to do so was irrational. It was his body. And *he* got to decide who touched it, not her. Better if she worried about her own body—particularly her neck.

"What did you learn about Gillingham?"

Anthony reached for his collar to fumble with the cravat. "That the man is a first-rate scoundrel and blackmailer."

Her black brows lifted in surprise.

"It seems Mr. Gillingham uses his club as a front to wring out his patrons' darkest secrets before he exploits that knowledge for his own financial gain."

"Emma told you this?" She couldn't hide the incredulity in her voice. Just how infectious were Anthony's charms if he could get the doxy to betray her employer in just one night? . . . On second thought, considering her own predicament, did she really have to ask herself that?

"Emma, no." He loosened the cravat before sliding it off his neck. "The staff is fiercely loyal to Gillingham, evading any personal questions regarding their employer."

Now she was really confused. "So how do you know about the blackmail?"

"Observation, my dear." His vest was next to go, dropped into the lap of the chair. "Gillingham is no one of any political or social importance, and yet, once inside the club, I witnessed how the mighty lords cowed at his feet. Evidently, the villain holds great sins over his lofty patrons' heads."

"And the locket?"

"A means of communication. All the doxies wear one. I assume, once a gent has been thoroughly doused in spirits, a lucrative secret is coaxed from the besotted fool, scribbled down on a piece of paper, and then stuffed into a locket before being passed on to Gillingham. I witnessed the exchange of such a locket between Gillingham and one of his wenches just as I was leaving."

"So what was so important about the address in *my* locket?"

He reached for the buttons at his collar. "I'm not entirely sure of that, but it stands to reason that the resident of the mysterious address owes Gillingham a great sum of money. In such a case, it's understandable why he desperately wants the paper back."

"And it took you hours to observe all this?"

The skepticism in her voice had him guessing—accurately—what she truly wanted to know. "I already told you, I didn't indulge in any pleasures with the doxy."

Sabrina gawked at the discarded shirt, now crumpled on the floor. Her eyes were transfixed at the movement of his hands, reaching for the buttons of his trousers.

"S-so why were you at the club for so long?" she stammered.

His trousers were undone, revealing a patch of sandy brown curls all clustered at the opening. He went to tug on his boots next. Thud went one boot onto the carpet. The second followed soon thereafter. She just watched him, mesmerized. She couldn't even remember what they were talking about.

He reached for the waistline of his tight-fitting trousers and jerked them down his hips. She gasped. The engorged sight of him caused her heart to miss a beat and her thighs to ache with unabashed longing. If he had been with another woman that night, he certainly hadn't had his fill of her.

Anthony came dangerously near. Close to her body, but more unsettlingly, close to her soul. She retreated a step, hoping the distance was enough to sever the powerful connection that had forged between them. It was not, however. The bond only strengthened. Dark green eyes, rough and turbulent, beckoned her near. She felt as if she had no control over her own movements, as if she was floating on air toward the formidable rogue. No, it was the other way around. He was advancing on her.

Thick arms slipped around her, pushing her up against a hard chest—and another hard part of him. She stifled a second gasp when she felt the sturdy tip of him poking into her abdomen, demanding her attention. Which she readily gave. How could she ignore *that* part of him?

"I haven't been with another woman since the day I met you." His voice was as rough as the look in his eyes. "I went to the club, intent on doing whatever it took to learn Gillingham's secrets, even if it meant sharing the doxy's bed. But once I got there I couldn't be with her. I didn't want to be with anyone else but you."

Those words were making her shake, with desire or

with love, she wasn't even sure. All she was sure of was that she wanted him deep inside her. Now.

Oh, she was a fool. Aching for something that would only bring her more heartache in the future. But she didn't care right then. Right then, the urge to be with Anthony was stronger than any voice of protest or risk of regret.

"I spent the evening playing cards, the doxy draped over my arm," he went on to explain. "When I lost every pound I had with me, I made the excuse that I was penniless, that I would have to come back to see her some other night. But I don't intend to return. I don't intend to spend my nights with anyone else but you."

His lips came down on hers in a thoroughly possessive, thoroughly demanding, thoroughly thrilling kiss. She teetered on her toes to better meet the hot thrusts of his tongue, stabbing into her mouth with a vigor that so aroused her, she could feel the moisture already pooling between her legs.

He moved over her mouth in deft and eager strokes. All the while, it seemed as though they were levitating toward the bed. When she felt the feathers press into her backside, she didn't care to think how she got there. All that she cared about was what Anthony was making her feel.

Her heart ticking faster than the seconds of a clock, she let go of all her fears, of all her doubts that they shouldn't be doing this again, that it was wrong. But it felt so right. And that was enough for now. Regrets could come at dawn. She already had a lifetime of regrets to nurse. What was one more?

His hand fisted around the hem of her skirt. Slowly, he pushed the garment up her legs, the fabric slithering along her thighs, leaving her trembling in the wake of the steady ascent.

When she was bare from the waist down, he broke away from the kiss and repositioned himself. Parting her knees, he kneeled between her splayed thighs.

In the candlelit room, she was wholly exposed to him. A sudden tickle of embarrassment encouraged her to bring her legs back together, but his hands clamped over her inner thighs, the heat from his palms branding her, stopping her retraction.

Slowly, he spread her legs wide again. "Don't hide yourself from me."

She was almost giddy with the emotions bubbling inside her. She was shaking for sure, her heart shuddering, her breaths coming out in quick and raspy pants.

"Let me look at you," he said with a gruff edge, his piercing gaze devouring her, making her sweat and her body ache.

"Let me touch you." His fingers combed through the dark and curly patch of hair between her legs, exposing more and more of her moist and quivering flesh to his searching green eyes.

And then, with a dark twinkle in those lustful eyes, he whispered, "Let me taste you."

He bowed forward. She gasped and tightened every muscle in anticipation. But he didn't touch her with his lips. Fingers still entwined in the thick curls of her apex, he only blew over the exposed flesh. A soft whistle of cool air, followed by a short puff of warm air.

She shivered violently at the shifts in temperature. Cold and hot bursts of air breezed over her damp and sensitive skin. Gone was any thought of modesty. She felt nothing but a throbbing want.

The tension eased in her muscles. Eyes closed, she dipped her head back against the pillow, and released a half sigh, half moan of pleasure when he finally dropped his head to kiss the dewy mound between her legs.

He was tender and gentle at first with his kisses. Soon, though, his mouth parted, opened wide to unleash the eager thrust of his tongue, which stabbed and stroked at the most sensitive part of her, leaving her gasping and digging her fingers into his hair to hold him firm against her pulsing flesh.

"Don't stop," she pleaded. It was a breathless request, yanked from her lips in a moment of desperate urgency. She didn't want the erotic moment to end. She felt a sense of panic at the thought that it would. But he couldn't stop. Not now. Not when every nerve in her body was tingling. And to make sure he didn't abandon her, she held him fast, giving him very little room to move.

She was burning inside. She was shaking. Nothing had ever felt so good . . . but she was wrong. He guided her thighs upward until she hooked them over his broad shoulders, giving him more access to her supple flesh.

Her stark cries of delirious pleasure provoked his tongue to swirl and dart with greater passion. The louder she grew, the more ardent he became with his thrusts, giving her what she demanded.

He licked and he kissed, whipping her into a state of pulsating arousal. Her fingers tightly knotted in his hair. Oh, sweet heaven, it was pure ecstasy.

"Anthony," she cried. She wanted release from the pressure building at her junction. Her innards twisted with the demand for that relief. And he gave it to her. His tongue laved over the quivering bud pulsing between the folds of her flesh, and she shuddered with unbridled relief, the strain and the throbbing draining from her loins. She felt so peaceful, so content when it was over.

"That was wonderful," she praised weakly, eyes still closed, breathing hard and fast.

He chuckled with a deep sound of masculine satisfaction. "You'll feel it again in a moment."

Unclenching her fists from his hair, she opened her eyes to look down at him. "I will?"

"Oh, yes, my dear, you will."

He kissed the insides of her thighs, and straightened to his kneeling position once more. It was then she saw his rigid shaft, still swollen with arousal. He had yet to have his own release.

Timid, but determined, she wanted to give him back the same pleasure he had given her. She wanted to be familiar with every curve and ripple of his body. She wanted to feel the heat of his skin burning under her palms. She wanted to hear him groan again and again, knowing all the while it was her touch that was evoking his candid responses.

But how? How to touch a man as jaded as Anthony and make him ache inside the way she ached for him?

She kneeled in front of him.

His questioning gaze, dark and intense, glazed over her. "What are you doing?"

She could hear the stress in his voice, sense the great need he had of her. Her answer was to lay a hesitant hand on his magnificent chest, her splayed fingers stroking the gnarled muscles that twitched and capered under her every caress.

He closed his eyes with a groan. "Oh, yes, Sabrina, touch me. Touch me anywhere you like."

She'd like to touch him everywhere, she thought with a sudden wanton impulse. "Show me," she said. "Show me how you like to be touched."

His lids opened, heavy with desire, an unmistakable hunger reflecting in the dark green pools of his eyes.

"Like this." He rested his palm over her fingers and guided her hand down the moist, sleek expanse of his midriff.

Sabrina watched in fascination as her hand moved lower and lower. Her fingers trembled softly when he brought her palm to the base of his shaft, and folded her fingers over his throbbing erection, bidding her to cradle the warm, hard length of him.

It was such an odd sensation, to feel the power of his manhood surging through her fingertips. She looked into his handsome face to find his eyes were closed again, his expression tight, as though he were concentrating hard to keep his lust under control.

She kissed his neck. He inhaled sharply. She nuzzled his jaw line with her nose, kissing him softly, her fingers still gripping his turgid flesh.

The noises he made, low moans and grunts of passion, mirrored the ones she had made earlier. She liked hearing those noises coming from him. She liked even more knowing she was the cause of them.

"Move your hand over me," he said. And to demonstrate what he meant, he steered her fingers up the length of his shaft and then back down again, stroking and rubbing at a swift and steady pace.

Sabrina could feel him growing larger in her palm. She studied his features, hypnotized by the expression of joy and need and pain she saw intermingling in each shift of his lips and brows. She wanted this man with all her heart. She hurt inside to have him. He made her feel alive. He made her feel happy.

She kissed his lips. A hard and passionate kiss. One she had never given him before. He stiffened when she pressed her body against his, a brief moment of surprise, but then he kissed her back with an urgency that matched her own.

"Sabrina," he broke away from the kiss, his voice a half groan, half growl. "I can't hold it in anymore."

She released him, trailing her fingers up his sweating back and twisting her arms around his neck. Lightly, she pressed her lips to his. "So don't hold it in anymore."

She could feel him shudder against her. "Take off your clothes," he bade in a hoarse whisper. "All of your clothes."

With only a brief hesitation, she rocked back on her heels, unfastening the buttons of her blouse.

Anthony didn't touch her. His smoky eyes followed her every move, though, and it felt as if his hands were roaming all over her, his gaze was so intense.

She slipped the blouse off her shoulders, dropping it to the floor.

"Now the skirt," he commanded.

Fumbling with the laces, she unfastened the ties and pulled the skirt down her hips, yanking the garment over her knees until she was free of it.

"Take off the chemise," came the next order.

She was anxious all of a sudden. Anxious to feel Anthony moving inside her. And knowing he would soon be buried deep within her, had her quivering with pleasure. Quivering so hard, in fact, her fingers kept groping at the laces of her undergarment with ill success. The knot wasn't coming undone.

"Allow me," he offered gallantly, brushing her fingers away. A few quick turns of his wrists, and the laces were loose. "Now take it off."

Her heart was pumping in her ears. She peeled back the shoulder straps, nudging the wool fabric down her arms and over the full swell of her breasts.

"Oh, yes, Sabrina, don't stop now." He narrowed his spicy gaze to her exposed breasts, her nipples tightening under the lazy caress of his eyes. "Let me see all of you."

She shoved the undergarment down her hips and wiggled out of it. She was bare before him. And he before her.

In an intimate and possessive gesture, one that sent a shudder down her spine, he raked his smoldering gaze over her. "Lie down."

She fell back against the bed. He nestled between her legs, the cusp of his swollen shaft nudging the portal of her womanhood.

"I've dreamed of you all evening," he said in a husky whisper. "Of touching you. Of tasting you." He thrust hard into her and she gasped. "Of being inside you."

The length and thickness of him filled her, her insides throbbing with want. He moved in swift and steady plunges. She clung to him in a desperate hold, and he to her, as if they could never get enough of each other.

The tension gathered between her legs, twisting and twining, just as Anthony had promised. She could feel the ache mounting in her thighs once more. It was magical, to feel the same intense explosion of sensations so close together. She cried out in release, Anthony surrendering to his desire moments later with a roar of his own.

The candles burned low around the room. One flickering dot of light in particular caused shadows to dance across the wall. The little flame puffed and puffed, as though gasping for air. Choked at last, the glowing light vanished.

Now only three candles burned in the room. Anthony noted the changes in the shadows as each light grew weary and died. The shadows became larger and darker, slowly embracing the bed.

He tightened his hold around Sabrina. She was asleep in his arms, so still and quiet. He felt protective of her, even against the shadows, as if they were trying to snatch her away from him.

What rubbish! No one was going to take her away, least of all the shadows. She was safe with him. And he intended to keep it that way.

For how long, though? he wondered.

Forever, answered a voice.

Forever?

Yes, forever.

Anthony rubbed his cheek across the crown of her hair and kissed her head softly. Forever it would be.

Chapter 24

❧

The procession of fine-crafted Town Coaches, each emblazoned with a noble family's crest, jammed the street for more than half a mile. It would take the rest of the morning just to reach the front steps of St. James's Palace, and caged with three restless women, Anthony did his utmost to refrain from scowling.

There were yards of flowing silk all around him, and the constant cries that he should not move an inch or he risked creasing the meticulously pressed gowns. Plumes were perched in tightly coiled coiffures: long, crooked plumes, so whenever a lady bobbed her head near a window to criticize the manner in which so-and-so descended from her carriage, Anthony had his nose tickled, or his ear jabbed, or his eye poked.

Struggling against the urge to yank those blasted feathers from everyone's hair, Anthony's frayed patience was further stretched by the wails of his youngest sister, insisting his sword's sheath was tearing into the hemline of her gown. The blade happened to be nowhere near her precious apparel, but to keep peace in the angst-ridden coach, he pressed his sword hilt more firmly to his thigh after each holler of protest, until he was sure he had marked his own flesh.

Despite his best efforts, Anthony wasn't able to keep that scowl from forming across his brow. But this was his penance, he reminded himself, for unsettling Cecelia's début ball, and he'd have to suffer it in silence.

By the time their vehicle had reached the palace entrance an hour later, Anthony's teeth were gnashed, his fingers were cramped around his sword hilt, the muscles in his neck and shoulders were knotted, and his face had been thoroughly whipped with feathers.

He was bloody grateful at that point to have no more siblings, for this would be his last presentation at court.

The viscount was first to descend amidst the fanfare of curious spectators on one side of the street, and anxious debutantes and chaperones on the other. His mother was next to step out in a resplendent gown of cinnamon-brown silk, with deep white ruffs around the neck, and long net gloves that went above the elbow. Ashley made her graceful appearance in sequence, her gown a demure shade of green, the sleeves slightly puffed, her shoulders wrapped in a diaphanous, mist-green shawl of fine silk. And then came Cecelia, adorned in dove white, her heelless slipper shoes peeking out from under the cascading fabric of her empire frock. All three ladies were a stunning sight, with perfected countenances of womanly grace, offering no testament to the farrago that had raged within their coach not too long ago.

And so the whirlwind ceremony had begun. The four of them passed under the ornately carved lintel, above them the balcony perched with chattering young ladies, all scanning the arriving *ton* below. Ushered into the long gallery, they crossed the Great Hall and made their way up the grand staircase and into the corridor, where they were met by a gentleman-at-arms. His mother presented the family card and they were escorted through antechamber after antechamber after antechamber.

Anthony ground his teeth in frustration. The palace had *not* been this large when he was last here for his own presentation, he was sure of it. The regent must have added another wing in all that time.

Maintaining his brisk and steady strides, Anthony trailed after his family, paying little heed to his surroundings, anxious only to get the whole blasted affair over and done with. So engrossed was he with his apathy, he didn't bother to glance sidelong when a bright green gem flashed in the corner of his eye. But when he heard the voice—that irritating, condescending voice—his gaze snapped up to peer sharply into one of the branching corridors.

The speed at which the procession was moving did not provide Anthony with more than a second to glimpse the figure. But that second was enough for him to recognize Luther Gillingham stepping into one of the royal chambers.

Anthony dug in his heels and stalked back over to the corridor's entrance, glaring down the elongated passageway.

It was deserted.

He gave his head a brisk shake. It couldn't possibly have been Gillingham. That nefarious scoundrel in the palace?

When pigs fly.

The viscount resumed his march. He was imagining things, seeing a resemblance where there was none. That had to be it. He *was* stretched tight between his obligation to Sabrina's well-being—and the lustful joy he found in his gypsy's arms each night—and the duty he now had of shuffling his sister about London. He was downright exhausted. A hallucination, though unsettling, wasn't unreasonable.

"Watch your step," hissed Ashley.

Anthony mumbled a whispered apology for having stepped on his twin's train. In his bewildered state, he hadn't noticed the party had finally reached the outer waiting room that led to the presence chamber.

The family card was passed into the hand of another lord-in-waiting who boisterously announced the Kennington clan to Her Royal Highness.

The women curtsied, Anthony bowed. Cecelia approached the throne and kneeled before Princess Caroline, who grasped the sides of her head and kissed her brow. His sister rose, curtsied once more to the Princess of Wales, and they all four backed out of the room, never giving Her Highness their backs.

And so, inaugurated into formal society by the uncrowned queen, Cecelia was now an accepted member of the *ton*, and it was time for her to find a husband and for Anthony to find the palace door.

"Bloody hell, where is it?"

Anthony scrambled in search of his top hat. He was late. Ashley was going to peck out his eyes. She'd wring his neck, too, if she ever discovered he was tardy because he had dallied to make love to his gypsy one more time.

But he couldn't seem to help himself of late. One look at Sabrina and he had an erection to tamp down. He could fight it off most of the time, but when the ache in his groin just grew too hard to bear, he sought out the comfort of her warm, wet, womanly passage. And she welcomed him into it with a desire that rivaled his own.

Ah, there it was! Anthony spotted the elusive top hat wedged under his bed. He gave it a firm yank and made a grimace at the crumpled rim.

Damnation, what he wouldn't do for a valet at this point!

With grim determination, he proceeded to smooth out the crinkles in the hat with his thumb and forefinger, smoothing the edges as he had seen his servant do before.

Satisfied the accessory was presentable, he glanced up to find his nymph snuggled on the bed, staring down at him with apparent fascination.

"How long will you be gone?" she asked him quietly.

"I don't know. These tedious affairs can go on for hours." He propped his elbows on the edge of the bed and leaned into her. "Can I have a goodbye kiss?"

Without hesitation, she bowed her head and pressed her lips to his in a tender kiss. Anthony felt his heart tighten. God, how he . . .

What? Cared for the girl? That was apparent. Lusted after her? Without a doubt. So what else did he feel rumbling in his breast whenever he looked into her soulful blue eyes?

"Anthony?"

He stroked her mouth with the pad of his thumb. "Hmm?"

"What if I have a baby?"

The wood planks shuddered and gave way beneath his knees—or so it seemed. "You couldn't possibly know so soon?"

"Well, no, but in time, I will."

He sighed and moved his thumb to trace the regal outline of her jaw. "I'll take care of you, no matter what happens."

That vow didn't seem to appease her. "And what will become of the child?"

"We don't know that you're going to have a child."

"But if I do?"

"Then I will make sure the child wants for nothing."

"Will you want the babe?"

The image struck him, cleaved to his heart with an unremitting hold. He saw the gardens of the family's country estate in full summer bloom, the sun sinking beneath the thick crop of treetops, bathing the freshly reaped land in a warm and fiery glow. He heard the laughter of both Sabrina and the little boy, as she chased him through the hedges and the aisles of thorny pink roses. He heard the squeal of delight when mother finally snagged mischievous son, and then saw as she whirled him through the air in the protection of her loving arms. Anthony saw himself, too, standing not too far from the garden's edge, gazing on in pride and devotion.

He closed his eyes briefly, willing the unfamiliar yearning into submission. He had never wanted anything resembling a family before. He'd always wanted, in the distant future, a docile wife to provide him with a necessary heir, nothing more.

But the vision of Sabrina and her son—their son—was an impression on his heart he couldn't smooth away.

"I'll make sure the child has everything he needs."

She pulled away from him, glowering. "He or she might want a father. Will you give the child that?"

What could he say? It was impossible. Sabrina should realize that. The world held no sympathy for a social outcast, and a child born of gypsy and noble blood was destined to be just that—an anathema.

He would visit Sabrina and any child she might bear. He would offer both all earthly goods. But he could do little more. A babe of gypsy and noble blood would never be accepted into society. He couldn't change that. And he couldn't give Sabrina false hope to the contrary.

"Sabrina, I can't be a father—"

"It's all right." She scooted off the bed, poised on the other side, a yawning rift between them. "I shouldn't have asked. I understand."

"No, you don't."

"Yes, I do." Her eyes glistened under the glowing candle flame. "I'm a gypsy—a disgrace. You have to hide me and our child from sight."

"Damnation, woman, you are no disgrace!" He stalked around the bed to confront her. "Society is the disgrace . . . but I can't change society. I can't change how it will treat you or a babe."

"I know."

Words quick and toneless, she mustered up an appearance of cool composition, but he saw past her bravado. He reached for her to comfort her, but she retreated from his grasp.

"Go," she said stiffly. "You'll be late."

"Sabrina—"

"I said I understand, Anthony." Their eyes met, both stormy and passionate and full of regret. "I'm no fool.

The world is cold and cruel . . . I know firsthand." Her voice softened. She inclined her head toward the door. "Go on."

There was a sudden scratching at the door.

"It's Vincent," she said. "He'll watch over me."

Anthony withdrew, his heart anchored somewhere near his ankles. Collecting his top hat, he headed for the door, giving Sabrina one last look.

She smiled. A tender smile. A plaintive smile. A smile that made him want to tear the world apart and build it back up again—so he and Sabrina could be together.

Chapter 25

❦

The room was still, except for the infrequent snorts and coughs from a tipsy Vincent, dozing on the chestnut brown sofa. There would be no game tonight. Sabrina didn't feel like playing a game. Resigned to spending her evening in quiet contemplation, she sat curled in an armchair, legs pressed up against her chest, chin resting on her knees, eyes gazing past the sheer white drapes to the murky shadows shuffling in the street below.

Her heart was heavy. Heavy with a mix of emotions. It seemed every passionate response she had ever known was now gurgling around in her chest, and each of those passionate responses was at odds with another.

Leading the wild herd of emotions was fury. Fury that Anthony wanted to hide any child they might have in shame. Then came sorrow. Deep, soul-wringing sorrow. Sorrow at the injustice of their predicament. If she cared anything for Anthony—and she did, perhaps more than she should—then she couldn't impose upon him the very wretched state of exile. A state she was all too familiar with herself. He might also be banished from his family, his friends, if he ever made any sort of respectable life with her. And losing one's family and friends—one's life, in essence—gouged a wound so deep in the soul, one might never recover. She couldn't put Anthony through that, not when she knew how truly horrific it was.

And then she felt the fear. Fear of what was going to become of her. Not fear of losing the cottage Anthony had promised her, but the fear of emptiness she was destined to endure when she moved into that cottage all alone. If Anthony came to visit her once in a while, how much more desolate would she feel when the time came for him to leave again? She would feel happy and safe while he was with her, and miserable and frightened when he was gone. And she would feel that swing of emotion over and over again: each time he came to call on her and then each time he trotted off to rejoin his old life.

An image of her standing on the threshold of an isolated cabin, watching in tears as Anthony's wiry figure grew more distant, jabbed in her mind. A child would offset the loneliness. An adorable, bouncing child, with a spirited laugh and the same captivating green eyes of its father. But what if she wasn't going to have a babe?

Sabrina couldn't go on like this. She couldn't spend her nights with Anthony, growing closer to him, wanting him, all the while knowing she could never be with him. When the time came for them to part, her heart would shatter. She had already lost everyone else in her life, and to lose Anthony too would be an affliction she could not bear.

She should go. Yes, that's what she should do. Go away. Now. Before she wholly lost her heart to the viscount. If she left now, the pain would still be there, chewing on her heart, leaving wounds and marks and scars, but those scars would heal in time. A long time. But they would heal. If she waited to go, she might never regain her bearing or her hope or her happiness. As it was, her future was bleak and dreary. Imagine it dark and full of despair?

She could make her own way in the city. She wasn't sure of it, but she could try. She had her fortune-telling skills. Ladies always wanted to know who they would marry, how much wealth they would have, what position in society they would attain. She could offer her services for a price.

Sabrina slipped soundlessly out of her seat before she had a chance to think too greatly on the matter. Her plan was sound, for now. She would work out any chinks as they crossed her path. All she knew was that she had to get away from Anthony. Far from him. Somewhere where the memory of him could fade away. Without him tugging on her heart, she had a chance for a new life. Maybe she could make the crossing to the mainland and become part of another gypsy caravan. It wasn't unthinkable.

Heedful not to disturb Vincent's napping, she crept through the room, gathering her belongings. Once she had everything in her bag, she brushed her gaze over the spacious bedchamber, taking in one last detailed look.

How could she say goodbye to Anthony? A double meaning in that. How could she pen a note of farewell when she didn't know how to write? And how could she leave him when she cared and . . . loved him?

The realization gripped her, choked her, squeezed the breath from her lungs. It was too late. She had already lost her heart to the viscount.

It didn't matter. She still had to go. She had no future with Anthony even if he possessed her heart.

In the end, Sabrina stepped closer to the bed. She fiddled with the beaded pouch secured at her waistband and spread it open. Inside, she reached for the gnarled cluster of vines. The very vines she had found on her travels with Anthony. The very vines the faeries had tied.

She laid the charm on his pillow. Before her doubts and fears could stop her, she quickly and quietly slinked out of the room.

Anthony was in fairyland. It was the first of May. Vauxhall Gardens were open for the season. He strolled down the graveled walk, making his way back to one of the amphitheaters where his family supped. A majestic avenue stretched before him, nine hundred feet long, lined with soaring elms festooned with thousands of sparkling lamps. The gardens glowed under the brilliance of the dappled lamps: an imposed starry sky over a miniature Eden.

He doffed his hat to a passing couple, a matter of reflex rather than deference, for he scarcely observed any of the faces he saluted. Indeed, he didn't *see* a distinction between aristocrat, commoner, or masked prostitute, nodding to each figure in turn. Rather he heard his surroundings, heeding the whispers that trailed after him. Whispers of "scandal" and an "unseemly ragamuffin." As soon as he caught wind of such comments, though, he blotted them out. It was becoming a bloody encumbrance, listening to the

chortles and remarks, trying to smother the impulse to
bark out that Sabrina was no unseemly wench, ragamuffin or any other such nonsensical term, and that it
was none of their infernal business what he did with
his time and with whom.

Of course, he hadn't lost all his wits to make such a
blasted reproof, but by God, he was sorely tempted. No
one actually thought anything less of him for the scandal. "It was just Viscount Hastings being his usual
rogue self," they would all say in some form or another.
What had everyone so nonplussed was his lack of "sexual" restraint during his sister's début ball, and with a
peasant no less! *That* had the mouths of the gossip mongrels watering with delight and his clenching in deep-
rooted frustration. A sham of a tale had never bothered
him before, truly nothing his addlepated contempo-
raries spoke of concerned him in the least. But this was
different. Sabrina was being abused. And the fury billowing inside him was growing harder to maintain.

Anthony reached the end of the walk and entered the
grove: a quadrangle, enclosed by a colonnade and tight
shrubby thoroughfares. There the orchestra, an assortment of some fifty musicians, were perched in their
Gothic box, their music sheets aglow from the brilliant
lamps that bedecked their musical pit. Scattered across
the quadrangle were the supper boxes, seating anywhere from six to eight diners, all of whom gaily partook of the roasted sweetmeats, biscuits, cheesecakes
and arrack punch.

Anthony lingered around the colonnade, not quite
ready to rejoin his family. His mother, Ashley, Daniel,
and Cecelia were ensconced in their box, conversing
over some triviality he assumed, as it was only the

countess and her youngest offspring who found the discourse engaging. Ashley listened patiently, nodding her head as a filial daughter should, while her husband slapped his milk-white gloves over his knee, more content to examine the freshly hewn lawn than his in-laws.

No, Anthony definitely wasn't prepared to link up with kin just yet.

Lulled by the harmony of clashing instruments, he settled his gaze on the spinning dancers and mused. A ghostly figure began to take shape on the dance floor. Two figures: he and Sabrina. A vague shadow at first, arms and legs soon sprouted, followed by the color of their dress. He saw his gypsy, as regal as any princess, smiling up at him, her body snug in his guarded embrace. It was a subtle seduction, their dance. An idle caress here. A tantalizing brush there. Their limbs lilted to the music, their bodies more aware, more aroused, with each lambent twirl.

But the gardens would clear out at such a spectacle. A gypsy and viscount dancing together would be an unpardonable offense . . . then again, waltzing with Sabrina in his arms, the two of them the only souls in all of Vauxhall, sounded strangely wonderful.

"Well, well, Lord Hastings."

The seductive purr gnarled Anthony's insides, shattering his warm vision. He silently cursed his blasted misfortune before turning a brittle smile to the Marchioness Livingston.

Cassandra returned his smile, just as brittle—but also smug. "I didn't expect to see you here this evening. Tired of the peasant girl already?"

His expression steely, he knotted his fingers behind his back to keep them from springing to the woman's incendiary throat. "I believe you have sharpened your claws on my backside long enough, Lady Livingston. Surely there is another, more worthy, object of your affection here tonight."

Please God, let there be another, he prayed. If he had to endure this woman's company for the rest of the evening, he was going to cause an even greater scandal than the one he'd stirred on the night of his sister's début.

"My affections are secure, I assure you," she said with terse confidence, and brought the rim of her flute to her lips. But before she partook of the sparkling spirit, she arched a cinnamon brow. "And you, Lord Hastings? Who is the object of your affection?"

He wasn't daft enough to play her little game. His voice was flat, hollow, quite a feat, considering the sinister brood of emotions she was roiling. "At present, I'm afraid my affection lies with none other than my sister Cecelia."

"Performing your brotherly duty? And how goes that duty? What gentleman here is worthy of our dear Cecelia's hand?"

He glanced at her askance. It was all he permitted himself to do. If he studied her sly feminine features for any great length of time, he might find his temper bucking too wildly to restrain. And he wasn't going to embarrass his youngest sister, yet again, by uttering an improper comment. He didn't want to play chaperone for the rest of the season to make amends for any slip of the tongue. And it was that horrifying obligation, rather than any tender brotherly devotion, that kept his tongue in check.

But one look at Cassandra and he found his vision assaulted with the sight of her well-endowed breasts, hiked up and snug together in her rich, carmine red gown of shimmering satin. *Look at me*, the cleavage seemed to holler. *Look at what you lost*. But it was a loss he did not regret. He was no more tempted by the woman's ample curves now than he had been on the night of the ball. More and more of late, no female captured his carnal interest—no female save one black-haired nymph with eyes of midnight blue.

"Madam, you show a great concern for Cecelia's happiness—at present. There was a time you appeared to care not a jot about her welfare."

He was referring to the vicious tales she had spread about him and Sabrina, tarnishing Cecelia's début, and they both knew it, though the marchioness insisted on being coy. "I haven't the faintest idea of what you mean, Lord Hastings."

He refrained from any comment, toes curling in his boots.

"I would never spoil Cecelia's chance at a respectable match," she purred on. "Here, I shall prove my sincerest wish for her enduring contentment. The gardens are not devoid of respectable gentry this evening. I will help you select a prime candidate for your sister." Her eyes glazed over the motley crowd in sharp assessment. "What about Lord Kingsley? He is the son of an earl. It would be an equal and very respectable match."

"He's a mere babe—and a fop at that."

"Very well. How about Lord Barrington? He's neither babe nor fop."

"He gambles too much," was his curt return.

"A trait all well-bred gentlemen possess. Really, Anthony, poor Cecelia may never wed if you are to be her matchmaker. What about Lord Redmond?"

"Too poor."

"With five thousand a year?"

"Too poor for Cecelia," he clarified.

"Lord Handford?" she suggested next.

Anthony's gaze settled on Lord Handford. The periwinkle blue of his waistcoat jabbed him in the eyes. "Hideous taste in fashion."

"Lord Middlebrook? Osbourne? Thorncroft?"

His gaze skipped over each of the suggested candidates. "Unattractive, a miser, a greater rake than I am." With a supercilious air, he'd dismissed them all—and felt like a wretch for having done so. Here he was, judging and condemning each man for faults, real or imagined, based on society talk, without bothering to acquaint himself personally with any of them. He was doing to them just what the rest of the world was doing to Sabrina. He was deciding who was fit and worthy of his sister's hand based on appearance and gossip, not character and integrity.

"Tut, tut, Lord Hastings," came the soft admonishment. "The way you do go on about your own kind. One would think you'd rather spend your time with uncultivated peasants."

His tight lips parted in exasperation, but he hadn't the chance to make any disparaging comment. The bell clanged in the distance.

"Time for the cascade!" Cassandra flashed him a dazzling smile. "I wish you luck in your search for the perfect mate—for Cecelia."

A clump of her skirt secured in her gloved hand, she swept up the train of her gown and gracefully flounced off to observe the entertainment.

He let her go, grateful her voice was no longer chafing his ears.

Heart thudding in his breast, Anthony took in deep and even breaths, watching the supper boxes drain of diners as the crowd amassed around the cascade. It was a fleeting source of entertainment, visible for only fifteen minutes each night, its start signaled by the sound of the tolling bell. The cascade was in fact an ornate construction of a mill, complete with gushing waterfall and mill wheel. The mechanical display set into motion when water poured over the wheel, bringing the whole animated scene to glorious life. It was a delight to all eyes. Fireworks sparked and exploded in the distance, a torrent of brilliant colors showering the earth.

It was magical.

And Anthony wished with all his heart that Sabrina was there to see it with him.

Chapter 26

Lanky shadows and swirling mist did not look very inviting. It all gave Sabrina a sense of impending doom. Her doom.

But she was just being foolish, she tried to convince herself. London was a foreign land. Of course she was nervous to wend through it on her own. But she had no choice in the matter. She had to get away from Anthony. She had to try to forget him. If she didn't, her heart would be eternally chained to his. And that was a tragic fate indeed. To be tied to one man without any hope of ever being with him.

It was too much for her to bear. She had to move on. She had to take a chance at a new life. She might even come to be happy again, if she ever found another gypsy home and family to join.

Sabrina poked her nose past the front door. The street was deserted. Slowly, she peeled back the heavy oak barrier and slipped through it, closing it softly behind her.

Safe. For now.

Her bag of belongings flattened against her chest like a shield of armor, she hastily moved away from the grand dwelling, glancing down either side of the walkway to confirm she was indeed alone.

The fog licked at her boots as she made her way in the direction of the north star. It was as good a bearing as any, she figured, the city as unknown to her as it was. She might as well follow that bright light in the sky and hope it guided her to some sheltered setting.

But a shrill voice inside her head insisted she stop, turn around, and get back inside the safe haven of Anthony's home. She didn't listen to that voice, though. It had taken her much too long to sneak away undetected, and she wasn't about to risk capture by slipping back inside Anthony's abode. It was just the shadows, the silhouettes of the gloomy buildings in the distance, that rustled her fears. She was in a strange new world. A dark and threatening world. And she would have to learn to conquer her fear of it. There was no choice but to accept and get accustomed to the darkness and fog of London. Why not sooner rather than later?

The sudden thought of always being alone in such a dour place made her pause and pivot. Her eyes went to Anthony's townhouse. Soft candlelight flickered through the draped sheers of the main floor windows. Such a warm and inviting glow, she reflected, as her gaze lifted to the second level, where another streak of light spilled through Anthony's bedroom window, a beacon summoning her home.

What rubbish!

She twisted back on her heels and headed stealthily through the shadows. Anthony's home was not her home. She had to accept that. She had to move away from any illusions to the contrary.

Sabrina lowered her eyes to her booted toes, watching them disappear beneath the churning mist with each hastened step. Her heels clicked the cold pavement in faint strikes. It was so hushed, it was a wonder she didn't hear the footfalls behind her before it was too late.

A hand broke through the thick shadows, smothering her lips before she could scream. She didn't think to struggle, not once she felt the cusp of steel prick her in the back.

"Rather good of you to come out of there," rasped a harsh voice by her ear. "Saves us the trouble of having to go in after you."

Us?!

Nerves humming, Sabrina listened to the steady approach of creaking axle wheels.

Sweat was pooling to the base of her spine. On impulse, she sent her heel swinging into her assailant's shin.

The ruffian cursed, lurched in reflex, but maintained his tight grip on her face, winding the blade around her waist and wedging it just under her chin.

She sucked in a sharp breath, trying to make some room between the cold cutting edge and her neck.

"Inside," barked the voice, nudging her toward the now stationary carriage.

The door opened from the inside, revealing another kidnapper, and the driver in the top seat made the band of three complete. Three villains. She could think of no one who would want her so desperately save Gillingham.

Her eyes wide, her breathing heavy and loud, Sabrina rooted her heels in the pavement, pushing back against one assailant's chest, while trying to evade the other's reach.

But a mighty shove sent her crashing to the floor of the carriage.

She gave a piercing shriek in the seconds before a foul sack was draped over her head, suffocating her.

"Stop with the hysterics or I'll squeeze 'til you're quiet."

And to support his threat, the fiend strengthened his hold on the sack, wringing the very breath from her lungs.

Sabrina grasped frantically at his fingers, hard as rocks. Her neck felt as if it was about to snap, the pressure was so great. Before she lost all her waking senses, she stilled. Quiet as a mouse, she sat in trepidation at the cat's feet, waiting to learn whether she would live or die.

When those thick fingers loosened their grip on her throat at last, she slumped forward, weak and light-headed. Sputtering, wheezing, she gasped for precious air. But she didn't touch the sack around her head. She didn't dare. Wherever the goons were taking her, they didn't want her to see where she was going. And she'd oblige them for now. She had little strength to defend herself against three hulking brutes. If she attempted to remove the sack now, she'd likely get a smack across the head for her efforts, and as dizzy as she still was, Sabrina couldn't risk losing consciousness. She had to stay alert. She had to gather her strength. She would need both when the time came to escape.

The carriage lurched into motion and took off at a high speed.

But that chance of escape grew bleak with each passing moment. By the time the carriage had rolled to a halt, Sabrina not only had a sack still muffled around her head, but her wrists were tied as well, trussed with thick, coarse rope that chafed her skin and made it blister and bleed. The blood had stopped flowing once she'd ceased trying to wriggle free of the binds, little dry blood clusters having formed over her tender wounds.

But she didn't feel the pain. Drenched in a cold sweat, her belly in tight knots, she thought only of her one chance to escape. And it was upon her, that one chance. She sensed the door of the carriage swing wide open, the weight inside shift as one kidnapper stepped down.

It was time, she thought. Heart throbbing, she waited for one brute to grab her by the ankles and haul her out of the carriage. The second her feet touched the ground, she was off.

Bound and blindfolded, though, she didn't get very far. Within seconds, two sturdy sets of hands pinched her upper arms, bringing her to a complete stop.

But her stark fear wouldn't allow her to submit quietly, and she kicked and thrashed 'til her toes stung.

It was only when the same burly hand as before came to close around her neck and squeeze, that she gave up the struggle entirely.

"So we have ourselves a little spit-fire fiend, do we?" The harsh laughter was followed by a wallop to her behind. "That was for trying to get away." Another hard smack. "That was for all the kicks." The brute then leaned in close to whisper, "And if you try any more tricks, you'll get one hell of a beating—and you won't have your skirt for padding next time."

The tears gushed forward, followed by the hot bile rising in her chest, burning her throat.

Sabrina was dragged. She couldn't fathom to where. But with each wretched step she was forced to take, the gripping hand of despair tightened around her heart.

To offset the panic welling in her breast, her thoughts turned to Anthony. At least he was safe—for now. So long as Gillingham believed she had the locket, he would not harm the viscount.

But the ruse could not go on forever. Gillingham wanted the locket. Since she didn't have it, he would eventually go after Anthony. After all, she was seen coming out of the viscount's home. Gillingham would naturally suspect she and Anthony were cohorts in some way, concealing the locket and its secret.

A chill fell over her. The panic was back. How was she going to protect Anthony? How was she going to convince Gillingham the viscount was not involved in this whole miserable affair?

There was a cruel irony to her present predicament. Having abandoned Anthony with the intention of forgetting all about him, she'd found herself in a situation where she could do nothing else but think of him. And fret over him. And yearn to be with him.

Forget Anthony? She was a fool to have thought it was possible. How could anyone forget such a man, with eyes like shimmering gemstones and a smile to warm the soul?

Sabrina was forced to stop. Orders were shouted to

open the gates. And they were massive gates by the sound of the rattling wail of rusted hinges.

But the true horror of it all didn't nestle in her gut until she heard the moans. Moans of such misery, her heart sank to her toes in an instant.

There were so many voices, so many whimpering pleas and aching howls. The din was like a death chant, suffocating her soul.

A fierce tug at her arm urged her to move on. But she wouldn't budge. Fixing her heels to the ground, she refused to go another step.

"That beating is looking ever more promising," came the gruff threat by her ear.

Curse that devil and his promises of pain! Did he think she would simply walk into hell without a whimper of protest? She wanted to rail and brawl and cleave to the fresh spring air.

But her captors were impatient and so much stronger than her, and she was whisked through the gates without a chance to resist, stumbling over her own feet in all the haste.

The low boom of heavy wood doors closing behind her echoed throughout the room, her bones shuddering in response.

Trapped.

"This way!" came the barked order, and she was pulled along in a roughshod manner, still unable to see her surroundings.

But her other senses were working just fine, and what she picked up on made her stomach churn.

A dank stench filtered through the thick burlap sack. A bitter odor of sweat and filth.

Her nostrils flared in offense of the stinging intruder,

so foul, it made her choke and gag. She whisked her head from side to side in a desperate attempt to fan away the pungent scent. But the rapid movements only sent pain to her temples, and she was compelled to steady herself. Once she did, she took heed of the oddly soft floor beneath her feet, so slimy and clammy, she could feel the icy wetness seep through her leather boots and bite her toes.

Sabrina shivered. Her salty tears brought her some mild relief, cooling her burning cheeks, all scratched and raw from the rough burlap sack.

But tears alone could not alleviate the crushing weight that was pushing down on her chest, squeezing her heart. A weight of utter agony, as she moved further and deeper into the hell that would become her home for the next few . . . hours? Days? Weeks? She had no idea. God forbid it was years. Years of isolation and perhaps torture, until she turned into one of those groaning, howling voices herself.

Another door opened.

The hairs on her arms bristled at the sound of the whining hinges. With a swift movement, the binds at her wrists were severed, and she was shoved inside a room. A small room, for she collided with a wall almost straight away.

The sack was the first thing to go, whipped off her head, the cool air dousing her flushed features.

But in the moments it took her to get accustomed to the light, it was gone. Darkness fell over her once more, the door swinging shut with a thunderous thump.

Alone.

Sabrina just stood there, quietly staring at the thin,

luminous crack under the door frame. How she wished she was small enough to fit through that crack and scramble on to freedom.

But maybe there was another way to escape? She glanced around and quickly discovered her eyes were of little use to her. Instead, her trembling hands went up to press against the wall. A rutted and dewy stone wall. She moved along the frosty surface, dust and debris crumbling through her widespread fingers.

Nothing.

The space was so small, she had circled every inch of it in a matter of minutes and found nothing. No hole in the corner, no weakness in the door. Nothing to help her escape.

Only a small barred opening high above her head provided the room with air and a faint source of light. Too faint to be practical. A ghostly pale glow from the outdoor lanterns filtered in, but with the vines twisting around the iron bars, obscuring much of the opening, only a bare trickle of illumination made its way into the . . . what? Dungeon? Is that where she was?

Sabrina suddenly found it hard to breathe. She was, in fact, gasping for air, but she couldn't seem to get enough of it. The thought that she might remain here, penned in this squalor for the rest of her days, ripped at her heart. She would die in confinement. Her entire life up to this point had been spent wandering in open spaces. Her spirit wouldn't endure two days in captivity before it withered away.

That, in the end, might be her sole means of escape, she concluded in sorrow.

Wedging her shivering body in a corner, she sank to the soiled ground, her knees pressed up tight against her chest, her arms twisting around her legs. There she sat, rocking and cradling herself, weeping for comfort.

God, how she missed Anthony. How much she ached to be with him at this very moment. To feel secure in his tight hold. To hear his husky and soothing voice. To see his beautiful green eyes smiling at her.

Someone was coming.

Gaze darting to the thin beam of light flickering under the door frame, Sabrina saw nothing yet, only heard the poundings of quick and determined steps making their way toward her cell.

At last, shadowed feet appeared beneath the door.

She took in a long, shuddering breath.

The lock snapped and the door swung open.

She instantly knew who it was. "Gillingham."

The rangy figure stepped into the dungeon, lantern in hand. He was alone. It would take only a second to slam her shoulder into his chest, send him stumbling backward into the corridor, and make a dash for her life.

But she didn't shift from her corner. One look into his eyes, murky brown pools of mud, and she was pinned to the spot.

Sabrina knew that look well. A look of disgust and loathing. A look she had so often received from *gajos* throughout her life. But there was something more beneath his piercing stare of disdain. A reflection of cruelty. And despite his slender frame, she sensed intuitively that he would snap her in two if she tried to tackle him.

The door closed softly behind him. "So you think you know who I am, do you?" His voice was scantly above a whisper, and yet so cutting, she could feel his every word jab her in the chest. "What is in a name? It reveals nothing about one's character. It certainly doesn't tell you anything about my capabilities—which are varied indeed."

Sabrina held her breath for a moment, as he set the lantern on the ground and crouched across from her. She saw more intimately the hard lines etched across his face. Lines of long-suffering frustration. And of resolve. Invincible resolve.

"I believe you have something of mine," he said in the same low tone, eyes dropping to her neck in search of the gold locket. "Where is it?"

There was no sense in pretending ignorance. His aura of impatience and brutality convinced her it would be foolish to tangle with him. But she wasn't about to reveal the truth either. To tell him that Anthony still had the locket would mean certain death for the viscount. And she would suffer grueling torment before she let any harm come to Anthony.

"I don't have the locket anymore." And then before Gillingham could clout her for her willful response, she added hastily, "I lost it in the struggle with your men."

But he didn't look like he was going to smack her. His fingers rested quietly between his spread legs. It was the fire stirred in his copper brown eyes that had Sabrina's teeth clicking together.

"So you've lost the locket? That is a shame." With a shake of his head, he made a *tsk*ing sound. "And here I thought this was going to be a simple exchange. Your peaceful death for my locket." He heaved a sigh of feigned distress. "I see it will prove more complicated than that."

"I told you, I don't have the locket," she grit through teeth and tears alike, gathering her crumpled wool skirt tight between her fingers.

He leaned in just a smidgen to whisper, "The trouble is, I don't believe you." Then rocked back on his heels. "Now, how to nudge your memory? Let me see. A fort-night in dark isolation might help you to remember the locket's location. But unfortunately, I can't wait a fort-night. So that leaves me with a rather grisly alternative."

Sabrina's muscles, pinched taut in apprehension, jerked wildly at the sound of the sudden shrill scream that ripped through the building.

Gillingham only grinned. "That must be Lizzy. Per-haps it's time we find her a replacement? I think you'll do very nicely."

Fresh, briny tears soaked her flushed cheeks. "W-what will you do with me?"

"Well, you see, very beautiful women like yourself, who happen to find themselves locked away in here, will occasionally find themselves chained to a wall, where re-spectable gentlemen—who pay a small fee of course—are free to make merry havoc with their bodies."

Sabrina gulped back a sob. She suddenly wanted to howl like all the other miserable souls trapped in hell.

But she kept her trembling lips pressed together. She wouldn't give Gillingham the sadistic pleasure of wit-nessing her fear. And to stop from shrieking, she bit the inside of her cheek hard, the warm blood seeping through the corner of her mouth.

"Why don't I give you some time to think about my proposition?" suggested the fiend, rising to his feet, lantern in hand. "And I advise you to think carefully on the matter. A quick death is so much more appealing than torture. You have until dawn to decide."

The boom of the closing door was like a death knoll.

A choice? It was the last thing she had. For torture or

no, she would never endanger Anthony's life. That was final and absolute.

And so, the sorrow she had tried to hold back from Gillingham's eyes now came rushing forth in a torrent of silent sobs, which only she heard and in which only she drowned.

Chapter 27

Anthony found the door to his bedroom unlocked. He paused in the corridor for a moment, glancing down both ends to find it deserted, before he entered the chamber.

His eyes went straight to the bed. It was the first place he always looked for Sabrina when he entered the room. He liked the thought of her curled under the covers of his bed, waiting for him to return, ready to welcome him into her outstretched arms. And he had great need of her arms tonight. The jaunt to Vauxhall, usually a mediocre event, had been trying and downright lonely. Masses had bustled all around him, and yet he had felt so isolated. Such a solitary condition had never affected him before. He didn't like the feel of it. And there was only one soul he could think of to banish the disturbing sensation.

But where was she?

His eyes suddenly narrowed on a tiny obstruction. There laid out on his pillow was a cluster of knotted vines. The very same cluster of vines he had once seen Sabrina grapple for with a bush.

He walked over to the bedside and picked up the gnarled twigs, caressing the charm in his palm, pondering its meaning. And it must have a significant meaning for her to have left it over his pillow in plain sight like that. But what was she trying to tell him?

Better yet, *where* was she?

"Sabrina?"

Anthony scanned the room, his gaze glazing over a snoring Vincent sprawled out on the sofa.

Pocketing the vines, he headed for the privy and knocked on the door, calling for Sabrina again, but he received no response. He opened the door to find the privy empty.

Heart beating a bit faster in his breast, Anthony went around the room, stalked across it was more like it, and looked behind the curtains, in the armoire, and even under the bed.

No Sabrina.

"What the devil!?" A sound blow to the shoulder stirred a somnolent Vincent to life, who, after rubbing at his eyes, looked up to find a brooding Anthony hovering above him. "Sorry about that, old chum." Vincent gave a gaping yawn, the air filling with the scent of brandy. "Seems I fell asleep."

"Where is she, Vincent?"

Still somewhat drowsy, Vincent made the unfortunate mistake of remarking, "Who?"

But the two gripping hands at his collar, pinching his airway, quickly roused him from his lethargy. "Oh, Sabrina. She's fine. She's right here." But when he caught sight of the empty room, he amended, flustered, "I-I swear she was here when I fell asleep."

"And when did you fall asleep?" demanded Anthony, a dark glow smoldering in his gem-green eyes.

"It was just after nine o'clock."

Anthony glanced at the clock. Half past eleven. He released Vincent and marched over to his writing desk, yanking open the top drawer and rummaging through the sheaf of papers. The twinkle of gold ended his search. It was still there, the locket. So no one had come in search of it.

Anthony grabbed the locket from its hiding place, stuffing it into his inner breast pocket. He turned next to examine the door. There was no sign of a forced entry. Had someone tried to break down the door, surely even a sluggard like Vincent would have heard all the commotion.

It appeared as though the door had been opened from the inside. And that meant Sabrina had willingly unlocked it. He was certain she would never have opened the door for one of his servants, so that left him with only one other possibility to consider—Sabrina had left him.

Anthony didn't bother to change out of his formal evening wear. He only moved over to the dressing table to divest himself of his hat and gloves. He was heading out to look for his gypsy. He wasn't going to abandon her to the streets of London. Not with Gillingham still out there searching for her.

Bloody hell! What was the girl thinking to have run off like that? Surely she still wasn't afraid for her future? Had he not promised to take care of her? Didn't she trust him yet?

London was such a treacherous place for someone so inexperienced. She knew nothing of the sectors to avoid or which folks to sidestep. How would she survive? Did she even have any money with her?

Impatience was taking root in his gut. Eager to begin his search for Sabrina, Anthony didn't even think of arming himself. He only strode toward the doorway.

Vincent called after him, expressing his grief and regret, asking if Anthony needed any assistance, but Anthony said not a word in reply. He was too furious with Vincent to exchange any more words. And forgiving his best friend—his former best friend—would all depend on what condition he found Sabrina in, for it was not a question of if he would find her, but when.

Anthony paused at the foot of the stairs and glanced around the front foyer. The grandfather clock tucked against the opposite wall caught his eye. He walked over to it and removed the locket from his coat before placing it in the belly of the clock. He wanted to be sure the locket was safe. If Sabrina's disappearance *had* something to do with the locket, he would need the jewelry to get her back.

The night air was crisp. Smoke and soot clogged much of Anthony's view of the sky. Only a few stars, the very brightest in the heavens, poked through the London smog.

Anthony was on foot, having decided a carriage would roll by too quickly for him to get a good look down every alley and enclave. But he couldn't decide in which direction to go first.

He glanced to the skyline at his left. Nothing but tall buildings with dots of light peeking through draped windows. He looked over to his right and saw the exact same thing. And then something struck him. An odd and strangely familiar sensation. That he had done this all before. That somehow, he had stood on his front stoop and gazed out into the dark beyond in search of Sabrina.

His dream!

The memory came back to him. He had dreamed of this moment back in the country, the night of the storm . . . the night he had kissed Sabrina for the very first time.

He remembered that kiss now. The warmth, the desire, the peace he had felt when he'd touched his lips to hers. It had been utter bliss to feel her in his arms after such a disturbing dream. A dream in which he'd searched through the darkness for her and wasn't able to find her.

But it was only a dream, he reminded himself. This time he would find Sabrina and he would not let her go again. She would be with him forever. He'd see to it. If he had to buy her a house in London, so be it. But never again would he wonder where she was or if she was safe. Never again would he feel this pang of abandonment, as though someone had just snatched away his soul and hidden it far, far away, where he could never find it.

Anthony retrieved the knot of vines from his pocket and fingered the charm. With a brief prayer, he set out toward the north.

But he didn't get very far. He caught sight of a shadowy figure shuffling about in the servant alleyway next to his house.

Thinking it a member of his staff, but not quite sure of it, Anthony called out to the figure to identify itself.

When there was no immediate response, his impatience prompted him to demanded a reply or he would summon the authorities.

The threat seemed to do the trick. The shadow stirred, hobbling toward him, and Anthony soon realized it was not one of his servants.

An old gypsy peddler woman emerged from the darkness, leaning on her crooked cane for support.

"I was only lookin' for somewhere to sleep," she huffed. "No need to holler at me. I'm goin' on my way."

For a moment, Anthony said nothing, looking after the decrepit creature with a mixture of guilt and remorse. But then the thought struck him.

"Wait." He came round to block her path and held out the charm in his hand. "Do you know what this is?"

The old woman squinted at the knotted cluster. "Perhaps I do."

"Will you tell me its meaning?"

"Perhaps I will."

His sigh was swift and exasperating. Anthony dug into his pockets and removed all the blunt he had, stuffing it into her eager hands.

"Now will you tell me?" he all but pleaded.

First, she tucked away the coins, then her gnarled fingers went to examine the crisscrossing vines. "Where did you find it?"

"On my pillow."

"Ah, a powerful gypsy love charm."

Anthony's heart bounced at the word. "Love?" He felt as if someone had just punched him in the gut. No, that wasn't true. He felt as if someone had just plowed a horse into his gut.

"Hmm." She nodded, still studying the twisting

vines. "Very rare to find a charm the faeries have tied. You place this on the pillow of the one you love so he or she will never forget you."

Slowly, Anthony recovered the charm from the old woman's grasp. "Thank you," he murmured, and turned to walk away, his soul in turmoil.

"Do you want more charms?" her voice croaked after him. He stopped and looked back at her. "I have lots of charms." And she proceeded to open her sack and riffle through the articles within.

Anthony could hear metal clanking and wood knocking, and he put his hand up in the air to disabuse her. "No, thank you. It's not the charm that I want, but the one who gave it to me."

"But my charms are better than hers. Look here. This will bring you luck." She held up a horseshoe. "And this will protect you from the evil eye." She pulled out a polished stone.

"Her?" said Anthony, taking a step toward the old woman. "Do you know the gypsy who gave me this charm?"

"No, no. Look at this." She shoved a rabbit's foot in his face. "This will bring you—"

"Please," he interrupted her sales pitch, his request earnest. "Can you tell me where she is?"

"Don't know where she is. But I can make you any charm that you need."

"I told you, it's not the charm that I want, it's the woman."

She sighed, disenchanted, and stuffed her charms and talismans back into her leather sack, moving on. "She's gone."

Anthony fell in step beside her. "Where?"

"She left with three men. In a carriage." Her crooked finger pointed down the street. "That way."

Anthony allowed the old gypsy peddler woman to pass him. He stared down the deserted and misty street after her.

The direction of "that way" wasn't very specific, but the mention of "three men" told him exactly where he needed to look for Sabrina.

The fury in his belly wreaked havoc on his innards. Anthony let the rage consume him, let it twist and worm its way into every pocket of his soul, for if he did not, fear would surely take its place.

Sabrina had not just found herself in trouble, she had found herself in the hands of Gillingham. And what that man could do to her . . .

Spinning on his heels, Anthony bounded up the steps to his home, bellowing for his horse to be saddled.

The door to the Lion's Gate opened without delay.

Anthony was expected.

Waiting for him were two hefty blokes, who escorted him down the corridor and into Gillingham's office.

Once inside the dimly lit room, Anthony searched the shadows for Sabrina. But there sat only a scoundrel, hunched over a desk, shuffling through a stack of papers.

"Have a seat, Lord Hastings."

Anthony didn't budge, too furious to acquiesce. Two burly hands had to cup his shoulders and push him down into the chair. It was only then that Luther Gillingham abandoned his papers to observe his guest.

"Where is she?" demanded Anthony.

"Where she belongs."

He bristled at the cool reply. "And what does that mean?"

"It means she belongs to me now, and I will decide her fate."

Not bloody likely, thought Anthony. Without the locket, Gillingham wouldn't be making any decision regarding Sabrina's fate. He would. "You *will* give her back to me."

"And why would I do that?"

"Because I have the locket."

Gillingham's eyes darkened. "Yes, the locket. My locket. I wonder how it found its way into the hands of a lord and a gypsy."

"Coincidence."

"Coincidence indeed." The fiend leaned back in his chair, fingers lacing over his midriff. "I assume it was you who attacked my men in the woods a fortnight ago, thwarting their efforts to capture the gypsy? And I know you've been hiding her here in London."

"What do you mean you know . . ." His words trailed to a stop. This was no mere mishap. Sabrina hadn't just stumbled upon Gillingham and his men. The scoundrel had been watching them for some time now. She had never really been safe.

Anthony gnashed his teeth. "You have very keen eyes."

"And yet the locket still eludes me."

"Then I propose a trade."

"A trade?" echoed Gillingham, with true interest or mockery Anthony wasn't sure. Either way, the exchange was going to happen, for bravado or not, Gillingham wanted the locket as much as Anthony wanted the gypsy. And neither was going to get what the other wanted without cooperation.

"The gypsy for the locket," said Anthony, studying the unflappable scoundrel, searching for any hint of a reaction. But the man remained as stoic as ever.

"I reject such a trade."

Anthony gave him a look of genuine disbelief. "Then how do you intend to get the locket back?"

"You're going to give it to me, of course."

"Not until you give me Sabrina."

"Is that her name?" Gillingham waved a dismissive hand. "It doesn't matter. I have something of greater value than that filthy gypsy's life. Something I'm sure you'll want to have."

Those words, filthy gypsy, uttered in contempt, made Anthony cringe inwardly. Is this what Sabrina had confronted her entire life? Disparaging insults? Threats to her safety? Did she ever have any peace?

Perhaps. With her family. Is it a wonder she grieved so boundlessly at their loss? And then he had come along, promising to stick her in some isolated cottage, denying her, and any child she might bear, protection from such vile abuse. The protection she deserved. The protection he had once so earnestly wanted to give her. And when his chance to offer her that protection had come, he succumbed to the unjust morals of the *ton*, discarding fatherhood and the woman he cared for.

It was a shameful realization.

"I want nothing from you but Sabrina," said Anthony.

"What about your family honor?"

He paused to consider the man for a moment. "And what does my family's honor have to do with this?"

"Well, the Kennington name will be tarnished once you are condemned for high treason."

"Treason! Are you mad?"

Fidgeting with the emerald ring on his finger, Gillingham returned confidently, "If you refuse to surrender the locket, you will be committing treason."

"Ridiculous."

"I warn you, Lord Hastings, I have the authority to do as I will. If you want your family free from persecution, you will give me the locket."

"Horse shit. Now give me the gypsy."

The cold façade crumbled. Gillingham slammed his fists against his desk top, knocking away a number of his papers, all fluttering to the floor in disarray. "I refuse to believe you give a tinker's damn for that vagrant!"

"I don't give a rat's bloody arse what you believe," was the curt reply. "I want the girl."

"The girl must die."

"Why?" challenged Anthony, as a sickening vision invaded his thoughts; an image of Sabrina's lifeless body floating down some watery channel, and him fishing her from the channel, cradling her limp limbs in his arms, howling at his loss. He quickly dismissed the disturbing thought.

The scoundrel stood in frustration, paced before his desk, then paused to demanded: "Do you think I would risk this nation's security for a gypsy's meager life?"

"Don't be absurd." Anthony rejected the suggestion at once. "Sabrina cannot jeopardize Britain's security."

Cupping the edge of the desk, Gillingham leaned forward. "She knows what is inside the locket, doesn't she?"

Anthony didn't answer.

"Doesn't she?" Gillingham pressed him again.

"*I* know what is inside the locket. If you want a prisoner, take me."

"What if I take your family prisoner instead?" A sadistic twinkle of delight flashed through his shadowed eyes. "What if I detain your father in the tower, humiliate your mother, ravish your sisters? Condemn you all as traitors?"

The viscount bounded for the desk. But two robust arms shoved him back into his seat.

"You see, Lord Hastings?" The fiend offered a satisfying smirk. "I have a hold over you. Your family honor is far more precious to you than a mere gypsy. You're not going to reveal what's inside the locket. I would destroy you. And your blue-blooded instincts are far too sharp to let such a fate befall you. You will do whatever I tell you. But I have no such hold over the gypsy."

Anthony all but growled, "Sabrina doesn't understand what's inside the locket. She can't even read!"

"I'm not willing to take that chance." Gillingham resumed pacing. "Now that locket is rightfully mine. It was stolen from me five years ago with very sensitive information."

Sensitive information? Anthony made an internal snort. Sensitive indeed. The scoundrel wanted money. Money owed to him, no doubt, by the unfortunate resident of the address in the locket.

Well, if mere wealth was the issue, Anthony would offer it in abundance. Whatever it took to get Sabrina back.

"How much?"

Gillingham paused and quirked a brow. "Pardon?"

"How much for the girl? That is what all this nonsense over British security is all about, isn't it? A ploy for money?"

"Oh, Lord Hastings." He shook his head like a disappointed father scolding a son. "Your paltry wealth could never entice me to betray my country."

His words triggered a memory. Anthony could clearly see in his mind the arena of the Lion's Gate, the tables scattered across the main floor, the patrons clustered together at each of the tables. He quickly skimmed over the faces of the gentlemen, recalling those he knew, remembering how he had once thought the group a rather eclectic bunch. But on closer reflection, he realized there was one similarity that all the men shared. Jeremy Fielding, the third marquess of Winbourne, for instance, wasn't always the present marquess. In fact, he was never destined to become the marquess. As second born, the man was devoid of a fortune and was impelled to make the military his career. It was only after his elder brother had died in a riding accident, that Jeremy sold his commission and assumed his place as the next marquess of Winbourne.

General-Major Archibald Adington had served under Wellington himself, so it was no secret the man was associated with the army. And then there was the politician, Lord Bradford Derwent, who, though he had never served in the army, had caused quite a stir when he'd made some rather ambiguous comments in Parliament concerning the war with the French. Comments that could be construed as treasonous. And then, of course, there was Vincent, another man involved in the war.

The implication was suddenly clear—though Anthony loathed to acknowledge it. "You're a spy."

"Very good, Lord Hastings. That's one matter resolved."

Anthony didn't want to believe what he was hearing. He just wanted to pay the scoundrel a hefty sum and be done with the whole ghastly business of bargaining for another's life.

But there was one piece of evidence he could not deny, something he had seen with his own two eyes—Gillingham at court.

Anthony had tried then to dismiss what he had witnessed, convinced it was only his imagination gone wild, but he could no longer refute the obvious. No ordinary scoundrel would have that kind of access to the royal palace, and Anthony was forced to accept the man's claim, however much he deplored it.

"And the locket?" asked Anthony next.

"The locket was stolen by a French spy. A royalist supporter who wanted to see the *ancien régime* restored in France. She joined my coterie some years ago, posing as an English patriot. Her loyalty was vigorously tested, of course, but in the end it was all just a ruse. She needed the information only my spies could acquire."

"And where is she now?"

"Dead. But we never did find the locket."

Anthony settled back against his chair in a daze, all sorts of baffling thoughts swimming through his head. "Then I assume your club serves as a front for your true intentions, and yet it is filled with British officers and politicians. Why spy on *them?*"

"To ensure there are no traitors. Should I happen upon a potential radical, the individual is encouraged to conform."

"Blackmail, you mean?"

"Precisely."

"And if you find you have trapped an innocent man?"

"He is released without much fuss—though perhaps stripped of a few coins."

Anthony grumbled, "Vincent, for instance?"

"Yes, Mr. Longhurst proved to be a threat only to himself. Not much of a card player, I'm afraid." Gillingham returned to his seat. "I see all this astonishes you, Lord Hastings. With so many balls to attend and whores to bed, I'm not surprised you haven't noticed our country is in peril. Daily I hear of conspiracies to overthrow the government. There is always a riot needing to be suppressed somewhere in England. Economic and social discontent is breeding violence. The people are clamoring for a revolution of their own. And surely you, Lord Hastings, as a member of the realm, do not want to lose your head on an English version of Madame Guillotine?"

Anthony made no reply.

"I didn't think so. Now let me paint you an even grimmer picture. *Habeas corpus* has been suspended. I have the authority to throw any suspected conspirator into the jail without trial or witness. I have executed a number of would-be conspirators, and yet, despite all of my best efforts to crush any sort of revolution, the threats to the crown and government persist. Now what do you suppose would happen here in England, if the frail political stability in France were to snap and the people there were to launch another revolution?"

Anthony let out a deep breath. "England would be inspired to launch a revolution of her own."

"Precisely. Now do you see my predicament? To keep England safe, I must keep France safe, too. An arduous task. And you, Lord Hastings, are making my duty all the more difficult by withholding the locket."

Brow wrinkled, Anthony remarked, "I don't understand."

"You don't need to understand."

"You had best make me understand, because I'm not about to let you murder an innocent woman over a scrap of paper inside of a locket."

"That scrap of paper has the power to hurl France into another revolution if it falls into the wrong hands." Gillingham adjusted his neck cloth, which had twitched out of place in his earlier outburst. "The current King Louis has two warring parties inside his moderate government: the ultraroyalists, who want the *ancien régime* restored, and the ex-revolutionists. Now the ultraroyalists realize they have very little chance of restoring the old regime, unless, of course, another French king was to come along and challenge the current King Louis for power."

"But there is no other French king."

"My spy in Austria believed otherwise." Propping his elbows on the desk, Gillingham leaned forward to whisper: "Shortly before she was killed, my agent managed to smuggle an address into England. I was away from London when the message arrived. Upon my return, I learned it had been stolen, and inside the locket was gone forever the location of a small Austrian village, where a young man, believed to be King Louis XVII, resides."

Anthony quirked a brow. "But the boy-king died in prison more than twenty years ago."

"Yes, that is the official report. A victim of tuberculosis, the young Louis-Charles was buried with the rest of the royal family. But my sources tell me the boy was smuggled out of the temple by royalist sympathizers and into Austria, another youth's body left in the boy-king's place. Once safely removed from the carnage of France, Louis-Charles was to remain in seclusion until such time as he could be restored to the throne. But something went wrong. The young king's sympathizers lost all trace of their monarch. Some sympathizers were beheaded, others fled France for their lives, and little by little, knowledge of the boy-king's whereabouts disappeared.

"When the time came for the government to establish a constitutional monarchy, an heir was needed, so the boy's uncle was proclaimed King Louis XVIII. And now he is responsible for France's recovery. And I am not about to permit another king to enter France and instigate a revolution."

Anthony remained thoughtful for a moment. Such plots and conspiracies seemed too flamboyant to be true, and yet, why else would Gillingham scour the countryside for the elusive locket these last five years? And there *was* an address scribbled on the scrap of paper. That much Anthony could acknowledge.

"What will you do with the alleged king in Austria once you find him?" wondered Anthony.

"First, establish his true identity. If he is Louis-Charles, I will ensure he never makes a bid for the throne."

"You will kill him?"

"Nothing so dramatic. It is unwise to murder a monarch. Should rumor ever escape of his second death, it, too, might trigger a revolution. Better to keep Louis-Charles alive—but out of sight."

"But Sabrina need not die."

"Yes, she must!" The dark and wintry glow in his eyes was back. "I have the lives of you and your kin in the palm of my hand. I would crush you all were you ever to betray me, but I have no such hold over the gypsy."

"I will guarantee she never reveals what is inside the locket."

"Preposterous!" Down went a fist. "She is a wandering beggar. You will have no more power over her than I."

"Then I will take her as my wife."

The offer had a peculiar impact on Anthony. Here he was, demanding the right to a wife. A more unlikely situation he could not have envisioned. And yet, pure instinct had propelled him to present the solution: one Gillingham would have to accept, since Anthony would *never* accept the forfeit of Sabrina's life.

"The law will give me authority over my wife," Anthony went on to explain the credence of his plan. "You would have a hold over both of us."

But Gillingham only snorted. "You would never take a gypsy for your wife. It would be social suicide."

Anthony heard none of his skepticism. The crushing impulse to whisk Sabrina away from brutality—away from an empty death—was the sole instinct he heeded. "I will surrender the locket if you will give me the gypsy. That is the final bargain."

Gillingham leaned back in his chair with a thoughtful gaze. "So you want to marry the wench?" He paused, then, "Very well. I'll bind you to her myself. You will be married at dawn. If the secret of the locket is ever revealed, her disgrace will be yours—and your whole family's. I will have you both executed for treason. Future Kennington generations will have no hope of ever showing their faces in England again. Do you understand?"

"I understand. Now where is Sabrina?"

He paused. "In Bedlam."

Chapter 28

Bedlam. A hospital—if it could be called such a place—for the insane. Anthony had only heard tales of the appalling conditions of imprisonment. It had been a popular excursion some years back for members of the gentry to tour Bedlam and its host of "abominable creatures." But Anthony had never actually seen the grotesque surroundings for himself. With no interest in the exploitation of England's mad citizens, he'd never participated in such a tour.

But now he was going to get a private look inside the squalid walls. A sight he would never forget, he was sure.

The looming wood and iron gates stood before him. Gillingham shouted for the doors to be opened, and it wasn't long before the feeble entrance rolled back on its rusted hinges.

The putrid stench smacked him across the face the moment the gates parted. Followed by the blast of foul air came the racket. A horrid din of desperate pleas and moans and cries of pain.

It got to him. All the hapless and forgotten voices weeping for salvation. And to think, Sabrina was among the wretched lot!

A burning, twisting need to save her from a soulless existence gripped him. He wanted her in his arms. Safe. He wanted to feel the warmth of her body, inhale the sweet scent of her hair, taste the briny sweat of her skin. Everything about her thrilled him. Made him feel alive. Like his true self. Without her, he was lost. He accepted that now. She was always on his mind, dwelling in his heart. He could sense her even when she wasn't near. All he had to do was close his eyes and remember. Remember the tender touch of her fingers on his flesh, stirring within him emotions of frightening depth. Remember the sound of her spirited laughter. A sound he had heard only once. A sound he hoped to hear again and again—for the rest of his life.

Anthony entered the hospital, escorted by Gillingham and his two hulking brutes. It was dark inside, so much that a torch was needed to light the way. Anthony would have preferred to stumble through the darkness, though. The glow of torchlight only made the pervasive squalor all the more evident.

He shuddered to think of Sabrina buried within the doomed walls. Walls that seemed to stretch on toward interminable blackness. It was an endless column of stone. Oblivion. And he suddenly felt as trapped as all the inmates hollering behind locked doors.

The entourage passed the whole of Bedlam, or so it seemed. Eternal corridors going this way and that. Finally, they came to a stop in an obscure corner of the hospital.

Anthony waited for the cell door to be unlocked, his

heart thundering. If so much as a scratch was on his gypsy, he'd tear out Gillingham's throat.

The door swung back. Huddled in a nook of the tiny cell was Sabrina, quietly weeping and rocking herself for comfort.

It hit him the moment he saw her. The feeling welled in his chest until he could scarcely breathe. He loved her. Every fiber of his being thrummed with renewed energy at the sight of her.

Anthony fell to his knees, and with a rough movement, yanked his shivering gypsy into his arms, so desperate with relief to feel her snug against him once more.

"Everything will be all right," he whispered by her ear, burying his face in her mussed hair.

But she wailed all the louder for his words of comfort, as if she didn't believe him, as though she considered him some figment of her imagination come to torment her with hollow promises of well-being.

"Sabrina, it's me." He cradled her moist cheeks between his palms and pressed a hard kiss to her sweet lips. "You're safe. No one will ever hurt you again."

He drank in the briny tears from her eyes, and then smothered her back in his embrace, stroking her long, sable locks in tender regard.

Her cries crushed his soul like no other sound. He didn't know what to say or do to convince her he was really there, that she was safe at last.

"Put your arms around me," he said to her softly. "Let me take you away from here."

Without hesitation, she slipped her trembling fingers behind his neck, and gripped him with the strength of an iron leg trap.

Carefully, Anthony scooped her into his arms, relishing in the relief and pleasure he felt at holding her so close.

Sabrina's sobs dwindled once out of Bedlam. Quietly, firmly she held onto him throughout the carriage ride back to the Lion's Gate, and even up the staircase to one of the club's bedrooms.

Once inside, Anthony revealed to Gillingham the location of the hidden locket. The villain would have little trouble entering the townhouse, he was sure, and then departing without anyone the wiser.

After the confession had been made, the door was secured, and Anthony and Sabrina were left alone in the room to await their wedded union at dawn.

The bathtub was first to catch Anthony's eye. It was at the far end of the room, but he could still see the steam drifting upward from the tranquil water.

He wasn't surprised to see the tin tub. A spy like Gillingham would have to be well organized, with an eye for detail, and a couple about to recite the wedding vows should have the decency of a bath before the considerable occasion.

It was still rather difficult for Anthony to accept he would be married by morning. It usually took weeks to acquire a marriage license. One had to post the banns first. Only the archbishop of Canterbury had the power to grant a special license, allowing a couple the privilege to marry at any time. And yet, Anthony was sure he would be married come sunrise. Somehow, he suspected Gillingham would have no trouble in obtaining the archbishop's permission.

He looked down to the woman in his arms and pressed a gentle kiss to her temple. She was still shivering, and he went straight to work to rectify that.

Anthony set her down to the ground, but she maintained her tight hold on him, shifting her hands from his neck to his waist. He didn't mind the close proximity. He, too, was still getting used to the fact that she was safe, and he didn't want to take his hands off her.

"Here, let's get rid of these." Slowly, he nudged and wiggled her damp blouse off her shoulders, then pushed down her skirt. The clothes lay in a heap on the floor and he added to the pile her wool chemise and boots.

Lifting her into the warm tin tub, he helped her settle into the water. But she didn't let go of him even then. And so, Anthony knelt beside the tub, stroking her backside and whispering soothing locutions into her ear.

In time, Sabrina's tremors subsided. But he continued to caress her, to rub his hands all over her body, shooing away the cold, and at the same time, convincing himself she was really all right.

He noted the wounds at her wrists, where she'd been bound, blistered and clogged with dried blood. He went to wash away the blood, but she winced when the water touched her in such a sensitive spot.

"I'm sorry," he whispered, and lightly kissed both wounds. Yanking at the knotted neck cloth fastened around his throat, he removed the white linen fabric and tore it in half, winding each piece around one of her injured wrists. "It will heal in time," he promised, then brought her head down to rest in the groove between his neck and shoulder.

He heard her sigh, and he felt like giving a sigh of his own, but he had to ask her one important question before he could really be at ease.

"Sabrina, I know Gillingham frightened you, but did he hurt you? Did he cause you any physical pain?"

When she shook her head against his shoulder, he released a long suppressed sigh of relief. It had haunted him, the image of her being tortured in Bedlam. Though she had no prominent bruises to suggest anything dreadful had happened to her, some torments could be concealed. Ravishment for one.

He closed his eyes, banishing the hideous thought. She was safe, he reminded himself. And safe she would remain, just as soon as they were wed.

"How did you find me?"

Her voice was weak and shaky, interrupting his reflection, and he nuzzled her brow with his cheek in a soothing gesture. "I offered Gillingham a trade. The locket for you."

"Where are we then?"

"In Gillingham's club."

Her head reared up, panic flashing in her sea-blue eyes. "Why?"

"Sabrina, there is something we need to discuss." He wasn't quite sure how to broach the subject of marriage. It had always been the furthest thing from his mind. Then again, was a proposal really necessary? The matter was already decided by Gillingham. He and Sabrina were to wed. He need only inform her of her fate—their fate. Perhaps the simple truth would suffice. "I offered Gillingham a trade," he went on to say. "But the villain refused it at first. I had to give him something more than the locket before he would surrender you."

"What did you give him?"

"My word . . . that I would marry you."

Her eyes rounded. Big blue pools of disbelief. "You can't marry me. I'm a gypsy. You said you could never—"

He placed the pad of his thumb over her lips to quiet her. "Sabrina, there was no other way to assure Gillingham of your silence. As my wife, you are bound to me, and I can guarantee you will never breathe a word of the locket's secret to anyone."

"But I don't know the locket's secret."

"Yes, but Gillingham doesn't trust your word. It had to be mine. If you want to live, we must marry at dawn."

She looked away, her gaze drifting to a corner of the room. So much had happened to her in so short a time. There was a lot to take in, he knew. And after a thoughtful pause, she asked him, "What was really inside the locket?"

There it was. The dreaded question. Should he tell her the truth? He didn't want to. Revealing the locket's secret would only risk her life further. But she had lost so much because of the locket. And in the end, she deserved to know the truth; to find some measure of peace in knowing why all this had happened to her.

With a deep breath, Anthony recounted the tale of the lost boy-king. When the story was over, he cupped her chin, lifting it until their eyes met. "Now you know everything. Now you understand why we must marry."

She nodded somberly.

The next morning, Anthony and Sabrina found themselves in a local chapel, standing before the altar. Both were dressed in the crumpled clothing they had worn the night before. Both looked a little stunned to be standing before the altar and reciting the wedding vows. With Gillingham standing in as best man, and his two brutish protectors attending as witnesses, the ceremony wasn't anything like Anthony had imagined it would be.

After a few binding words, he was married to Sabrina. The minister made the sign of the cross, blessing the union, and Anthony glanced down at his side to observe his wife for the first time.

His wife.

The new Viscountess Hastings seemed somewhat bewildered at the sudden change in her circumstance. Anthony was feeling that bewilderment himself.

The formal announcement of their nuptials would appear in the next printing of the *Times*. Gillingham's doing, of course. For the present, however, two dozen cards had been sent out, all hand delivered across the city to only the most famed gossips, proclaiming the couple's attachment. Soon all of London would know about the marriage.

The deed was done. Sabrina was safe from Gillingham forever. Now Anthony need only explain all this to his family.

Chapter 29

The Viscountess Hastings stood alone in the bedchamber, her mind a whirl.

A gypsy wedded to a *gajo*. It caused her own brow to raise in wonder. Not two days ago, Anthony had vowed he could never be with her because of her gypsy blood. And now he had married her?

Bafflement soon gave way to a ticklish hope. Hope for her future. One that didn't look quite so bleak anymore. She had married the man she loved. That alone was cause for great joy, for she had never believed her wants would ever come to pass.

But something else gave her vast hope. Anthony had saved her life. In so doing, he'd defied a sacred canon: to never marry an outsider. She could think of only one reason why he would flout convention and risk the wrath of his family and friends. He must love her, too.

Sabrina glanced over to the bed. Her eyes searched the covers for any sign of the charm, but she saw nothing. The knotted cluster of vines was gone. Had An-

344

thony found the charm? Or had a servant mistaken it for trash and tossed it away? She wished she could ask her husband what had happened to it. She wished she could tell him everything that was swimming around in her heart.

But Anthony wasn't home. He had gone to inform his family of his recent nuptials. And it was her distress over that impending encounter that had her pacing.

She could do little else but wait. Wait and pray that Anthony's confrontation with his father would not be as brutal as her own had been.

Anthony made his way through the bustling London crowd. He needed to expend the energy burning inside him. A brisk walk to the West End was an agreeable tack.

The stroll also provided him with an opportunity to mull over in his mind what he was going to say to his parents once he arrived at their door. How to explain why he had married a gypsy? The truth was unthinkable. He was sworn to silence about the locket and all the trouble it had caused, but he did need to come up with some sort of reasonable explanation.

That he loved Sabrina wouldn't matter a fig to anyone. He could already hear his father's bellows, demanding to know why he hadn't just made the girl his mistress instead of his wife. And it was to that question Anthony was in want of an adequate answer.

His quick stride suddenly slowed to a more leisurely jaunt. It was not just the reactions of his parents he had to dread. Gossip amongst the *ton* was going to be in a state of frenzy. Sabrina was going to be abused by every haughty patrician in the city, the country, too. That she now bore the title of viscountess would make nary a difference to anyone. She would be given the cut direct. She would become the social pariah he had feared. And there was scant he could do to avoid any of it.

London wasn't even privy to his wife's true heritage—yet. The announcement in the wedding cards only stated Lord Hastings, heir to the Wenhem title and estate, had married Sabrina Kallos. There was no further detail given. But her name alone signified she was neither a member of the gentry nor had she any English blood. And an outsider was rarely, if ever, accepted into the fold of the British aristocracy.

Anthony approached the West End. As he neared his parent's home, his pensive thoughts gave way to ones of agitation. It was bloody ridiculous that he had to go through this charade. That he had to confess to his parents his supposed misdeeds like some rowdy schoolboy. So he had married the woman he loved. Was England really going to fall apart because of it? Granted he had been coerced into the marriage, but he wasn't adverse to the way things had turned out. Having Sabrina with him for the rest of his days brought a warm feeling to his heart and a sense of peace he had never felt before. It felt *right* to be with her. It always had. He'd just never admitted it to himself before—or to her. But he would remedy that. Just as soon as he returned home he would reveal to Sabrina his true feelings for her.

Anthony sighed inwardly. For all his wealth and prestige, neither could buy him true freedom. The freedom to do as he willed. Sabrina had been right. There was a chain around his neck. And he had not noticed how tight it was until now.

An old acquaintance approached from the other end of the street, and Anthony gave a nod in acknowledgment, but the gentleman walked past him without reciprocating the greeting. A simple misunderstanding, Anthony concluded. The man obviously hadn't seen him. But then, when Anthony noticed Lady Stanton drag her daughter over to the other side of the street, rather than pass him by, he realized something was dreadfully wrong.

He didn't have too long to dwell on it, though. Baffled and restless, Anthony finally reached the front steps of his parents' opulent townhouse. He was admitted by the butler and informed the earl was expecting him in the study.

Anthony suddenly felt his neck cloth was too tight, and he tugged at the ruffled linen to loosen its grip on his throat.

But his advance toward the study was curtailed by a wild shriek and a hard smack across the back.

Whirling around, Anthony caught Cecelia's hand in mid-air before she had a chance to clout him.

"How could you?!" she cried.

It had begun.

Anthony rallied up his inner strength and ushered Cecelia into an adjacent parlor, closing the door behind them to bar the servants any view of the row that was about to commence.

His mother was already in the room. She had her back to him, and said not a word, only stared ahead through the window at the brooding storm clouds gathering strength in the distance.

Anthony's gaze shifted from his mother to Cecelia.

He saw more than plump tears in his sister's emerald eyes. He saw . . . hopelessness.

Anthony could feel it inside him, a gnawing sense of guilt. To save one life he had ruined another. And now he had to accept the consequences of what he had done.

"How could you do this to me?" Cecelia's weeping garbled some of her words, but he understood her grief plain enough. "I'm ruined!"

"That isn't true," he assured her, not certain he had the authority to make such a claim, but he wasn't going to watch his sister fall apart before his very eyes, so he had to say something of comfort. "The season will go on for you."

"This season is beyond repair, as is the rest of my life." Her dress and petticoat swished at her abrupt twirl, as she stalked over to a nearby table to collect a copy of the wedding card.

The sight of the tear-stained announcement of his nuptials, the smeared ink running down the card like so many broken dreams, wrenched at his gut.

"Who is she?" Cecelia demanded, pointing her trembling finger to the announcement. "Who did you marry? Not that same peasant you were seen with on the night of my début ball, is it?"

"Cecelia—"

"Is it?" she cried.

When he gave no answer, the card was tossed to the floor, and two dainty feet danced all over the announcement in a fit of rage and sorrow.

"How could you do this to me?" she wailed again in disbelief, her dancing fit at an end. "Who will want me now?" she whined with the voice of a little child. "No one will ever marry me. Our family is disgraced. I will die an old, lonely maid."

She suddenly screamed and lunged for him again. This time, Anthony didn't try to stop her, but let her clout him soundly. "Do you hate me that much?" Her eyes burned with a dark energy he had never seen before. "You have never liked me, you were always closer with Ashley, but do you really hate me so much? Enough to destroy my life? If you wanted to be an eccentric fool and marry some peasant, why couldn't you have waited until *after* I was wed? *Why?!*"

Anthony could not explain to her the reason he had come up with. To his father, surely, but not to Cecelia. He had nothing to offer her but an apology. He received a firm smack for it.

"You're sorry," she imitated with scorn. "My life is in tatters thanks to you and you're sorry." Another smack.

This time, the countess turned away from the window and approached her hysterical daughter, folding the howling girl in her arms.

She gave her son a cold and piercing look, and without any affection in her voice, informed him his father was waiting for him in the study and that he should not keep the earl waiting.

Anthony quietly withdrew from the room, Cecelia's sobs following him out the door.

He was numb. He couldn't feel anything right down to his toes. He had known this was going to be difficult, but he had not expected it to be *this* difficult.

Truthfully, he hadn't thought very much about his family and the response they would have to his nuptials. He had thought only of saving Sabrina's life. And he had no regret in that regard.

Yet the devastation in his sister's eyes, the cold and lifeless stare of his mother was a blow he had not been prepared for.

And there was more to come. Anthony had reached the entrance to his father's study. He felt awkward having to knock. He had done it countless time before, but this time was different. This time, for the first time, he felt as if he would not be welcomed by his father.

Anthony opened the door and stepped into the study. The earl was seated at his desk, his hands resting on his cane, gazing pensively out the window. He did not acknowledge his son when he entered the room, but continued to stare ahead.

Anthony did not interrupt him. He waited for his father to say the first words. And it took a while for the earl to abandon his meditation and confront his son.

"Sit down, Anthony."

He did as his father requested.

The earl kept his eyes averted from his son's while he spoke. "You understand you have caused this family much grief."

"Yes, I know, Father."

"Then may I ask the reason why?"

Anthony took in a deep breath. There was no sufficient answer he could give. The deed was done. The reason mattered not, but it was a matter of formality to have some explanation given.

"I compromised the girl," said Anthony. "I felt it my responsibility to do the honorable thing."

That word, responsibility, seemed to trigger something within his father, who twitched slightly before he lifted his gaze to finally meet his son's. And the disappointment Anthony saw reflecting back at him was heart wrenching.

"You have never done the *responsible* thing before and married one of your mistresses. Why this one?"

"She was an innocent, unlike the others."

"I see." The earl swiveled in his chair and looked back toward the window. "You have certainly chosen an inopportune moment in which to demonstrate your sense of responsibility. Here, I have begged you for years to take up the reins of the estate, and to do your filial duty as my heir, but I see my requests meant nothing to you."

Anthony felt the tension in his chest mounting. The hurt in his father's voice was like a cutting sword to his heart. But he could not tell the man the truth. Not a soul could ever know that for once in his life, he *had* done something responsible by saving his gypsy's life.

"Well, something must be done, you understand?" The earl moved a hand toward his eye. Anthony thought he spotted the glistening of a tear, but it was gone before he could get a really good look.

That his father might be shedding tears was more than he could bear. He had never seen his proud father cry. And the thought that something he had done could reduce the earl to such a state was suffocating.

"Cecelia needs to be protected," said the earl gravely. "We will head back to the country for the remainder of the season. Perhaps, in a year or two, we will return to London, providing the scandal has settled somewhat, and try to launch her début once more. God willing, she will still be able to make a respectable match and find some happiness."

Anthony flinched at the word "happiness." The very thing he may have denied his sister from ever finding.

"You, of course, are not permitted to return."

A bemused expression crossed over the viscount's face. "What do you mean?"

The earl's steady gaze remained on the window. "You are not welcomed here or at the estate in Sussex."

"For how long?"

"For so long as I live."

Anthony got up from his chair, leapt from it was more like it. "Banishment? I don't believe you would do that to me."

"And I never believed you could do this to me. So you see, we are both disappointed in the other."

In brisk, long strides, Anthony took to pacing, his fingers twined and locked behind his back. "In a few years, the gossip will die down. A new scandal will erupt and captivate the *ton*. Cecelia will find herself a good husband and all will be well again. Banishing me isn't necessary."

The earl's golden-tipped cane slammed into the floorboards, resounding throughout the room. "You have married a worthless wench with no breeding or fortune. You have disgraced the Kennington name. Banishment is indeed necessary. If I had my way, I would disinherit you, but the estate is entailed to my first-born son. That being the case, I will not welcome your *wife* into my home so long as I live. Nor will I admit you or any offspring you might have. I never want to meet your heir, Anthony. I never want to look upon his face and be reminded of the shame which you have brought upon me." The earl took in a deep, ragged breath before he resumed. "In addition, your allowance is hereby severed. What funds you possess are yours to keep. Your townhouse in London belongs to you still, but if you have any measure of respect remaining for your youngest sister, you will never venture near this city so long as she remains unwed."

Anthony couldn't believe what he was hearing. He could scarcely utter the next question past his lips. "And where do you expect me to live?"

"There is the old manor house in Northampton, once belonging to your mother's father. It was entrusted to you on your twenty-first year—not that you've ever shown an inkling of interest in the management of the property. I've already sent word to the land steward there. He and a scant number of servants are expecting you. You may reside within the manor's walls until my death, when, at such time, the Wenhem estate will pass on to you."

The cold, businesslike tone of his father squeezed at his heart. "You cannot mean this."

"I suggest you pack up your London household and depart as soon as possible. Don't give the gossip mongers more fuel to keep this atrocious tale alive. The quicker you depart, the quicker the talk will burn out."

Banishment? To never see his family again? Surely his father was just angry and overreacting. He couldn't mean to cast him away like this.

Anthony tore off the blasted neck cloth that was suffocating him, and wound it around his palm instead, his fingers turning a bright crimson red.

"Father—"

"Do not try to contact me again. If you have any business regarding the estate, contact my land steward or my lawyer." The earl's hard voice dwindled slightly as he ordered, "Now leave."

Anthony was torn. He wanted to stay and fight with his father, to make the man see reason. But the earl's hands were visibly trembling. He was trying to keep his emotions under a tight hold, and Anthony feared, if he pushed his father any further, those emotions would burst and trigger an apoplexy.

In the end, he held back what he wanted to say, and, somewhat dazed, left the study in long, fluid strides.

Banishment? The word had such a deafening ring to it. A sense of finality where Anthony saw none. His family was among the living. To cut himself off from them as though they were dead was unthinkable. True, he had not always been on good terms with all his kin, but he could not imagine losing them all forever.

He *would* try to reconcile with his father. Anthony was adamant. He would give the aging earl some time to recover from the surprise of what had happened, and then he would strike up communications. A letter at first. Perhaps a brief visit during the holidays. Surely by then the anger and hurt would have diminished somewhat.

Anthony wasn't entirely certain his conviction wasn't misplaced, but he held onto the hope nonetheless, that one day his family would forgive him.

The sight of a pale Ashley standing at the far end of the corridor roused within Anthony a brutal instinct for survival. If *she* abandoned him too, he would be lost. It would break his heart to never see her or his beloved nieces again.

"Don't say it!" Anthony barked the moment he reached her and she opened her mouth to speak. "Don't you dare tell me you will never see me again!"

A sob bubbled to the tip of her tongue, and she bit her trembling bottom lip to quell the sound of her sorrow. "I have my girls to think of, Anthony."

He grabbed her by the upper arms. "The girls are too young to bear any scars from this event. By the time they reach marriageable age, this will all be forgotten."

"But your wife will always be a gypsy. That will never change. Not even in fifteen years. Oh, why did you do it, Anthony?"

"Ash, please, trust me. I had to do it. There was no other way to save . . ."

"To save what? Our family name? Your pride? Did you think of any of these things before you married the girl? Were you foxed, is that it? There is a way to end the marriage, Anthony. A procedure you could initiate."

"No." He released his hold on her arms. He was numb and cold and he couldn't take much more of this. "I have to go, Ashley. But I *will* see you again."

He moved toward the entrance, not sure he had the strength to make it back to his own townhouse. His brother-in-law met him at the door rather than the butler. Daniel held out his hand, which Anthony silently accepted.

"Give it some time," Daniel said in a hushed voice. "It might all work out in the end. I don't know why you did it, but I'm sure you had your reason."

Anthony mustered a silent nod of appreciation before he left the building. He remained on the front stoop for a while, just staring at the storm clouds brewing in the distance.

As the fog lifted in his mind, he became more aware of the passing whispers and looks of disdain.

He had known Sabrina would be subjected to those very looks and whispers, but he had not anticipated he would be the recipient of them as well.

By taking an outsider for his wife, he had become an outsider himself.

And Anthony wasn't so sure he could live with that.

Dark clouds whirled, as a fork of blue light stabbed into the earth, followed by the distant groan of thunder.

Sabrina was traveling to her new home. And she had been traveling to it in silence. Anthony spoke scarce a word to her, with reason, though. The confrontation with his family had been ghastly. That they'd abandoned London in such haste told her so plain enough.

She looked over at her husband. A brooding faerie king, lost, and bewildered at his loss. He had once had everything and everyone at his beck and call, and now such certainty was gone.

Her heart ached for him. She understood the turmoil swirling in his soul. She understood the time he'd need to come to terms with all that he had lost. She, too, had fretted in silence. Anthony was no different in that respect. And yet, he *was* different.

Something about him had changed. Perhaps his grief had altered him. Or perhaps it was just the jitters of a naïve wife making her imagine such a thing.

But in truth, that fledging hope of marital joy she had nurtured in her heart seemed to be dwindling.

Such tenderness he had shown her on the night before their wedding. Such devotion . . . such love. Had it all been in her mind? She'd not had a kind look from him all day, nor a word of encouragement. Just one little gesture was all she needed to know everything was going to be all right.

But her husband had withdrawn into his woe, leaving her to fuss and obsess over the same redundant thought: *He loathes me*.

She tried to dismiss the terrible notion. After all, this was the man she loved. This was the man she was sure loved her in return—in part anyway. He had given up so much for her. Surely it was done out of some feeling of love? Surely love could not dwindle and die so quickly?

But one event repeated itself over and over again in her mind, rousing her doubt. Prior to their leaving London, Vincent had come to call on Anthony, desperate to see his best friend. But Anthony had barred him from the townhouse.

Now Sabrina was left with the irksome task of trying to figure out why Anthony had turned so cruelly against his dearest comrade. Was the viscount merely miffed at Vincent's lack of supervision on the night she was abducted? Or was Anthony furious that Vincent's carelessness had eventually led to his marriage?

She didn't want to dwell on it. But she knew it might be true. Anthony might regret having married her. And if it was so, that hope for a salvaged future would be nothing more than a wistful memory.

The horses cantered at a steady gait, turning a bend and clearing a wooded grove. In a lush valley, a small manor house came into view. Well, small in comparison to Anthony's other country estate. But it was still a good deal grander than anything Sabrina had ever imagined she would end up living in.

The home was quaint in appearance, two levels high

and built entirely of stone. The greenery blanketing the walls was thick, concealing much of the rugged gray stone beneath, which occasionally peaked through a sparse patch of ivy.

A pepper of servants lined up in front of the house, seven to be exact. The ladies were smoothing their aprons, the men fingering their lapels, and such fussing prompted Sabrina to do a little grooming of her own.

The carriage rolled to a halt. Anthony was first to step down, leaving her inside the vehicle to comb her fidgety fingers through her mussed hair. Next, she tended to the crinkles in her skirt, then checked to make sure her boots weren't too muddy.

Satisfied she was presentable, Sabrina took a hesitant, and rather uneven, step out of the carriage. All eyes went to her. Big round eyes of astonishment.

It shouldn't bother her, being gawked at in such a manner. It wasn't the first time eyes had broadened upon hearing *her* announced as the new viscountess.

But it did bother her. It made her feel an imposter. As if she had no earthly or divine claim to be Anthony's wife.

"Mrs. Chadwick," said Anthony, a cool and official tone to his voice. "As head housekeeper, you will oversee the servants until my butler arrives from London with the remainder of my belongings."

Mrs. Chadwick gave a deep curtsy. "Aye, my lord."

"You will also report all domestic matters to Lady Hastings, and follow her explicit directions in the governing of the household."

Mrs. Chadwick gave the flustered Lady Hastings a critical eye, but then nodded in obedience.

Sabrina, on the other hand, wasn't so agreeable. Her

heart was in her throat. She knew nothing of running a household. She had never even lived in a house before! It was her custom to do everything for herself, from laundry to cooking to cleaning. She couldn't ask anyone else to do it for her, nevertheless order someone about. She was better qualified to *be* one of the servants, not govern them. And that disparaging truth had her opening her mouth to protest such an arrangement.

But Anthony had one more order to dictate.

"And Mrs. Chadwick, see to it that the local seamstress is summoned in the morning. Lady Hastings is in dire need of apparel befitting a viscountess."

Sabrina closed her mouth, her heart sinking to her toes.

Chapter 30

〜⌒◯◯⌒〜

The flames spit and crackled, puffing warm air into the spacious room. Sabrina crouched before the fire, her back to the window and the wild spring storm soaking the land beyond. In her hand she held a towel, wrapped around the handle of an iron pot. And in that iron pot bubbled some sugar, slowly melting to the golden thickness of honey.

At the sound of a cough and the shuffling of papers, her eyes abandoned the snapping flames in favor of the restless man shifting only a few feet away from her.

Anthony was engrossed with a stack of calculations. A list of past market sales, of tenant names and rent dues, of servant wages and household expenses. He appeared lost. But she could offer him no help. She could gather meadow grass and twist it into rope. She could spot a prize thoroughbred in a crowd of endless studs. She could even grind a dead lizard into powder and turn that powder into a magical potion. But what good would all those skills do her here?

Another garbled cough drifted through the room. For much of the evening, Anthony's cough grew more frequent and more intense. Back in London, after the visit with his parents, a fierce spring storm had lashed out at him, and ever since, he had shown signs of an approaching sickness.

On that matter, at least, she was quick to find a remedy.

Sabrina poured the melted sugar into a glass, then added a few tablespoons of honey, followed by some water. Stirring the concoction to a gooey consistency, she abandoned the hearth and walked over to the desk, setting the glass on the parchment-littered surface.

"Drink this," she instructed.

Anthony gave the glass a curious inspection. "What is it?"

"A remedy for the cough."

After a brief pause, he shrugged, and drank down part of the potion. Resting the half empty glass on the desk, he returned to his work, surveying the stack of papers in front of him.

Sabrina pretended his stiff demeanor didn't mean anything, that Anthony was just brooding and she should let him brood in peace, give him some time to get adjusted to his new life—with her. But despite her attempts to rationalize his cold behavior, the gnawing fear in her chest intensified, cleaved to her heart with a vicious hold.

He blames me for the loss of his family, his friends . . . his life.

Her fingers curled into her palms. What right did he have to blame her? *She* had lost everyone dear to her, too. Or did her grief and suffering mean nothing because she was a gypsy?

Sabrina gave a weary sigh. There was a dark cloud of misfortune hovering above her head, always threatening to shower her with another tragedy. She was tired of it. It was time she moved out from under it.

For far too long she had trusted the members of her kin to take care of her. For far too long she had accepted whatever fate had thrown her way. Her wants, her dreams were always a nuisance, conflicting with her ordained destiny.

But now there was neither kin nor destiny to determine the course of her life. Now there was only her heart to guide her. And her heart yearned to fight for Anthony. To claw and to battle through his doubt and fear, to yank him from his oppressive grief. It was time she did what she wanted. And what she wanted was her husband's heart.

"It's late," she said softly, and placed a gentle hand on his wrist. "Why don't you put the papers away until morning?"

"Go on to bed." He shifted his hand, reaching for another leaf of paper. "I have a lot of work to do."

As did she. It would not be easy dragging her husband from his melancholy. He was evidently resistant to any such attempt.

But it would be a worthy fight.

"I don't know which bedroom is ours," she said, hoping to draw him out of the study; hoping a night's rest, together in each other's arms, might offset the sorrow in his heart and bring a new sense of hope to their marriage.

For a moment, Anthony abandoned the study of his papers, lifting his eyes to meet hers. And they were such dark eyes, shadowed by the flicker of candle flame. "Your room is at the end of the corridor. Ask the housekeeper to show you the way."

And he was back to his examination of property taxes and estate dues.

Was that it? she wondered. One abrupt announcement of their separate bedrooms and she was to accept their wedded life was over? That he no longer cared anything for her?

Not bloody likely.

She drew in her grief like a whirlpool would a lost ship, her features settling into peaceful repose.

Lightning engulfed the room, and her eyes briefly lit upon a bright red cushion at the far end of the study.

She headed for it, her fright of storms replaced with anger. Red-hot anger. Anger that she could lose the most precious being in her life because of his own stubbornness.

The pillow sailed through the air. It missed its intended target—Anthony's head—but landed within a few feet of him, and so still accomplished its goal, which was to gain the viscount's attention.

"Something troubling you?" he drawled.

"Why did you marry me?"

A light was back in his eyes. A fire. Something other than empty pain. It was a relief to see, even if the fire was directed at her.

"Do you think me such a blackguard that I would allow an innocent woman to be murdered?" he said.

"Duty? Mere duty made you save my life?"

"What else?"

What else indeed. He had forsaken his privileged existence out of a sense of obligation? She didn't believe it. She didn't *want* to believe it.

Her own eyes sparked with fire. "So what do you plan to do with me now?"

"I don't *plan* on doing anything with you."

She made a prominent noise of disbelief, something akin to a snort and scoff. "You've given me command of the servants, you're going to take away my clothes in the morning and replace them with *gaji* rags. And you want me to believe you're not planning anything?"

The papers slammed onto the desk. He was out of his chair and moving toward her. The flames hissed and danced as he sauntered past the hearth, his large body stirring up a breeze, fanning the dwindling fire to life.

"Those *gaji* rags are the attire of a viscountess," he said with unsteady calm, coming to a stop only inches away from her. "Command of the household staff is the duty of a viscountess. *You* are a viscountess."

"No, I'm not!" She fanned out her skirt. "This is who I am, Anthony. A gypsy. I don't *know* how to be a viscountess. And changing me into one won't bring your family back. They will never accept me no matter what clothes I wear or what chores you give me. I will always be an outsider."

Something flashed in his emerald eyes. A sense of understanding? Or of pain? Or perhaps a combination of the two? She couldn't tell. And she didn't have a chance to ask him.

He turned away from her.

She reached out for him. He stiffened at her touch and she withdrew her hand from his arm.

"Anthony, I know what you're feeling." She moved to face him, his brooding features aglow from the bouncing firelight. "I lost my family, too. But you still have a home." And her hands swept over the room to indicate her point.

His voice dropped to a rough whisper. "A house without a family is no home. Those were your words."

"I could be your family."

She wasn't sure he had heard her, she had uttered the proposition so softly. But then his eyes lighted on her, a rather stunned pair of eyes, and she realized he had heard her clearly. And it was the truth. It was all she had ever wanted from him. A life together. A family.

She'd been aware of that desire for a long time now, ever since the day they had talked of faeries and nymphs. It was then she had realized how much she wanted to be with Anthony. It was then she had bemoaned how impossible it was to be with the man she truly wanted, since neither of their worlds would accept them as a couple.

But now, both rejected, they had a chance to build their own world. One with no social bonds. One where they could find joy again.

Sabrina rushed on with her argument, wanting Anthony to see he had not lost everything after all. "You still have me and you still have a true friend."

The thoughtful look he gave her quickly turned to one of confusion. "Who?"

"Vincent."

The rough edge to his voice was back, any wistful contemplation wiped clear off his face. "Don't mention that scoundrel's name."

"That scoundrel is more of a friend to you than any lofty *gajo* in London. That scoundrel came to your door, hoping to see you and make amends. He *wants* to remain your friend. You're a disgrace because you married me. I'm no fool to that truth. But by staying at your side, Vincent risks your disgrace becoming his, yet he still won't abandon you."

"That scoundrel also fell asleep and allowed this whole blasted—"

Anthony looked away from her again, but this time she grabbed him by the arm and pulled him back in her direction. "He allowed what? This whole blasted tragedy to occur?"

It was a twisting blow to her gut, hearing the truth, from her own lips no less, of what she had suspected—and dreaded—all along. Anthony *did* regret marrying her. He *did* regret ever having saved her life and forsaken his own.

She let go of his arm, trembling, fighting against the suffocating urge to surrender to her grief. There was no hope for them if he loathed her. There was no hope for them if he regretted the day he had rescued her from Bedlam.

"Don't be angry with Vincent because you find yourself wedded to me," she said, voice cracking. "Be angry with yourself instead. If you didn't want to make the sacrifice, you should have left me in that dungeon to die. Then we would both be free of this hell."

And before her knees gave way under the pressure of her splintering heart, she walked out of the room.

Anthony sat alone in the darkened study. Save for the occasional spat of lightning and the low burning embers of the fire, there was little to distract him from the haunting words of his wife.

If you didn't want to make the sacrifice . . .

He'd certainly wanted to make *a* sacrifice. His bachelorhood for Sabrina's life had seemed a paltry forfeit. Exile from his family was a much greater price to pay.

He reached for the cough syrup, drinking the last of the soothing liquid. His parched throat coated, he was feeling much better. And that had him thinking about how much better he had felt, in body and soul alike, since the day he had met Sabrina. She had changed his life, made him realize he could be more than just a rogue. She made him want things he had never wanted before, like a family of his own.

Anthony burrowed into his pocket, withdrawing a knotted cluster of vines. He fingered the charm, given to him with love. He thought of a pair of stormy blue eyes, of a gentle hand reaching out for him in trust and hope. And then he thought of an existence apart from those blue eyes and tender touch, and he realized it would be true hell, a life without Sabrina.

A peace settled over him. A kind of acceptance. He had his gypsy. Without her, there was nothing. No joy. No hope for the future. And as much as it hurt to lose his kin, it was unfair of him to take his grief and frustration out on her. She had lost her family, too. She understood better than anyone what he was feeling. And she was the only one who could take away his loneliness.

You still have me, echoed her words in his mind.

But he had to wonder about that now. After the abysmal way he had just treated his wife, he wasn't so sure she would be willing to forgive him.

Chapter 31

Dawn broke. Pale blue light streamed in through the unmasked window, rousing Sabrina from a deep and troubled sleep.

She had dreamed of Anthony last night, that he had come to her room and kissed her softly on the cheek. The wonderful, loving gesture had warmed her to the very depth of her soul. And she wished with all her heart it had not been a dream.

Opening her eyes, she gazed out the window toward the breaking dawn . . . but a gnarled cluster of vines obscured much of her view.

Sabrina squinted at the knotted bundle, the very same charm she had once left on Anthony's pillow.

Her heart pattered. So Anthony had had it all along. But why give it back to her?

Wait! If Anthony had snuck into her room to give her the charm, then that tender kiss . . . might not have been a dream.

A mixture of hope and dread tangled up in her belly.

Hope for a future not lost after all. And dread that her newfound hope might be dashed yet again. Anthony had given her the vines. But what did it mean? To him anyway. He knew not the tale of the faeries. Not really. He knew the faeries had tied the knots, but he didn't know why. He didn't know it was a love charm.

Perhaps he just wanted to return it to her, to do away with any memory of her . . . Or perhaps he was trying to tell her something? Something more promising?

The cluster in hand, Sabrina rolled off the bed and sprinted for the door. Dressed in the same clothes she had worn the previous day, she didn't pause to change or even comb through her tousled locks. Instead, she headed straight for the stairs and clamored down the wooden steps.

Hailing the housekeeper, eager to know where Anthony had gone, she was informed the master was out in the garden.

But the blasted manor had one too many passages, and it took Sabrina a few minutes to wander through the unfamiliar causeways before she finally located one of the doors leading out to the estate.

Once on the green, her heart was in her throat. She scurried around the exterior of the house, scanning the property for a sign of her husband.

It didn't take her very long to spot the lone figure perched on a boulder near a cluster of young trees. Anthony leafed through a small book nestled in the palms of his hands, oblivious to her company.

Eyes longingly fixed to the man she loved with every thread of her soul, Sabrina remained rooted to the spot. It squeezed her heart, pinched her lungs, the yearning to be with her husband, to share in a wonderful life with him. She thought she had lost all chance of such a fate, but now . . .

She took in a deep breath. *Don't be foolish*, she chastised herself. *Don't expect all your dreams to come true.* One night it appeared Anthony had loved her, the next night it appeared he had not. Now he loved her again? It was best she guard her heart for a time, until she discovered exactly what Anthony had meant by leaving her the charm.

Her heartbeats savage, she gripped the vines, each step hesitant as she approached Anthony from behind.

The soft rustle of grass distracted the viscount from his reading, and he raised his head, a thoughtful reflection in his glistening green eyes. He set the book aside.

Sabrina paused a short distance away from him, her body thrumming in expectation, and unfurled her palm to reveal the cluster of vines. "What does this mean?"

"It's a charm," he said, a soft timbre to his voice. "You place it on the pillow of the one you love so she will never forget you."

Her heart missed a beat. He knew its meaning. But how? And what did he mean by love? She realized she couldn't blindly accept his words. After all, last night she was the cause of all his pain. She was nothing more than a burden. And today everything had changed?

She didn't want to risk being hurt again. She didn't want to release the joy pounding on her chest. A second devastation would be too much to bear.

Anthony took advantage of her stunned silence to hastily snatch her into his arms and pull her between his parted legs. His sinewy thighs locked around her hips, holding her flush against him.

"I love you, Sabrina." It was a gruff whisper, prickling her skin and making her shiver. "Don't ever think I regret taking you for my wife. My life without you would be barren."

She could feel her heart throbbing, demanding she accept his words as truth. Delving deep into his lucid eyes, she searched for clarity, for truth . . . and she found it, gazing back at her candidly, lovingly.

That once so unlikely light of hope inched back into her heart, the oppressive darkness that had settled in its place retreating.

But the joy spilling through her was tapered by her next thought. "And your family?"

Warm palms cupped her cheeks. "I will learn to live apart from them. But I could never learn to live without you."

The heartfelt pledge possessed the power to heal all the wounds in her soul. Warmth spread through her, tickled her, doused her in a glorious blanket of comfort and peace and joy. Such joy she had never felt in all her years. She wanted to dance and laugh and shout.

She kissed him instead. Took his lips in hers with a possessive instinct that left them both breathless when it was over.

"And I love you, Anthony."

He hugged her tight. "I know."

"The charm!" She suddenly remembered. "How did you know its meaning?"

"On the night you were abducted I met a gypsy in the street, an old peddler woman with a sack of talismans and a trove of wisdom."

An image came to mind, of a hobbling figure making her way through the deserted streets of London. It was that lonely fate Sabrina had wanted so desperately to avoid. And now, looking into her husband's soulful eyes, she knew such a fate would never befall her; she knew she had found her true home.

After a brief pause, Anthony went on to admit, "I wrote a letter to Vincent this morning."

More surprises. "You did?"

"I invited him up for a visit, once we've settled in, and all."

Her lips brushed his in a gentle kiss. "What else have you been doing this morning?"

"Reading this." He picked up the book and spun her around, so her back was pressed snugly against his chest. Perching his chin on her shoulder, he read, " 'Sonnet to a Lady Seen for a Few Moments at Vauxhall.' "

"A poem?"

"About a temptress seen for an instant under the twinkling lights of Vauxhall. I'm going to take you to the gardens one day, and dance with you under the dappled lights and starry sky."

"Why?"

"Because it's a magical place and I want you to see it. I've dreamed of us dancing in the garden for some time now, wrapped in each other's arms, lost to the music and the stars and our hearts."

She took in a shuddering breath, so overcome with serenity and bliss. Twisting around in his embrace, she gave him a tender smile. "Then you'll have to teach me a *gajo* dance."

He smiled back, the same mesmerizing smile he had showered her with since the day they'd first met. "If you promise to teach me how to mix that cough syrup."

"Of course, I will." And she kissed his throat for good measure. "Feeling better?"

"In more ways than one. I feel like a man who has found his place in the world at last." His brow came to nuzzle her cheek. "Loving you, loving our future children, this is where I belong."

She sighed at his whispered words, so sultry and truthful. And she knew whatever happened in the future, however much she changed to adapt to her new life, one thing would remain forever constant—her adoring love for one unforgettable rogue.

Epilogue

The steed hopped the low wooden fence without hesitation. Hooves pounded over crisp fallen snow as an eager rider made his way across the wintry glen.

I'm late, he thought. *She's going to kill me.*

He would have stayed home that day had it not been for the summons of his tenants, concerned with the structure of the bridge at the far end of the property. Anthony had gone that morning to inspect the bridge, the only link between the tenant farmers and the local village, to find it was indeed damaged. Heavy snowfall and ice had weakened the structural supports, and if not attended to soon, the bridge was bound to collapse. A foreman had to be summoned in the morning.

It was near luncheon when he'd set out for the manor, plenty of time remaining before the ceremony was scheduled to begin. And he would have arrived in time had the wails of a lost and trapped sheep not interrupted his journey home. It had taken nigh an hour, with the help of one very distressed shepherd, to hoist the snared animal from the pit it had tumbled into.

Now he was late, and bounding for the manor house—or more precisely, the little church structure nestled at the rear of the house.

A few minutes later, the steed came to a skidded halt just yards away from the sacred entrance. Dismounting, Anthony hastened inside the holy dwelling, sweating and smelling of sheep fleece. A true country bumpkin, as his father would say. Not that he minded anymore. The title suited him just fine.

Sabrina was pacing in front of the altar. She glanced up at him with a disapproving glare, then wrinkled her nose as he approached. He offered her a contrite smile and a quick peck on the cheek before turning his attention to Vincent, who looked ready to faint from the strain of two wiggling infants in his arms.

" 'Bout bloody time," he heard his best friend whisper.

"May we begin?" the rector wondered.

"Yes, of course," returned Anthony, and took his place next to his wife.

Vincent turned to face the altar, the rector lifted his spectacles to his nose, and soon the ceremony was underway.

When at last the blessed water hit the scalp of the first gurgling infant, a loud wail of protest ripped through the hushed surroundings. But when the water hit the scalp of the second infant, all Anthony heard was a soft yawn.

And so, with little fanfare, Edan and Gabriel respectively were christened into the Kennington family, the twin boys, no doubt, to be a joy, and perhaps a bit of a handful, to their parents.

But only time would tell.

We know you expect the very best love stories written by utterly extraordinary writers, so we are presenting four amazing love stories—coming just in time for Valentine's Day!

Scandal of the Black Rose by Debra Mullins

An Avon Romantic Treasure

What is the secret behind the Black Rose Society? Anna Rosewood is determined to find out. Dashing Roman Devereaux has his own reasons for helping Anna—even though he *thinks* she's disreputable. Soon, their passion causes scandal, and what they discover could be even worse . . .

Guys & Dogs by Elaine Fox

An Avon Contemporary Romance

Small town vet Megan Rose only sleeps with a certain kind of male—the four legged, furry kind! But when she finds herself on the doorstep of millionaire Sutter Foley she starts changing her mind about that—and more! But how can she like a man who doesn't love dogs?

Pride and Petticoats by Shana Galen

An Avon Romance

Charlotte is desperate—driven to London to save her family's reputation, which is being assaulted by Lord Dewhurst. He's insufferable, but sinfully handsome, and soon she finds she must play the role of his bride, or face the consequences.

Kiss From a Rogue by Shirley Karr

An Avon Romance

Lady Sylvia Montgomery has no choice but to involve herself with a band of smugglers, but she needs help, which arrives in the irresistible form of Anthony Sinclair. A self-proclaimed rake, he knows he should seduce Sylvia and have done with it. But he can't resist her . . .

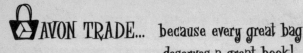